PARIAH

DAVID
JACKSON

PAN BOOKS

First published 2011 by Macmillan

This edition published 2012 by Pan Books
an imprint of Pan Macmillan, a division of Macmillan Publishers Limited
Pan Macmillan, 20 New Wharf Road, London N1 9RR
Basingstoke and Oxford
Associated companies throughout the world
www.panmacmillan.com

ISBN 978-0-330-52026-3

1 3 5 7 9 8 6 4 2

A CIP catalogue record for this book is available from
the British Library.

Typeset by CPI Typesetting
Printed and bound by CPI Group (UK) Ltd, Croydon, CR0 4YY

PARIAH

After taking his bachelor's degree and then a PhD, David Jackson became a full-time academic. He is married, with two daughters and a menagerie of animals. *Pariah*, his first novel, was Highly Commended in the Crime Writers' Association Debut Dagger Awards.

Also by David Jackson

The Helper

Acknowledgments

Thanks first and foremost to Will Atkins, Editorial Director at Pan Macmillan, for believing in me and in my novel, for giving me a chance, and for his incredibly astute editing; to Mary Chamberlain, for spotting me in the slush pile and for her superb copy-editing; to all the staff at Pan Macmillan, for working tirelessly behind the scenes; to the author Margaret Murphy and the judges and organizers of the Crime Writers' Association Dagger Awards, for their stamp of approval that means so much; to Mandy and Rob, for their keen interest and enthusiasm; and to Karolina and Kate, for their invaluable advice. Last, but certainly not least, I want to thank Bethany and Eden, just for being.

For Lisa, for providing the support and encouragement that carried me to this destination; and for my mother, for instilling in me the love of books that put me on this path in the first place.

ONE

She draws a breath, and the icy air crackles like fire through her lungs. The cry that she pushes out into the night is driven by the burning pain. Thick blood bubbles from her nose and trickles down the back of her throat. She coughs, and something clicks in her chest. A busted rib, she thinks.

Slumped between overflowing garbage bags, she waits. And counts.

One . . . two . . . three . . .

She has always counted. When she was tiny – in a parallel universe it seems now – her parents listened to her interminable counting and optimistically packaged her up as a child prodigy. Stepping from dream to dream, they conjured up futures for her involving nuclear science, brain surgery, accountancy, high finance.

She wonders what they would think of her now. Lying in a stinking vacant lot, her body battered and broken. Craving a hit of heroin to numb the pain.

. . . six . . . seven . . . eight . . .

She can count while thinking of other things. Like her mind is working on two levels. A useful skill, maybe, in some walk of life. Not so much in her own, though. In her life, it would often be far better if the numbers could eclipse all other thoughts.

. . . twelve . . . thirteen . . . fourteen . . .

She tends to think of people in terms of numbers. She sees them as having big numerals painted on their foreheads. Her customers especially, most of whose real names she doesn't want to know. Like Sammy Sixty-Nine, for example, his appellation deriving from his exclusively oral sexual preferences. Then there's Freddy Five-O, with his uncanny ability to climax after precisely fifty thrusts – no more, no less. And not forgetting, at the other end of the scale, poor old Two-Stroke Tommy.

She saw this movie once. *The Producers*. Laughed all the way through. Not because it was especially humorous, which it wasn't, but because one of the actors was called Zero Mostel.

Oh, to have a few more johns with that moniker, she wishes.

Lights dance in her eyes. She is not sure if they are real or imagined. One too many blows to the head maybe.

She forces out another cry, hears her plea reverberating off the featureless brick walls. Hears something scuttling away from her in the trash. The pain in her chest is worse now. She starts her count from the beginning again.

One . . . two . . . three . . .

She decides she has done well to stay in the life this long without more such beatings. Some of the girls she knows have had real numbers done on them. Like Moira, for example, who lost all her front teeth in one assault. Irony is, many of the tricks she turns view the absence of incisors as a bonus.

'Hey! Who's there?'

She struggles to push open her swollen eyelids, and can just make out a figure on the other side of the vandalized chain-link fence. She lets out a groan, the most she can manage. A flashlight comes on and searches her out. She winces as it stabs at her eyes.

'You okay?' the man calls.

Yeah, sure, she thinks. Lying here in garbage, freezing my ass off, is just a hobby of mine.

The man starts coming toward her, playing the cone of light over the ground in front of him. She counts his steps, and wonders who this might be, what his intent is. Maybe he's the Good Samaritan. Yeah, right, because New York is just overflowing with those.

More likely is that he's a scumbag. A lowlife with a hard-on who can't believe his luck at coming across a piece of ass who is currently incapable of resisting his amorous advances.

Yes, she tells herself, the scumbag theory is definitely the most statistically likely.

It sits oddly with her that she is hoping to be correct.

The man stops after fifteen paces, then scans her form with the flashlight. Despite her profession, this seems such an invasion. She tries to pull herself into a ball, and her body protests at the effort.

'It's okay,' he says. He shines the light onto his other hand, and the metal badge he holds there gleams and twinkles. 'I'm a cop.'

A cop. Great. In her experience, being a cop is no indicator of where one sits on the moral spectrum.

'You a working girl?'

She nods, thinking, We gonna play Animal, Vegetable, Mineral now?

'So who did the fandango on your face? A john? Pimp?'

She turns the slits of her eyes on him, and as if sensing her discomfort, he lowers the beam. All she can see is a large silhouette against the night sky – a human-shaped hole in the starry canvas. Again she wonders if he is a good or a bad man. She hopes that he is evil. She hopes that he is a child molester, a rapist, a serial killer, a man who rips babies limb from limb with his teeth. She hopes that there is not an altruistic bone in his body.

'I'm gonna come a little closer, okay?'

. . . sixteen . . . seventeen . . . eighteen . . .

He kneels down in front of her, turns the flashlight toward his chest.

'See, I ain't gonna hurt you. We're gonna get you fixed up.'

She can see his face now. And despite its being bathed from below in a ghostly yellow glow, she cannot tell herself that she finds malice there, cannot convince herself that this man intends anything other than to offer help.

The acceptance of that makes her want to weep, and she has not shed tears in a long, long time.

She looks at the man and waits and counts, and it is only brief moments before a second hole appears silently in the sky and sends a spear of flame into the head of her benefactor.

She sees the cop's expression twist into puzzlement as his body pitches forward. The side of his head smacks into the ground and he lies there, his eyes still open and the flashlight still in his grasp as he twitches.

She watches in horror and sadness as the second man steps closer to the body. In the reflected light she can see the gun in his hand, and she counts as two more tongues of fire lick out at the cop's skull.

As the cop's twitching stops, her own trembling grows. She peers up at the assassin.

'I did what you wanted, right? Exactly how you said, right?'

The man pauses before answering. He still holds onto his gun.

'You did.'

'I was on cue, too, right? I called out at exactly the right time, right? Soon as you flashed that light at me?'

'Yes, you did.'

'So I did good? And now you'll keep your promise?'

There is another pause, worrying in its length.

'What promise was that?'

'To let me go. You told me. You promised. You said that if I did everything exactly as you said, you'd let me go.'

'Yes, I did say that, didn't I?'

'And . . . so, now we're done. You got what you wanted, and so you have to let me go. Like you promised.'

'Like I promised.'

'I ain't gonna say nothing, if that's what's bothering you. Just . . . let me go. Okay?'

'Yes. Okay. You can go now.'

He raises the gun. She starts to count.

She doesn't get beyond one.

In the car he cries.

He feels hot tears coursing down his cheeks as he unscrews the still-warm silencer from the Colt.

A mixture of emotions stirs within him. Before tonight he has never killed. And to do so at such close range, in such cold blood, is intensely empowering. It is a feeling he tries to suppress. He can understand now how this could easily become habit-forming, and that must not happen. He has to remain in control, to adhere to his plan.

He cries also from relief. He has postponed this for too long. And now he wonders why he procrastinated. No longer does he have to suffer the agony of debating what to do and how to do it.

What he does not experience is remorse or sadness, but then he never thought he would. In fact, he is surprised at how satisfied he feels.

It has begun, and it cannot be undone.

The next killing is inevitable.

TWO

Despite their increased numbers, they are quieter than usual.

Normally, at a scene like this, there would be jokes and laughter and general chit-chat. About how fucking cold this Christmas is going to be, about how the latest caps on overtime suck, about how shitty the current police recruitment policy is. But this time it's different. This crime involves a Member of Service. A brother. There is a need for reverence here. The audience gathers around the mouth of the vacant lot as if about to sing a hymn or utter prayers.

Detective Second Grade Callum Doyle approaches the throng with some trepidation. Anyone not familiar with him might puzzle over the slight bounce in his step on such a solemn occasion. Closer inspection might offer a hint that Doyle is not full of the joys of winter. If they can tear their gaze away from his startling emerald eyes, they might notice the slight crookedness to his nose – another relic from his boxing days.

He makes a quick scan of the surroundings. This section of East Third Street is mostly residential. Low-rise tenements, their faces zigzagged by fire escapes. Building lights are on everywhere. Despite the freezing weather, a bare-chested man is hanging out of a fourth-floor window, binoculars trained on the scene below. A cordon formed from sawhorses connected by yellow crime-scene tape keeps the gathering public at a respectable distance.

Pressed against the tape, two elderly spectators fill plastic cups from a steaming thermos. Doyle wouldn't be surprised if they'd brought sandwiches too.

Seeking protection against the bitter cold, he burrows his hands deep into the pockets of his leather jacket, then turns his attention back to the people on his side of the barrier. He keeps his head high, knowing what certain elements are thinking. He's ready for them – possibly too ready. He warns himself not to be too eager to react.

His mind begins to sift the various officials here into categories: the uniforms, the night-watch detectives, the Homicide dicks, the Crime Scene team, the Medical Examiner. And then there are the detectives from his own tour, none of whom is supposed to be on duty for several hours yet. But when something like this happens, word gets around quickly and sleep is demoted to an unnecessary luxury.

As he reaches the periphery of the crowd, faces glance at him and swiftly turn away again. There are whispers, nudges. Doyle feels his intestines forming reef knots.

First to venture toward him is the lieutenant. Morgan Franklin – Mo to his friends – is tall and wiry and approaching fifty in a nosedive, but all of this belies his strength and aura of authority. Doyle has often wondered what it is about the man that causes others to hang on his words and swing at his command.

'Cal,' he says, the simple greeting carried on a white puff of breath.

'There's no mistake, then?' Doyle asks.

Franklin shakes his head. 'I wish there was.' He looks up at the cloudless sky. 'This is gonna be tough on you. In more ways than one. You know that, don't you?'

Doyle just stares. He does know it, but hearing it from somebody else's lips hammers it home.

The assembly parts like the Red Sea, and a squat man emerges and shuffles over. Norman Chin, MD, has stiff black hair that sticks out like the bristles of a toilet brush, and the magnifying effect of his glacially thick glasses lends him the appearance of a demented owl. But Doyle knows that behind the geeky facade lies a tough Brooklynite whom one derides at one's peril.

'Who wants the report?' he asks the lieutenant.

Doyle chips in. 'Me. I'll take the case.'

Franklin looks at him. 'You sure? Could be a poisoned chalice.'

'He was my partner. I knew him best.'

Chin pulls his lapels together and stomps his feet. 'Can we toss a coin here or something? This cold, my toes are about to snap off.'

Franklin thinks for a moment, then nods his assent.

'Okay,' Chin says, and turns to face Doyle. 'Cause of death in Parlatti's case was three gunshots to the right rear side of the head. Cause of death for the girl was probably also three shots to the head, but from the front.'

'Probably?'

Chin shrugs. 'I'm covering my ass. She had the crap beaten out of her. The injuries she sustained might have led to her death. Whatever, the three slugs in her brain didn't cure her.'

'Can you give us anything on the weapon?'

'Small caliber, judging by the holes. Powder burns on the skin of both victims, suggesting close range. Oh, and no exit wounds, indicative of low-velocity ammo. If the slugs haven't deformed too much, the lab will be able to tell you more. What I do know is that there's no sign of any cartridge cases near the bodies.'

'Jesus,' Franklin says, and Doyle knows they're thinking the same thing: that this has all the hallmarks of a professional hit. Blowing somebody's head off with a Magnum .44 is for amateurs and opportunists, since it has the disadvantage of alerting everyone within a five-block radius to what you've just done. Besides, it's messy. You want a swift, efficient and quiet kill, then use something like a .22 at close range. With the peace and tranquility of your neighbors in mind, fit the gun with a silencer and use low-power shells. It might seem like a pussy's weapon to you, but two or three of those projectiles bouncing around somebody's dome still gets the job done – no muss, no fuss.

'Were they killed here?' Doyle asks.

'I'd say so. Doesn't look like a dump job. Nah, I'd say they were whacked here within the past two hours.'

'What about the girl? Find anything there?'

'She's a user. Track marks on her arms and legs. One of your uniforms thinks he's seen her before, on the streets. Thinks she's a local pross.'

Shit, thinks Doyle. What the fuck was Joe Parlatti – who was married, no less – doing on a vacant lot with a known hooker?

Chin seems to have read his mind. 'There's no sign of any sexual activity immediately prior to death. But I can't rule it out totally. I'll know more when I get 'em back to the ranch.'

'And the beating she took?'

'Again, no signs that Parlatti did the deed. His knuckles are clean, and I couldn't find any gloves. What I did find was his wallet still in his pocket, his detective shield in his left hand and a pocket flashlight in his right hand. Battery must be dead because the switch is on.'

'Okay, thanks, Doc. Any chance you can bump this one for us?'

'Already top of my list. Watch this space.'

Chin walks away, muttering something else about his frozen extremities. Franklin says to Doyle, 'You wanted the case. Go work it.'

9

Doyle heads into the crowd. He receives a couple of sheepish nods, one or two grunts. Nobody for a high five then, he thinks.

He has worked with these people for a full year now. He was beginning to think he had finally become accepted. Now this.

'Who found them?' he asks nobody in particular.

Evasive silence. Then: 'You taking this, Doyle?'

This from Schneider, a bull of a man with a stiff carpet of slate-gray hair. Doyle recalls remarking that it looked as though his head had been dipped in iron filings and a magnet pushed up his nose.

'That okay with you, Schneider?'

Schneider smiles viciously and chews his gum. Doyle looks around at the others, challenging them to declare any allegiances. It takes a while for one of them to pipe up.

'Kid over there. He's a student, on his way home after a party. Feels the need for a piss, looks for somewhere away from the street . . .'

Doyle is already on his way to the youth standing near one of the radio cars angled into the sidewalk, his arms folded and his head bowed.

'Hey, kid. You okay?'

The student looks up. His eyes and nose are red with alcohol and the cold. 'Yeah, yeah. I just . . . I never seen a dead body before, you know? Much less two of them.'

'Sure. So can you tell me what happened?'

'Yeah. It was like I was telling the other cops before. I been drinking, see, and with the cold air and all, I really needed to pee.'

'So you stepped into the lot. You really have to go all the way to the back wall to do that?'

It's one of the few fragments of information Doyle was given before he arrived. Two DOAs found in the far corner of a vacant lot. One his partner, the other a woman who was not his wife. All the ingredients for one of the shittiest days imaginable.

'No, no. I just went about halfway down. But when I was doing my thing, you know, I saw this light.'

'A light?'

'Yeah. A little light. And I wondered what it was. So I went down there to take a look. And that's when I found them.'

'And the light was . . . ?'

'A flashlight, in the guy's hand. It was really dim, like the battery was dying, you know? But it was just enough so I could see them. There was a lot of blood, but it didn't look like blood, because it was so black, you know? And the girl's face, it was wrecked, man. I thought she was wearing a mask at first. And you know what the really freaky thing was?'

'What?'

'Literally while I was standing there, the flashlight went out. Slowly dimmed, and then just went out, totally. Man, was I spooked. It was like . . .'

'Like what?'

'Like . . . his soul just left him. I know it sounds crazy. He already looked stone-cold dead when I found him. But that's how it felt at the time. Like his life was draining out of him while I watched.'

An image enters Doyle's brain. A memory. Of standing over a body drenched in blood. He is aware of the life force leaking away, and is powerless to prevent it. He is crying in frustration . . .

Doyle shivers, and blames the cold. He asks the student a few more questions, thanks him, and returns to the crime scene. Slipping wordlessly between his colleagues, he enters the lot. It is brightly lit by banks of floodlights. He can hear the thrum of the generator that powers them. Members of the Crime Scene Unit are scouring the weed-pocked ground and sifting through garbage. Doyle gets as close as he can without disturbing them. Close enough to get a good look at the bodies.

The woman is young. Perhaps not yet twenty. To the uninitiated she might appear older, but her line of work adds years in that way. She is wearing a faux-fur jacket that ends at the waist and a skirt that extends not much farther. The signs of a severe assault are not hidden behind her face mask of caked blood. Her features are contorted and misshapen, her nose looking like a squashed strawberry. Her mouth is open and the tip of her tongue is wedged in the gap where one of her teeth has been smashed out.

He has seen this woman before. Well, not her exactly, but quite a few like her. She's another corpse, another DOA. As yet she doesn't even have a name. She's paperwork, she's tracking down friends and family and acquaintances, she's interrogating suspects. She's his job. She's what puts bread and butter on his table.

At least, that's what he's learned to tell himself at scenes like this. It's a defense mechanism that doesn't always work. Sometimes the sheer waste of it all still gets to him. Sometimes he cares a little too much for his own good.

And then there's Joe, and for him Doyle cannot make even the pretense of detachment. That crumpled lifeless mass lying there in a puddle of its own blood is the body of a man who, just yesterday, was telling Doyle a joke about a blind beggar and a nudist. This was minutes after they had worked in perfect harmony in the interview room to get a confession from a suspected rapist. Which in turn was not long after they had spent over three hours freezing their asses off doing surveillance from a rooftop coated in pigeon shit.

There are strong ties here that Doyle cannot and does not choose to deny. They make him wonder whether he made the right decision in requesting this case: he knows that the end of

Parlatti's journey is the start of a new one for himself, and that it's going to be a rough ride. But they're also the reason he doesn't trust anybody else to get to the bottom of it.

He sighs, slowly and heavily, and feels as though he exhales more than just breath.

He looks around the enclosed space. He guesses that the chain-link fence separating it from the street has been broken for some time, making it an ideal dumping ground. Against the walls are huge piles of boxes and bags, overflowing with garbage. The air is thick with the stench of rotting food, making Doyle grateful that December is not noted for its muggy nights. The mountains of junk have converted a perfectly rectangular area into a landscape filled with dark, forbidding recesses.

Doyle heads back toward the street, conscious of the sea of faces studying him. He pushes through, finds the lieutenant. Franklin is instructing a couple of his men to initiate a door-to-door. Doyle waits for him to finish before delivering his thoughts.

'The killer's not somebody Joe knew as a friend, not someone he trusted.'

'Okay. Why?'

'Because a friend could have killed Joe anywhere. He could have talked his way into Joe's apartment and done it there, or in his car. Anywhere.'

'I'll give you that. What else?'

'Although the killer wasn't a close acquaintance, he knew a lot about Joe. Or he was hired by somebody else who knows a lot about Joe.'

'Why so?'

'Because last night was Wednesday. And every Wednesday night, without fail unless he's on duty, Joe hooks up with some buddies at a bar on First. They sink a few beers and then move on to a pool hall farther down here on Third Street. At midnight precisely, Joe leaves the pool hall and walks down here, past this lot, and on to the subway station at Houston to catch the F train.'

Franklin removes his hands from his pockets and holds them up.

'Wait a minute. That's kind of a leap. Why does the hitter have to know all that info? Maybe he's just following Joe around. He sees an opportunity, gets the drop on Joe, forces him onto the lot and . . . and that's it.'

Doyle catches the way that Franklin puts a stop sign on his mental journey past the fence bordering the vacant lot, as if he cannot yet fully accept what has happened to a member of his squad.

He shakes his head. 'I don't think it went down like that. First of all, Joe wasn't the kind of guy you just sneak up on, even with a couple beers inside him. Even if he was, the killer wouldn't know that. All he would know is that this guy's a cop, and cops have guns, and cops have street smarts. An amateur or your average stupid mutt might take a chance, but from what we've seen, our hitter was careful. He wouldn't want to risk this thing blowing up in his face. Besides, we have to fit the pross into this somehow.'

'Yeah, I was wondering about her. Somehow I don't see Joe as the type to—'

'He wasn't, and I'm certain that Norm will confirm that. I don't believe he beat the shit out of her either.'

Franklin nods, and Doyle can almost hear the wheels turning. 'So explain to me how Joe ended up like this. If it wasn't for sex, what was he doing with this girl?'

'Joe had his flashlight and his shield out, right? That means he went in there looking for something, and that he needed to identify himself. Suppose the girl was already in there, that she'd already been beaten up.'

'Okay, so Joe finds the girl. He tries to help her. He's distracted. The killer sees an opening . . .'

'No, there's too much chance involved. I think this was a set-up. I think the girl was involved, but not out of choice. That's why Joe's at the back of the lot with a flashlight in his hand. He's trying to help her, only he doesn't know he's just walked right into a trap. He doesn't know he's just been led to a spot where nobody on the street is going to see or hear anything.'

'And that would require the killer to know that Joe was going to come past this spot at about this time.'

'Exactly. He would also know that Joe couldn't ignore something like this. Most people, they hear noises in a dark corner, they cross the street to avoid it. Not Joe. Not when somebody's in trouble.'

Franklin draws breath through his teeth. 'Jesus. She was *bait?* If you're right, that's a clinical kill.' The roof lights of the radio cars bounce colors off his face as he looks around. 'Okay. Put the word out. We want anything on someone looking to buy a hit. Also anything on the movements of known professional hitters. Find out where the pross worked, see if anyone saw her being picked up tonight. Look at the scumbags Joe put away – anyone who might have had a reason for wanting him dead. And somebody needs to speak with Maria.'

Doyle picks up on the expectation dangling on the end of those words. 'Yeah, I know. My first port of call when I'm done here.'

Franklin frees a hand from his pockets, slaps Doyle on the arm to send him on his way. Doyle walks toward the uniforms, intending to find out more about the prostitute.

The name carries to him on the thin air, not quite hidden in the snatches of conversation. It cuts him, and he snaps.

'Fuck!' he yells. 'You fuck!' He runs straight at Schneider. The self-assured smirk drops from Schneider's face, but it is all he has time to do before Doyle piles into him, slamming him into a tenement wall.

The other cops are quickly on Doyle. Arms snake around him and pull him away. He watches Schneider bounce himself off the wall and prepare to come barreling back at him, but then something stops the man in his tracks. He has seen the figure of Franklin standing there, condemnation written on his gnarled face.

'What the fuck, Doyle?' Schneider growls. 'You feeling guilty about something?'

'Fuck you, Schneider,' Doyle answers. 'That's my partner lying back there. My partner, get that?'

'Yeah, I get it. Your partner. Kind of like a running theme with you, huh, Doyle?'

Doyle struggles to free himself for another pop at Schneider, but the hold on him is too strong.

'You keep your shit-stirring thoughts to yourself, you fat fuck! I got nothing to be ashamed of. And I don't ever want to hear that name from your mouth again, you got me?'

Schneider is laughing now, taunting him.

'Enough!' Franklin commands, and an anxious silence descends once more. 'We have two homicides to solve here. One of them's a cop. Somebody you all worked with. Show him the respect he deserves by acting professional and doing your jobs.'

Schneider straightens his tie and brushes something off his sleeve. The grip on Doyle is relaxed, and he yanks himself free. As he heads toward his car he gives himself a mental slap for his stupidity. He knew something like that was probably coming, so he should have been more prepared to handle it.

Today was always going to be a bad day. He's probably just made it a hundred times worse.

THREE

'Cal! Hold up, man!'

Tony Alvarez catches up with Doyle as he reaches his car. He has the smooth voice and looks of a nightclub crooner – a guy who could steal away the girl on your arm with just a glance or a word. Doyle has lost count of the number of different females he has seen him with.

'You want company?' Alvarez asks. Like the others, he has probably had only a couple of hours' sleep; unlike them, he has the appearance of a man who has just walked off the shoot for a clothing catalog.

Doyle looks at him. 'I'm tired, I'm pissed off, and my partner's just been found dead in a stinking lot. Do I look like I need to hear about your latest roll in the sack right now?'

'You want company,' Alvarez says, a statement this time. Without invitation, he jumps into the car.

Doyle shakes his head and climbs behind the wheel. He starts the ignition and pulls the car away.

'You sure you want to take the risk of associating with me like this? Maybe I'm taking you to a dark alleyway to shoot you in the head too.'

'Don't make this more than it is,' Alvarez says. 'Schneider's an asshole. Nobody else in the squad believes anything he says.'

'They were putting on a pretty good act back there.'

'Schneider's been on the team a long while. Compared with him, you're still the new kid on the block. He's made a lot of good collars in his time, so when he speaks, people feel they have to listen. Doesn't mean they can't make up their own minds about things. Give 'em a chance. They'll come round.'

'Yeah, well, fuck 'em. I've been here a year already. That should be long enough for anybody. Maybe I could speed things up a little by knocking Schneider's teeth out for him. Stop him spreading that shit.'

'Schneider's as bad as anyone for believing rumors. He's a drinking buddy of Marino's – you know that, right? That's where his poison comes from.'

Doyle thinks about this. Danny Marino. One-time husband of Laura Marino. Hers was the name Schneider let loose. A name that still sends tingles down Doyle's spine.

'Hard to believe,' he says.

'What?'

'Joe. Him being dead. Gonna be a while before I can accept that.'

'Gonna be even harder for his wife,' Alvarez answers.

They have to ring the doorbell several times before they get a response from within the Parlattis' apartment. The building is in Carroll Gardens, in Brooklyn. Not as many Italians in this neighborhood as there were back when Cher found Nicolas Cage here in *Moonstruck*, but they're still around. Just don't go looking for Luigi to bake you a loaf, or Vito to cut your hair. The small family-run businesses have mostly been driven out by all the bars and boutiques and antique shops. And now the Italian headcount in Carroll Gardens has just been reduced by one more.

'Joe!' they hear. 'You know what time it is, Joe? What the hell do you think this is, coming home at this hour? And where's your goddamn keys?'

The detectives wait, say nothing. What they need to say can't be delivered through a door.

Doyle hears the slight scratching noise of a cover being slid back from the peephole. Knowing he is being examined, he tries to assemble his features into an expression that is neither too serious nor too happy.

He hears the locks being taken off. The door opens. Maria Parlatti is belting up her pink robe over a body that is not yet ready to be vertical, and her hair looks like it could have starlings nesting in it. She stares at them through bleary eyes. The anger has gone, to be replaced by a whole new range of emotions.

She knows what this is, Doyle thinks. She's a cop's wife. This is the visit that every cop's wife dreads, and she knows.

'Hi, Maria—' he begins, but she cuts him off.

'Shit, guys, what's he done this time?' She laughs, but it's forced. 'Come in, come in. Let me put some coffee on.'

They follow her into the small living room. This hour of the morning, it's still pitch black outside. Maria has put on a single lamp that at other times might make the room seem cozy; right now it just seems funereal. The police commendations hanging on the wall make the place feel like a shrine, and the small plastic Christmas tree and few sad hangings of tinsel do nothing to lighten the atmosphere.

'Sit, please sit,' she says, urging them toward a battered brown sofa. 'Just don't use the recliner, okay? Joe is very possessive about his recliner.' She laughs again, and Doyle knows the tears aren't that far behind.

It goes like this sometimes. You can never tell. Some people, they collapse in a heap as soon as they see you – maybe even faint. Others wail hysterically. But there's a surprisingly large number that go into denial. Even after you've told them – practically spelled it out for them – you're still not sure when the hammer is going to strike the bell. Doyle still remembers that day from his time in uniform, when he drew the short straw over explaining to a distressed woman that her husband had been decapitated in a traffic accident. He took at least an hour over it, thought he did a good job. Sensitive, and not too graphic. When he went to leave, she asked him what time the hospital visiting hours were.

The detectives glance at each other. They don't want to sit unless Maria joins them, and right now she seems far too wired to do that.

Doyle tries again: 'Maria, about Joe—'

'Jesus, I must look a mess,' she interrupts. Her hands fly to her disheveled dark hair, try to tease it into some order. 'Sorry fellas, I'm afraid I'm not one of these women jumps out of bed looking like a supermodel.'

'You look fine,' Alvarez says.

'Well, thank you, Tony. From the man who's seen any number of women first thing in the morning, that has to be a real compliment, huh, Cal?'

'Maria—'

'Coffee. I mentioned coffee, didn't I? How d'you take it?'

'Not for me. I . . . we just want to talk for a while, if that's okay.'

Maria's eyes dart as if seeking another distraction, something else to move the conversation off-topic. She tightens the belt on her robe again, tying up her vulnerability.

'He send you here to do his dirty work? Which is it, too drunk or too ashamed? He get himself into some kind of scrape? Never mind, I don't want to know. He can't be trusted to get home to his wife, then I don't want to know.'

She turns then and starts to head toward the kitchen, but Doyle stops her. It can be put off no longer.

'Maria, Joe was killed tonight.'

She halts, her back still to them. She doesn't say anything for a long time. Then: 'You're sure? That it was Joe? Did you see him?'

'Yes. I saw him.'

She turns toward the detectives again, then pads across the carpet and sits on the sofa. Doyle sits down next to her. She can't look him in the eye, and he's glad of it.

'Tell me,' she says.

'He was shot. His body was found on a vacant lot in the East Village.'

'A vacant lot. What was he doing on a vacant lot? He wasn't working, was he? He went to play pool. He was meeting his pals.'

Alvarez speaks up: 'We're not sure of all the details yet, but the way they were found—'

'*They?* There was more than one? Who else?'

'There were two killings,' Doyle says. Better to hear this now, from them, than later on the news. 'The other was a female. A prostitute.'

'A prostitute,' Maria says flatly. 'A fucking whore?' She jumps to her feet again.

'No, Maria. Listen. It's not—'

'I have a new job, you know?' Maria says. Her lower lip is quivering. The tide is ready to break. 'At Barnes and Noble. It's not much, but it helps to pay my tuition. Because I'm taking night classes too. Trying to better myself. Get some qualifications. I never really took an interest in high school.'

'Maria—'

'But I'm so goddamn tired all the time. When I hit the pillow, I'm out for the count. Was a time I never could have slept without

21

knowing Joe was next to me. But last night I didn't even know . . .
I wasn't even aware . . . And our love life? What happened to that?
Where would I get the energy or the time for that? So if Joe . . . I
mean, if he felt the need to go elsewhere, I can understand that.
But a whore?'

'Maria, let me finish. We don't think he was with her the way
you're saying. Our belief is he went to help her because she'd been
beaten, and that's when they both got shot.'

Maria's eyes are glistening. 'You're not just saying that? Not
trying to make me feel better? 'Cause I don't want that. I don't
want lies.'

Doyle stands up and approaches her. 'We wouldn't lie to you.
Far as we can tell, that's how it went down.'

She considers this. 'You really think he died trying to help
somebody?'

'Yes, we do. Come on. Sit down over here.'

They both sit again. Maria puts her hand to her mouth, and
tears run over it. After a moment she says, 'That's Joe for you.
Always willing to lend a hand.' She cries some more, then says,
'You get the bastard who did this?'

'No. Not yet. But we will. We're hoping you can help us
on that.'

'Me? What do you mean?'

Doyle squirms on the sofa. 'The thing is, we don't think Joe
was picked at random. We think he was targeted. Somebody had
it in for Joe. He talk about anything like that recently? Any threats?
Anything he was worried about?'

'No. Nothing specific. He's a cop, and cops get threats all the
time, right? But nothing serious. Nothing like . . . like this.'

Doyle looks up at Alvarez, who nods back. They are done here
for now.

'Okay, Maria. We're gonna leave you now. You think of

anything we might need to know, just call me. We'll come talk to you again soon, okay?' He takes Maria's hand in his. 'You take care of yourself. Call someone over. Don't stay alone, okay?'

Doyle stands up, but Maria stays where she is.

'Joe was a good man,' she says. 'That's how he would have wanted to go. Helping somebody.'

Doyle leads the way out. The detectives close the apartment door behind them. Alvarez heads for the stairs, but Doyle hesitates for a moment.

When he hears the wail of grief that vibrates through his whole body, he knows it is time to go.

The detectives remain immersed in their own thoughts until they are back in their car.

'You think he was playing away?' Alvarez asks.

'What?'

'Joe. Him not getting any at home, you think he was poking somebody else's fire?'

Doyle twists in his seat. 'What the fuck, Tony? Just for once, can you bring your mind above waist height? You know, not everybody is like you. We don't all feel we're going to explode unless we empty our load five times a day.'

Alvarez puts his hands up in surrender. 'Okay, man. I'm just saying, okay? Just putting the thought out there, like we would for any other homicide.'

Doyle lets the subject drop and guns the engine. He knows Alvarez is right. If a guy's wife thinks that the idea of him seeking comfort elsewhere is not so outrageous, then neither should they. Wives don't always know everything about their husbands.

Just as cops don't always know everything about their partners.

FOUR

Back in Manhattan, they fuel up on a breakfast of sausage, eggs, toast and coffee, and then spend the rest of the morning tracking down and interviewing Parlatti's pool-playing buddies. There are four of them, and each one confirms without the slightest conflicting detail that they downed a few beers and then played in the pool hall until midnight. After that, Joe went his way and they staggered theirs. Joe seemed his usual affable self, either oblivious to or unconcerned about any danger he might have been in. There is zero about the men that suggests to the detectives they should be considered as suspects, and they have zilch to offer on reasons for his murder.

In the afternoon Doyle and Alvarez turn their attention to the prostitute. Although a couple of uniforms claim to have seen her on the streets, they don't have a name for her. Armed with a crime-scene photograph of the dead girl, the detectives go on the hunt.

The daylight hours are not the best time to find a hooker on the streets of Manhattan. Gone are the days when it was impossible to stroll around the Times Square area without being propositioned by females, males and various combinations thereof. You want some pussy now, then check out the classifieds at the back of the free sheets or call up an escort agency or use the Internet. If you're really set on doing things the old-fashioned way you can still find company on the streets, but only if you look hard, and almost always after dark.

It takes a lot of legwork before the detectives strike lucky. As they approach a massage parlor on First Avenue, a tall Latino girl with startling red streaks in her otherwise raven hair comes click-clacking out of the front door.

'Hey, Floella!' says Doyle. 'You working indoors these days?'

Floella Cruz chews her gum and blinks at each of the cops in turn, her expression both puzzled and wary.

'When I can get it. They were short-staffed in there.'

'Many hands make light work,' says Alvarez.

'You should try it,' she answers, glancing down at his groin. 'Take some of that stiffness out of your posture.'

Doyle knows that most prostitutes would prefer to work inside where it's safer and warmer, but that for many it's not an option, especially for the crack addicts who find it almost impossible to handle fixed hours.

'And when you're not here?' he asks.

'I'm in my Trump Tower apartment, checking my share prices. Come on, fellas, what's this about?'

When Doyle produces the photograph and holds it in front of her face, Floella nearly falls off her heels. As she steps back, her short leather jacket opens up and her large pale breasts almost leap for freedom from the dayglo-pink bra.

'Fuck!' she cries. 'Is that Scarlett? Fuck! What happened to her? Is she dead?'

'She's dead,' Alvarez confirms. 'You know this girl?'

'Not real well. Scarlett is all I got for a name. Girl's only nine-teen. Shit, what's the world coming to when a girl's got to start turning tricks at nineteen?'

'How'd you know her?'

'Just from seeing her on the streets. Girl's pretty new around here. I gave her some of the benefits of my extensive experience.'

'When'd you last see her?'

'About three, four nights ago.'

'Where?'

'Eleventh, Twelfth Street. Somewhere around there.'

'She tell you anything about any of her johns?'

Floella puts a finger to her temple as she thinks. A theatrical pose. Her jacket swings open again, affording the detectives another view of her plump assets.

'Nobody in particular,' she says finally. 'I mean, we talked about some of the crazy shit we get from time to time.'

'Like what?'

'Like this one guy she had, liked her to lick his bald head while they fucked. And then this black motherfucker, wanted Scarlett to put a cork up his ass and take it out with a corkscrew . . .'

'Okay, okay,' Alvarez says. 'But she didn't mention any real psychos? Nobody she thought would try to hurt her?'

'No.'

'What about cops?' Doyle asks, and he catches the sidelong glance from Alvarez. 'She go with any cops?'

Floella smiles and jiggles her breasts in invitation. 'Honey, do cops do that sort of thing? I mean, aren't you highly trained to keep your weapons holstered and out of sight at all times?'

Doyle sighs and Alvarez says, 'Speaking of which, do you have a carry permit for those?'

As Floella laughs and turns toward Alvarez, Doyle feels a surge of irritation.

'Who's the pimp?' he demands. Again he picks up on a glance from Alvarez, which tells him that the note of anger in his voice has not been missed.

'I . . . I dunno,' Floella says, and it's clear that she too has detected the change in the air.

'Floella, I'm gonna ask you one more time, and I don't want to have to come looking for you again. We're working a double homicide. Your girlfriend here was beaten until the snot flew out of her ears, and then she had three bullets put in her head. The other victim is a cop. My partner, in fact. So you can guess how I'm feeling about that right now. I'll ask you again: who's the pimp?'

'Okay, but you didn't hear it from me. Tremaine Cavell. Most know him as TC.'

'Where can we find him?'

'Prob'ly hanging with his boys. He owns an auto repair place on Houston. The Pit Stop.'

Doyle pulls a card from his pocket. 'Thanks. You think of anything else, give us a call. Oh, and put those away before you get frostbite.'

They are walking away when Floella says, 'She counted. Only other thing I know about her. She counted a lot.'

'Yeah,' Doyle says. 'She still counts with us too.'

At the Pit Stop, a group of young black men is gathered around a brand new silver Mercedes SL convertible, red leather interior. One of the men is doing all the talking, showing off his new acquisition. Despite the cold, he wears a tight black sleeveless T, emphasizing his muscular arms and chest. Around one wrist is a gold Rolex; heavy gold chains are on the other wrist and around his neck. His hair is braided in cornrows. His face is boyish, the only thing putting any menace on it being a small moon-shaped scar high on his cheek.

As Doyle and Alvarez walk in off the street, the gang descends into silence and focuses its energy in a collective stony glare.

'Tremaine Cavell?' Doyle asks the apparent leader.

The man chin-points at Doyle. 'Who you?'

Doyle flips open his wallet, flashes his own gold. 'Detectives Doyle and Alvarez.'

Cavell looks to his boys, a hint of amusement on his lips. He gets a rumble of laughter in return.

'Yeah, thass me,' he says. 'Friends call me TC.'

Doyle turns to Alvarez. 'Close friends get to call him TC.'

Alvarez smiles. 'The indisputable leader of the gang.'

Doyle points to a short, rotund man in blue mechanic's overalls. 'That Benny the Ball?'

'Yeah, and you Officer Dibble,' Cavell says. 'Now what you want?'

'Information. On one of your girls.'

Cavell puffs out his already-substantial pectorals. 'I got more honeys than Winnie the fuckin' Pooh, man. You gonna have to get more, like, specific.'

'I'm talking about the girls who turn tricks for you, Tremaine.'

Cavell puts a finger to his neck chain. 'Me? Running hookers? Nah, man, I don't do that shit. Who gave you that?'

'All right, Tremaine. This ain't a vice bust. I just want to know about one girl. Blond, age nineteen. Goes by the name Scarlett.'

Cavell folds his arms. 'Never hearda her.'

Doyle surveys the faces of the other young men in the garage. Their faces, like their souls, are hard. He wishes that, just for once, people in this city would be a little more cooperative.

He drops his gaze to the Mercedes. 'Nice ride.'

There is a sudden softening in Cavell. He lowers his arms, becomes more animated.

'You like that, huh? It got DVD, multi-CD, GPS. Shit, it even got a Playstation in the back . . .'

Doyle sits down on the vehicle's hood. He doesn't do it lightly, but throws his whole weight on there.

'Whoa!' Cavell shouts.

Doyle bounces heavily up and down a few times. 'Good suspension too,' he says. He is aware of the consternation among Cavell's boys, but he knows that Alvarez has his back.

Doyle points to his left foot. 'Will you look at that? Damn shoelace coming untied again.' He lifts his foot, plants the heel securely on the fender.

'Oh, man . . .' Cavell says, raising his arms to the sky.

As Doyle reties his lace, he pretends to peer at something on the spotless hood. 'I think you got some dirt on here, Tremaine. Some tar or something, man.'

He reaches into his pocket, pulls out a bunch of keys.

Cavell is getting worked up into a frenzy; his voice goes up an octave. 'What the fuck?'

Doyle leans over the hood, brings the jagged teeth of a key within millimeters of the paintwork.

'Aiight!' Cavell screams. 'I know the bitch, yo. Thass all I'm saying. I know the bitch. Aiight?'

Doyle slides off the car and points a finger at Cavell. 'Gotcha, TC.' He drops the keys back into his pocket and swaps them for the photograph. 'This her?'

Cavell takes a look, then a closer look. 'Shit!' He turns to his buddies and says, 'Bitch be dead. Fuckin' bitch be dead, yo,' like it's a line from an updated *Wizard of Oz*.

'You sound awful cut up about it, Tremaine.'

'Shit, you don't know how fuckin' *inconvenient* that is.'

Doyle suddenly feels like getting his keys out again and playing tic-tac-toe on the Mercedes.

'Inconvenient? Yeah, I guess that just about sums it up. What's her real name?'

'Danielle O'something. A mick name like yours. O'Hara, yeah thass it.'

'Right. Hence the street name.'

'What?'

'Scarlett O'Hara. Frankly, my dear, I don't give a damn.'

Cavell turns to his crew for enlightenment, gets no help there. He says, 'First of all, I ain't your "dear." Second of all, the fuck you doing wasting my time if you don't give a shit?'

Doyle sighs. He flicks the corner of the photograph. 'You do this to her?'

'Hell, no. Why I wanna go waste my own merchandise?'

'What about the beating she took? You behind that?'

'No. What fool gonna pay for a ho looks like she Herman Munster's sister?'

'Ever take a hand to her? Slap her around a little when she gets out of line?'

'Not my style. My charming personality is all I need to get the ladies on my side.'

Around the garage the others smile and nod, as if profound truth has just been uttered to a gospel congregation.

'Any idea who might have killed her?'

'Ain't that your job?'

'When'd you last see her?'

'I checked her ass out last night, 'bout seven, seven-thirty.'

'What about later? Toward midnight?'

'Nah. I was too busy getting it on my own self, know what I'm saying?'

'Did she call at any point, let you know who she was with?'

'I don't need no running commentary. She doing her job is all I gots to know.'

'She ever talk to you about any johns she was worried about? Anyone who threatened to hurt her?'

'No. Tell you somethin', though: whoever did this is gonna be hearing from me.'

'Nice to know you care.' Doyle fishes out a card. 'Okay, Tremaine, this is how it's gonna be. You hear anything, and I mean *anything*, about the person who did this, you call us. And just so you know, we ain't about to let this drop. This ain't a show we're putting on here, this is for real. Any part of you want to know why this is so serious?'

Cavell just shrugs.

'Because your girl Scarlett wasn't the only one killed last night. A cop was murdered too. You know anything about that?'

'No. Real shame, though. Now I really am cut up.'

'Sure you are. Just know that it's personal now, and that if I hear anything about you holding out on me, I'm coming right back. And next time I won't be so nice.'

With that, Doyle licks the back of his card and pastes it on the inside of the Mercedes windshield.

'Call me,' he says.

He and Alvarez head out of the garage, but pause on the side-walk. Cavell and his boys have pulled together into a tight knot.

Doyle calls back to them: 'You know what they're saying on the street about TC, don't you?'

'What's that?' Cavell says.

'Word is, he's a pussy.'

FIVE

Doyle cups his head in his hands, supporting its weight before it rolls off his neck and thuds onto his paper-strewn desk.

The desk is in a squadroom in a building of white stone and red brick close to Tompkins Square Park, which is in an area of the East Village sometimes referred to as Alphabet City. There are only four avenues in Manhattan with single-letter names; running from west to east these are Avenues A, B, C and D. There was a time when it was said that A was for the Adventurous, B for the Brave, C for the Crazy, and D for the Dead. Was a time when this was one of the most violent, drug-ridden areas of the city. Was a time when the main reasons to visit the park were to shoot victims, shoot dope, or shoot your load into a hooker.

Those fun-filled days are gone. Most of the scum have been driven out. Drug dens have been replaced by shops, bars and nightclubs. Property prices have soared. Alphabet City is about as dangerous as Alphabet Soup.

Well, okay, maybe that's an exaggeration.

Maybe there is still the occasional burglary, the odd mugging, the infrequent assault, the surprising rape.

And yes, perhaps murder does sometimes feature in the crime figures.

But, hey, nobody would want to see the dedicated cops of the Eighth Precinct being put out of a job, now would they? Got to throw them a few tidbits to prevent the vultures from circling overhead.

Doyle is finding this particular morsel difficult to digest. At his left elbow is a teetering column of brown accordion-style case files, each associated with an investigation in which Joe Parlatti was involved. Inside each file is a '61', the form completed when a crime is originally reported, plus a stack of DD5s, the Detective Division follow-up reports familiarly known as 'fives'. Doyle has been plowing through these for hours, a task not aided by the fact that some reports are out of place and others are missing. He is searching for an event which, however seemingly innocuous at the time, could have lit the fuse with Parlatti's name on it.

Around Doyle, other detectives are performing similar duties. One is systematically and noisily pulling open and rifling through the contents of file cabinets. Another is sifting through the rap sheets on some of the perps that Parlatti arrested, rousted or otherwise encountered during his police career. Another is working the phone, trying to ascertain the current whereabouts of the likeliest suspects.

And so it goes on. It is tedious work. Unglamorous work. The sort of daily grind that is never reflected in TV cop shows. Doyle is aching to get back on the streets, but at the same time he is beginning to feel a lack of sleep settling on his shoulders.

Lieutenant Franklin leaves his office and enters the squad-room, overcoat on and briefcase in hand. He approaches Doyle's desk, weariness in his walk.

'I'm going home. You should too.' He gestures toward the detectives who are only a few hours into the evening tour. 'Leave this for fresher eyes.'

Doyle glances at his watch and is surprised to see that it's past seven-thirty.

'Over nineteen hours since Joe got it.'

Franklin absent-mindedly taps the head of the bobbing

leprechaun on Doyle's desk. A 'welcome gift' from the squad when he first arrived.

'You're thinking not much to show for it.'

Doyle shrugs in reply. Most of the squad on one case for nearly a full day, and not one whiff of a lead. It isn't looking good. He is not alone in having at least a couple of dozen other cases waiting in the wings, and the numbers are building. Criminals are inconsiderate that way: never willing to give a busy cop time to catch up. At the moment, Joe's case is at the top of everybody's priority list, but it won't stay there forever. Every detective working a homicide knows that unless something breaks in the first forty-eight hours, more often than not you can forget about it. Despite any other reassurances of the city's COMPSTAT figures, homicide clearance rates continue to blot the record.

'I have a bad feeling about this, Mo.'

Franklin closes his eyes. It seems an effort for him to open them again. 'Tomorrow,' he says. 'We'll get a break tomorrow.'

He leaves the squadroom, looking every inch a man already in his twilight years.

Doyle runs the same gamut of emotions every time. He parks, gets out of his car and looks lovingly up at his apartment building, thinking how fortunate he is to be living here.

By the time he has planted his foot on the first step, the unease has already set in. He imagines the curtains twitching, the neighbors peering out at him and nudging their partners and pointing to his rust-bucket of a car and muttering about the area not being what it was.

The building is a brownstone on West Eighty-seventh Street, close to Central Park. It has wrought ironwork and stone lions above the doorway and the original stoop and hardwood floors. And he could never afford to live here. Not on the salary of a New

York Detective, Second Grade. Not even if he were ever to make First Grade – an increasingly unlikely prospect, in his view.

He has his wife, Rachel, to thank for this place. Which is okay: he's not so Neanderthal that he can't live with that. But she in turn has her parents to thank for the apartment. Which is not so okay. Doyle hates the thought of being indebted. He especially hates the idea of being indebted to two people who refuse to recognize or approve of anyone unless they're rich, white, right wing, and not a member of the Police Department.

Doyle turns the key in the lock of his apartment door and pushes it open. He hears raised voices, laughter, and feels drained by the prospect of having to dredge up polite conversation. When he identifies the owners of the voices, things don't seem so gloomy.

He walks up the short hallway, glancing at the framed black-and-white photographs taken by Rachel, especially that one of Amy wearing a summer dress and a goofy smile.

In the living room there are more photos on the walls, including one of him shirtless, which he keeps asking Rachel to consign to the bedroom. Tan leather furniture surrounds a glass coffee table atop an Aztec-pattern rug. In one corner of the room is a small desk with computer equipment.

'Evening, ladies,' he says as he enters.

The two women parked on the sofa turn their heads to face him. Their bodies are still angled toward each other, and Doyle feels slightly awkward at the suspicion that he has just cut into one of those deep discussions that men must never be allowed to hear, on pain of death.

The visitor's name is Nadine. She is blond, petite, and never wears a bra. She is, Doyle knows, twenty-four years old, but looks as though she has never escaped her teens. At the moment she is wearing a clingy silk dress. Her legs are crossed, and the dress rides high over her bare thighs. She has kicked off her shoes, and her button toes curl and uncurl as she beams at him.

If you could capture and bottle the essence of sexual desire, you'd have to call it Nadine. The girl can't help it. It's just there. Whenever she walks into a crowded room it's to the accompaniment of male jawbones hitting the floor. What makes it worse, in Doyle's view, is that she seems oblivious to her powers, and therefore makes no attempt to counteract her allure. Not that he's sure how she could ever achieve that. She could put on a hazmat suit and still have the ability to straighten the Tower of Pisa.

More surprising to Doyle is that Nadine is married. To his boss, Lieutenant Morgan Franklin. A man who is twice her age. It's a fact that constantly causes Doyle to battle the cynic within himself. Love is unpredictable, he reasons; it shines through in the most unexpected of circumstances. This is a bond which has nothing to do with the substantial inheritance that came to Franklin when his mother died. It has no connection to the colossal house in Westchester County they now own in addition to their Manhattan apartment.

'Hello, Cal,' Nadine says.

Two words, Doyle thinks to himself. A perfectly commonplace, matter-of-fact greeting. So why does it sound like she's just invited me to take her clothes off?

'Hi, hon,' says the sofa's other occupant.

Already feeling the guilt of keeping his eyes glued on Nadine for a split-second longer than is advisable, Doyle shifts his gaze to his wife. Rachel is wearing a baggy red Gap T-shirt and faded denim jeans. Her long dark hair is tied back in a loose ponytail. Her expression is saying to him, *Look, I know you're a guy and Nadine is, well, Nadine, but can you just remember that this is your wife sitting here watching you drool like an elderly St Bernard?*

In return he flashes her a twisted smile that says, *You're jealous, even though there's nothing to be jealous about, and I love you for it, and that's why I like to tease you.*

And she smiles back and arches an eyebrow that says, *Keep on doing it, buster, and see what happens.*

And *that*, Doyle thinks, is what makes the difference. The telepathy. The ability to convey volumes of information without uttering a word. Nadine, in all her eye-catching glory, is still just candy when it comes down to it. What he sees in Rachel's eyes is what he first saw all those years ago when she was showing him around a crummy studio in Washington Heights. For some reason he found himself opening up to her, and it was only some time after she told him he could do better than this that he realized she wasn't talking about the apartment. It was later, too, that he discovered she wasn't some lowly junior, but that in fact her father owned the realty company and a lot more besides.

What he also sees in those eyes is the look of devotion and conviction that he saw when she was forced to defy her parents' warnings to stay away from Doyle, opening a family gulf that still tears her apart.

Doyle inclines his head toward one of the bedrooms. 'Amy gone to bed?'

'Uh-huh,' Rachel says, and it sounds to Doyle as though there is still a hint of admonition in there somewhere. 'She left you this.'

She leans forward, slips a sheet of paper from the coffee table and holds it out to Doyle. He takes it from her and stares fondly at the colorful drawing of the house and the deranged-looking animal that towers above it. Some penciled writing begins tight in the top left corner and gradually droops to the bottom right:

this is my rabit. his name is Marshmallow. he cam
in my yard and I gave him a carot. the end.

'That's pretty good,' Doyle says. 'She get any help with this?'

'Listen to the cop,' Rachel says to Nadine. 'Why do they have to be so cynical about everything?' She looks again at Doyle. 'Would it do any harm to believe that this is all your daughter's own work?'

'Why Marshmallow?' he asks.

'Because he's pink and white and fluffy. Jeez, where did you go to detective school?'

'Well, we're still not getting a rabbit,' Doyle says and drops the paper back onto the coffee table.

From the corner of his eye he catches Rachel mouthing something to Nadine, and she responds with a conspiratorial giggle.

'I had a rabbit once,' Nadine says. 'I used to sneak him up to my room and cuddle him in bed.'

'Yeah?' Doyle says. 'What did Mo think about that?'

This sets her rolling about in girlish laughter, while Rachel sits there emanating further warnings that anything pertaining to whatever Nadine does in bed is strictly off-limits.

Rachel clears her throat loudly. 'You eaten yet?'

Doyle flops into an easy chair, knocking a newspaper off its arm. 'No. I've kinda got past it. I'll make a sandwich or something in a minute.'

As he hears himself say these words, he knows there is a tone there that Rachel will tune into.

'Rough day?' she asks.

'Kind of.'

He pauses, and the two women, both police wives, know not to interrupt his silence.

Finally he says, 'Joe was killed last night.'

There is an audible intake of breath from Nadine, like a cry in reverse. In Rachel, Doyle detects a slight slump, as though something within her has just fallen away. They live with this worry every day, Doyle realizes, that their loved ones may not come home. And the fear is driven into them even more when a member of service is killed, and they are reminded that the protection offered by a badge and a gun can be as fragile as life itself.

'Joe *Parlatti*?' Rachel asks, the shock evident in her voice.

Doyle nods. 'It'll be all over the news by now.'

Rachel glances at the television, but makes no attempt to switch it on.

'What happened?'

'He was found dead on a vacant lot. We think he went in to help out a hooker who'd been beaten and dumped there. The killer got both of them.'

There is another whimper from Nadine, who has her hand clamped to her mouth as if she is about to cry or vomit.

Rachel's eyes flutter closed, and it looks as though she is thinking a prayer. 'God, Cal. You know who did it?'

Doyle shakes his head. He doesn't want to be any more negative than that, doesn't want to give voice to the feeling that the killer has been so careful and devious that they may never catch him.

'So that was my day,' he says. 'Sorry to bring the mood down.'

Rachel reaches across and consoles Nadine by rubbing her thigh. Doyle has now lost the urge to read any eroticism into the action.

Nadine gets up. 'I should go home,' she says. 'Wait for Mo to get in.'

'He's on his way,' Doyle says. 'Left before me.'

'He is? Okay.'

Rachel leaves the sofa too, and goes to fetch Nadine's coat.

'I'm sorry, Cal,' Nadine says. 'To hear that about Joe. I know you worked well together.'

Doyle nods. He is almost sorry he brought the subject up.

This perfunctory conversation contrasts jarringly with the levity, the easy chatter of a few minutes earlier. He feels like he has just told a dirty joke at a party, unaware that all the attendees are nuns.

Rachel brings back the coat, then sees Nadine out.

'You want a beer?' she asks when she comes back.

'Nah. I just want to sit a while.' He leans his head back against the chair. 'What'd Nadine want?'

'Just company. I think she's still finding it hard to adjust to being a cop's wife. The long hours, not knowing if your husband is safe.' She retakes her place on the sofa. 'You know, we do have a phone here.'

Doyle realizes that it's no longer Nadine she is talking about, but herself.

'What do you mean?'

She goes to say something, then changes it to a simple 'Nothing.'

'No. Tell me what's on your mind.'

She looks down at her hands as she scratches at something in her palm, saying nothing. When she finally looks up, a tear escapes and runs down the side of her nose.

'It could have been you, Cal. Joe was a good cop and a nice guy. He shouldn't be dead, and it must be cutting you up inside. But if it can happen to him then it can happen to you. I need to know you're safe, Cal. When you're out there doing what you do, I need to know you're okay. Can you imagine what would have gone through my head if I had turned on the TV and heard that a detective from the Eighth Precinct had been found dead with a hooker?'

As she says this, her other eye sends down a tear to join the first. Doyle gets up and crosses over to her. He sits next to her and pulls her into his embrace, absorbing the warmth of her body and enjoying the comfort it brings, but also sensing the slight heaving of her shoulders as she cries more freely.

When they finally part, Rachel reaches her hand up to wipe the wetness away from Doyle's own cheeks.

'Just call me, okay? Not every hour. Not even every day – I know how hectic it can get for you. But once in a while. Especially when something like this happens.' She smiles at him. 'Deal?'

'Deal.' He hugs her again, seals the contract with a kiss.

She ruffles his hair as she stands up. 'I think you need that beer now.'

She walks away, still talking as she tries to lighten the mood. 'You know, Amy's got her Christmas dance show on Saturday. She'll be getting a medal, and she really, really wants you to be there.'

'I'll be there. Promise.'

She pauses at the door and smiles teasingly at him. 'I got a ticket for Nadine too. She'll be there, in case it makes any difference.'

'Who? That dumpy broad? Why should that matter to me?'

'Right answer,' she says, laughing.

She disappears into the kitchen, then comes back a minute later clutching a cold bottle of Heineken. He takes it from her, stares for too long at the vapor tumbling down its sides.

'What?' she says. 'Tell me.'

'Joe wasn't just any member of the squad. He was my *partner*.'

As he stresses the word, he notices a shift in Rachel's posture, like she expects what's coming.

'Yes, I know. And?'

'One or two of the guys, they're making noises about that, giving me a hard time. Because of what happened, back in my old precinct.'

Rachel's lips tighten. This subject has not been discussed for many months. There is an unwritten, unspoken rule that it never will be again. Which is understandable, Doyle thinks, given that it nearly destroyed their marriage.

'That's bullshit,' she declares. 'And you can tell them I said that. Joe had to be somebody's partner, and he just happened to be yours. What occurred with that woman a year ago has no connection with what happened to Joe last night. I'll fix you a sandwich.'

She turns on her heel and marches back to the kitchen, a stiffness in her figure that was not there previously.

SIX

Tony Alvarez begins to think he must be getting old or sick or something. Not so long ago he would have been hitting the bars and clubs about now, working his charm, making his moves. Or else he would be in bed, bouncing it against the wall to the tune of some female vocal accompaniment beneath him. Instead, here he is, sitting in front of an empty pizza box, two empty beer cans, and an empty TV program. He feels a little like Homer Simpson. Okay, he didn't get much sleep last night, but that was never an excuse he would have made before now.

He worries about getting old. His father, God rest his bones, passed only a month after his fiftieth birthday. Tony doesn't want to go when he's fifty. Or even ninety, for that matter. The only plan he has for his police pension is to stock up on the huge supply of condoms he's going to need.

Since he has to blame his apathy on something, he decides to blame it on the fact of Joe Parlatti's death. Man, he thinks, that is some serious shit. Joe was a nice guy – everybody liked him. Stands to reason that a good guy getting whacked like that – someone he worked with, no less – is bound to affect a man's libido. Keeping the old johnson at half mast tonight is just paying the proper respect.

He is still in his work clothes, and he notices that there is now a tomato stain on his striped shirt. Anything less than sartorial perfection is also unlike him, and this only serves to confirm to himself how badly his state of mind has been altered by today's events.

Enough of this shit, he thinks. Bring back the old Tony.

He gets up and heads toward the bathroom, stripping as he goes. He takes a long, hot shower, trying to wash away the grime from his body and his mind. Images flash in his brain. Of Joe, lying amidst the garbage, three small holes drilled into his skull. Alvarez tells himself that he shouldn't have to think about such things. He is young. He should be able to think about women and beer and having fun. And today, somebody robbed him of that youth.

As he rinses the shampoo from his hair, he lets out a shout, a roar of anger and emotional pain. The noise fills his head, distracting him from the images. For now at least.

When he steps from the shower cubicle and wraps a warmed towel around his waist, there is a ringing in his ears. It takes him a second or two to realize that it's coming from his cellphone. He walks back into the living room, finds the phone in the pocket of his jacket.

'Hello?'

'Tony, it's Vic, down at the house. I hope you don't mind me calling you like this.'

Vic is one of the detectives on duty at the station house. He will know that Alvarez has put in a very long day, and that there has to be a good reason to disturb him now.

'Go ahead, Vic. What's up?'

'I took a call just now. Very weird. Guy won't give his name, but says he's got something on the Joe Parlatti case. I ask him for the details, but he refuses. Says the only person he'll speak with about it is you.'

'Is that it?'

'No. He gave me a number you can call him back on. Said it can't wait, neither. You want to hear what he has to say, you need to call him straight away. Oh, and one other thing . . .'

'What's that?'

'I don't know if it means anything, but he said to tell you that Fancy and Choo-Choo send their regards.'

TC, Alvarez thinks. Tremaine Cavell.

He dips a hand back into his jacket pocket, takes out a notebook and pen.

'Okay, Vic, thanks. You got that number?'

He writes it down and hangs up. He looks again at the number, starts dialing, but changes his mind. Moving into the bedroom, he opens a drawer in his bureau and pulls out an Olympus voice recorder and a TP-7 cable. He plugs one end of the cable into a jack on the recorder, and pops the other end into his ear. Switching the recorder on, he dials the number he's been given.

'Yeah, who that?'

Nice telephone manner, Alvarez thinks.

'Tremaine, it's Detective Alvarez. I hear you want to talk to me. You got something for me?'

'Nah, man, not on the phone. What I got for you got to be face to face.'

'You prepared to meet me at the precinct station house?'

Cavell barks a laugh. 'Fuck that shit. Only time you get me in there is when you arrest my ass. Niggers see me walking in there without ten cops on my back, I might as well write my obituary now.'

'Okay, so where?'

'One of my girls got a crib on West Seventeenth. Meet me there.'

'What's the full address?'

Cavell gives him the building and apartment numbers, and

Alvarez scribbles them below the phone number that Vic gave him.

'Okay, let me get in touch with Detective Doyle—'

'Whoa! Hold up! I ain't throwing no party here. This is me and you, man. That's it.'

'Detective Doyle was with me earlier today. He's working the case with me.'

He hears a sigh from Cavell. 'You don't get it, do you? What I got for you is some heavy, heavy shit. A cop like Doyle be the last motherfucker I want around me when I break this out.'

Alvarez feels like a bony finger has just stroked his spine. What's the problem with Doyle? Why exclude him?

'What makes you think I'm any better than Doyle?'

A pause. 'I don't. Let's just say your name didn't crop up in what I heard.'

'And you want to take that risk? Why the good citizen act all of a sudden, Tremaine?'

'Because some motherfucker took out one of my bitches, and that makes me mad. So if the only way I can get back at him is through you, then that's what I have to do.'

Alvarez considers this, and knows that he's hooked. Tremaine is too stupid to make up a story like this, and too unadventurous to follow through on such a lie. He knows something, and he wants to capitalize on that knowledge.

'All right, Tremaine, I'm coming over. This better be worth it.'

He hangs up, then switches off the recorder.

Quickly drying himself off, he dresses in jeans, Timberlands and a woolen sweatshirt. He shrugs on a tan overcoat, then clips his Glock to his belt and drops three more loaded magazines into his pocket. He picks up his cellphone and the recorder, with the intention of returning the latter to the bedroom drawer, then thinks better of it and slips both gadgets into his other side pocket.

As he heads out into the night, his thoughts are troubled by one thing. Or, rather, one person.

And it's not Cavell.

Alvarez parks up on West Seventeenth, close enough to get a good view of the apartment building Cavell specified, but not directly in front. He turns off his lights and remains in the dissipating warmth of his Toyota for a good ten minutes while he watches the five-story walk-up.

He sees nobody go in and nobody come out, and as far as he can tell, there is no sign of anybody else keeping an eye on the building from out here on the street. The only indication that anyone is aware of his presence comes when a coiffured poodle takes an interest in his car's front bumper. The dog's owner, a middle-aged man in a long coat and wide-brimmed hat, warns the pooch that the cute-looking driver probably isn't ready for that level of intimacy, and they continue on their merry way.

Alvarez takes out his cellphone and voice recorder, then connects up the cable microphone and inserts the earpiece. He searches the phone for the last number he called, then redials. As he listens to the ring tone, he switches on the Olympus.

'Yeah.'

'It's Detective Alvarez, Tremaine. I'm gonna be a little bit longer. My car's decided it's too cold to move.'

'Fuck is this, man? You want to hear this shit or not? I don't need to be taking no risks like this.'

To Alvarez, Cavell sounds a little flustered. Not quite the cool gangsta image he had adopted in the garage.

'All right, Tremaine. Keep it puckered. I'll be with you in fifteen, twenty minutes tops.'

'Aiight, but any more than that and I'm gone.'

Alvarez hangs up. He disconnects the recorder and puts it into the glove compartment, then drops the cellphone back in his pocket. He pulls his Glock, checks the indicator telling him there's a round in the chamber, then reholsters it.

When he climbs out of the car and locks it up, the cold hits him. He feels as though he will freeze to the sidewalk if he stands here too long.

He walks toward the building, glancing into the interior of each vehicle as he passes it. At the lobby door he doesn't ring the bell for Cavell's apartment, but instead buzzes the superintendent.

When the super opens the door, Alvarez flashes his badge and ID.

'I need to speak with one of the tenants. Unannounced.'

The super, a gray-haired, grumpy-looking man, has spaghetti sauce around his mouth and is still chewing.

'There gonna be shooting?' he asks, losing a strand of spaghetti as he does so.

Alvarez says, 'Well, it's not on my to-do list.'

The super sucks the pasta back in, chews some more.

''Cause I don't need no holes in my building. And not in my tenants neither. I just want a quiet night. Good food, cold beer and *Barbarella*.'

'Your wife?'

'I wish. The movie. Jane Fonda stripping off in zero-G. My wife, she looks more like *Henry* Fonda.'

Alvarez is already heading for the stairs. 'Enjoy the movie,' he says.

'No holes, remember,' the super calls after him, and then Alvarez hears a door shutting.

He takes the stairs two at a time, but with stealth, listening as he goes. Outside apartment 3C he puts his ear to the uniform slab of a door.

He doesn't fear Cavell. Cavell is a young punk. But Alvarez doesn't like the fact that, right now, Cavell is calling the shots and acting kinda weird. And so it seems sensible to Alvarez, especially acting without backup like this, to proceed with some caution.

If this is some kind of trap, Alvarez thinks, then Cavell will believe he can breathe easy for a while, his victim not expected for a good fifteen minutes yet. He's not going to stand there with a cannon pointed at the door for that long. And if he's got anybody else in there with him – say a whole bunch of his homies laden with artillery – then it's likely that they will be equally at ease for now. There'll be some conversation. A couple of jokes. Maybe even some detailed description of what fun things they are going to do to that spic cop when he walks in.

But Alvarez hears nothing. Not a murmur. He is not even certain that Cavell himself is in there.

He draws his gun and lowers it to his side, then knocks on the door. It is only seconds before the door opens and Cavell's face appears in the gap. He is wearing a gray Hilfiger hooded zip-up over a blue T-shirt. He looks slightly surprised.

'That was fast, man. You get the car—'

Alvarez snaps his gun hand up and aims the weapon at the center of Cavell's forehead. With his other hand he pushes the door wide open to get a view into the apartment.

'Turn around,' he orders.

'Yo, what the—'

'Turn around. Now!'

Cavell does as he is told, raising his arms slightly in surrender as he has probably done a hundred times before. Alvarez puts the muzzle of the Glock to the back of Cavell's head, then places his left hand on his shoulder. He pushes him forward into the apartment, kicking the door closed behind him.

He marches Cavell into the middle of the living room, his eyes darting as he moves. The room gives off to a small kitchen area and there are doors into two other rooms. Alvarez picks one and guides Cavell toward it.

'Open it!'

Cavell pushes open the door and stumbles in, Alvarez tight behind him. A bedroom. All pink and lilac and teddy bears. A huge unmade bed filling the space. Some kind of black skimpy nightwear on the end of it.

'The closet,' Alvarez says, and Cavell twists his head slightly toward him.

'The closet? You think you Inspector fucking Clouseau or something? You think I got fucking Cato hiding in there?'

Alvarez jabs the gun muzzle hard into Cavell's skull. 'Do it!'

Cavell sighs and steps over to the closet. Alvarez stays near the doorway, his gun on Cavell's back but his eyes constantly flicking back to the living room and that other unopened door.

Cavell yanks open the closet. There is a sudden movement within. Alvarez tightens his trigger finger. A red shoe falls from the shelf and lands at Cavell's feet, and Alvarez steps down the pressure on the trigger.

'Back that way,' he says. He keeps his gaze fixed on Cavell as he retraces his steps. As Cavell passes, he puts the gun back to his head.

'You don't gotta do that,' Cavell complains.

'Shut up! Open the other door.'

They cross the living area, and Cavell follows his instructions. Alvarez doesn't need to enter the tiny bathroom to see that it's unoccupied.

'Happy now?' Cavell asks.

'No,' Alvarez answers. 'Against the wall.'

Knowing the drill, Cavell puts his hands high on the wall, alongside a window looking onto the street below. Alvarez kicks his feet apart, displacing his center of gravity so that any attempt to come away from the wall will have him falling flat on his face. Keeping his gun in place, he pats Cavell's armpits, then down both flanks. He checks Cavell's waist, then drags his gun down Cavell's spine and runs his free hand over the man's legs. Straightening up, he does a similar run along Cavell's arms. Finally, he dips his hand into the hood of Cavell's sweatshirt.

'Stay there,' Alvarez says. He walks back to the apartment door and sees that it has a locking bar. He fixes it into place, just in case some friends of Cavell's should decide to pay a visit.

'Now I'm happy,' he says, putting the Glock away.

Cavell straightens up, drops his arms and turns to face Alvarez.

'The fuck you gotta do all that shit for, man? I tole you I was trying to help you out.'

Alvarez is warm after the exertion and the stress of the last few minutes. He takes off his coat and slings it over the back of the sofa, then folds his arms and looks around the room. It's clean and tidy. Vases of dried flowers on the coffee table and on the kitchen counter. On one wall, a poster of the good-looking black doctor from *ER*.

'You like that guy, Tremaine?'

Cavell curls his lip at the insult. 'Like I said, this my girl's place.'

'One of your hookers?'

'One of my own private collection. I don't like to mix business with pleasure.'

'Uh-huh. So why bring me here, Tremaine? What's all this about?'

'I got a message for you.'

'A message, huh? Who from?'

'Can't say.'

'Can't or won't?'

Cavell just shrugs.

'Okay, so why not tell me on the phone? Or send me a letter? Or a fucking carrier pigeon?'

'Don't know. I was just told this is the way it has to be.'

'You always do what you're told, Tremaine? Whose bitch are you being right now?'

Cavell flares his nostrils and bares his teeth. Alvarez knows that the slur got to him, but when Cavell bites on his bottom lip, he realizes it's not enough. Somebody, somewhere, has a grip on Cavell's testicles and is threatening to squeeze.

'And why do I have to keep Detective Doyle out of this? What's that all about?'

Again Cavell shrugs, and Alvarez accepts he's wasting his time.

'All right, Tremaine, give me the fucking message. And this better have something to do with the case we're working, or I'll run you down to the station house so fast your ass won't be able to keep up. So spit it out.'

Cavell licks his lips, acting like he's about to give a damn speech. He's looking nervous too, Alvarez thinks. Almost ready to pee himself. What the fuck is going on here?

'The message is . . .' Cavell begins.

Alvarez waits for the rest. He notices that beads of sweat have broken out on Cavell's forehead. So much for the street-hard pimp.

'Yeah?' he prompts.

'The message is . . . you got too close.'

For a second, Alvarez feels he is in a surrealist painting. Or reading a foreign pamphlet in which the text has been badly mistranslated. Cavell's words just don't fit any mental template he knows how to process.

And now he feels he is being dicked around.

'The fuck you talking about, Tremaine? Is that it? That's your fucking message? That's what you dragged my ass all the way across town to hear? Get your coat, Tremaine. We got a trip to make, and don't plan on seeing your woman in her skimpy shit tonight. Second thoughts, bring the frillies with you. You can wear them for the nice big cellmate I'm gonna hook you up with.'

Cavell holds his palms up, his shoulders high. The body language of someone who is trying to plead his case.

'Serious, man. That's what I been told to say. You got too close. Dude said you'd understand what it means.'

There is a wavering pitch to Cavell's voice now, Alvarez notices. Like he really needs to hear confirmation that his words have struck some big-ass bell in the mind of the detective.

'Don't mean shit, Tremaine. Let's go.'

He beckons to the pimp, but Cavell doesn't budge from his position near the wall. He waves his hand at Alvarez.

'Hold up. I got more. Something else I got to deliver.'

Alvarez raises an eyebrow. 'What?'

'A note. Over there, on the counter.'

Alvarez looks to where Cavell is gesturing. Lying on the kitchen counter is a white envelope. Alvarez steps over to it and picks it up. It weighs little, and bears no writing on the front. He glances at Cavell, then pushes his thumb under the sealed flap and rips it open.

Inside, there is a single sheet of paper, folded once. He opens it up and reads the typewritten text:

Bang. You're dead.

Alvarez feels his heart pound harder. He senses that he's been dropped into the middle of a situation he doesn't fully understand. He doesn't know whether to be afraid or angry.

He glares hard at Cavell and flaps the note at him. 'You write this, Tremaine? This your idea of a fucking joke?'

Cavell is shifting his weight from foot to foot. 'I don't even know what's in the fucking note, man. Just take it and leave, okay? I done my part. Take the note and get the fuck out of here. That's what's supposed to happen.'

Alvarez shakes his head in an effort to clear his confusion. 'What are you talking about? What do you mean: supposed to happen? I ain't going nowhere until you start talking some sense.'

Cavell just stares back. His eyes are bulging. His chest is heaving.

And then he does something totally bizarre.

He begins talking to himself.

Or, rather, to an imagined person behind him.

He twists his head so that it is angled over his shoulder and says, 'We done, right? I done what you said. We straight now.'

Alvarez whips his gun out. He doesn't know why, or what he is going to do with it, but it seems the prudent thing to do in the face of this insanity.

He levels the gun at Cavell's face. 'What's going on, Tremaine? Talk to me, man.'

Cavell continues to stare and to suck hard on the air, like he's having trouble getting enough oxygen into his system. Alvarez rushes toward him and puts the gun to his nose, squashing it against his face.

'Who you talking to, Tremaine?'

He puts his left hand around Cavell's throat and forces him back against the wall. Cavell almost screams his protest: 'My back, man! Watch my back!'

The shock of Cavell's cries sends Alvarez reeling away from him.

He looks Cavell up and down and thinks, I frisked the guy. He's not strapped. What did I miss?

It strikes him then how warm it is in this apartment. The heating is turned up high. And yet Cavell – the man who earlier today was wearing a sleeveless T-shirt in near-freezing conditions – is now hiding his muscles under a zip-up sweatshirt.

Alvarez takes up a two-handed shooting stance, the gun aimed at the exact center of Cavell's chest.

'Take off the sweater,' he orders.

'What? No, man.'

'Do it, Tremaine, or I start shooting.'

Cavell's eyes seem to shiver in their sockets.

Do it! Alvarez barks.

Slowly, shakily, Cavell reaches for his zip and starts to slide it down. He talks over his shoulder again. 'I have to do what the cop is asking. Don't do nothing now, okay? Stay cool.'

He takes off the sweater, lets it drop to the floor.

'Now the shirt,' Alvarez says.

Cavell consults his invisible friend again. 'It's okay, man. This ain't nothing. Just ride it out.'

He pulls the T-shirt over his head and lets that drop too. His muscular torso glistens with a sheen of perspiration.

'Turn around,' Alvarez tells him.

Cavell swallows, his eyes saying to Alvarez, *I hope you know what you're doing.*

Slowly, he turns to face the wall, and that's when Alvarez sees it.

The package is taped high up, nestling in the deep channel between Cavell's shoulder blades. The hooded top had covered the bulge, and Alvarez had missed it in the pat-down.

Shit!

Alvarez raises his eyes from the sights of his gun and refocuses on the package. There are wires – for a microphone of some kind. Somebody has been listening in to everything that has been said in this apartment.

But this isn't just a listening device.

Alvarez recalls what was in the note. The note which Cavell hasn't yet seen . . .

. . . and that's when he decides it's the moment to get out of here.

In that instant, time slows to a trickle. Alvarez turns toward the door. Run, he tells his legs. Run like fuck!

But it is like trying to swim through treacle. He can see where he needs to be, and he knows what he needs to do to get there, but he's like a toy with a dying battery.

A sudden realization descends on him that he will never reach his goal. Not like this. Not unless he can sprout wings and fly.

And then his wish comes true. He is flying. Flying while the heat and the light and the pressure overwhelm his body and tear it apart.

Sitting in the hired Ford van, behind its blacked-out windows, the man listens to the reverberations of what he has just done.

His finger is still on the button, pressing so hard that the nail has turned white. He removes it, watches the blood rush back.

It worked. There were moments when he had his doubts, when he worried that he was trying to be too clever, too ingenious.

He had worried, too, about the amount of explosive to use. A bigger charge could have been stashed in the apartment somewhere, but it carried the risk that Cavell would have run away from it at the first opportunity. Turning Cavell into a human bomb like that, along with a microphone that would reveal any attempt to remove the package, was a stroke of genius. He can still picture the moment when he told Cavell. He'd put a gun to Cavell's head, forced him against the wall, slapped the bundle onto his back. Stepping away, his gun still raised, he revealed to Cavell what he'd just done. The expression of disbelief and horror on the pimp's face was so exaggerated it was comical.

Even with Cavell's big muscles and the hooded sweater there was only so much explosive that could be taped to him without it being obvious, but that didn't matter. C-4 detonates at a velocity of 18,000 miles per hour. You don't need much of that shit to take out a whole roomful of people.

And if Alvarez *had* found it, so what? It would have simply meant pressing the button that little bit sooner.

But Alvarez missed it in the frisk, didn't he? A trained cop, years on the job, and he missed it. Ha! How delicious was that?

It meant that the message could be delivered, offering Alvarez the chance to puzzle over what it was he had done wrong. And yet he suspected nothing. Even when confronted with the reason for his imminent demise, he was still too stupid to grasp its implications.

It meant too that the note could be given to Alvarez, allowing him to contemplate the sounding of his death knell.

But above all, it meant that everything that Alvarez said and did right up to the moment of his annihilation could be overheard.

The man in the Ford leans back and reviews his accomplishment here tonight. He feels like he should be lighting up a cigarette, the way they do in the movies after great sex. In the distance he can hear sirens, and he knows he will have to drive away soon. But he will allow himself to revel for a moment longer. This has been so much more satisfying than the killing of Joe Parlatti.

SEVEN

When the phone rings, Doyle doesn't know where he is. As he reaches out to his bed table he blinks his eyes until the hazy lights on his clock sharpen into recognizable numerals.

It is five-thirty in the morning.

Shit, he thinks. Telephone calls at this time of day carry only bad news. There's a law about it somewhere.

Next to him, Rachel groans her disapproval and pulls the duvet over her head. When Doyle's fumbling hands finally locate the handset, he answers the call with a mouth that feels like it's filled with cotton wool.

'Hello?'

'Cal? It's Mo.'

The tone is subdued.

'Okay, Mo, what is it?'

There's a lengthy pause. 'It's not good, Cal. There's no easy way to tell you this.'

Doyle is wide awake now. 'Spit it out, Mo.'

'Something happened last night. To Tony Alvarez. He was killed.'

And now Doyle begins to wonder whether, in fact, he is still sleeping. Whether his mind is filled with dark imaginings of his deepest subconscious. He swings his legs over the side of the bed.

'Killed? How? Where?' There are a million other questions on his lips, but these will do for now.

'There was an explosion at an apartment on Seventeenth Street. Alvarez was there with another guy, still unnamed. I only found out about this an hour ago myself. I don't have all the details yet.'

Doyle stares into the darkness of the bedroom. His questions have all run away, as if his brain has decided it doesn't want to know any more about this because it's all too terrifying.

Franklin cuts into his thoughts. 'Cal? You're the first one on the squad I've told about this. I don't think I need to say why.'

Doyle nods, not thinking that Franklin can't see him. Mo is preparing him. Forewarned is forearmed, and all that.

Franklin continues: 'The killing was in the Eleventh, so it's their case at the moment. But you know how quick these things get around. By the start of the day tour, everybody'll have heard about this. I just thought . . . Well, I just wanted you to know.'

Doyle clears his throat. 'Yeah. Thanks for the heads-up, Mo. Appreciate it.'

'Okay, Cal. See you in a couple hours.'

'Yeah. Yeah.'

He ends the call. Sitting on the edge of his bed like this, he begins to notice how cold the room is.

Two cops dead in the space of twenty-four hours. Could it be any worse?

Well, yes, if they were both partners of yours.

He leaves the house before Rachel and Amy are up. He doesn't want to tell Rachel about it just yet – doesn't want to discuss it with anyone – and if he sits there moping over breakfast she will know that something is wrong.

He doesn't go directly to the station house, but instead drives the streets for a while, killing time and thinking. Eventually, he pulls up at a near-empty diner and seats himself at a booth in the corner. He orders sausage, eggs and coffee, but finds that his stomach will permit entry only to the coffee. After pushing the food around his plate for a while, he finally gives up and heads off to work. He times his arrival to be as late as he can make it, seconds before the start of his shift.

As he walks through the doorway he hears a loud fake cough, warning of his presence. Silence descends as he moves toward his desk. He waits for the first wise-ass remark, but nothing comes his way. Not yet, anyway. It might be because Mo Franklin is standing at the front of the squadroom, like a teacher keeping order among his pupils.

Jay Holden, a shaven-headed black cop who ran with street gangs in his youth, is the first to speak.

'We're all here now, Mo. How about you put an end to all the rumors?'

Doyle has always liked Holden. He is his own man – never to be swayed by the unsupported opinions of others. He waits until he gets all the facts, and then he makes up his own mind.

Franklin perches himself on the edge of an unoccupied desk. Tony Alvarez's desk.

'I wish I could say to you that all we have here are rumors, that none of it is confirmed yet, that it's all likely to be so much bullshit. Unfortunately, that's not the case. Detective Tony Alvarez was killed in the line of duty last night.'

They know it already, but still they groan, curse, lower their heads.

'What happened, Mo?' somebody asks.

'Tony was following up on the Joe Parlatti hit. He went to an apartment on West Seventeenth to meet someone who claimed to have information.'

Puzzled, Doyle looks up at Franklin. A lead on the Parlatti case? What lead? Why didn't Tony bring him in on it?

Franklin carries on: 'It was a trap. The apartment was booby-trapped somehow. A bomb. The guy Tony was meeting was killed instantly – blown to bits. Tony was brought out alive, but only barely. He didn't survive the journey to the hospital.'

There is a moment of silent reflection before Schneider pipes up.

'The news channels are saying the explosion on Seventeenth happened at about ten o'clock last night. How come we're only just getting to hear about Alvarez getting caught in that?'

'The bomb went off in the Eleventh Precinct, so none of our guys were on-scene. When Tony Alvarez was carried out of the building he had no ID on him. It was hours before the Bomb Squad declared the apartment clear, and another couple hours before the fire department said the building was structurally safe to enter. Eventually, they found Tony's shield in his jacket, which had been blown across the room.' He pauses. 'I got a call only hours ago myself. I had to . . . I had to ID the body.'

This seems to mollify Schneider for the moment. He nods almost imperceptibly and tosses his gum around his mouth.

Holden asks, 'We have an ID on the other DOA?'

Franklin looks relieved to drag his thoughts away from the vision of Alvarez's shattered form. 'We think it's a pimp named Tremaine Cavell, street handle TC. The apartment belongs to a girlfriend of his.'

What?

Doyle's mind is racing now. A follow-up with Tremaine? All the more reason for not cutting him out. So why the hell would Alvarez do that?

Holden says, 'And Cavell fits into this how?'

Franklin's eyes flicker toward Doyle. The lieutenant seems reluctant to supply an answer, so Doyle does it for him.

'Cavell was pimping for the pross found with Joe. We tracked him down yesterday, but he didn't give us much.'

Schneider's mouth is provoked into action again. 'Wait a minute. Have I missed something here? Yesterday you and Alvarez go talk to this pimp scumbag, who gives you zip. Later that same day, Alvarez goes to see the same scumbag, only this time without backup. More specifically, without *you*, Doyle. You wanna explain to me how this situation came about, Alvarez going into a potentially dangerous situation without his *partner*?'

The emphasis on the word 'partner' is like a sharp jab in Doyle's ribs. He doesn't feel that Alvarez was truly his partner – they just happened to come together and work jointly for less than a day. But he knows that the others won't see it like that.

He studies their faces. All eyes are on him, and irrespective of their feelings toward Schneider and the way he phrases things, it is clear that they think an answer is warranted.

The problem for Doyle is that he doesn't have one.

He opens his mouth, unsure as to what words are about to spill out, but Franklin gets there ahead of him.

'I can answer that. Cavell phoned the station house last night, looking to speak to Tony. Tony called him back on his cellphone, but he was careful. He recorded the conversation.'

'And we have it?'

'We do. Tony's car was found near the apartment on Seventeenth. The digital recorder he used was in the glove compartment. I asked the Eleventh Precinct to send me a copy of the discussion between Tony and Cavell.'

As he says this, Franklin reaches into his jacket and takes out his own voice recorder.

'This will get back to you anyhow, so you may as well hear it now.'

He switches the machine on, and the detectives listen in rapt silence as the recording plays through to its end. When it reaches the part where he is mentioned by name, Doyle feels the pressure of numerous gazes being directed his way.

Schneider says, 'So, Doyle, what puts you on the blacklist of a slimy mope like Cavell? Any reason you can think of why he might not want you there last night?'

'You heard what I heard, Schneider. He wanted Tony there alone. He didn't want *any* other cop there, not just me. He used my name explicitly because Tony brought it up that he should call me. If you'd have been working with Tony yesterday, it would have been *your* name on that recording.'

'Oh yeah. That's right. You and Alvarez were *working* together. Just like you were *working* with Joe Parlatti, who also happens to be dead. And if we all care to cast our minds back a little further . . .'

'Oh, fuck you, Schneider,' Doyle says.

'Fuck you too, Doyle. All's I'm saying is that it don't take no Sherlock fucking Holmes to see a pattern developing here . . .'

'All right!' Franklin yells. 'Can it, you two, for Christ's sake. I lost two of my finest detectives yesterday. Two people I was proud to call my friends. They were your friends too. Bickering like schoolgirls is going to get us nowhere.' He aims a finger at Schneider. 'If you think that Detective Doyle had anything to do with the death of any police officer, in this squad or anywhere else, then you put it in writing. If you don't want to do that, then I don't want to hear any more insinuations.' He takes his eyes off Schneider, addresses the whole group. 'From any of you. Understand?'

He gets a few nods in return.

'That said,' Franklin adds, 'there's a bit more I need to tell you. This may be nothing, but it may be important, so you need to hear it.'

Doyle catches a brief, almost apologetic, glance in his direction. Shit, he thinks. What now?

'When Tony was being put in the ambulance, he said a name,

"Doyle." Then he said three more words: "Got too close." Like I said, Tony was on the edge of dying right then. He may have just been rambling. Any thoughts?'

Schneider's response is to expel air from the corner of his mouth in a kind of *pfff* sound – his way of letting the room know where his opinions lie.

Holden's comments are a little more lucid. 'Maybe Cal and Tony were on to something without even knowing it. *Too close*. So close, Tony had to die.'

Schneider decides he needs to be vocal again. 'Yeah. You need to be careful, Doyle. You could be next.'

Holden ignores him and presses on. 'That stuff from Cavell about some heavy shit going down. If he really was about to toss something juicy to Tony, that could have been a good reason for someone to whack both of them.'

Franklin nods thoughtfully. 'That's assuming Cavell really did have something to deliver. If this went down the way the hit on Joe did, Cavell was probably just being used as bait. Any other theories?'

'A cop killer.'

This from LeBlanc, an ambitious young cop who only recently traded in his white shield for a gold one. Always sporting the most fashionable spectacles, although Doyle suspects that he wears them only to appear brainier than he is. Older, wiser heads might not have dared to voice LeBlanc's idea, but Doyle is sure that it has entered the minds of all of them.

'For some reason,' LeBlanc says, 'the killer just doesn't like cops, period. He's working his way through them, one by one.' He looks across at Schneider. 'In which case, maybe it doesn't have to be Cal who's next. Maybe it's any one of us.'

'Nice thought, kid,' Schneider answers. 'Cheer us all up, why don't you?'

'Even so,' Franklin says, 'we have to take it into consideration. Could just be we have a psycho cop killer on our hands.' He raises a warning finger and wags it at each man in the room. 'I don't want to lose any other members of my squad. From now on, you have to be on your guard at all times, you hear me?'

He gets nods again, but more vigorous this time. Now and again, it's nice to hear how much your boss loves you.

And then there is another period of silence, while every detective here weighs up the implications of having to be aware of everything around them, at all times of the day. The killer has shown himself to be a person of astounding ingenuity and resource. From now on, even taking a crap could be fraught with danger.

Who says a cop's life is dull?

'There's another possibility,' Doyle says. He has been thinking about this ever since the wake-up call from Franklin. What the lieutenant said about the last words of Alvarez lends it even more currency.

'Maybe I really am the link in this. Maybe this is some warped way of trying to hurt me. Those words of Tony's, using my name and then "got too close". Maybe what he was saying was that he got too close to me.'

Franklin is staring at him, his expression grave. 'You know anyone might want to get at you like that?'

Doyle looks round at Schneider. 'Outside this room, no.'

This raises a couple of snickers, which tells Doyle that there are at least one or two people on his side.

Franklin says, 'That'd be one crazy way to hurt somebody, Cal. I hope to God you're wrong about that.'

Not as much as I do, Doyle thinks.

EIGHT

Barely five minutes after the men in the squadroom finish trying to fathom what is happening to them, the lieutenant takes a phone call from the Chief of Detectives. The Chief of Ds tells Franklin, amongst other things, that even though the death occurred within the confines of the Eleventh Precinct, the Alvarez case now officially belongs to the Eighth, being as it seems to have a solid link to the Parlatti case, which was already theirs. In his turn, Franklin relays the word from above to the squad, and it's all systems go.

Doyle makes it his first task to learn what he can about the events of last night. It's a job that takes longer than he hoped, mainly because the required information seems to be distributed across about a dozen people from the Eleventh Precinct, the Manhattan South Homicide Task Force and the Bomb Squad, not all of whom are immediately contactable.

Next, Doyle calls the Medical Examiner's office for a prelim on the Alvarez and Cavell autopsies. He manages to speak to Norman Chin, who informs him that Alvarez's fatal injuries were sustained solely as a result of a massive explosion, the epicenter of which lay in the immediate proximity of one Tremaine Cavell. It is Chin's conjecture that the bomb was either being held by Cavell, or was somehow attached to his upper torso, this being difficult to confirm owing to the current absence of said upper torso.

The conclusion being, Doyle thinks as he ends the call, that Cavell had somehow been turned into a human bomb. So, strike the notion that Cavell had any hot information to reveal. He was being used, just as Scarlett had been used to kill Joe.

Tired of having a phone clamped to his ear, Doyle abandons his desk and heads out to the apartment of Cavell's girl on West Seventeenth. There he speaks with the building superintendent, whose primary concern seems to be that his warning about making holes in his walls was ignored, his building now possessing one very large hole where a third-floor window used to be, thank you very much.

There is only a handful of tenants in the building when Doyle is there. Others are out at work; some have evacuated and are refusing to return until they are 100 per cent certain they are not likely to have their asses blown off. From those remaining, Doyle extracts nothing in the way of a lead.

His next visit is a return one to the Pit Stop. He finds a few of Cavell's buddies there; others require further legwork. To each of them he puts the same questions: Do you know where Tremaine went last night? Do you know who he met with?

These boys are incensed. They want revenge. They will do whatever they can to track down the motherfucker who smoked TC. But as far as how to carry out that mission goes, it's clear to Doyle that they don't have a clue where to start.

With time ticking away, hour after fruitless hour, Doyle begins to fear that there are no clues to be found. The killer is that good. So good, in fact, that if the police are to have any hope of catching him, the perp may have to lend them a hand.

He may have to continue his killing spree.

The clothes hang loosely on the man's thin frame. The battered corduroy coat looks ready to slip off his narrow shoulders, and his wrinkled beige pants billow around his bony legs. He walks with his head tilted to one side, like he's trying to keep ear drops in place. His left arm does not beat time to his walking pace, but instead dangles and bounces off his side as though it's a length of rubber.

Doyle takes another bite from his beef sandwich and watches through his car windshield as the man pushes through a doorway farther up the block here on East Eleventh Street. He waits five minutes, finishing his sandwich and coffee before stepping out of his car and heading toward the building the man has just entered.

He swings open the heavy front door, forcing it back against powerful springs that slam it shut when he lets it slip from his grasp. He is in a small, musty lobby containing a noticeboard, a desk and a single unoccupied chair. He pushes through the next set of double doors and enters a dimly lit corridor. There's a smell of sweat here. From Doyle's right comes the hissing of a shower at full blast; from his left, the unmistakable pounding of gloved fists, the shuffling of feet, and the yells of men who live for the controlled release of aggression.

Doyle heads left, breathes deeply of the testosterone-filled atmosphere. The ever-present bounce in his step becomes more pronounced now, until his gait is more of a swagger. He remembers how it felt to be on the edge of threading a path through the supporters and the detractors, the cheers and the catcalls, his sole intent to knock the living daylights out of another man.

He enters a large hall. On the far side, a man in a sleeveless white T-shirt and sweat pants takes powerful swings at a punch-bag, while another huge man studies his technique with a critical eye. The center of the gym is taken up by a boxing ring. A white man and his black opponent, both of whom would be mean-looking enough even without their headgear and gumshields, dance around the canvas looking for openings. Dotted around the ring, other men watch and throw out words of advice and encouragement.

Seated on a wooden bench near the wall, still wearing his coat, is the man Doyle has followed. A bag of potato chips is on his lap, and he brings handfuls of them to his mouth with his one good arm. His eyes do not shift from the sparring fighters as Doyle makes his way over and sits next to him on the bench.

They sit there like this for several minutes: not saying anything to each other, just watching the boxers, assessing the skill, the art, of the men corralled together in that small roped-off square.

Finally, Doyle says, 'My money's on the white dude.'

The man next to him brings another mound of chips to his mouth, munches on them thoughtfully.

'I coulda taken him,' he says in all seriousness.

Doyle's eyes slide to his neighbor. Yeah, he thinks, you could. Back in the day.

As an eight-year-old kid fresh over from Ireland, Doyle had it tough growing up in the South Bronx. It might not have been so bad had his father migrated his family into one of the few remaining Irish communities in the borough. For some reason unknown to Doyle, he chose instead to bring them to an area inhabited predominantly by blacks and Hispanics. Of the white minority in Doyle's neighborhood, few could lay claim to any Irish ancestry, and even then it was an Irishness distanced from them by several generations. The problem for Doyle was that he *sounded* like he had just walked off the bogs, and for that he was teased mercilessly. Rare was a week that went by without his getting embroiled in at least one fist fight.

Tired of trying to keep her young son out of trouble, Doyle's mother decided that if he was going to fight anyway, then he might as well learn how to do it properly. Her solution was to sign him up in the nearest boxing gym.

Doyle learned a lot in that gym. Not just about how to defend himself, which he did with great success, but also about life itself. It was here that Doyle was coached by a black ex-cop named Herbie Chase. As a boxer, Doyle was above average in ability but never top class, and it was Chase's fascinating stories of life on the streets that eventually convinced Doyle to apply for the Police Academy. But there were others in that gym who showed a lot more boxing promise.

Like Mickey 'Spinner' Spinoza, for example – the man now seated next to Doyle.

Right into his teens, Doyle looked up to Spinner as a role model. The guy was five years older and not as bulky as Doyle – he was a lightweight, in fact – but back then he had a perfectly sculpted physique. And his technique – boy, was that something to behold. That guy could *move*, man, and his punches would shoot out with the speed of an arrow and the force of a sledgehammer. Doyle always envisioned that Spinner was destined for great things in the boxing world.

And then life played one of its cruel jokes. As blows go, it looked nothing. A jab to the side of the head that Spinner shouldn't have even noticed. But he dropped as though his legs had just disappeared. Just lay there, drooling and twitching.

They diagnosed a brain hemorrhage. It had probably been waiting to pop in his head for months, maybe even years. When it did, its effect was like being hit by an express train.

Spinner recovered eventually. But not fully. He pretty much lost all use of his left arm, and the left side of his face would always droop lower than the right, but at least he had his life back, right?

Wrong.

Spinner's life was in that gym. Was in the ring. Boxing was what kept him off the streets. When he was told he would never box again, Spinner did what many other of his South Bronx compatriots had done: he slipped into the murky world of drugs and crime.

Doyle lost contact with him. As the years passed, Spinner became a fading memory of unachieved greatness. Then, six months ago, he showed up at Doyle's precinct station house in the East Village. Desperate for money to feed his drug habit, he offered the only thing he now possessed: knowledge. From that point on, Spinner became Doyle's confidential informant.

Doyle continues to stare at the pathetic figure next to him. Spinner is now just a husk, his muscles having wasted away as quickly as his dignity. And yet, Doyle knows that there's a part of Spinner that still wishes he could be in that ring right now, showing that pasty-faced kid what *real* boxing is.

'Took a while for me to find you today,' Doyle says. 'What happened to that cellphone I gave you?'

'Threw it away. Never did like those gadgets. Damn things give you cancer. I think that's why they call them *cell*phones – 'cause they rot away your brain cells. And my brain don't need to lose no more of *them*.'

'Uh-huh. I hope you wiped the numbers from it before you sold it.'

Spinner gives him a disapproving look. 'You here to bust my balls over a phone?'

'No. I got bigger fish to fry.'

Spinner pushes more chips into his mouth, then something in the fight grabs his attention. 'Keep that chin in,' he shouts, and soggy pieces of potato chip fly from his mouth. 'Jab, Jab! Follow through, you son of a . . .' He leans toward Doyle. 'Look at that, will ya? He coulda had him. Even a slow lunk like you wouldn't have missed an opening that wide.'

Doyle smiles. Like Spinner, he wants to be up there so much his biceps are twitching. It's a feeling that never leaves.

Spinner asks, 'This fish, it's already been fried and it's carrying a gold shield, am I right?'

'Actually, I got four dead fish. My partner, Joe Parlatti, was killed along with a hooker, night before last.'

'That one I heard about.'

'Last night, another cop got it. Detective Tony Alvarez. Blown to pieces while talking to a pimp named Tremaine Cavell.'

'That I didn't know. So that makes two.'

'Two what?'

'Come on, don't pretend you're here because of a pimp and a hooker. They're nothing to you. You're here because of your cop buddies. Far as you're concerned, the others, they're just collateral damage.'

It's a cynical view that Doyle finds all the more irritating because he knows it to be true. 'Whatever. The point is, I need to find who did this.'

'Parlatti – you said he was your partner, right? That must be tough for you, coming on top of the Laura Marino thing.'

Doyle shrugs. 'The timing could have been better, sure.'

'And this other cop, this Alvarez guy . . . ?'

Doyle hesitates. 'Yeah, he kinda started working with me when we lost Parlatti.'

Spinner stops eating. He slides himself along to the end of the bench.

'Hoo, Cal, buddy. Is this safe, me sitting so close to you like this? It's starting to sound like you got some kind of curse on you, man. You upset any voodoo witch doctor or something lately? I mean, the odds against three strikes in a row . . .'

Doyle holds up his fingers. 'Two. That's two strikes. Parlatti and Alvarez. Laura Marino has nothing to do with this. Now get your skinny ass back here before I add another dead acquaintance to my list.'

Warily, Spinner shuffles back to Doyle's side.

'Whaddya want from me, Cal?'

'Anything you can get me. These were calculated hits. Very clever, very professional. Whoever did these is no mutt; he knew exactly what he was doing. I need you to ask around for me. Anyone talking about offing cops. Anyone looking to put out a contract on cops. Find out if we got any big hitters come in from out of town, like that.'

Spinner nods, his eyes back on the fight. 'Tell me what you got so far.'

Doyle gives him a summary of what the investigation has revealed since the night of the first murders, which to his mind is a big fat zero.

'I'll see what I can do,' Spinner says. 'But I have to tell ya, if this is just some lone sicko out there . . .'

'I know.' Doyle stands up. 'Take it easy, Spinner.'

'Yeah. And you watch out for that left hook. Sometimes it just comes from nowhere.'

As soon as Doyle steps out of the gym, he knows his day has just gotten a whole lot worse.

Parked directly in front of him is a gray Chevrolet Impala. A man sits on the car's hood, smoking a cigarette. He wears a midnight-blue suit, skinny black tie and charcoal overcoat. Lank black hair fans out across his forehead, and he stares at Doyle from eyes set deeply beneath thick eyebrows. His cheeks are hollow, and become even more concave when he draws on his cigarette. He looks like he's on his way to a funeral. As the one in the coffin.

Doyle throws his hands up in despair. 'Jesus H Christ, Paulson. What the fuck are you doing here?'

Sergeant Paulson takes the cigarette from his thin lips, blows a cloud of smoke in Doyle's direction.

'Nice to see you too, Doyle. Been a long time. I was just passing through, you know, and I thought to myself, Hey, wouldn't it be nice to hook up with good old Callum Doyle again? We could talk about old times, swap some stories . . .'

'Passing through, huh? If you knew I was here, then you know what I'm doing here, right? I'm having a meeting with a confidential informant. Emphasis on the *confidential*. That means being discreet, Paulson. Look at you. You might as well put up a neon sign saying "The Cops Are Here". Jesus, do you even remember what it was like to be on our side of the fence?'

Paulson pushes himself off his car and pretends to look hurt.

'Aw, gee. Don't be like that. We got history, you and me.'

'Yeah, history. Meaning, in the past. Now get the fuck out of here, before I do something I regret.'

Doyle turns and starts to walk back to his own car, but he can hear the clicking of Paulson's shoes as he trails after him.

'Can't do that, Doyle. I feel this burning need to talk to you. If not here, then it'll have to be somewhere else.'

Doyle stops on the street, his fists bunched. Watching the fighters train back there has put him square in the mood for landing a haymaker on someone. If not Paulson, then he has a good second choice in mind.

There was a time when informants were more or less regarded as a cop's personal and private property. Undisclosed sums of money and favors were traded in dark and dingy locations, the fact of these meetings and the identity of the CI often never being revealed to anyone else.

That time has long gone. Nowadays, CIs have to be formally registered with the Police Department, which entails a tree's worth of paperwork and a list of signatures that seems to involve everyone up to the US President. Partly for reasons of 'investigative transparency', but partly also to ensure the safety of the detective involved, meetings with CIs have to be logged.

Doyle regards himself as a man not predisposed to breaking rules. Save in circumstances when those rules are stupid. And on the odd occasion when they prove inconvenient. So, naturally enough, he called in his whereabouts when he came over to the gym here on East Eleventh. He trusted his colleagues not to go blabbing his location to all and sundry, and especially to members of the Internal Affairs Bureau.

Most of his colleagues, that is.

Doyle turns around, folds his arms, and waits for Paulson to reach him.

'So talk,' he says.

Paulson looks from side to side. 'Here?'

'I ain't going for coffee and donuts with you, Paulson. Talk.'

Paulson takes another puff on his cigarette. 'You're an interesting man to know, Doyle. Things seem to happen around you, like you're a source of cosmic disturbance in the universe.'

'It's my animal magnetism. All the chicks love it.'

'I think you're underestimating your power. What I'm talking about is a destructive force. Enough to start people dropping like flies all around you.'

'Ah, you're referring to my deodorant.' Doyle raises his arm. 'You wanna take a sniff?'

Paulson taps his finger on his cigarette, watches the slug of ash drift to the sidewalk and roll away.

'The wisecracks are all very funny, Doyle. But they don't make this any less serious. This situation, cops dying, it's making a lot of pen-pushers sit up and take notice. 1PP is buzzing with this right now. They're getting nervous. They're looking at the connections. And you know what? There's one obvious connection staring them right in the face.'

Doyle can picture the brass in NYPD headquarters at One Police Plaza, running around like soon-to-be-headless chickens and wondering who's wielding the hatchet.

'And you see it as your job to try to prove them right, is that it?' Paulson looks shocked.

'Not at all. Me, I think there's nothing there to find. Just like there was nothing to find a year ago.' He pauses. 'Jeez, was it really a whole year ago? Seems like yesterday.'

It's a vivid memory to Doyle too. He recalls only too well being cooped up in that interview room, just him and Paulson. He remembers the quick-fire salvos of questions, the devious attempts to trip him up, the insults and veiled threats. He remembers how much he hated Paulson's guts, how close he came to leaping out of his chair and closing his meaty hands around Paulson's throat. It was a point in Doyle's life at which his career, perhaps even his freedom, were nearly brought to an end, and he resented with ferocity the fact that this shadow of a cop could have so much power over him.

And now, like a bad smell, the wraith-like figure is back with his poison.

'So it's just coincidence that you end up on this gig? All the dirt-diggers in IAB, and you're the lucky guy gets the spade.'

'Let's just say I already had a vested interest in your precinct.'

The object of interest being me, Doyle thinks.

'Like I said, Paulson, what do you want?'

Paulson takes a last long inhalation of nicotine. He drops the stub to the sidewalk and grinds it out with a polished shoe before finally blowing the fumes out through his nostrils.

'The best way for you to think of me is as someone who can be a lot of help to you. Regard me as your benefactor, a force for good in your life.'

'There being every reason for me to think of you in that way.'

Paulson shrugs. 'The alternative is to feel embittered and victimized. No, in a situation like this you need to promote some positive energy. Look at it this way: anytime any criticism comes your way, anybody even hints that you might be wrong, you can point me out and say, "See, kindly Sergeant Paulson here has been dogging my every step, turning over every stone in my path, and he's found nothing, not a crumb of incriminating evidence." You see how that would work, Doyle? I could be the best defense a cop could possibly have.'

'And that's what you intend to do – stay on my case like that?'

Paulson leans forward and lowers his voice. 'Don't worry. It's our secret. Nobody else needs to know I'm helping you out like this. Otherwise where would we be? Everyone would want such personal service.'

Doyle can feel his blood approaching boiling point. He has to look away from Paulson as he tells himself to calm down. Then he faces the man again.

'Listen to me very carefully, Paulson. You want to get your kicks from watching me, that's fine. But do it from a distance, okay? A very large distance. We got a cop killer on the streets, and I'm gonna do everything I can to get him. I don't care whether you believe that or not – I think it's in your nature to regard anything a real cop tells you as a lie – but just don't get in my way. Understand?'

Paulson says nothing at first. He digs into his pocket, pulls out a cigarette pack and opens it.

'Will you look at that. I'm out. Don't suppose you got any smokes on you?'

Doyle turns and walks away. 'So long, Paulson. I hope you feel proud.'

As he nears his car, he notices a white envelope that's been pushed under his windshield wiper. He reaches over and takes it out. The words 'Detective Doyle' are typewritten on the front of it.

He looks back at the retreating figure of Paulson.

'Hey! Hey, Paulson!'

Paulson stops and turns around. Doyle waves the envelope in the air. 'You been near my car?'

Paulson doesn't answer. He smiles and gets into his Chevy.

Doyle stands there for a while, staring at the envelope. He takes a good look around him for anyone that might be watching, then opens his car door and climbs behind the wheel. He examines both sides of the envelope, flexes it, sniffs it. Using his car key, he slits it open as carefully as he can. He slips out the single sheet of paper and unfolds it, holding it gingerly by the corners.

As he reads the typewritten note, he knows that his life will never be the same again.

NINE

Doyle enters the squadroom, his eyes zeroing in on his target. Schneider is at his desk, stabbing his podgy index fingers at a keyboard.

Doyle halts in his tracks and sniffs the air like a cat testing the breeze. Schneider raises his head and shows a puzzled frown.

'What's that I can smell?' Doyle says. 'Is that cheese, Schneider? You been feeding the rats again?'

Schneider interlaces his hands behind his head and leans back in his creaking chair, a big smile of satisfaction on his face.

'I don't know what you're babbling on about, Doyle. Something happen to ruin your day?'

Doyle digs into his trouser pocket and finds a coin. He flicks it in a high arc toward Schneider. The coin hits him on the chest and rebounds onto the floor.

'Here. Drop another dime on me. Buy another wedge of cheese. Buy a whole fucking truckload of cheddar, if it makes you feel any better.'

Schneider looks down at the coin, leaves it where it lies. 'Anybody in bed with IAB, it's most likely you, Doyle. All those cops turning against you like they did, that could easily drive a man crazy. Wouldn't take much for the rat squad to flip a guy like that. Maybe it's the rest of us ought to be worried.'

He makes a grand sweeping gesture with his arm, as if to claim that he speaks for all the other detectives.

Doyle shakes his head and wills his legs to take him away from here before he inflicts some serious physical damage. As he heads toward Franklin's office, he can hear Schneider tittering to himself.

The lieutenant's door is wide open. Doyle raps on it without pausing in his stride, then closes the door behind him. Franklin leans back in his chair, taking his shoulders perilously close to two large cactus plants behind him, and watches Doyle intently.

'What was that about?' he asks.

Doyle slides out a chair and plonks himself onto it.

'Nothing. Just Schneider being Schneider. You know how he is.'

Franklin continues to eye him. 'You've got something.' A statement, not a question.

'Yeah,' Doyle says. 'Yeah.'

He reaches into his pocket and takes out the envelope, then tosses it onto Franklin's desk.

'Found this under the wipers on my car.'

Franklin wheels his chair forward and bends over the envelope, peering at the name on it.

'You had it dusted yet?'

'No, but I'm not hopeful.'

Franklin nods, then picks up the letter almost fearfully, as if anything more than a feather-light touch might cause it to disintegrate in his fingers.

With a great deal more care than Doyle himself took, he eventually extracts the note and reads it through.

Detective Doyle,

So how does it feel? Have you realized yet what is happening to you? I hope so. I hope you're not such

a lousy detective that you could still possibly be
thinking that this is all just mere coincidence.

It hurts, doesn't it? When people you know
die. And not just people. Your colleagues. Your
friends.

I understand, because I've been there. In fact,
I'm still there. Alone. Painfully alone.

You put me there, Doyle. You put me into a
state of isolation more hellish than any prison.
You destroyed my links with humanity.

And now it's your turn.

I'm cutting you off, Doyle. From now on, you're
on your own.

I know you don't think I'm kidding. You saw what
I did to your partners. If you don't want anyone
else to die, you need to keep them away from you.

If you don't, next time they might not die so
quickly.

Start enjoying your own company.

Franklin sets the letter down.

'Looks like you were right,' he says. 'You're the focal point.'

'Ain't I the lucky one?'

He didn't want to be proved correct. Yesterday, when he made
the suggestion, it seemed only a remote possibility, one he was
almost embarrassed to voice. Now it's a certainty. Ridiculously,
he wishes he hadn't said anything, as if the very utterance had
made it come true.

'If this is kosher,' Franklin says, 'it kind of shifts the whole
nature of the investigation.'

Doyle nods. 'Onto me, I know.'

'You prepared to have the NYPD looking into every aspect of your life?'

Doyle thinks about this. He's a victim here, and in theory that's how he should be treated. But that's not how it'll ride. The Schneiders and the Paulsons of this world will do what they can to make sure that the digging beneath Doyle's skin is taken right down to the bone, exposing as many raw nerves as they can on the way. So is he prepared for that?

'I got nothing to hide,' he says.

Franklin waves a hand across the letter. 'You got any idea who could be behind this?'

'Nope. Everybody loves me. Just ask Schneider.'

'Speaking of which, we have to let them know. If this sicko is prepared to carry out these threats . . .'

'Then everyone I work with could be in danger. I understand that.'

'We have to play it safe.'

'I understand. Really.'

'And I can't team you up with anyone else right now. Not till we catch this fruitcake.'

This isn't such a blow to Doyle. If Schneider's preaching has worked as intended, nobody will want to partner him anyhow.

And then Doyle suddenly realizes where this might be leading.

He says, 'Just . . . don't take me off the case.'

Franklin opens his mouth and then closes it again, as if re-thinking his words.

'Mo?'

The hesitation goes on a little longer. Then: 'Work alone, Cal. Let the other cops do their jobs. Put up with their questions. In the meantime, do what you can to work out who's behind this. But do it alone.'

Doyle stares into Franklin's flinty eyes as he tries to read the subtext. He senses that the lieutenant is granting him a huge concession, that he's acting against an impulse to preempt any possible danger to the members of his squad. For now, at least.

Doyle nods his gratitude. In return, Franklin chin-points at the door and the squadroom beyond.

'Come on,' he says. 'Let's get it over with.'

As Franklin reads out the message, Doyle waits for the reaction to set in. He waits for the gathered detectives to start making the sign of the cross at him and yelling, 'Unclean, unclean!' He waits for them to shuffle their chairs to the far corners of the room and tie handkerchiefs across their faces.

Instead, he gets a welcome surprise.

Because what he sees on the faces of his colleagues is outrage. He sees a band of men and women who do not take kindly to being goaded. A threat? Against a cop? Against New York's finest? What the fuck is that? Bring it on, shit-for-brains. We're ready for you.

And what Doyle learns in that moment is that the receipt of the note is one of the best things that could have happened to him in the present circumstances. Because now there is an enemy. Nameless, yes; faceless, yes – but an enemy for all that. What these people needed to hear more than anything was that there is an external agent responsible for this mayhem – that it has nothing to do with the poor schmuck sitting just a few feet away. It's how it should be: cops on one side, criminals on the other, and never the twain shall meet.

Doyle senses the wave of relief that washes over the squad as they acknowledge the changed situation. They are comfortable with this. This is something they can get their teeth into. Doyle can almost feel the melting away of some of the antagonism against him.

But not from everyone.

It's Schneider who remarks, 'Has anyone checked to see if that note is in Doyle's handwriting?'

It is a curious venture, trying to work out who hates you and why.

Cops get threatened all the time, and Doyle has had his fair share of being on the receiving end. But what people say and what people do are usually two very different things. Your occasional perp, aggrieved at being caught, arrested and possibly sent to prison, may promise to carry out all manner of unspeakable acts on you, your family, and even your pets. But usually it's all talk, most of them having neither the intelligence nor the wherewithal to put their plans for revenge into effect. Of the more powerful and resourceful criminals that Doyle has consigned to living in a box – and there have been a good number – most are level-headed enough to realize that it's all part of the game. They do wrong, they get caught, they go to prison, no hard feelings. Such is the nature of their enterprise. To attempt to exact revenge does not make good business sense, and becomes sheer lunacy when it involves stirring the wrath of the NYPD.

And so Doyle is having a hard time coming up with a list of potential subjects, especially those possessing the ingenuity and audacity displayed so far. All he can do is err on the generous side, adding to the list even those who probably don't remember that it was Doyle who arrested them in the first place.

He spends hours working his way through old case files, reading and rereading his DD5 reports to refresh his memory, making the occasional phone call to check a fact, a detail, the present whereabouts of a con. It's the same process he went through with Joe Parlatti's files, only this time it's personal, and that makes it hard to be objective. Now and again he adds a name to his list, together with a few notes about them, but almost every time a nagging voice says to him, Do you *really* think this guy could be doing this?

There's one name he doesn't set down on his notepad, even though it should probably go at the top of the list. It's a name that doesn't appear in any of the arrest records or mugshot books currently spread out in front of him.

He doesn't want to go down that path. Not yet. Not until it starts to look like it's the only one still untrodden.

Doyle tosses his pen onto the desk. He digs the middle finger and thumb of his right hand into his eyeballs, trying to squeeze out the tiredness. He stretches his arms out to the sides, hears his vertebrae and shoulder blades complain. He looks at his watch. Six-forty p.m. Way past the end of his shift. The faces that started the day with him have all been replaced by new ones. He knows he should go home, get a good night's sleep. See something of Rachel and Amy.

Oh, shit!

What was it I promised Rachel last night? About keeping in touch? About how I would call her from the station house to let her know I'm okay, and especially when shit like this is happening?

And how many times have I called today, when we have another cop in the morgue and I've received a note from the killer?

He reaches for the phone, knocking over a paper coffee cup as he does so. There was only a cold mouthful left, but it seems to spread like a river that has just burst its banks. He grabs a Kleenex and tries to mop up the murky deluge as he dials home.

He gets a ring tone, but no answer. Eventually, the answering machine cuts in and he hangs up.

Strange. Where would they be now?

Normally they would be sitting down to eat at this time. Or Rachel would still be cooking the meal. In any case, they would be in the apartment.

Unless . . .

Unless Rachel has already heard the news about Tony Alvarez, and she's pissed that her thoughtless husband has forgotten his pledge to keep her informed. In which case maybe she's felt the need to escape, and has whisked Amy off to a McDonald's or a pizza parlor.

Yeah, that's it.

Doyle takes his cellphone from his pocket and speed-dials the number of Rachel's own cell.

It goes straight to voicemail, and Doyle cancels the call.

She's really pissed all right.

He snatches a few more Kleenex from the box and does his best to dry off the pages of his reports before turning his attention to them again. He stares at the pages for another half-hour, but not with the same degree of concentration he had earlier. Thoughts of Rachel keep crowding his mind. He pictures her sitting in a diner somewhere, staring into space and not eating, while Amy wolfs down her chicken strips and fries with bucketfuls of ketchup.

At seven-fifteen he repeats the calls – home first and then Rachel's cell. Nothing has changed. Rachel has decided on a tit-for-tat approach. You don't want to call me? Fine, I don't want to accept your calls.

It's the only possible explanation.

Because the alternative is unthinkable.

The alternative being that the piece of shit who left that note wasn't just talking about cops. He was saying that anyone – *anyone* – Doyle spent the slightest time with could be in grave danger.

But no. That's just blowing this thing out of all proportion. Give it time. Give Rachel time. Even better, buy some flowers – she likes freesias – go home and wait for her.

The phone rings. An outside line. He snatches up the handset.

'Hello?'

'Cal?'

'Rachel, I'm sorry. I know I was supposed to—'

'No, Cal. It's me. Nadine.'

'Nadine.'

'Yes. I was supposed to meet up with Rachel tonight. I'm at your apartment building. Only, she's not answering. She said to be here for seven, and now it's nearly twenty past. And she's not picking up the phone either. Is she . . . I mean, has she said anything to you about a change of plan or anything?'

Stay calm. This is nothing. She's forgotten, that's all.

But Rachel doesn't forget things like that.

Doyle is on his feet now. He is yanking his coat from the back of his chair and babbling something at Nadine. Telling her something must have come up, or another appointment slipped her mind. Some garbage like that.

And then he is through the squadroom door and clattering down the concrete stairs.

Racing to find his wife and child.

TEN

When he pulls up in front of his apartment building, he sees that Nadine has decided to wait on the front stoop. She is cocooned in an immense fake-fur coat, like she's just come from Narnia – but still she looks frozen. Doyle scrambles out of the car and heads toward her, hurrying but at the same time trying to appear untroubled. He likes Nadine – she's a good friend to Rachel – but this is not her concern. He doesn't want to experience the embarrassment of revealing to her the details of this minor domestic dispute. Because that's all it is: a tiff. Really.

'Nadine,' he says. 'You should have gone home. No point standing out here like this.'

She stares at him, and he can tell that his cloak of tranquility has a pretty open weave.

'I was just a little worried, Cal. It's not like Rachel to arrange something and then just not be there. Has something happened?'

Doyle is fumbling for his door key. He wants to get in there and check out the apartment. Maybe she's left him a note. Dinner's in the dog – that type of thing. Something that will confirm that she's furious with him. Something that will reassure him that she is safe and well, if perhaps a little emotionally unbalanced right now.

'Honest to God, Nadine. It's cool, really. Nothing to get worked up about.'

'Cal.'

His name is delivered in the tone of a mother who is interrogating a chocolate-covered son about missing cookies. A single drawn-out syllable that manages to say, *I am not going to leave you alone until you tell me what this is all about.*

Doyle can loiter here no longer. And if Nadine is not going to be shaken off, then so be it. Let her suffer the discomfort of being an intruder into a couple's private affairs.

'Okay, we had a little falling-out over something, that's all. I didn't call her when I was supposed to, and now she's pissed. Either she's up there, refusing to answer the door, or else she's taken Amy out for dinner and turned her cellphone off. She's trying to get back at me.'

Nadine says nothing for a while, which tells Doyle that she may now finally be satisfied and that he can get on with sorting this mess out.

He puts his key into the lobby door and opens it.

'So go home, Nadine. Let me fix this. I'll get Rachel to call you.'

'Okay,' she says through a weak smile. 'If you're sure.'

He steps into the lobby, is on the verge of shutting the door behind him.

And then he sees it. His mailbox poking its tongue at him.

It's a white envelope.

For a few seconds he cannot move. Doesn't dare confirm his worst fears.

'Cal?'

It's Nadine. She is still behind him, obviously bemused by his behavior.

He snatches out the envelope, looks at the writing on the front. 'Detective Doyle.' Exactly as it appeared on the letter that was left on his car.

Now the ability to breathe has become something of an ambition. This can't be happening.

He's been here. The son of a bitch has been here.

Doyle rips open the envelope in one savage motion. Fuck the forensics.

His eyes try to absorb the whole message in one go.

```
Dear Detective Doyle,

What are you doing here?
Didn't you understand my previous message?
I said I was cutting you off.
That means from EVERYONE.
Especially your lovely wife and daughter. Rachel
    and Amy.
After what happened to your partners, did you
    really think I was kidding?
Big mistake.
Maybe next time you'll know better.
```

And then Doyle is bounding up the staircase, ignoring Nadine's confused cries from below. Adrenalin is surging through his system. He reaches his apartment door, snatches out his Glock. An inner voice quotes his training at him, cautioning him to use the softly-softly approach. He tells it to shut the fuck up. He puts his key into the door, swings it wide open and steps in, gun at the ready.

'Rachel!'

He moves speedily through his apartment, eyes scanning, finger firmly on the trigger.

'Rachel!'

He kicks doors open. The bedrooms. The kitchen. The bathroom.

Nothing. There is nobody here.

He stands still in the center of the living room, his chest heaving, his gun still grasped in a two-handed combat stance.

A noise behind him. He whirls, his trigger finger tensing. Nadine jumps back, startled.

'Cal? What the hell's going on?'

'I don't know. Something. I don't know. There's a guy. He wants to hurt me.'

He knows he's not making much sense. He can see the puzzlement and fear on Nadine's face. But there's no time to explain. He has to find Rachel and Amy. But how? Where to start?

He lowers the gun, starts to look at the apartment through different eyes. Searching not for people, but for signs of disturbance. Clues hinting at a struggle. Another note perhaps.

But he sees nothing. The apartment looks exactly as it always does – tidy but not obsessively so.

He holsters the Glock, then takes out his cellphone. He tries Rachel's number again. This time he gets a ringing tone instead of voicemail.

Nadine says, 'Cal? Where's Rachel?'

He raises a hand to silence her while he listens.

Answer. Please God, answer.

'Hello?'

It's a woman's voice, but it doesn't sound like . . .

'Rachel? Is that you?'

'Who's calling, please?'

'My name is Callum Doyle. I'm trying to get hold of my wife, Rachel Doyle. Is this . . . I mean, am I calling . . .'

'Mr Doyle, could you hold on a minute, please?'

No, I can't fucking hang on, he wants to say, but the sounds from the handset become muted, like the phone has just been smothered. He can hear snatches of a muffled conversation, but cannot make out the words.

'Cal? Who is that?'

It's Nadine again, and once more Doyle requests her silence with a raised finger.

The voice comes back on the line.

'Mr Doyle, my name is Nurse Lynley. I work at Bellevue Hospital. We have your wife here.'

'At the hospital? Put her on, please. I want to speak with her.'

There is a slight pause. 'Mr Doyle, your wife can't talk right now. She's been badly beaten.'

Doyle feels his legs start to buckle. His breath comes out in a long quiver that he finds difficult to shape into words.

'Beaten?'

'Yes. We received an anonymous phone call. Your wife was assaulted and left in a parking lot. An ambulance picked her up and brought her straight to the ER. We're doing all we can for her.'

'All you can? How bad is she? She'll live, won't she?'

Another pause. 'Mr Doyle, your wife is in a critical condition. Her injuries are extensive. The doctors are doing everything they can . . . Mr Doyle, are you able to come over to the hospital?'

Doyle is almost shaking now. He hears how carefully the nurse is choosing her words. Worse, he knows what she's leaving unsaid. What it amounts to is that Rachel is clinging to her life by a thread.

'Yes,' he answers. 'I'll come now. You're . . . you're sure it's my wife?'

'She had this cellphone on her when she was brought in. Also, her driver's license.'

'I'll be right over,' he says, and then, 'Wait. My daughter. A little girl. She should have been with my wife. Is she there too?'

'I'm sorry, Mr Doyle, but nobody else was found with your wife.'

He ends the call, turns toward Nadine. She has a hand to her mouth, and her eyes are wide. It's clear that she has caught the gist of the telephone conversation.

'What's happened?' she says. 'Tell me what's happened.'

But Doyle cannot speak. He thunders toward the door. He needs to help his wife, make sure she recovers fully from this vicious attack. He needs to find his beautiful innocent daughter.

And then he needs to track down and kill the son of a bitch who has so savagely ripped into his family.

He takes the stairs two at a time. He hears Nadine's clatter from above as she struggles to rush down the steps in her heels. She calls for him to wait, but he's like a train with no brakes. He keeps going until he's out on the street, seconds away from leaping into his car and launching it like a rocket.

'Cal! Wait. Please. She's my friend. She's the only real friend I've got in this damned city.'

That stops him. He is surprised by her words. Although she is fairly new to the city, he has always thought of her as Miss Popular.

And so he pauses for a while, waiting for Nadine to catch up.

'You should go home, Nadine,' he says when she is at his shoulder.

'Open the car. I'll drive. You're liable to take out half the traffic in New York.'

He is reluctant, but when she shows him the whiteness of her open palm he finds her difficult to resist. He hands her the key.

'It's the ER at Bellevue. You know how to get there?'

'Head east, turn before we hit the river, right? Get in,' she says.

She starts the car up and pulls it out into the traffic, then signals at the next turn to take her back toward Central Park West.

'Why is she in the hospital, Cal? What did they say on the phone?'

'Somebody beat her up. I think it's bad. They beat her up and dumped her in a parking lot.'

'Oh, Jesus. Is she going to be okay?'

'I . . . I don't know. They wouldn't say.'

'She'll be okay,' Nadine says. 'Rachel's a fighter. All cops' wives are fighters.'

'That include you?'

'I forced you into taking me along now, didn't I?'

Doyle looks out of the passenger window at the buildings going by. He wishes he hadn't let Nadine drive at this snail's pace. He also wishes that he was in a squad car, so that he could put on the lights and sirens, then floor the gas pedal.

Nadine says, 'You knew, didn't you? That something might have happened. Even before you went into the apartment you suspected something was up.'

'I had an inkling. I hoped I was wrong.'

'Why? The inkling, I mean. What's going on, Cal?'

Cal opens his mouth to speak, and then something occurs to him. Does this count? Talking to Nadine at the apartment. Getting in a car with her. In the killer's estimation, does this cross the line regarding close contact?

'Nadine, pull over.'

'What? What are you talking about? We're nowhere near the hospital.'

'I know. Just pull over and get out of the car. You need to go home. Now!'

She glances across at him. 'No, Cal. Not until you explain all this to me.'

Doyle thinks, She's a fighter, all right.

'I'm in danger. Everyone who gets close to me is in danger too. That means you, Nadine.'

'Why? What kind of danger?'

'Mo hasn't told you about any of this?'

'No. He hardly ever talks about his work.'

There is a bitter edge to her voice. A suggestion of discord between her and Franklin. It comes as no revelation to Doyle. His view has always been that this marriage contract was a trade of Nadine's dizzying curves for the lieutenant's new-found wealth. Body for bucks – an age-old barter. But right now he has too many worries of his own to go diving into that murky pool.

'You heard about Tony Alvarez though, right?'

She nods. 'It was on the news. An explosion of some kind. They're saying it may not have been an accident. That it may have been deliberate, and that there might even be a cop killer on the loose. Are they right, Cal? Is that why you're in danger?'

'Yeah, but not in the way you're thinking. After Joe was killed, Tony took over as my partner. They both died because of me. Somebody's trying to hurt me through the people I'm close to.'

'How do you know that?'

He tells her about the two notes he received, and he can see the shock, the disbelief on her face. Which is fair enough, since he's finding it difficult to accept this himself.

'So that's why I think you should go home, Nadine. If this guy's willing to kill my partners and knock my wife about, then harming you is something he probably won't think twice about. I don't want the responsibility of that.'

He watches her as she mulls over his words. When she nods her head he thinks at first that she's conceding, but her expression tells him she's merely signaling the end of an internal argument.

'I have to see that Rachel's okay. She'd do the same for me.'

If he were not so strung out, Doyle would smile. The belle has balls.

After Nadine has taken a right onto the service road that runs alongside the FDR Drive, she voices another of Doyle's fears.

'Cal, did the hospital say anything about Amy?'

Doyle shakes his head. 'No. They don't know where she is.'

He stares at the tall gray-brown building looming up ahead of them and wonders what he will find there. He wants to walk in and see Rachel sitting up in bed. A few cuts and bruises, but nothing a little extra make-up won't mask. She'll be sipping the insipid brown stuff that hospitals dare to call tea, and telling him how she left Amy playing at a friend's apartment. She will tell him that she'll be able to go home soon, and that she needs to be a bit more aware of her surroundings in future, so as not to get caught like that again. She will tell him that she was furious at him for not calling, but only because she loves him so intensely. She will tell him how much Amy loves him too, and that his little girl can't wait to show him the picture of a dragon she drew today.

And everything will be okay again.

On the way to the emergency room, Doyle steps around a man on crutches, dodges a drunk with blood streaming down his face, and keeps on marching until he reaches the reception counter. Behind the counter two nurses are laughing and joking. One of them manages to slot the words 'donut' and 'anus' into the same sentence, and the other – a redhead – laughs even harder. The redhead's hair is an alluring auburn rather than shocking ginger, and is formed into soft curls. She has pale skin and a laugh that hints of mischief and adventure in the bedroom. She reminds Doyle of a girl he once knew in Ireland – an older girl who gave the impression of knowing all the secrets of post-pubescence – and so it is *her* name badge he examines first. Her name is Nurse Lynley.

His first thought is that things can't be all that bad. Nurse Lynley, the woman he spoke to on the phone, is too filled with joy. She has had a good day. Nobody assaulting or abusing her. No costly mistakes. Nobody in her care dying.

'Hi,' he says. 'My name's Doyle. I spoke with you on the phone.'

And then it is as if a rain cloud has moved across her head, darkening her features. The sudden sobriety shocks Doyle into the realization that, like him, she is a professional who is used to dealing with death and injury on a daily basis, and that, like him, she has to make sure it doesn't warp her view of life. It's why cops tell jokes at murder scenes. It's why nurses tell jokes about the anatomical applications of confectionary. It says nothing about your satisfaction with the day you're having.

It's a mirror that Doyle finds unsettling to face.

When the nurse comes around the desk and takes him by the arm and leads him off to a small side room, he is only vaguely aware of Nadine trailing behind. In the room itself he sees a small table and plastic chairs, a coffee machine, a sink with two unwashed mugs. Nurse Lynley is talking to him, but he feels like he's bobbing up and down in a choppy sea, catching brief snatches of conversation each time he comes up. The isolated fragments make little sense to him. He stares into the sink. The faucet is dripping into one of the mugs: *plop . . . plop . . .*

The cry from Nadine breaks the spell. His brain wakens again, and he sees the nurse searching his face. Jesus, she is so like that girl back in Ireland. A real tease she was. Proud of her body and keen to impart its mysteries to all of us grubby boys. What was her name again? Helen something . . .

'Mr Doyle? Do you understand what I'm saying to you?'

He blinks, tries to clear his fogged head.

'Yes. No.'

So she tells him again, and this time his brain drops its shield and allows the painful arrow of truth to penetrate.

Rachel, his beautiful Rachel, has died of her injuries.

ELEVEN

No.

This can't be right.

He must be getting confused. Thinking about the time Amy was being born. Rachel lying on a hospital bed, pressing a mask to her face between the screams. The midwife issuing her instructions – when to push, when not to. The blood, so much blood. And then the sudden change in the atmosphere in that room. The *wrongness*. Everybody galvanized into a course of action that clearly signaled a problem. He remembers being ushered out of the room, still looking into Rachel's eyes, calling her name. And her words back to him: 'You wait for me. You wait for *us*. Me and this baby, we're not going anywhere.'

And so he waited. Through all the talk of placental abruptions and blood loss and transfusions, he waited.

When she came back to him, her tiny gift of life cradled in her arms, he cried. And she said to him, 'You don't get rid of me that easily.'

It became kind of a joke after that. Whenever they argued, and they sulked about it for a while, and they got back together again, she would repeat her mantra.

You don't get rid of me that easily.

So, yes. That must be what he's thinking about. It's the

hospital environment and the stress. They're taking his memories and twisting them into horribly warped hallucination.

He looks at Nurse Lynley.

'I want to see her.'

She stares back at him as though in appraisal. As if she is assessing his strength for this.

'Mr Doyle, I'm not sure it's a good idea. Your wife . . . She won't look the same to you. Especially after the work the doctors have done on her. It can be a shock to some people.'

'I want to see her. Where is she?'

The nurse tilts her head as she considers the request. 'Come with me.'

He follows, passing Nadine who has tears in her eyes and a sheen of wetness on her cheeks. They head down a brightly lit corridor. A scrawny man on a gurney shows them a toothless smile. A black porter whistles 'If I Were a Rich Man'. Nurse Lynley pauses at a pair of swing doors. Gives Doyle a look that asks, *Are you sure you're ready for this?*

They enter. The room is empty. Except, of course, for the body on the steel table.

Doyle swallows, and wills himself forward. He has to see, has to be sure.

He sees her hair first of all, shoulder length and dark. Normally glossy, but now matted into thick tendrils. He wonders why he can't see her face properly. What have the doctors put over her face?

And then he realizes that what he's looking at *is* her face.

It is all the colors of sorrow. Purples and blues and browns. And it is so misshapen. Her nose is spread sideways across one cheek. Her lips and eyelids are like lightly inflated balloons. One side of her head is concave, and the ear seems to have dropped several inches.

Doyle has seen worse before, but never on someone he loves. And that's what makes all the difference. That's what closes the gap.

He takes a few more steps forward, feeling a growing tightness in his chest. Like he is going into cardiac arrest. Like he is going to be grateful to be in the vicinity of medical experts any second now.

And then it overwhelms him. He lets out one huge sob that fills the room, and he pitches forward as his legs finally give way. He reaches his arms out to stop his fall, and feels his hands slam into the cold metal table. He stays like that, bent over, head buried between his outstretched arms.

A hand alights on his back, rubs gently. He knows it's Nadine, and he can sense that she is crying.

He hears Nurse Lynley's steps as she comes forward.

'Mr Doyle? Is there anything I can get you? Some water?'

Doyle sniffs and raises his head. His eyes move from the nurse to Nadine – one patiently concerned, the other on the verge of being inconsolable – and he doesn't know which emotion to release first. His anger . . .

. . . or his sheer relief and gratitude.

He says the only thing that seems appropriate in the circumstances:

'It's not her.'

Nurse Lynley's response comes in a flash, like it's automatic.

'Come outside,' she says. 'Let's find you someplace we can talk.'

Doyle knows what she's thinking. That he's in denial. She's seen it so many times before.

'It's not her. This is not my wife.'

Her lips tighten slightly. 'Mr Doyle—'

Nadine cuts her off. 'Cal. Come on. Let's go.'

In response, Doyle grabs the sheet that has been draped across the body on the table, then yanks it back, exposing the naked upper torso. The action elicits a gasp from Nadine and a glare of annoyance from the nurse.

'Look at her, Nadine! Look at her ribs! She's like a damn glockenspiel! And here . . .' He takes hold of the cadaver's arm and lifts it. 'You see those? Track marks. She's a junkie. You see a wedding ring at all? You see any marks where there *used* to be a wedding ring?' He turns toward the nurse. 'You got her clothes? Her possessions?'

Nurse Lynley glances at a red plastic tray on the counter by the sink. Doyle goes over to it. He lifts the scraps of material he finds there – a thin red blouse, a translucent black brassiere with red trimming – and shows them to Nadine.

'You think Rachel would wear any of this stuff?'

The tray also holds a small open purse. Doyle tips out its contents. He sees Rachel's driver's license, and also what looks like her cellphone, but the other items are unfamiliar to him.

'Take a look at this lipstick, Nadine. And this perfume. You think this is Rachel's style?'

Nadine shakes her head. She looks like a child, upset and confused. Nurse Lynley appears even more dumbfounded, perhaps mortified at the thought that she has made a dreadful error.

'I don't understand,' the nurse says.

Doyle keeps the phone and ID, and tosses the rest back into the tray. 'Don't worry. It's not your fault. You've been had. We've all been had.'

He heads out of the room, Nadine once again following at his heels like an adopted puppy.

'Cal, wait. If that's not Rachel, then where the hell is she?'

He has no answer. The relief he feels is tempered by the fact that he still doesn't know that Rachel and Amy are safe. His mind races to come up with ideas for locating them.

His cellphone rings. He removes it from his pocket and looks at it. It's not a number that's stored in the phone's address book. He answers it.

'Hello?'

'Cal? Is that you?'

He stops, Nadine almost crashing into his back.

'Rachel? RACHEL?'

'Cal, where are you?'

'I . . . I'm at Bellevue Hospital.'

'Yes, but where? And why have you got your cellphone? Are you okay? You sound—'

'Yes, I'm okay. Where are you?'

'I'm at Bellevue too, but I can't find you. I've had everyone looking for you.'

Doyle brings his free hand to his forehead. This conversation is making absolutely no sense to him. Why shouldn't he have his cellphone?

He looks up at the people milling around him. A short bald man carrying flowers and trying to figure out which way to go. A young man pushing an elderly lady in a wheelchair. A small child in a fur-trimmed duffel coat, a pink balloon tied to her wrist.

'Cal?'

The little girl stares at him, smiles . . .

'Cal? Are you there?'

. . . and then she runs. She comes straight at him. Her face radiates sunshine and daisies and moonbeams and castles and fairies as she dodges around the short bald man and the old lady in the wheelchair, and she is opening her mouth and shouting something, one word over and over, a word that means everything to Doyle, a word that puts the world back on its axis and the stars in their rightful places, and that word is . . .

'Daddy!'

He bends at the knees, ready to scoop up the incoming human missile, and as he does so he catches a glimpse of somebody else at the payphones. A woman, turning to check on her child, staring in disbelief at what she sees. Such a familiar figure to Doyle. Such a part of him.

Rachel!

And as he gathers Amy up into his arms and whirls her around, he checks his wife on each rotation, sees her come closer and closer, until she too becomes swallowed up in the maelstrom and they all spin around together, hugging and kissing and laughing and crying and oblivious to what is beyond their reach.

When they settle, when they calm, and some of the love has been doled out to Nadine too, there are answers to be sought.

Rachel says, 'God, Cal, I thought you were dead. When they couldn't find you—'

'Who? Who couldn't find me?'

'The nurses. I was told you were in the ICU, but they didn't know anything about you. They tried the operating rooms, and there was no sign of you there either. I didn't know what to—'

Doyle takes hold of her upper arms. 'Slow down, Rach. Rewind this a little. Who told you I was in the ICU?'

Rachel takes a breath. 'I got a phone call tonight. It was a really crackly line, and the guy sounded foreign – Indian or Pakistani or something – so it was really hard to understand what he was saying. He said he was a doctor at Bellevue, and that you'd been brought in with gunshot wounds to the chest. He said you were in a pretty bad way, that it was touch and go whether . . . whether . . .'

She breaks down then. Doyle wraps her in his arms, whispers

reassurances to her as she sobs into his chest. Over her shoulder, he looks at Nadine, then nods toward Amy and the hospital exit. Nadine gets the message, takes Amy by the hand and starts to lead her out of the building.

Amy says, 'Why is Mommy crying?'

Nadine answers, 'She's just happy to see your Daddy, sweetie. Come on, let's go see if we can find the car.'

When they have gone, Rachel surfaces again. 'What's this all about, Cal? Did someone make a mistake?'

Doyle shakes his head. 'It was deliberate. Somebody's idea of fun. I was told you were hurt too. Bastard beat up an innocent woman and left these on her.' He takes the cellphone and driver's license from his pocket.

Rachel gapes at the items. 'I've been looking for those! I was convinced I put them in the car's glove compartment this morning. When I went to get them later on, they were gone. I thought my mind was playing tricks on me.'

'He must have broken into the car somehow, looking for things that belonged to you.'

'Who, Cal? Who the hell would play such a cruel trick on us?'

'I don't know. I really don't.'

'What about the woman? The one who got beat up? Couldn't she tell you anything?'

Doyle looks at her, biting his lip. His vision suddenly blurs, and he blinks it away.

Rachel says, 'Oh, God, Cal! She's dead? And you thought it was . . . Oh, Jesus!'

She latches onto him again, pulling herself as close as she can get. He savors the intimacy while he can. There are other things he needs to say to her.

'Come on,' he says. 'Let's get out of here.'

They head toward the exit, his arm around her shoulders,

keeping her safe against him, wishing he could be her protector forever.

She doesn't suspect yet, he thinks. She doesn't know what's coming.

He hears footsteps hurrying along the corridor behind him.

'Mr Doyle! Mr Doyle!'

He turns, and Rachel turns with him. He takes her hand in his, and waits for the caller to catch up with them.

Nurse Lynley stops in front of them. Her eyes slide to Rachel, then back to Doyle.

'This is—'

'My wife, yes.'

The nurse nods at this final and undeniable confirmation of the mistaken identity. 'Mr Doyle, I'm so sorry. We try to be as careful as we can about identifying victims. It's just that—'

'It's okay,' he says. 'You're not to blame. I don't plan to file a complaint or sue the hospital or anything.'

In gratitude, she flashes the briefest of smiles. 'Mr Doyle, would I be right in thinking that you're a detective?'

Doyle stares back into her green eyes, looking for a hint of mysticism that helped her divine that particular piece of information.

'Yes, I am. How did you . . .'

'There was something else on the victim. It fell from her clothing when she was brought in. An orderly left it at the reception desk.'

Nurse Lynley dips into a capacious pocket on her uniform. Doyle knows what her hand will contain even before it's withdrawn.

A white envelope. The words 'Detective Doyle' on its face.

Doyle takes the offering, thanks the nurse. He feels the familiar turmoil in his stomach.

She says, 'I don't understand what's going on here, and maybe you'd prefer not to tell me. Maybe you'd prefer not to talk about this to anybody. But there's a woman back there who is now a murder victim. The thing you need to know is—'

'The hospital has to make a police report, I know. And you'll have to mention my connection with all this. I understand.'

She shows another hint of a smile, grateful to him for not making this difficult for her.

'I'm glad you've found your wife. Goodbye, Detective.'

She turns then, and goes briskly back to her business. Doyle gazes down at the envelope, knowing that he can't delay in opening it.

'What is it?' Rachel asks.

'The son of a bitch has been sending me anonymous messages. This is his latest. His chance to gloat.'

Doyle rips open the envelope and unfolds the note it contains.

```
Dear Detective Doyle,

Fooled you!

    Did you like it? As practical jokes go, you have
to admit it was pretty damn good. Go ahead, laugh
about it.

    Next time it really will be your family on the
slab. I can get to them, and there's nothing you
can do to stop me.

    You getting the message now, Detective? People
just aren't safe when you're around them.

    Why don't you go away and think about it? Far away.
From everyone. Think about it real hard, and maybe
then you'll get some idea of what you put me through.

    Sweet dreams, Detective.
```

'What's it say?'

'Crap you don't need to hear.' He folds the note over, then tucks it and the envelope into his pocket. 'Let's go.'

His mind is made up now. All that remains is to figure out how to break it to Rachel.

He worries about his plans.

It seems to him that he plans things meticulously, knows exactly what he wants to do, but when it comes to implementing them he just gets, well, carried away. Like he starts off as the driver and suddenly finds himself in the passenger seat.

He hadn't set out with any intention of killing the girl.

His objective was just to rough her up a little. Well, a lot, actually. Enough to keep her in the hospital for a while. Get her into the ICU, drips in her arm, monitors on her brain activity – all that shit. Long enough to get Doyle in there. Give him a little scare.

He'd done his research. The hooker was roughly the right height and shape, her hair was long and dark, and she wasn't too skanky-looking as whores go. Her face was nowhere near as attractive as the one on Doyle's wife, but that wasn't so important. When he was done with her, the face was the last place people would be looking for recognizable features.

So he called her up. Told her he'd traveled all the way from Chicago for a business meeting and wanted to relax a little before heading back to the Windy City. Put her at ease by telling her to meet him at his nice hotel on Seventh Avenue.

There were many things he didn't tell her, of course.

He didn't tell her she would never make it to his hotel. Didn't tell her that she wouldn't even make it out of her own apartment building. Didn't tell her that his call was just a ruse to get her out of the apartment without her feeling that, at that very moment, she was about to be attacked.

He was waiting for her in the hallway. It was black out there because he'd removed the light bulb. He waited patiently until he heard her take the locks off. Waited until the door opened and a dirty yellow light leaked out and she stepped into the gloom and turned to lock up.

And then he pounced.

He rammed into her back, driving her through the door and into the apartment. She yelped, then whirled to face him. He saw first the shock and then the fear. He'd expected that reaction. He believed he cut an imposing, formidable figure. Although the ski mask and the baseball bat may have added to the effect.

He expected also that she'd run. Maybe even put up a fight. This was a woman of the streets, after all. She would have learned something about how to handle herself.

So he didn't wait. Didn't try to reason with her. He just let the baseball bat do the talking. Let it sing through the air on its way to connecting with her ribcage with such force that he heard bones crack. Let it whistle a little before bouncing off the back of her skull.

And then he closed the door behind him. Stood panting over the woman who was now balled up on the floor, her blood-streaked hands spread across her head in a pathetic attempt at protection.

So far, so good. He'd stuck to the plan. The next phase should have been straightforward: smack her around a little more, throw her into the van, dump her somewhere and then give the hospital a call.

Except that's not how it went, was it?

What actually happened was that he got a little over-zealous. The old baseball bat became a little too verbose. Became a veritable chatterbox as it arced and swung and pummeled and smashed.

Not how it was meant to happen. Not at all.

Hell, why would he have bothered putting on a ski mask if he hadn't intended the girl to survive? What would be the point in that?

So why the deviation? Why the fuck didn't he just stick to the sequence of events that he outlined at the beginning?

Thinking about it now, he realizes that a part of him – a subversive element buried within his subconscious mind – has been having other ideas all along. It concocts its own, darker plans. It allows him to think that he's just being businesslike, that he's just taking one logical step at a time. And when the moment is right, it asserts itself and shows him as the monster he truly is.

And right now, looking back on what he did to that wretched human being, 'monster' does not seem too strong a word.

Especially since he enjoyed it so much at the time.

TWELVE

At Doyle's request, he drives Rachel home in her car. He tells Amy to ride in Daddy's car with Nadine, and waits for the whines. Instead he gets a 'Yay!' So much for being pleased to see him.

Doyle takes his eyes off the road for a glance at Rachel. Little more than a murmur or two has escaped her lips since they left the hospital.

No biggie, he thinks. She's been through a lot. Me, I got plenty to say. I just can't find the words.

'You okay?' he asks.

She doesn't look at him. Just keeps staring straight ahead.

'This is hard for me, Cal. I haven't experienced anything like this before. It's scary.'

'I know, babe.'

'I don't know what the hell is happening to us. Who could do something like this?'

'I really don't know. But I'm gonna stop him. Okay? I'm gonna get this sonofabitch.'

They lapse into silence again. Doyle can sense a pressure building up in his wife.

'You said you'd call me.'

A few simple words, but Doyle knows there's an avalanche of emotion waiting just behind them.

'I know. I tried. I couldn't get through to you. Obviously you had no cellphone, and—'

'When? When did you try?'

Be careful here, he thinks.

'Earlier this evening. It's been kinda hectic today.'

'I understand. What with the death of Tony Alvarez and all.'

Shit. This ain't gonna work out well.

'You heard about Tony, huh?'

'Yes, I heard. Eventually. You want to hear how my day went? I spent the morning trying to come to terms with what happened to Joe. Then I spent the afternoon doing exactly the same thing for Tony. And for most of this evening it looked as though I would have to do it all over again. Only this time for you, Cal. For you.'

'Look, I'm okay. We're both okay. He was just trying to frighten us, that's all.'

'Well, he did a damn good job. I've been worried ever since you told me about Joe. And when I heard about Tony, you know what my first thought was after I got over the shock? I thought, Christ, I need to call Cal. I need to find out what's going on, check he's okay. Because that's what wives and husbands do, Cal: they check on their loved ones when bad things are happening around them. And then I thought, No, why should I call? He should be calling me, just like he promised less than twenty-four hours ago. He should care enough to pick up the telephone and pass on a few reassurances to his wife and daughter that he's not wearing wings just yet.'

Her words are broken by sobs, and she brings a hand to her mouth to stifle them.

'Hey,' he says. 'Hush. It'll be okay.'

'Don't shut us out, Cal. Whatever happens, we're in this together. Remember that.'

He just nods then. He has an answer, but he knows she's not ready for it.

Not yet.

They park the cars and congregate on the front stoop. It's clear to Doyle that Nadine has detected a frostiness in the air that has nothing to do with the icy December weather. When Rachel invites her in, it's voiced without conviction. Doyle can almost see the subtitle that says, *Don't you dare say yes to this invitation*. Nadine reads it too, and declines despite Amy's pleading. She says her goodbyes to each of them in turn, promising Amy that she will come to see her rabbit when she gets one, then gets in her car and drives away.

In the apartment, all conversation is between Doyle and Amy, or between Rachel and Amy. Anxious to restore the third side of the triangle, Doyle follows Rachel into the kitchen. She keeps her back to him as she opens and closes cabinet doors.

'Rach.'

'I have to fix something for Amy. She hasn't eaten yet, and it's already way past her bedtime.'

Her voice is flat, emotionless – her way of telling him how mad and upset she is.

'Rach.'

'Can you get Amy in the shower, please?'

He stays in the doorway for a while, watching Rachel and wondering how she manages to keep her back aimed in his direction no matter where she moves to in the room. Eventually he slips away.

He coaxes Amy away from the TV, bribing her with a ride on his shoulders that he feels he's not making as much fun as it usually is. He helps her undress, and talks her into carrying her dirty clothes to the hamper. He struggles to push all of her strands of hair under a Clifford the Dog shower cap, then lifts her into the shower and heads back to the kitchen.

Rachel is warming something up in a pan on the stove. Her arms crossed, she watches the pan like it's the most fascinating thing in the room. Which maybe it is to her right now.

'Amy's in the shower,' he says, because he needs to say something even though it does nothing to make him more interesting than the pan.

'Thanks,' she says over her shoulder, still not turning, still not facing him.

He leaves her to her thoughts and goes into the bedroom. He starts to do what has to be done.

In the background he hears Amy singing a nursery rhyme. Something about cheeky monkeys and what they get up to on a bed. She can hold a tune too, unlike either of her parents.

He continues with his task, but remains alert to the distant drone of family life. He smiles at Amy's usual complaints when the shower is turned off before she's had a chance to flood the floor. Later, he hears the chink of cutlery against plate as she eats, her mother constantly reminding her to take another mouthful. He hears the trip back to the bathroom, the garbled chatter of Amy as she speaks through foam while getting her teeth brushed.

These noises, devoid of interest to anyone else, are precious to Doyle. They represent normality. He bitterly resents having them stripped from him.

Five minutes later Rachel enters the room, a monotone sentence already on her lips. 'You should say goodnight to your—'

She stops then, as she takes in what she did not expect to see.

'What are you doing?'

Doyle straightens up, drops a clumsily folded shirt onto the bed. 'I'm packing, Rach.'

'Why?' she demands, the question tainted with hurt and anger.

'I have to get out of here.'

'Bit of an over-reaction, wouldn't you say? I give you one little bit of criticism—'

'No. Rach. You don't understand. This has nothing to do with what you said to me earlier. You were totally right about that.'

She gestures at the suitcase on the bed. 'So, then, why?'

'I don't have a choice. In order to protect you, I have to leave. Simple as that.'

She shakes her head. A tiny movement of both disbelief and negation.

Doyle says, 'Rachel, what happened in the hospital tonight was a warning. The sicko who wants to hurt me was showing us what he could have done for real, to you and Amy. He's already proved he has no qualms about killing people. We've got five dead bodies already. I don't want to see any more, especially members of my own family. That's why I have to go, so he'll leave you alone.'

'What if I don't want you to go? What if I think the best way for you to protect us is to be here, by my side? Does my opinion count?'

Doyle sighs. 'That note the nurse gave me? It wasn't the first. Whoever's sending them keeps telling me that anyone I stay in close contact with is in danger. For whatever twisted reasons, he wants me on my own.'

'Why? I don't understand.'

'Me neither. All I know is that I can't stay here, because he'll come here too. With me gone, you're safe.'

She lowers her eyes as she considers his words. When she lifts her gaze again he sees her sadness.

'How long, Cal? How long are you going to be away?'

He shrugs, then counters his uncertainty with a smile of optimism. 'We got a lot of people on this. He can't keep this up for long. I might be moving back in tomorrow night. Keep my side of the bed warm.'

She tries a smile, but it's a half-hearted attempt that tells him she's not convinced.

'Let me say goodnight to Amy,' he says.

As he brushes past her she touches a finger to his arm.

'Cal?'

He stops and looks into eyes that are now brimming with tears.

'I don't want you to leave,' she says.

He takes her in his arms then, presses her whole body against him, wishing he could carry this closeness with him when he walks out the door.

Rachel asks, 'Where will you go?'

'A hotel. Somewhere I don't have to mix with people.'

'That's a pretty lonely existence. That's not you, Cal.'

'It's for one night. A couple at the most. I'll call you all the time, I swear.'

She runs a finger under one eye, catching a tear. 'You'd better, if you know what's good for you.'

He takes her face in his hands, plants a big kiss on her mouth. 'Give me five minutes.'

He leaves the bedroom, walks across to Amy's room. She's sitting up in bed, looking at a book about something called a Gruffalo.

'Daddy!' she says when he walks in.

'Hi, pumpkin. You ready for sleep yet?'

'Oh, no. But I am a little bit tired. Is it late now?'

He perches himself on the edge of her bed, and she wriggles over to make more room for him.

'Yeah, it's late. I'm going to bed myself soon. I've got a lot of work to do tomorrow.'

'Catching bad guys?'

'That's right: catching bad guys. And it's going to keep me so busy, I might not even be able to come home for a day or two. What do you think of that?'

She shakes her head emphatically. 'Not good. I don't want you to stay away, not even for one day.'

'I'll come back home as soon as I can, honey. I promise. Meantime, you be good for Mommy, okay?'

'Okay,' she says, begrudgingly. 'And then maybe when you come back, you can bring me a rabbit?'

'We'll see,' he says. He takes the book from her, tucks her and her toy bears into the bedclothes, then leans over and kisses her on the cheek. 'Goodnight, Amy.'

'Night, Daddy.'

He rises from the bed, steps toward the doorway and the light switch.

'Daddy!'

Amy is sitting bolt upright in bed again, as if awaking from a nightmare.

'What is it, hon?'

'Tomorrow is my dance show. I'm getting a medal. You have to be there.'

Shit! The show. He'd forgotten all about it.

'I, uhm, I'll do my best, honey, okay? I'll try to be there, I really will.'

'You promised.'

'I know, Amy, I know. Let me see what I can do, okay?'

But he knows he's not going to be there. And as he repeats his goodnight wish and turns out the light and closes the door, he feels like a complete heel. He feels like the sort of father he swore he would never be. Like his own father, the bastard.

He knows how much little things like this mean to a child. In the grand scheme of things it's nothing; to a six-year-old girl it's everything. The empty seat in the theater tomorrow will create a bigger emptiness in her heart – one that he may never fill. He knows this because of all the holes that were opened in his own heart as a kid. They never close over, not fully.

For that alone – never mind all the other things – Doyle swears vengeance. You want to break my daughter's heart, then go ahead. Just know that when I catch you, I'm gonna tear out your own heart and make you eat it, you fuck.

For what he can afford, the Cavendish Hotel near Union Square seems decent enough, although the reception staff are none too happy about a booking for an indeterminate number of nights, what with all the Christmas shoppers swarming into town at the moment. In the end Doyle stretches himself to a three-night reservation, extracting in return (inequitably, it seems to him) a verbal agreement that the hotel staff will do their utmost to keep the room available for longer if required.

His room is clean, the carpet isn't too threadbare and the bed isn't too concave in the middle, but Doyle can't settle. Things aren't where he expects them to be. The smells are different; the noises are different. He's not used to a bathroom without a window, and a view from the bedroom that's fascinating only if you have a thing for bricks. Worst of all, he's alone. He cannot reach out for the warmth of his wife in the bed next to him; he cannot lift up his daughter and smell the shampoo in her hair.

Doyle throws his clothes into drawers, then calls Rachel on the phone. He lies about how comfortable he is here, and understates the truth about how much he's missing his family. After the call he kills some time reading the hotel information brochures, then murders another hour or so staring at the flat-screen TV. It just makes him wonder how long it'll be before living in a box like this drives him insane.

Despite his tiredness, he is bursting with a high level of contained energy. To release it, he does some sit-ups and push-ups, then takes a shower. But still he feels like a caged lion with claustrophobia.

When he can stand it no longer, he escapes his room and goes in search of the bar.

The bartender is a swarthy Greek called George. Doyle asks him if the hotel has Guinness on tap, but they don't.

'Okay, make it a whiskey. Irish. Be as generous as you like.'

When it's poured, he raises the glass. 'To absent friends.'

He knocks it back, slams the glass down on the counter. 'Hit me again, George,' he says.

And keep on hitting me till I'm numb.

THIRTEEN

When Doyle gets into the squadroom at seven-thirty that morning, he sees that Franklin is already in his office, deep in conversation with the sergeant heading up the midnight tour. As Doyle sits at his desk it's as though it causes a buzzer to sound somewhere, because he sees the two men raise their heads and look across at him through Franklin's window. A dead giveaway to Doyle that he's the subject of their discussion.

Two minutes later, when the sergeant walks out to tidy up the tail end of his tour, Franklin beckons Doyle to enter. Wishing he'd stopped off to buy some Tylenol this morning, Doyle blinks against the pain he experiences with each step toward the lieutenant's office.

'You want to talk to me about what happened last night?' Franklin asks.

Doyle is unsure as to what his boss already knows. So he tells him everything. Finishes by placing the latest letter from the killer on Franklin's desk.

Franklin coasts a hand over his thinning hair. 'Shit, Cal! What a fucking mess.'

It's something Doyle can't deny, so he doesn't even try.

Franklin says, 'You sure Rachel and Amy are safe? We need to send some uniforms over?'

Doyle considers this. He knows that Rachel would hate the

idea. 'No. I think they're okay. I've done what that bastard wanted.' He pauses. 'You hear anything on the victim?'

'A hooker from the West Side. From what you've just told me, it was probably only the fact that she didn't look a whole lot different from your wife that got her killed. Shitty reason to die.' He blows air in exasperation. 'This'll hit the desks of the brass this morning, Cal. You know I can't sit on it. Somebody's gonna make a connection, somebody else is gonna make a recommendation, and I'm gonna get a phone call.'

'How long do I have?'

'Who knows? Hours? Minutes? To be honest with you, Cal, I'm not even sure I'm doing the right thing waiting for that call.'

Doyle leans forward, rests his arms on the edge of the lieutenant's desk. 'Mo, please don't pull me off this just yet. Not until you have no choice. I can't be pacing a hotel room while all this is going on.'

Franklin picks up a pencil, taps it on the arm of his chair while he considers his next move.

'You don't look well to me, Cal.'

Doyle blinks. Does he look so obviously wrecked?

Franklin says, 'I think maybe you should have called in sick today, at least for this morning. Maybe you'll feel better around, say, after lunch, when I'm in meetings at 1PP.'

It dawns on Doyle then. He's just been given a pass.

'Yeah,' he says, 'I do feel kinda nauseous.' Which isn't that far from the truth.

He gets out of his chair and moves toward the door. 'Thanks, Mo.'

Franklin waves him away. 'Get out of here before I catch whatever it is you got. An affliction like that could be the death of an old guy like me.'

The five-story tenement building on Suffolk Street in the Lower East Side stinks of piss and stale cooking. On the second floor, Doyle pounds his fist on the door of apartment 2A for the fifth time.

A few yards away, a neighboring door opens and yellow light spills out into the dark hallway. A huge black woman in an indecently short nightdress steps out as if entering the spotlight on a stage. Doyle waits for her to start singing.

'Hey! You ever think of using the damn doorbell?'

'It ain't working,' Doyle says, and pounds again.

'Hey, hey! Your momma ever show you how to knock on a door? Politely, I mean. Like this.' With surprising grace, she extends a pudgy knuckle and raps lightly on her own door. 'You see?' she says quietly. 'These apartments ain't so big. Don't need no sledgehammer to make yourself heard.' She straightens up, raises her voice again. 'Now show some consideration, you damn ignoramus.' She hefts her bulk back into her apartment and slams the door with a force that is sure to wake up the whole building.

Doyle sighs and raises his fist again, holding it poised in the air when he hears the locks being taken off.

The door opens, and Doyle is greeted by a face that is less animated than many he's viewed in the morgue.

'Jesus, Spinner. It's like waking the dead. You always sleep through people taking your door off its hinges?'

Spinner pries open one encrusted eyelid. 'I need my beauty sleep. Ugly lunk like you could do with a bit more of it yourself.'

Doyle says, 'You waiting for me to produce a bottle of wine before you invite me in?' but then doesn't linger for an answer before pushing the door open wider and stepping over the threshold.

The living room is a wreck. Unwashed dishes everywhere. Dark stains on the table and the carpet. There's a smell of blocked drains. In various stacks on the floor are collections of items that

Spinner hasn't fenced yet – DVD players, GPS units, game consoles – all neatly packaged in brown cartons. Stamped onto each of the boxes is the outline of a squat-bodied bird with a long tail, sitting on a branch.

'Christ, Spinner, how can you live like this?'

He steps over some boxed hi-fi speakers and heads toward the bedroom.

'Hey!' Spinner says. 'Did you hear me say you could go in there? Hey!'

Doyle opens the door, and takes one brief look at the chaos inside before his eyes alight on the bedside table. On top of the table is a length of rubber tubing and an empty hypodermic syringe.

He turns back to Spinner, closing the bedroom door behind him.

'No wonder I couldn't get you out of bed. You got wasted last night, didn't you?'

Swaying on his feet, his eyes half-closed, Spinner shrugs. 'What's it to ya? You looking to bust me for it?'

Doyle advances on him, grabs him by the bicep of his good arm, drags him into the bathroom. He kicks aside a mound of damp towels, then reaches for the shower control and turns it on full blast.

Spinner says, 'Cal! What you doing, man?'

Doyle brings his other hand to the nape of Spinner's neck and pushes his head into the jet of water.

'Cal!' Spinner yells, then splutters and coughs. 'That's fucking freezing, dude. Cut it out! Cut it out!'

Spinner struggles, but Doyle holds him there for a full minute, ignoring the protests. Finally, he releases him and steps away, trembling with his own fury. Spinner whirls himself out of the spray, and flattens himself against the cracked wall tiles as he sucks air back into his lungs.

'What you doing, man? What the fuck you have to do that for?'

Doyle picks up a towel and does what he can to dry his hands on the sodden fabric. He throws it at Spinner.

'Dry yourself off.'

He leaves Spinner there and moves back into the living room. He rests his hands on the back of a wooden chair as he tries to calm himself. A minute later, he hears Spinner enter the room behind him.

'You didn't have to do that.'

Doyle pushes himself off the chair and turns around. 'Look at yourself. Look at this fucking shit-heap of an apartment. Look at what you do.' He kicks an empty cardboard box, sending it sailing across the room. 'Selling stolen toys so you can pump more crap into your veins. What kind of life is that, Spin?'

Spinner rubs the towel under his chin. 'It's my life. Not yours. Mine. You don't have to live it.'

'And you do? Jesus, Spinner, what happened? What went wrong? You could have had a lot better than this.'

Spinner snorts a humorless laugh. 'Yeah, I coulda been a contender.'

Doyle closes the distance between them, and for a brief instant he feels like he's about to slap Spinner across the face. His hand comes up, but instead of striking him he takes a fistful of his grimy T-shirt.

'It's no joke, Spinner. It's sad. It's pathetic. There was a time I looked up to you. I actually wanted to be like you. And now you're just... you're just a...'

'A cripple.'

Doyle stares at him. 'What?'

'Go ahead, say it. I'm a cripple, an invalid – whatever term you want to use.'

'No, that's not what—'

'It's okay. Say it. Everybody else does. I hear 'em. They make jokes about me. You think I don't know what I used to be? You're right, I was good. I really think I could have been one of the best fighters in the country, maybe even the world. But do I have to take all the blame for what I am now? No, I don't think so. Doesn't matter how many times I run through my history, looking at all the stupid things I did, I can't find nothing explains why I had to be punished like this. So go ahead. Criticize me all you want. You don't want to deal with me no more, find yourself another sewer rat for your information. There's plenty other cops want what I got to sell.'

Doyle releases his grasp, tries to smooth out the extra creases he's just added to Spinner's shirt. 'Spinner, I didn't mean—'

'No. You know what? Fuck you. Get the fuck out of my crib. I don't need this grief.' He pushes Doyle hard in the chest. 'Go on. Get your ass out of here.'

Doyle looks for a long time into Spinner's face, and sees only fading echoes of the man he used to be. But he's right. It's not all his fault. He was dealt a bad hand, excuse the pun. And now he's hurting.

Doyle turns away and drags his feet toward the door. Stops after only three paces.

'What are you waiting for? Get the fuck out before I throw you out.'

'I can't,' Doyle says.

'What?'

Doyle faces Spinner again. 'I said I can't. I need you, man.'

'Ha! You *need* me. Yeah, right. You got a great way of showing it too. Makes me feel all warm inside the way you keep giving me so much affection.'

'No, seriously. I need your help. Things are bad for me right now.'

He detects a change in Spinner's stance. A slight softening. 'Bad how?'

'The cop killer? He's not smoking cops just for the sake of it. He's doing it to get at me. He's been sending me messages. Last night he killed a hooker and had me believing it was Rachel. For some reason he wants to isolate me, make me afraid to go near other people. He's trying to turn me into some kind of kiss of death.'

Spinner throws his towel down onto the floor – a gesture that tells Doyle he's just achieved the opposite effect of dredging up sympathy.

'Well, ain't that just dandy? You listen to any of what just came out of your mouth? About killing people close to you? And now you're where? Here, in my apartment, talking to your old buddy Spinner about how much you need him.' He stabs a finger angrily into his temple. 'Real clever, Cal. Real fucking intelligent.'

Doyle puts his hands out in front of him. 'Nobody knows I'm here, Spin. Not a soul. And before you ask, no, I wasn't followed. I made sure of that.'

But Spinner hasn't finished. 'Or is it maybe just that I'm expendable? Is that it, Cal? You can risk coming to me because it don't matter all that much if I get whacked. One less cripple in the world—'

'Jesus fucking Christ, man. Will you listen to me for one fucking minute? I'm coming to you for help, as a friend. The PD's getting nowhere on this. I need other sources. You want to know why I got so crazy a few minutes back? Because I wanted you clean. I wanted your head in shape so you could put everything you have into this. I'm that desperate. You may be all I got.'

Silence. The crunch point. Either Spinner buys this now, thinks Doyle, or I'm out on my ear.

Slowly, Spinner stoops and picks up the towel, then drapes it over the back of a chair. As if that makes any difference in a room that looks like it's had a hurricane blasting through it.

'I already asked around. After we talked last time. Nobody knows nothing. Or if they do, they're not telling me.'

'I need you to ask some more. Dig a little deeper.'

'How long you been running CIs, Cal? You know it don't work like that.'

Doyle nods his acceptance. On TV, in the movies, the cop meets his informant in a shady corner, inquires about the armed robbery at the First National Bank, and surreptitiously hands over a few bills. The next day, the snitch brings him a full list of the gang members, probably with their whereabouts, phone numbers and shoe sizes too.

Well, that's not how it goes in real life. Anyone who goes around asking career criminals direct questions about specific nefarious activities is liable to end up studying aquatic life at the bottom of the East River. Informants stay alive by being reactive rather than proactive. They listen, they remember, and they sell. Sometimes what they hear can be key to breaking a big case, but it's all down to being in the right place at the right time, and to gaining the trust of the right people.

Spinner says, 'But I'll do what I can, okay? Because you're a buddy, right? Because we go back a long way. Because there was a time when you and me, we weren't so different.'

Silence descends again. The two men face each other in the room, both lost in their thoughts, their memories. Both recalling a time when they had the same dreams for a better future. Both wondering how it was possible for their paths to diverge so greatly, and yet for them still to be thrown together in this crummy apartment.

FOURTEEN

The door. He remembers the door vividly. It's painted in cream and has a crack running down its center panel. The handle is in aged brass, and there are finger marks all around it.

And it's swinging shut. Slowly, to be sure, but it's definitely swinging shut. He is certain about that, oh yes. He can still see it now. Moving.

Doyle snaps himself out of it, focuses on what's happening on the sidewalk ahead of him. Two uniformed cops, outside of a bodega here on 120th Street. They have responded to a call to deal with an EDP – an Emotionally Disturbed Person – and have been trying to reason with the man for the last ten minutes.

The man, who looks to Doyle to be homeless and in his early fifties, points back to the bodega as he speaks. Despite the intense cold he has no coat, but it doesn't seem to bother him. His tirade becomes more animated, and Doyle notices how the cops tense when the man rips open his shirt. Even from here Doyle can see the vicious pink scar that runs all the way down his chest. The man points to it, then up at the sky. From the way that the cops glance at each other, Doyle guesses that the man has started blaming aliens or satellite death rays or some such for his disfigurement.

The debate goes on for another ten minutes before the cops eventually calm the man down and convince him to pull his shirt together and go on his way. Even then, the man stops every few yards and yells something at the waiting officers.

Good job, boys, Doyle thinks. Now let's see how you handle this one.

He gets out of his car, starts walking toward the two officers. His stride is steady, purposeful, but the cops are unaware of his approach. It's only when he's a few yards away that they turn to face him, still shaking their heads and laughing over their previous encounter.

The smiles evaporate when they see Doyle.

Officer Danny Marino points a warning finger. 'Get the fuck out of here, Doyle. If you know what's good for you . . .'

'I got a question for you, Marino.'

'Stick it up your ass. I'm outta here.' He starts walking around to the driver's side of his radio car.

'Not good enough, Marino. I need an answer.'

He starts to follow, but Marino's partner, a testosterone-infused gym rat called Smits, blocks his path.

'You heard him, Detective. He doesn't want to speak to you.'

Doyle looks him hard in the eye. 'This doesn't concern you, Smits. Step out of the way.' He tries to go around the man-mountain, but finds himself facing a wall of muscle again. Only this time Smits compounds his mistake by putting a restraining hand on Doyle's chest.

Doyle slaps the hand away, then shoves Smits backwards so hard that he has to windmill his arms to maintain his balance. His back thuds into the patrol car, rocking it on its suspension, and for a second or two, Smits appears surprised that anyone would have the temerity to do such a thing. But then a pearly-white grin spreads itself across his face. Like he's been looking forward to an opportunity like this for a long time.

He launches himself off the vehicle like he's a charging bull, head down and eyes up, nostrils flaring.

It's an easy one for Doyle. He uses Smits's huge momentum against him, standing his ground then quickly sidestepping and landing a full-force punch on his opponent's cheek as he sails past.

Smits shakes his head, puts on a smile as if to pretend that the blow was like being hit by cotton candy. But it's obvious to Doyle that the man is already beaten. He just doesn't know it yet.

When Smits bellows and comes back at him, it's without confidence. Doyle can see the uncertainty, the fear in his eyes. When Smits shoots his arm out, it's easily blocked, and Doyle counters with one, two jabs to the chin. He finishes with a swinging round-house to the jaw that feels to him as though it should take Smits's head off his shoulders. When it collides, saliva flies from Smits's mouth as he crashes against the door of the radio car and slides down it, his eyes rolling back in their sockets.

Doyle's thoughts turn back to Marino a millisecond too late. He catches a flash of rapid motion in the corner of his eye, just as something whips into his skull with a sickening crack that makes Doyle wonder if his brains are about to spill out. He falls headlong toward the white and blue sector car, almost tripping over the feet of the befuddled Smits. His hands come up instinctively to protect his face, and he feels sharp pain as his forearm smacks into the stiff metal support strut holding the windshield.

He knows this could be the end for him, but instinct comes to his rescue again and he allows gravity to yank him down as he whirls to face his attacker. This time the millisecond is in his favor, as Marino's baton skims the top of his head before it collides with the vehicle's side window, shattering it and showering Doyle with a thousand glinting fragments of glass.

Doyle knows there can be no delay in his reaction. As Marino pulls his arm back for the coup de grâce, Doyle pushes himself up and off the sidewalk. He throws his whole weight behind his right fist, driving it hard into Marino's solar plexus, so hard he swears he feels it connect with the man's spine. It's like uncorking a champagne bottle: there's an explosion of gas and wet spray from Marino's mouth, and his eyes look fit to shoot out in the same direction. Doyle doesn't wait to find out if Marino is still combat-fit. He follows with an uppercut to Marino's chin that practically causes the cop to levitate above the sidewalk before crashing down into a crumpled heap.

With Marino rolling on the ground, clutching his belly and wondering why he can't suck up any oxygen, Doyle glances at Smits again and sees that he's fumbling for his sidearm. Doyle whips out his own Glock and levels it at Smits.

'Don't do it, Smits. So help me God, I'll take you out.'

Smits slowly withdraws his hand. Tries to glare at Doyle through eyes that don't seem altogether in sync.

Doyle alternates his aim between Smits and Marino, alert for any sign that one of them wants to try his luck. He's oblivious to anything that exists outside of their own three-cornered world, and starting to realize how absurd that world has become. He feels ashamed that he's had to draw down on these officers like he's a gunslinger from a spaghetti western. His shame turns to embarrassment when he hears the whoops and cheers coming from farther up the street. He risks a glance upwards, sees that an audience has gathered to watch the fun. A knot of black kids, all astride their bicycles.

'Shoot 'em,' one of the kids shouts.

'Yeah, go on. Dead those motherfuckers.'

Great, Doyle thinks. Me being such a fine example to the impressionable youth of this city.

Seconds later, Marino regurgitates his last helping of coffee and donuts onto the sidewalk.

'Gross,' says one of the kids. 'Yo! Watchoo waitin' for? Put that motherfucker outta his misery.'

Doyle moves closer to Marino, kicks his shoe. 'You gonna answer my question now, Marino?'

Marino struggles a bit more for breath. 'Fuck you, Doyle. You fucked my wife and then you murdered her. The only help you'll get from me is to put you in a body bag.'

'That was a bullshit beef and you know it. I was cleared.'

'Just 'cause it was written up unsubstantiated, doesn't make you clean. You're a disgrace to the service, Doyle. You want to shoot me too now? Go ahead, pull the trigger, you piece of shit. Waste me like you wasted all your partners.' He looks up at Doyle, a pain-twisted smile on his face. 'Yeah, word gets around, don't it? Finally, people are starting to know you for what you are.'

'I didn't kill them. I didn't kill anyone. If the word's getting around like you say, then you must know that somebody else is doing this, somebody looking to hurt me. You have any idea who that someone might be?'

Marino tries to laugh, but ends up coughing and spitting out bile. 'If you're thinking it's me, then you go right ahead. Because if it's not me this time, it'll be me next time. After what you did to Laura and me, you deserve everything you get.'

Doyle wants so much to pull back his foot and fire a well-aimed kick into Marino's groin. 'If I find out you got anything to do with this, you're a dead man, Marino. You hear me? A dead man.'

Doyle walks away then, holstering his gun. Behind him, he hears Marino getting to his feet amid the jeers from the watching kids.

'Anytime, Doyle. Anytime. Who's going to help you now? You got no friends left. You're a nothing, Doyle. A nobody. Have a nice life, while you still got one.'

Doyle doesn't look back. He just keeps going until he reaches his car. He opens the door and gets in, then winces as he touches a hand to the swelling on his head.

Well, you handled that just fine, Detective, he thinks. Real nice job, you stupid prick.

Doyle enters the squadroom like a late pupil who's trying to sneak into class without the teacher spying him. Only when he is convinced that the lieutenant is still out at his meetings does he breathe a sigh of relief and settle at his desk.

At two-thirty p.m., Doyle's cellphone rings. He plucks it from his pocket and stabs at the answer button.

'Hello.'

'Doyle? It's me. Spinner.'

He sounds excited. Elated almost.

'Spinner? What's up?'

'I think I'm onto something.'

'So fast? How?'

'I got a meeting fixed up. Some people I know. They want to talk about who whacked your two partners.'

And two hookers and a pimp, Doyle thinks. But then they don't count, do they?

'What people, Spinner? Are you sure about this? What's in it for them?'

'Not on the phone. Later. Meet me at the usual place. Five o'clock.'

'Spinner! Hold on, man. I don't like the sound of—'

But the line goes dead.

Doyle prays that Spinner isn't about to go the same way.

He gets to the boxing gym at four o'clock, a full hour early. He sits in his car and waits, his eyes trained on the entrance to the gym.

There's no sign of Spinner entering or leaving, and at four-forty-five Doyle decides to check the place out.

He leaves his car, walks along the block and into the gym. Inside, he takes a good look around, finds the usual assortment of pugilists, trainers and other regulars. But no Spinner.

He leaves the building, goes back to his car and sits there for another half-hour, still watching. At five-thirty he goes back in for another reconnaissance, again with no success. Near the door he hails a man who has a brick-shaped head and no discernible neck.

'You seen Spinner lately?'

The man has to twist his whole upper torso to shake his head.

'Spinner? No, he ain't been in today.'

Doyle leaves and returns to his car.

This ain't right, he thinks. The whole thing stinks. Why the hell would anyone call in a small-time crook and junkie like Spinner to reveal what they know about a killer on the loose?

And that's when he really starts to worry.

He worries enough to fire up his engine and take the car screaming around to Spinner's apartment building.

He worries enough to take the steps two at a time as he races up to Spinner's floor.

He worries enough to draw his gun and kick open Spinner's door without even bothering to knock.

And then he stops worrying. Because Spinner is there in his apartment, sitting on his wooden chair facing Doyle. Wearing a big smile.

A red smile.

On his neck.

Worrying won't help him now.

FIFTEEN

There's a lot of blood. A hell of a lot of blood. But that's not the worst of it . . .

Spinner's head is tilted back and his eyes are open, staring at a spot above the doorway like he has a crick in his neck. The gash in his throat stretches almost from ear to ear, gaping and glistening. His clothes are sopping and sticky with his own blood. The dining table has been dragged from its usual position and set directly in front of Spinner. On it there's a tape recorder and a microphone. And a hammer.

Spinner's hand, his good hand, rests next to the recorder. Two six-inch nails have been driven through it, holding it firmly to the table's surface. All the fingers of the hand have been smashed with the hammer, crushing and flattening them into a single useless bloody mass. Like raw hamburger.

It must have been the ultimate torture for a man like Spinner. For a boxer of such promise to lose the use of one precious hand was devastating enough. To lose the second, there in front of his eyes, would have destroyed any spirit left in the man. Had his persecutor not finished him off, Spinner would probably have done it himself.

Doyle can almost hear the screams, see the agony and pleading in Spinner's eyes as the hammer crashes down time and time again, destroying his fingers, destroying his hope.

Doyle wants to cry over the waste of it, to rage at the stomach-churning cruelty of it. But what rips at him most is his own culpability.

'Jesus Christ, I'm sorry,' Doyle whispers to his friend. 'I'm so sorry.'

It's some time before he can put his mind back in order. He knows what he should do now. He should back out of the room, put in a call to Central. Get the experts down here while he protects the crime scene.

What the fuck. He's in enough trouble as it is. What's one more transgression going to add to his load?

And so he steps across the sodden carpet. Checks that the rest of the apartment is empty before returning to the body.

He looks again at the tape recorder. Taking a pen from his pocket, he uses it to press the eject button. The player's door springs open, but there's no cassette inside.

He frowns, then turns his attention back to Spinner. He leans in for a closer look, and that's when he sees it. Shiny and wet, it's tucked deep into Spinner's throat wound. Doyle takes his pen and pokes it gently into the fleshy chasm, pressing it against the foreign object. Whatever's in there, it's wrapped in some kind of plastic material.

Trying to apply the minimum of force, he teases the object out, farther and farther until it's protruding from Spinner's throat like some distorted second tongue. He goes off to the bathroom, and comes back with a wad of tissue. He wraps the tissue around his fingers, then uses it to grasp the edge of the object and pull it all the way out. As it comes free, a bubble of blood distends from Spinner's trachea and pops softly.

With great care, Doyle unrolls the plastic bag. He puts it down on the table and props it open with his pen, then reaches inside with some fresh tissue between his fingers.

What he brings out is a cassette tape. The words 'Detective Doyle' are written in pen on its label. The handwriting is Spinner's.

Doyle slides the tape into the recorder, snaps the lid closed, then presses the play button.

At first he's not sure what he's listening to. Some heavy rock music is playing really loudly, but beneath that is also the sound of faint sobbing. Doyle gradually realizes that the killer had turned on the stereo and ramped up the volume to mask what was happening here in the apartment. The crying is Spinner's.

And then: 'No. No. I won't do it.'

Doyle wonders what it is he's refusing to do, but he doesn't have long to ponder it. The next sound he hears is a bang like a gunshot, followed by a howl of excruciating pain that causes Doyle to leap away from the table and put his hands to his ears.

'Sweet Jesus,' Doyle yells to drown out the screams. 'Sweet fucking Jesus.'

When he can bring himself to listen again, the music has been turned right down and Spinner is talking to him.

'Cal? It's me, buddy. I have to read something to you, okay? I have to read this, so here goes.' There's a pause, then a slight rustle of paper, and then Spinner talking through his tears again. ' "Detective Doyle. You did this to me. You were warned, but you didn't listen. You were supposed to stay away from everyone you know, but you didn't. You came to see me. You are the reason I'm going through this right now. It's all your fault. When will you ever learn?" '

There is another faint crackle of paper, then the sound of footsteps retreating. Doyle waits for the tape to go dead, but suddenly Spinner pipes up again. His words come out in a rush, like he knows he has little time left.

'Cal, I'm sorry, man. I let you down. I didn't want to—'

It's as far as he gets, and Doyle thinks the recorder's stop button must have been pressed while he was in mid-sentence. But he's wrong. There is still sound. A gurgling, choking sound. The sound of a man who's just had his throat opened up.

Doyle stands in the chaotic, blood-soaked apartment, looking down at his old friend from the Bronx. Listening to his death throes.

He stands there until the tape reaches its end.

And he weeps.

He's hardly flavor of the month when the crowd arrives. Holden and LeBlanc are okay: the worst they give him are pitying looks and shoulder shrugs that say, *You're under pressure, so we understand why you're acting like such a rookie dork right now.*

The Crime Scene detectives, and especially the photographer, are a different matter. They're kind of upset that a precinct detective decided it would be okay to go tramping through the apartment, moving stuff around before they've had a chance to record the scene and look for clues and shit. They're funny that way.

Norman Chin takes it to another level again. Anything to do with a dead body, and especially *within* a dead body, he regards as his domain. He doesn't like the idea of detectives who don't know their ass from their olecranon process poking their grubby little retractable biros into the innards of his corpses. And in his own inimitable style, he's happy to tell anyone who would cross such a boundary what he thinks of them.

And so when Lieutenant Franklin arrives on the scene, the furrows on his face already spelling out the word 'grim', and finds that everyone and his brother are united in a 'we-hate-Doyle' campaign, it comes as no surprise to Doyle that his boss feels the need to join in.

'Go outside,' Franklin orders, his eyes glowering at Doyle.

'Mo, can we talk about this?'

'Outside, Detective. Now.'

The use of his job title is a sure signal to Doyle that to protest further would not be the most prudent course of action. With feet-dragging reluctance, he turns his back on the scene and heads out of the apartment.

On the stoop outside, two uniformed cops stare at him as he walks by. He steps down to the sidewalk, huddling into his leather jacket as he stares at the flashing roof lights of the radio cars. Five minutes later, Franklin joins him.

'Not one of your better days,' Franklin says.

Doyle glances at his boss. 'You could say that. You pissed at me?'

'You want the truth, yes, I am. It's bad enough I have to spend most of my Saturday afternoon stuck in dreary meetings on the upper floors of 1PP. But when I finally get out in time to meet my wife for some Christmas shopping, my cellphone never stops ringing. First of all from a very irate captain who's been briefed by a very irate duty sergeant that two of his men have had the crap beaten out of them by one of my detectives.'

'That's not the whole—'

'Then I get a call telling me that despite nobody knowing anything about your location or your actions today, you've suddenly phoned in to say that you're at the scene of a homicide. Of your own CI, no less.'

'I was trying to be—'

'And then, when I get down here, I discover that you took it upon yourself to walk all over a crime scene with the finesse of a bulldozer. So, to repeat my answer to your question, yes, I am a tad irritated that a member of my squad has decided to start World War Three without the knowledge or permission of his superior.'

Doyle waits for a moment. 'Can I talk now?'

Franklin sails an open palm out from his waist. 'Be my guest.'

'I admit I didn't follow procedure up there, but this is no ordinary homicide. This was done to hurt me. It was aimed at me. Spinner's a buddy of mine. We go . . . we *went* back a long way. His death's on me. Seeing him like that, what he went through, it hit me kinda hard.'

He gets no show of sympathy from Franklin. 'And this morning? What was that all about? First you have an unlogged meeting with a CI, and then you go out and beat up two cops.'

'They started it,' Doyle says, then realizes how childish it sounds.

'The way I heard it, not only did you kick the crap out of them, but then you even went so far as to draw your weapon on them. In full view of members of the public, no less.'

'Mo, it wasn't as simple as that. Christ, they're making me out to be some kind of cop-hating vigilante. I went to see Marino to ask him a simple question—'

Franklin stops him with raised hands. 'I don't care why you went there, although I can guess. What I care about is how it made you look, and by implication how it makes me look. Jesus, man, I turned a blind eye for you this morning. Against my better judgment I allowed you to stay on the job. At no point did I even hint that you could stop acting like a police officer and become some kind of maverick who thinks he can do whatever the hell he wants.'

'Mo, I'm sorry, okay? I don't know what else I can say. It's not like I got up this morning and thought I'd give myself a shitty day or anything. I've kinda had my fill of shitty days recently.'

'Yeah, well, maybe you should do something about it. Take some time to chill out a little.'

'I don't need . . .' Doyle begins, then realizes that Franklin isn't simply offering some friendly advice. He searches the lieutenant's face for a sign that he's wrong.

'You're taking me off the case.'

Franklin shakes his head, but his expression tells Doyle that it's not to convey better news. 'You're off all your cases, Cal. You're off the squad. Temporary R&R.'

'Mo, that's—'

'The call came through, Cal. I already spoke to the Chief of Ds. The word's come down from on high. You're out.'

'Well, fuck them. If they think I'm going to—'

'I'm not giving you choices here. For Chrissake, there are people dying all around you. Can't you see that? How many more do you want on your conscience before you decide to leave it alone? You're out, Cal. It's a done deal. And if you want my honest opinion, you're lucky you've still got your gun and shield after the cock-ups you made today.'

Franklin turns then, heads back up the steps of the apartment building.

Doyle calls after him, 'This case is all about me, Mo. I'm the best chance you have of catching this guy.'

'Go home, Detective,' Franklin says. 'That's an order.'

He disappears into the dark lobby. The two uniformed cops stationed at the door send semaphore signals to each other with their eyebrows.

Doyle takes a step toward the building, but no farther. He knows he can't fight this.

'I can't fucking go home!' he yells. 'Tell me where the fuck I'm supposed to go now!'

But there's no answer. Just the noises of the city going by like a river around a stone.

SIXTEEN

'Hello?'

Her voice. He really needs that voice right now.

'Rachel?'

'Cal! Honey! How are you?'

'I . . . yeah, I'm good. What about you? And Amy?'

'Oh, Cal, you should have seen her today. Danced her little heart out. I never knew she could dance so well.'

Yeah, the dance show. Amy getting a medal. One of those milestones in your child's development you just can't miss. And he wasn't there for her. He let her down.

'It's the Irish in her. All the Irish can dance a good jig. I wish I coulda been there.'

'Yeah, I do too. But, well . . .'

'Yeah. Did she miss me?'

'She's been asking for you all day. She's saved a dance just for you. For when you come home.'

'That's nice. Tell her I can't wait to see it. Tell her I'll bring her a little present home.'

'I will. That'll be soon, won't it? You coming home, I mean.'

'Are you kidding? With your husband on the case? How long can it take?'

'It's already been forever.'

'Yeah. Yeah, I know. Just . . . keep your chin up, okay? For Amy's sake.'

'I . . . okay. But it's not the same without you here. I don't even know what day you're coming home. It's not right, Cal. It'll be Christmas soon. We need to be together, as a family.'

'Hey, shush. You think there's any way I'm not going to be there for Christmas? I'll be home way before then.'

'You promise?'

'Swear to God. Maybe I'll bring an early Christmas present for you, too.'

'Just bring *you* home, Cal. Safe and sound.'

'Don't I always?'

'I mean it, Cal. I don't want to be called out to a hospital again. I don't want the next time I see you to be in a morgue. I don't want . . .'

Tears again. And not just in Rachel.

'Rachel. Rachel. I'm fine, and I'm gonna stay fine. Keep an eye on that apartment door. I'll be back before you know it.'

'Solve the case, Cal. Just solve the case.'

How? When he's virtually a prisoner in this fucking hotel?

'I . . . yeah. I'll solve the case.'

'Cal?'

'What?'

'I love you.'

'I love you too, honey.'

And that's the only thing he's got right now.

He lies on his bed for half an hour, hands clasped behind his head. He stares at an abstract painting on the wall and wonders what it's an abstraction of. He realizes that his brain just isn't wired in a way that will allow him to move beyond the colored circles and squares he can see. Decides that the only circle that will take him to a higher plane is the rim of a beer glass.

The bar on the first floor is almost deserted. Just a middle-aged couple tucked into a corner booth, whispering sweet somethings and exchanging meaningful smiles.

They're married, Doyle thinks. But not to each other. Call me cynical . . .

He takes a stool at the bar, and George the swarthy Greek glides over like he's on casters.

'Irish?' he asks.

Doyle says, 'Yeah. Is it the way I walk?' But when that just gets him a puzzled frown he adds, 'No, better just make it a beer. Gimme a . . .' he scans the bottles in the refrigerated cabinet behind the bartender, ' . . .a Heineken.'

One bottle of Heineken later he's back on the whiskey, throwing it down like prohibition's due to start in the next five minutes.

Doyle is a man for whom alcohol can loosen the tongue and free the spirit when he's in the right company. But an indifferent Greek and a couple who have now resorted to furtive groping do not the right company make.

He tries closing his eyes and transporting himself to an Irish bar – a true Irish pub in Dublin or Cork or somewhere like that – listening to a ceilidh band and joining in the craic and eyeing up the pretty lasses. But it's difficult when George turns up the volume to hear the latest on strife in the Middle East, and the woman in the booth – who Doyle now thinks to be at least a hundred beneath that slab of make-up – begins making peculiar mewling noises, like a cat with laryngitis.

Surrendering to the depressing tawdriness of it all, he pays his tab and leaves.

He meanders aimlessly for an unmeasured period of time, letting his feet take him where they will. And where they take him is to more familiar territory in the East Village. Despite an alcohol-tainted compass they steer him past the trendy bars, guide him away from the 'happening' nightspots, thread him through the Saturday-night revelers whose dress sense seems to flip a finger of defiance at the bitter cold, and eventually land him at Gilligan's on Avenue A.

Gilligan's has nothing to do with the Island and everything to do with an ex-cop from the Eighth Precinct named Patrick Gilligan. Long dead from cirrhosis of the liver, Patrick handed the establishment down to his son, also named Patrick but known to his regulars as Paddy. Paddy has never been a cop – never wanted to be – but he probably gets more of them through his doors on an average day than many station houses.

Something at the back of Doyle's mind warns him that it's a mistake coming here. He should turn around now and move on to a watering hole where he can be just another anonymous lonely drunk. But the alcohol-fogged bulk of his brain dismisses the notion of caution as the outpourings of a spineless wuss, and gives him a mental shove through the door.

It's like being Black Bart in the Last Chance Saloon. The laughing and joking stop abruptly as people catch sight of the man who has just walked in. These are men and women who would normally be slapping him on the back or shaking his hand or offering to buy him a drink or simply saying hello. Now they merely shuffle out of his way and offer each other mutterings and whispers and 'look-who-it-is' glances.

Doyle's heart sinks. He expected more from his fellow members of service. But it's too late to back out now. He's come in for a drink, and he's going to have a fucking drink. So fuck the lot of you.

He moves to the bar, takes one of the many stools that have suddenly become unoccupied. At the other end of the bar, Paddy's employee Terry is polishing glasses with a concentration and fervor that are disproportionate to the task.

Doyle watches him for a minute, hoping to catch his eye. But Terry's making sure his eyes are not up for catching anywhere in Doyle's zone.

'Hey, Terry! Any danger of some service down this end?'

Terry doesn't shift position or even acknowledge Doyle's presence. He glances up at one or two of his customers, checking that he has support, then returns to removing imaginary specks of dirt from the glass in his hand.

'Terry! You gone deaf on me?' Still getting no response, Doyle waves a hand in the air. 'Hey, Terry! Get the fuck over here, man!'

Terry looks at his other customers and shrugs at them as if to say, *Look, this ostracism thing ain't working on this nuisance.* He puts the glass down, then gravitates to the other end of the bar as if he's straining against the pull of an elastic rope. When he reaches Doyle, he slides his hands back and forth along the edge of the polished mahogany counter.

'Look, Cal. No offence or nothing, but everyone knows where you're at right now.'

'You don't say. And here's me thinking I forgot to take off my Bin Laden mask tonight.'

Terry lowers his voice, which Doyle thinks comes a bit late if the aim is to keep this away from the other customers. 'Cal, please. Do me a favor, okay? You coming in here, people are gonna start leaving in droves. It ain't good for business, you know? Be sensible about this, Cal. Think about what you're doing to the place.'

Doyle stares at Terry for a good ten seconds, not believing what he's hearing. He tears his gaze away, and aims it at the people behind him. Most of them are looking his way. Not talking, hardly drinking. Just looking and waiting to hear his response.

Doyle turns back to Terry. He sighs.

'All I wanted was a quiet drink. A Guinness. You know how long I been coming here, Terry? Ever since I joined the Eighth.

A whole year now. I thought I made a few good friends in that time – some of them are in here tonight, in fact. But I understand why people are worried. In their shoes, I think I would be too. They don't want to be afraid of getting killed just because they smiled at me, or said hello. So, really, I do understand, and I think you're right. I should spare a thought for them and for the health of your business.'

For the first time since Doyle walked in, Terry smiles, and a load seems to drop from his shoulders.

'Thanks, Cal. I knew you'd understand. I appreciate it.'

'Yeah,' Doyle says, and gets up from his stool.

Before he has even thought about the consequences, Doyle has whipped out his Glock from its holster. He presses its muzzle into Terry's forehead. Behind him he hears gasps of astonishment. He knows that a number of the cops here are already reaching for their own weapons, but he doesn't turn around.

'There you go, Terry. I'm making it easy for you.' He raises his voice so everyone can hear. 'See, everyone? I'm not his friend. I'm *making* him talk to me. I'm *making* him pour me a drink. Does that work for you, Terry? You don't have to be afraid, because you ain't my friend. All you have to do is pour me a drink every time my glass is empty. That goes for everybody else too. I ain't looking for friends here tonight. You don't have to talk to me. You don't even have to come anywhere near me. Just leave me be, and let me drink. That's all I'm asking. So how about it?'

There has probably never been a bar as busy as this that is now as quiet as this. Doyle keeps his eyes locked on Terry, whose only movements are involuntary through his sheer terror. Doyle knows at his very core that this is wrong, that he shouldn't be doing this. But he's beyond caring. He keeps the gun in place and waits for an answer. Or for someone to shoot him in the back, which seems a distinct possibility right now.

'Give him a drink.'

A figure emerges from a door behind the bar. Paddy Gilligan himself. A broad, powerful-looking man. A big goofy smile on his face.

'Do I pay you to be standing there looking like an idiot when there're customers to be served? The man has a thirst on him. Give him a drink. And the rest of you: don't you have better things to do than stand there gawking at the sight of a man ordering a Guinness? Jesus, they must be sad lives you're living.'

He says all this without anger or reproach. He just keeps that wide disarming grin affixed to his face. Friendly but firm: an approach that he's used to manage many a situation that's threatened to get out of control in his bar.

He'd have made a good cop, Doyle thinks.

He lowers the gun. Allows the suitably ashamed Terry to tend to the Guinness. While Paddy looks on, master of all he surveys, the customers return to their drinks and resume their conversations. The entertainment's over, folks.

Paddy strolls over to Doyle.

'Hear you're in a spot of trouble,' he says.

'More than a spot. Closer to a deluge.'

Paddy smiles and nods. 'As long as it's through no doing of yours, you got no problem getting served in this bar. Ever.'

Doyle stares into Paddy's eyes – as blue as his own are green – and thinks about this gesture. It's much more than a small kindness; it's an act of bravery from a man who has heard the stories and knows it could get him killed.

'You're a good man, Paddy.'

'I'm an Irishman. Like yourself. If there's a fight to be fought, we don't run away.' He gestures to the settling pint of Guinness. 'A drop of the black stuff there will help you remember where you came from and what it all means.'

Doyle picks up the glass and raises it to Paddy.

'*Sláinte,*' he says.

Paddy smiles again, turns to Terry. 'Whatever he wants, on the house.' He looks again at Doyle, gives him a mischievous wink, and is gone.

Doyle closes his eyes, takes a long draft of the heavy liquid, feels its silky smoothness flowing down his throat, and tries once again to take himself far away from this madness.

SEVENTEEN

It was too good to be true.

He has kept his place on the bar stool all night. Kept his peace, kept his dignity, kept himself to himself. The alcohol has done its work, coursing through his blood system, slipping into his capillaries and seeping into his cells, carrying him into that other-world where personal troubles are put into their proper perspective when viewed against the greater machinations of the universe. In short, getting him totally shit-faced.

With his physical isolation now accompanied by a self-induced mental isolation, the voice doesn't carry to him at first. He's aware only of a sound that seems to be steadily rising in volume while all other noises are diminishing. It's a while before his brain recognizes the voice being broadcast in all directions, and registers that the words it carries are being aimed specifically at him.

'To me, it's like owning a dog,' Schneider is saying somewhere behind Doyle. 'You got a dog that's dangerous, you have to do something about it. Say it's vicious, like maybe it's biting people, or attacking other dogs, or chasing the mailman. Do you think it's right to let a dog like that run around our streets? Or say it's not even the dog's fault. Say it's not even mean. It's just sick. It's carrying a disease of some kind. Any other animal it gets close to is likely to get sick too, maybe even die. You think it's okay to let that dog out? Don't you think it should be impounded? Maybe even put down?'

Doyle hears some noises of agreement, and a few laughs, presumably from Schneider's drinking buddies. He does his best to tune it out, and he gives Schneider no signal that he's heard any of his tirade. He doesn't want to give him the satisfaction.

'Ain't no different with humans,' Schneider continues, even louder now. 'We got a guy who's running around killing people, we lock him up, right? As cops it's our job, our duty. But what if he says it's not his fault? His story is that wherever he goes, the people he mixes with drop dead. Sounds pretty flaky, right? Personally, I'd have a hard time believing a story like that. But, hey, it's nearly Christmas, right? Let's show the guy a little charity. Give him a little latitude. Hard-nosed cynical cops that we are, let's suspend our disbelief just for once.

'So the guy's just a walking disaster area. King Midas with a twist: everything he touches turning to dead. What do we do with him? Let him walk? Give him the opportunity to drop a few more innocent citizens in their paths? Fuck no!'

The support for Schneider is more vocal now. He even gets one or two cheers. Give him his due, Doyle thinks, he knows how to play to the audience. Any minute now I'm gonna be the subject of a lynching.

He can feel dozens of eyes burning into the back of his neck, waiting for him to rise to the bait. Many of them have already demonstrated their sympathy for Schneider's view. A few, or so he hopes, will want him to cut Schneider down at the knees.

Doyle still doesn't turn. Instead, he beckons Terry the bartender over and asks for a whiskey.

'Irish?'

'Scotch. On the rocks.'

Terry gives him a look of faint surprise, but nods and fetches a tumbler.

''Course,' Schneider is saying, still on his soapbox, 'the ideal situation would be if our hypothetical individual with the extreme social disease decided to do something about it himself. Him being somebody regards himself as a responsible public servant, he'd probably choose to do the right thing without pressure from anybody else. Not wanting to be a danger to the people he calls his colleagues and his friends, he'd probably choose to stay away from the places those people are known to frequent.'

From the back room, Paddy puts in an appearance. It's the first time that Doyle has seen him wearing an expression of annoyance. It's a look so dark that Doyle feels he's on the verge of closing down the whole bar.

Paddy glances at Doyle. He's looking for confirmation. Doyle shakes his head almost imperceptibly. Paddy's eyes question this.

Doyle slips from his chair and takes hold of the glass of Scotch. He turns slowly, his legs not as steady as usual, his eyes not as focused. He takes in the sight of all those faces turned toward him. The sense of expectation is almost a force, drawing him into making some kind of response. They want a word, a gesture, an act. It's a fight-or-flight moment. What will he do now?

Blinking, squinting, Doyle makes out the big ugly mug of Schneider through the crowd. He's seated at a window table with some pals. He is grinning and chewing. Even when he drinks, he chews.

Doyle starts toward him. He knows he's drunk, but he tries to keep his path straight as he pushes onwards. The other customers move aside, letting him tunnel through. Many of them will have seen him pull his gun earlier; some will be afraid that this time he'll use it.

The three other men at Schneider's table are cops too, but not from the Eighth Precinct. Doyle recognizes their faces, but doesn't know their names. They watch him intently as he gets closer to them, and Doyle suspects that if he were more sober he would be able to feel their tension. Right now he doesn't give a shit. He just wants Schneider.

Schneider doesn't move from his chair. He takes a sip of his beer, tries to appear nonchalant. When Doyle stops just a couple of paces away, Schneider stares up at him.

'What's up, Doyle? You got something you want to share? Maybe add your two cents to the little debate we got going on here?' He laughs. His drinking buddies laugh along with him.

Doyle laughs a little too. 'Nah. I just want to show you something. A little trick I learned a long time ago.'

This throws Schneider. He doesn't appear so confident now. He looks to his pals, who just shrug.

'I got no time for tricks, Doyle. Especially with you. You got something to say, say it.'

'Come on. What are you, chicken? Look . . .' He holds the glass high, showing it to everyone around, then sets it down in front of Schneider. 'Scotch on the rocks. Your favorite tipple, right? It's yours. Win or lose this little contest I got in mind, the drink's yours.'

Schneider looks again to his comrades, who are signaling for him to go for it.

'A contest? What kind of contest?'

'Kind of like a strength contest. Don't worry, I ain't gonna hurt you. I'm sure your pals will see to that.'

Schneider barks another laugh. '*You* hurt *me*? Ha! Anyone gets hurt here, Doyle, it's gonna be you.' He gets up from his wooden chair. 'All right, magic man. What do we do?'

Doyle puts his hand out. 'First of all, you gotta take my hand.'

Schneider looks with uncertainty at the proffered hand. He wipes his own palm down the side of his pants, then folds his meaty fingers around Doyle's.

'That's a good grip you got there, Schneider. You been working out with it, maybe? On your own, with some skin mags?'

This gets a laugh from the crowd, and Doyle can see how it irritates Schneider.

'Just get on with the stupid contest.'

'All right. When I say go, you pull me toward you, and I'll pull you in the opposite direction. Ready?'

'I end up on my ass, I am so gonna slug you, Doyle.'

'Stop whining. You ready or not?'

Schneider shifts his stance, plants his feet to prevent him being shoved off balance.

'Ready.'

'All right . . . Go!'

Schneider yanks hard on Doyle's arm, but instead of resisting, Doyle allows himself to be hauled in. As he collides with Schneider's chest he loops his left arm around the man's neck, holding him securely in position.

Taken by complete surprise, Schneider doesn't know how to react. 'What the fuck . . .'

'Just hold it like that. A couple more seconds . . .'

'Doyle, get the fuck off me . . .'

And then Doyle releases him. Without another word, he turns and starts to walk away. He can see the bemused expressions of the onlookers, and can only imagine the bewilderment on Schneider's face.

'What the fuck was that?' Schneider calls, but Doyle keeps on walking.

'Doyle! Hey, Doyle! I'm talking to you!'

As he reaches the door, Doyle stops and turns. Schneider is looking at him, his palms out, trying to make sense of it all.

'Think about it,' Doyle says. 'There's somebody out there hurting people I know and like. People I get close to. He always seems to know where I am, who I speak to. Maybe he's watching me tonight, through that window behind you. What's he just seen?

Me buying you a drink, shaking your hand, giving you a big hug like you're my best buddy. Enjoy the rest of your night, Schneider.'

As the bar erupts, Doyle takes the last couple of steps toward the door. Just before he leaves he gets a grinning Paddy Gilligan in his sights, returns the mischievous Irish wink he received earlier.

And then he's gone.

In his dream, the door isn't moving.

He's standing there, staring at that cream door with the crack in its panel. He's willing it to move, but it doesn't. He looks for lines on the blue patterned carpet – any kind of marker by which to measure the progress of the door closing. It doesn't help. That slab of wood is in exactly the same position it was when he entered the room.

He moves to the door and pushes on it, but it won't budge. He leans on it, drives his shoulder into it with all his might. Gradually, inch by inch, the door opens up. He gets an arm through the gap, then a leg. Straining and squeezing, he eventually gets the rest of his body into the room beyond.

That's when he sees what was preventing the door from opening.

Body parts. Hundreds of them. Legs, arms, torsos, all piled on top of each other in a grotesque hill of lifeless flesh and bone.

He finds himself desperate to know who they belong to, and so he steps up to the mountain and begins to pull at its sides. Cold sticky cobs of gore come away in his hand. He flicks them away, tries again. Gradually he bores inside, but all he can see is wet redness and shiny gristle.

And then something drops into his man-made tunnel. Something round and heavy. It plops onto the bed of human meat and rolls toward him. As it gathers speed, a similar-sized sphere drops from above and chases after the first. Then comes another, and another. Doyle feels like a lone pin at the end of a bowling alley, about to be struck down by any one of these balls heading his way.

But as they get nearer to him they slow down. He tries to make out their precise nature, but only when all of them come to rest at his feet is he able to see them for what they are.

Human heads. With faces he recognizes. There's Joe Parlatti, staring at him with uncomprehending eyes and an open mouth. There's Tony Alvarez, and there's Spinner, and there's . . .

He decides to get out of there when the heads begin to scream at him.

They let out unpunctuated wails of torment and pain. Long drawn-out cries that can snap hearts and break minds. Doyle scrambles for the door, manages to squeeze himself through the gap as he did before. He pulls the door shut, muting the hellish sounds beyond. Resting his head against the cracked panel, he tries to regain his breath, his composure. He counts to ten, slowly turns.

Then, like Ebenezer Scrooge, he encounters the final ghost – the one he dreads most.

She is facing him, her arms out to him, pleading. Tears are running down her cheeks. She wants to know why.

But Doyle has no answers. All he can do is stare right through the ragged hole in Laura Marino's chest . . .

And scream.

He sits upright in bed, knowing that he has just screamed himself awake.

He's drenched in sweat. Shaky from the nightmare he has just lived. Laura Marino's heart-rending face is still imprinted on his brain.

'It was moving,' he mutters to himself in the blackness. 'The fucking door was moving.'

He swings his legs out of bed, then pads naked to the bathroom. He fumbles for the light. Steps through onto the cool tiles. He squints at himself in the mirror over the sink. Not a pretty sight. He doesn't know what time it is, but he hasn't slept nearly enough to get the alcohol out of his system.

He moves over to the toilet, takes a pee that seems even to him to last forever, then goes back to the sink and fills it with lukewarm water. He splashes handfuls of it onto his face, his hands rasping against the roughness of his stubble. He dries himself on the fluffy hotel towel, then steps back into the main room, turning off the light as he enters.

He doesn't know what it is – a sound, an odor, a flash of movement just before he doused the light – but he suddenly realizes that he's not alone in this room.

EIGHTEEN

He tries to act as though he hasn't noticed a thing. He knows he's at a disadvantage for several reasons. First of all, he's still under the influence of numerous pints of Guinness. Second, he has just blinded himself with the lights in the bathroom, while the intruder's eyes, on the other hand, are presumably fully accustomed to the darkness. Third, he cannot remember precisely where he put his gun when he got undressed. Last, but not least, he is as naked as the day he was born, which leaves him feeling kind of defenseless.

Straining to build a mental map of the room in front of him, he stumbles his way back to the bed and tries to make up his mind as to what to do now.

The gun, or the light switch?

His best guess is that his Glock is in the drawer of the bed table. But he could be wrong about that. And even if he's right, he can't see well enough to shoot anything.

So, he thinks, It's the light then. But what's the point in that? It might blind the guy for all of two seconds, but I still don't have a weapon, and he might just decide to start blasting away.

Final decision – the gun first. He reaches into the drawer, acting all nonchalant like looking for tissues or some such, then dives for the light switch, hoping to get the drop on the guy. Okay, it's not exactly the most foolproof plan in the world, but hey, I don't have many options here.

Of course, if he's mistaken, and there's nobody else in the room, then he's going to feel such a dick.

He sits on the edge of the bed, puts his head in his hands and lets out a groan.

'God, my head,' he mutters. 'I so need a painkiller for this.'

He stretches for the drawer, slides it open, dips his hand inside. Nothing. Except a Gideon Bible. Which in his experience doesn't make the best of weapons.

'Jesus, Mr Doyle, you are the world's worst actor. I hope they never send you undercover on any narco busts, that's the best you can do.'

Doyle turns toward the voice coming from the corner of the room. A lamp flares into life, and he squints to make out the figure seated next to the circular writing table.

'I guess you're looking for this,' the man says, waving Doyle's Glock in the air. 'Boy, do you sleep heavy. I should have put the TV on while I was waiting, all the difference it'd make to you.'

Doyle blinks a few times at the familiar face. Tries to match it up with a name in his mental record book. The guy is big. Looks like he hits the weights. He has a wide jaw and dimples in his cheeks. His thick black hair has a pronounced widow's peak.

'I think you were having a bad dream there, buddy. Something about a door? What's that about? You get stuck in a revolving door one time?'

Then it clicks. 'Sonny Rocca.'

The man smiles. A big white grin. Perfect teeth.

'I'm flattered. You remember me. I didn't realize I'd left such a lasting impression. I'm touched, really.'

'I like to take a mental snapshot of those people I'm gonna have to visit again someday.'

'You planning to come see me again? That's nice. Please, drop in anytime. I'll make you some cannoli. My grandmother's recipe.' He touches forefinger and thumb to his lips, kisses them away. *'Perfetto.'*

'You still running errands for Tweedledum and Tweedledee?'

Doyle watches Rocca's face cloud over, and he knows he's stung him.

'If you mean am I still in the employ of Mr Bartok and his brother, then the answer's yes.'

Doyle nods thoughtfully. 'So they still won't have you, huh?'

Sonny Rocca grew up in Little Italy, that area of Manhattan north of Chinatown that has been home to Italian-Americans since the immigrant influx of the late nineteenth century. As a teenager Rocca ran with gangs, got involved with petty crime and auto thefts. His one avowed ambition in life was to become a true mobster, a made man, a goodfella, a wiseguy.

The problem was that not one of the families would take him into its bosom. For one thing, his mother wasn't Italian; she was Norwegian – as blond and fair-skinned and non-Mediterranean-looking as they come. It's one of the reasons that Rocca has always overplayed the Italian side of his heritage, sometimes to the extent of sounding like a stereotype in a badly written play.

These days, as others have proved, full Italian blood isn't the essential ingredient it used to be, but Rocca has other baggage too. Three years ago he became engaged to a girl who was the beloved niece of a high-ranking mobster. Naturally, his actions were purely tactical: he never really loved the girl, as he frequently proved through his bedding of other women. All was fine until she found out about his infidelity and called off the engagement, at which point Rocca found his ladder of success hauled away and some very mean individuals put in its place.

Schooled as he was in the ways of organized crime, Rocca settled for the next best thing. A family partnership that was willing to accept him with open arms. The Bartok brothers.

Lucas and Kurt Bartok are not Italian; like their composer namesake they are of Hungarian descent. As such, they don't give a rat's ass for the Cosa Nostra or its codes of conduct. They work alone, and they have carved out quite a comfortable niche for themselves, thank you very much. Occasionally they resort to acts of violence, and when they do it can be so extreme as to make even the Italian mobs balk. The elder brother in particular, Lucas, has a penchant for disemboweling people with a meat hook. Legend has it that Lucas once used his butchery skills to carve an enemy into many pieces before having the choicest cuts delivered to the victim's family members as Thanksgiving presents.

What saves the Bartoks from a nasty collision with rival organizations is the activities of the younger brother Kurt. Very much the brains of the outfit, Kurt's specialty is information. His sources tend to be police officers he has turned using bribes, coercion or both. The information he gleans from the cops is extremely useful not only in safeguarding his family's own criminal undertakings, but also as a commodity for selling on to other outfits, thereby keeping them sweet. All told, it's a highly successful operation – an example to us all as to how to run a profitable and expanding business. Corporate America should be proud.

The reason Doyle knows all this is because three months ago he collared the Bartoks and Rocca for their part in a raid on a warehouse owned by a firm called Trogon Electronics. Naturally, with the lawyers they could hire and the people they could buy, they beat the rap before it even got to court. But word is that the Bartoks, and Lucas in particular, have never forgiven Doyle for his temerity. In his turn, Doyle feels no love for the Bartoks or their employees; hence his barb about Rocca's inability to follow his true calling.

The struggle to maintain his composure is clear on Rocca's face. It's a while before he finds his jovial side once more. 'Well, I think you know much more about that than I do, Mr Doyle. About people not wanting to accept you, I mean.'

Touché, Doyle thinks. How quickly word gets around.

'How'd you get in here, anyway?'

The disarming smile again. 'I ain't just a pretty face, you know. I got skills, talents. The way I can get into places, some people think I can walk through walls.'

'So you paid someone at the desk to make you another key card. Yeah, that's mysterious all right. Look, you mind if I put some pants on? I'm feeling kind of exposed here.'

'Sure, go ahead.' With Doyle's gun he gestures to the phone on the table. 'You want I could call room service, get some fresh coffee sent up?'

'Nah, that's okay. You won't be staying that long.'

Doyle stands up, but stumbles slightly and has to put his hand against the wall to steady himself.

Rocca says, 'You sure about that caffeine? You look like you could do with it.'

Doyle frowns, finds his boxers and pants, and pulls them on. Being in a room with a criminal pointing your own gun at you is bad enough; being naked to boot is downright humiliating.

He sits on the bed. 'All right, Sonny, what do you want? This payback time? Is that it? Lucas Bartok not able to sleep at nights with the thought of his arresting officer still walking the streets?'

'Come on, Mr Doyle. I wanted to cap you, I coulda done it while you were counting sheep or opening doors or whatever.'

'Maybe you got instructions to make me suffer first. That's more Lucas's style.'

'Believe me, if Mr Bartok decided he wanted you dead, he'd come and do it himself, and then you *would* be wishing I got to you first. No, you got it all wrong. I'm here to offer you some assistance.'

'Thanks, but I don't need a maid. The hotel's got its own housekeepers.'

Rocca laughs. 'You're a funny guy, Mr Doyle. That's what I like about you. Always with the jokes, even when you got nothing left to laugh about.' He leans forward on the chair. 'See, what I hear is that you've been dumped. And I ain't just talking about a wife or a girlfriend here; I'm talking about *everyone*. The whole world has put you out with the garbage.' He shakes his head. 'You know, every time I think about that I find it hard to believe. How is it possible for one person to be so obnoxious that the whole world turns against them? That really has to be a first. You should get in the record books for that one.'

'*Au contraire*, Sonny. People are *dying* to meet me.'

Rocca slaps his palm on the table, laughs even louder. 'See, there you go again. The jokes. *Dying* to meet you. That's clever. Very funny.'

'I got plenty more, you want to hear them.'

'Another time, maybe. Another time. But seriously, this thing about people dying wherever you go, that must be a bit of a downer, no?'

'It does kinda take the shine off the day.'

Rocca jabs his gun toward Doyle. 'Exactly what I thought. I can see how that could start to get a little depressing after a while. Mr Bartok thinks so too. Which is why he'd like to talk to you.'

'Don't tell me. He wants to make me an offer I can't refuse.'

Rocca jabs again, and Doyle starts to worry about the position of Rocca's trigger finger.

'Don't think I don't get the reference. *The Godfather*, right?'

'I can do it in a Marlon Brando voice if you prefer.'

'So how about it? You willing to come with me and have a little chat with Mr Bartok?'

Doyle glances at the bedside clock. 'Now? It's two in the morning.'

Rocca looks askance at him. 'It's Saturday night. The city's still rocking. Come on, Mr Doyle, live a little.'

Doyle sighs. 'You mind if I finish dressing?'

'Please. It's cold out there. Don't want you to catch your *death*.'

Doyle points a finger and thumb at him, pistol-style. 'I see what you did there. You're catching on.'

He finds the shirt he tossed on the floor a few hours ago. It's a little crumpled, but it'll do. It's not like he's going for a job interview.

'Speaking about catching my death, what about you? You not afraid to step outside with me, case it leads to you getting your head blown off?'

He isn't looking directly at Rocca as he asks this, but he catches sight of him in the wall mirror. He sees that Rocca is temporarily flummoxed, as though the notion that this might be putting him in danger has never occurred to him. It takes Rocca a few seconds to come up with a response.

'If this guy knows anything, and from what I hear he knows a lot, he'll understand that nobody hurts the Bartok family or anyone who works for them. Maybe you cops can't find him, but believe me, Mr Bartok would hunt him down and the outcome would not be pleasant.'

To Doyle the reply lacks conviction, but he lets it go and finishes dressing.

'You done?' Rocca asks, getting up from the chair.

'All except my nine. You mind if I have it back? I still feel naked without it.'

Rocca hefts Doyle's gun in his hand. 'It's okay with you, I'll hang onto it for a while.'

Doyle shrugs. 'All right. Just don't look at me to save your ass when the boogeyman starts shooting at us.'

He watches Rocca's face, and again the reaction isn't what he expected. He can't fathom it, but something's going on in Rocca's mind. Maybe he really is starting to worry about this assignment.

They head toward the door. 'Nice jacket,' Rocca says. 'Quality leather. You like my suit?'

Doyle gives him the once-over. 'Sharp.'

Pleased with the compliment, Rocca puffs out his chest. 'It's Italian.'

'I might have guessed,' Doyle says.

NINETEEN

The car is a fully specced Lexus. Rocca drives, with Doyle slumped in the back, allowing himself the short-lived luxury of feeling like a VIP. Both men know that, at anytime, Doyle could make a play to retrieve his gun and take control of the situation, but what's the point? This isn't a kidnapping; it's a lift to a meeting. At the moment, Doyle feels no need to give Rocca any grief.

They drive over to the Meatpacking District – a small patch of west Manhattan into which once were crammed a couple of hundred slaughterhouses and packing plants, and where the air hummed with the odor of dead flesh. Now most of the meat-processing companies have gone, to be replaced by clubs and bars and restaurants, and the smell on the night-time breeze is mostly that of money.

Rocca maneuvers the Lexus into a small space in an alley alongside a converted warehouse. He parks tight against the wall, leaving no room to climb out on the passenger side. Rocca gets out and opens the rear door for Doyle. At once, Doyle hears the rhythmic booming from within the building, and realizes that the place is now a nightclub.

'The Bartoks like to strut their stuff on a Saturday night?' he asks.

'Something like that,' Rocca answers.

'Yeah, I bet that old Lucas has got some really fancy moves.'

They walk around to the street. To the consternation of the line of people waiting to get into the club, they go straight up to the entrance. Rocca nods to the doormen, who part to allow them entry.

Inside, the noise is deafening. A steady bass pounds Doyle from all sides. The floor vibrates and he can literally feel the sonic waves rippling through his body. It's not the most invigorating of sensations to a man whose brain is crying out for sleep. Doyle's discomfort isn't alleviated by the colored spotlights playing over the crowds and occasionally dazzling him with an intensity that makes him feel like his retinas are being fried.

The dance floor, which seems to take up most of the cavernous area, is packed. Sweaty, half-dressed bodies gyrate and undulate in their alcohol- and drug-fueled private heavens. Doyle isn't sure where he's meant to go, until Rocca taps him on the shoulder and points the direction.

As they thread through the crowd, Doyle tries to make sense of the geography of the building. The ceiling seems to be as high as the floor is wide, and like the walls, its red bricks have been left unplastered. On one wall, iron staircases lead up to two metal walkways, one above the other. Doyle presumes that the doors he can see on each of the two levels lead to offices. Some of the lights that have been blinding him are fixed to the underside of the walkways. Guarding the entrance to the staircase nearest him is a burly looking security guard. On each of the stories above him, Doyle can make out similar-shaped figures watching the pulsing mass below for signs of trouble. Also dotted on the walkways are a number of dancers. Presumably employed by the club, they wear even less clothing than the customers, and their movements are just that little bit more synchronized and professional.

Doyle is ahead of Rocca, moving toward the staircase. He's finding it difficult to swim a straight path through the human tide.

Just as a space clears ahead of him, a girl blocks his route. She wears a white shirt tied high under her breasts and exposing a muscular, perspiration-beaded midriff. As Doyle's gaze drops to her tartan micro-skirt, he thinks to himself that he's worn wider ties than that. Her hair is tied into pigtails and she's licking a huge lollipop as she contorts her body before him with the agility of a belly dancer. The whole naughty schoolgirl effect is helped along by the fact that she looks barely sixteen to Doyle. She doesn't say anything, but her intentions are unmistakable as she looks Doyle in the eye, plays her tongue around the lollipop and beckons him toward her with her index finger.

Given his lack of human contact lately, and with his defenses lowered by the alcohol still in his system, Doyle finds the invitation difficult to refuse. Somehow he manages to override his baser instincts.

'Sorry,' he says, yelling to be heard. 'I have to go see the school principal. I think I may get detention. If not, I'll see you behind the bicycle sheds later.'

He's not sure if she's heard him, but she seems to get the message. Shrugging, she turns on her heel and skips away. Just before she melts back into the crowd, the hem of her skirt flicks up and Doyle gets a glimpse of black thong. He turns to Rocca behind him, sees that he's grinning again.

When Doyle finally breaks through to the stairs, it's the security guard's turn to step in front of him, only he's not as easy on the eye as the schoolgirl was. In fact, he has a face like a constipated pug.

'Hey, you wanna dance?' Doyle asks. 'I can do a pretty mean salsa if you're willing to take the woman's part.'

The behemoth shuffles closer to Doyle, the scowl on his face suggesting that tripping the light fantastic isn't the physical activity he has in mind right now.

Doyle feels a hand on his shoulder, and Rocca steps in front of him and issues the secret nod. With apparent reluctance, the guard moves to his left by a few inches. The man feels like an immovable monolith of lead as Doyle squeezes past him.

Clanging up the metal stairs and onto the first walkway, Doyle gets a closer look at the dancers shaking their booties there. The sight of all that jiggling firm young flesh starts to get his pulse moving to the beat of the music, until Rocca taps him on the shoulder and points the way up the next set of stairs.

The upper level is like the lower. More dancers, more heavies, more doors. Rocca indicates one of the doors halfway down, and as they head toward it, Doyle can't resist leaning over the railing for a top-level view of the crowd. He realizes how vast the interior of this place is, but also how difficult it could be to make a quick exit from up here if the need arose.

Rocca knocks and waits. The door opens a crack, and another muscleman peers out at them. If it's one thing the Bartoks aren't short of, Doyle thinks, it's somebody to take the lids off their peanut butter jars. Another Masonic exchange of nods, and they're in. As he passes the bodyguard, Doyle tips his own head to the man, who looks at him like he's just fallen off his shoe. Doyle figures that he hasn't quite got the hang of the gesture.

As Doyle walks across the polished wood floor, the bodyguard closes the door behind him, dampening almost all of the sound from the nightclub. Doyle takes a quick look around the plush office before his eyes settle on the man seated behind the huge oak desk in front of the window. Lucas Bartok.

Bartok the elder is not a pleasant man. Anyone who knows of his reputation for violence and sheer cruelty could tell you that. But with Bartok it goes further. It's somehow ingrained on his face. You only have to glance at that mug to see how deeply it's etched with his sourness and malevolence, like notches on the butt of a gun. And don't, whatever you do, look into those eyes. You will flinch at what you see. And if you can bear to maintain your gaze, those eyes will drive you insane, make you unable to stop yourself from trying to imagine the warped picture of the world that this man must have.

Lucas Bartok is cross-eyed.

So cross-eyed it makes you want to laugh. But if you do laugh, if you even give a hint of a smile, the merest quiver of your lip, then you'd better be prepared to meet your maker, because Lucas Bartok, sensitive soul that he is, will gut you like a fish.

Still, Doyle thinks, I'm here at his invitation. He's got to be a little welcoming, no?

No.

It's only when Bartok looks up from his paperwork (at least he *seems* to be looking up) that Doyle senses he's made a mistake coming here. Bartok's expression turns from quizzical to surprised; and then, when recognition sets in, he is clearly enraged. He alternates his gaze between Doyle and Rocca, sometimes appearing to look at both of them simultaneously.

'What the fuck?' he says. 'WHAT THE FUCK?'

He gets up from his chair, comes around the desk, walks right up to Doyle.

'I remember you. You fucking piece of shit. What the fuck do you think you're doing walking into my office like you own the fucking place?'

Doyle waits for the spittle to stop landing on his face, then looks over to Rocca.

'I think he's talking to you.'

Rocca bows his head to stifle a smile that's threatening to break out and call for his execution.

Bartok's eyes light up like two misaligned lasers. 'I never forget a face, especially a stupid fucking mick face like yours. I remember what you did to me, hauling me into jail like that. Like I'm some kind of street scum. You got real nerve coming here. I oughtta—'

'Boss,' Rocca says.

Bartok whirls on him. 'You shut the fuck up, you stupid fucking wop. Did I ask you to speak?' He walks over to Rocca, needing to vent his anger on somebody. 'You know, I don't even trust wops. I don't know why the fuck we let you stay. Your kind are worse than the fucking spics, what with your . . .'

As the tirade continues, Doyle decides he wants out. He feels as though his appearance here has tripped a wire that's sent a missile hurtling toward him. Waiting for it to land is not a good idea. At the same time, experience has taught him that, with men like Bartok, you don't ask, 'Please may I go now?' That would be weakness, and these men prey on weakness. The thing that Doyle has learned always to bear in mind in any confrontation is that he is the representative of right against wrong. He is the authority figure. No matter how scared he is or how chaotic the situation, he has at least to present the appearance of being the man at the wheel.

'Hey, Lucas,' he interrupts. 'When you've finished auditioning for a job as a race relations officer, I'd like to go back to my hotel. I've got some serious sleep to catch up on. So goodnight and thanks for the hospitality.' He turns to leave, but the bodyguard steps in front of the door. Doyle remembers that Rocca still has his gun.

'No, you don't,' Bartok says, wagging his finger from side to side. 'This is my territory now. We play by my rules. Try acting the big tough cop here, see how far it gets you. I only got to snap my fingers and you're dog food. You decide to waltz in here, you better have a reason. And you better hope it's good enough to convince me not to call in my Dobermann, 'cause he's pretty hungry right now.'

Doyle knows that the sensible thing to do would be to attempt to clear up this little misunderstanding. Somehow, wires have become as crossed as Bartok's pupils. They need to be untangled. Doyle needs to inject a little calm, a little reasoning into a situation that's on the edge of detonation.

But at the same time he's feeling really pissed. Pissed that he's been dragged out of his bed in the middle of the night. Pissed that he was led here on a false promise. Pissed that he's been subject to so much abuse and disrespect.

And so it's infuriation rather than diplomacy that drives out his words as he looks at Sonny Rocca again.

'Are you gonna explain things to this dimwit before his bulb blows?'

Rocca opens his mouth to speak, but thinks better of it. He's clearly afraid of saying the wrong thing, perhaps even of making his presence felt in the company of his lunatic employer. Bartok doesn't wait for an explanation, and comes storming toward Doyle.

Doyle thinks, This is it. I've gone too far. Bartok's lost it.

Bartok stops inches short of colliding with Doyle. 'You're lucky you can still walk, Doyle. Most men, they'd already be dead by now. Only reason I haven't skinned you alive yet is I'm curious. Curious as to how a piece of shit like you has the balls to come here, to my club. Now, you wanna say something to me, or do you wanna try throwing more insults at me? Go ahead, Doyle, make a joke. Say something about my . . . appearance. See what happens.'

In his head, Doyle is trying to come up with a plan. A plan that involves overcoming three experienced and violent opponents without the aid of his gun, and then fighting his way out of a packed nightclub containing a further assortment of armed and dangerous goons who are undoubtedly prepared to kill first and ask questions later.

On this occasion, Doyle's brain lets him down. He blames the alcohol still swirling around up there.

Behind him, Doyle hears the door open. His ears are assaulted by the music again.

'Good evening, gentlemen,' says a voice. 'Detective Doyle. Glad you could make it.'

The door closes, and the new arrival strolls across the room. As he walks over to the desk, he takes a comb from his inside pocket and slides it through his greased-back dark hair. He lowers himself with great precision onto the leather chair, then opens a drawer, pulls out a vanity mirror and checks the result of his combing. He's nattily dressed in a navy pinstripe suit, the arrowhead of a white handkerchief poking from the breast pocket. His facial features are aquiline, but set with tiny piss-hole eyes that would be of no use to any bird of prey.

Watching all this in silence, Lucas Bartok's jaw drops.

'You invited this pond-life into our club?'

Kurt Bartok takes his time replacing the mirror before looking up at his elder brother. 'Yes, I sent for him. Is there a problem?'

Lucas rounds on his sibling. 'Yes, there's a fucking problem. You know who this is, don't you? You do remember what he did to us?'

Kurt waves his hand dismissively. 'He's a cop. That's what cops do. Sometimes they make mistakes, like Doyle did in taking us on. We won, he lost. You should be proud of that.'

'What I will be proud of is when I take this asshole and force him down my garbage disposer.'

'Really, Lucas, you need to stop taking things so personally. No wonder your blood pressure's so high.'

'My blood pressure's fine. Leastways it will be when this Irish cocksucker is out of my sight. What's he doing here, anyhow?'

'Don't worry, I'm not inviting him to a surprise birthday party for you. It's business, that's all. Detective Doyle and I have a few things to discuss.'

'And you were planning on telling me this when?'

Kurt makes a foppish hand gesture toward Rocca. 'Didn't Sonny explain everything in my absence?'

'No, he fucking didn't. That stupid guinea doesn't know shit. You ask him the time, he tells you where the big hand is.'

A half-smile plays across Kurt's thin lips. 'Yes, I know what you mean. I'll speak to him about it.' He turns to Rocca. 'Sonny, see me afterwards.'

'Yes, Mr Bartok.'

Jesus, Doyle thinks. I wasn't so far off when I told that girl I was going to see the school principal.

He looks across at Rocca, standing there with his head lowered and his hands clasped, obviously seething with anger and embarrassment. Gee, it must be nice to feel such a part of the family.

Lucas Bartok starts to button up his jacket. 'You want to lower yourself to the level of dealing with *that*, then that's your fucking problem. Just don't expect me to hang around.'

'I wasn't, Lucas.'

'Good. 'Cause I'm gonna find me some cleaner air.'

He starts toward the door. As he draws level with Doyle, he pauses and jabs a finger at his face. 'You do anything to hurt my little brother, and I mean *anything*, then don't even bother to keep breathing, Doyle, because you're a dead man. Hell, you might be a dead man anyhow. I ain't decided yet.'

TWENTY

When Lucas has left the room, Kurt Bartok gestures toward a chair on the other side of his desk. As Doyle wanders over and takes a seat, Rocca and the other henchman take up positions behind and to either side of their boss. They stand quiet and still, like two stone lions.

'I hope my brother didn't upset you too much, Detective. He has very forthright opinions about some things.'

'Nah. He's just a big cuddly bear. He should do kids' parties; they'd love him to bits.'

Bartok's expression becomes dark. He leans forward slightly. 'Let's get one thing straight before we start. You never mock a member of my family. *Never*. Do you understand?'

Doyle remembers now why he always regarded Kurt as the more dangerous of the two brothers. With Lucas, what you see is what you get. There are no hidden depths, no subtleties. If he says he's coming at you, then start running or get ready to fight for your life. With Kurt it's a different story. He's his brother wrapped up in a false skin, able to shed it at anytime. He is not handsome by any means, but he can be a perfect gentleman, and that seems to attract people. He's the college graduate: the one who got his brother's share when brains were being handed out. He can be convincing too, able to bend wills with his logic and voice of reason. And that's where the danger lies. Because he puts you at your

175

ease, makes you believe he's your friend, your ally. If and when he strikes, you'll never see it coming.

Doyle recalls the time he arrested this crew. Rocca and the Bartoks, cooped up in the pen at the station house. Lucas throwing himself at the sides of the cage, cursing and raging about how he was going to tear the place apart and rip the limbs from every cop he found. But Kurt just stood there. Impassive. Watching. Studying every move that Doyle made. Seemingly making mental notes of everything that was said. Doyle remembers thinking to himself then that Kurt is the one to be wary of. He's the real threat in that cage.

'So, to business,' Bartok says, all sweetness and light again. He relaxes in his seat, then pats down his sculpted hair. 'I hear you've landed yourself in a little predicament.'

Doyle has already decided he's going to play a defensive game here. Let Bartok do all the talking.

'You heard that, huh?'

'I didn't have to listen very hard. You're the talk of the town. You're probably the only person that everybody wants to discuss, but nobody wants to be near. A unique position to be in, don't you think?'

'It's nice to have a specialty. I can also whistle through my nose.'

Bartok hums a note of amusement. 'It's good that you can make light of it. Although I don't really think you find it so humorous. I think that, deep down inside, it's killing you.'

Doyle mulls over his next words carefully. Bartok isn't buying his feigned lack of concern. He sees right through that, and he plans to keep scraping away at that raw nerve until Doyle is a gibbering neurotic mess, malleable in any way Bartok chooses.

'Look, I appreciate the interest in my psychological well-being and all, but I don't need to be talking to no Sigmund Freud right now. You got something for me, put it on the table.'

'You're an impatient man, Detective. I can see that you don't like to wait around. I think that's one of the reasons this is so difficult for you. You want to be out on the hunt, not left at home like some abandoned housewife.'

Doyle puts the tip of his index finger on Bartok's desk. 'On the table.'

Bartok tents his fingers in front of him. 'You've been asking a lot of questions lately.'

'I usually find it's the best way to get answers.'

'You're asking, "Why me? Who's got me in their sights?"'

'You been reading my diary? Try the pages on my bachelor party; they're a lot more fun.'

'I don't need to read your personal outpourings to know you're desperately in need of a friend right now, Detective. Perhaps I can be that friend.'

'No offense, Kurt old buddy old pal, but when I get that desperate I'll talk to the trees. Sometimes they make a lot of sense, did you know that?'

'Can they tell you who killed your two partners?'

Here we go again, Doyle thinks. 'Two partners plus a few other people.'

Bartok shrugs. 'A pimp, a couple of whores, a junkie fence. I don't think you're really interested in them.'

It's Doyle's turn to lean forward. 'Now you got *me* getting heated. I'll make you a deal. You don't tell me how to do my job, and I won't make jokes about the birds flying around in your brother's skull.'

Doyle can see Bartok's jaw clenching. There is visible annoyance there, but tempered by the acceptance of a fair point.

'All right,' says Bartok. 'Allow me to rephrase: Can your arboreal friends tell you who killed all those people?'

'No. Can you?'

'Not at the moment.'

'What I thought.'

'But I believe I could find out.'

'You do, huh? And what makes you think you can do that?'

Bartok pats at his hair again, preening himself. 'Detective Doyle, in case you don't already know it, my business is information. It's how I make my livelihood. I keep my ear to the ground, my nose to the air.'

'That's a neat trick. Can you put your thumb up your ass at the same time?'

Bartok ignores him. 'It's the information age, Detective. Data is the new commodity. Tapping into the right sources can be like drilling into an oil well or a gold mine. The talent lies in finding the right places to look.'

'Uh-huh. You wanna give me a clue as to what those sources might be?'

Bartok laughs. 'Don't give up your day job, Detective. If that's your best attempt at negotiation, you'd never make an entrepreneur. Now, are you interested?'

'Let me get this straight. The guy who's popping all these people connected to me, you're saying you know who that is?'

Bartok raises a corrective finger. 'Not quite. I'm saying I can find out who it is.'

Doyle pauses for a moment. There it is, the bait is being dangled in front of him. But Doyle knows it hides a nasty hook.

He says, 'For a price.' A statement rather than a question.

'Ah, now you're starting to get the hang of business practice. A little blunt, perhaps, but we can work on that. Yes, like everything in life, it has a price.'

'And that price is?'

'Don't worry. I don't want your money. I know you're running up large hotel and laundry bills at the moment. I'm more interested in a like-for-like deal. My information for your information.'

'Information on what?'

'Oh, I don't know. I'm sure there's a whole range of juicy nuggets you could toss my way.'

'Give me a for-instance.'

'A for-instance? Hm, let me see. Well, rumor has it that some of the men of your precinct are assisting in an undercover operation to catch one Ramon Vitez in the act of selling large quantities of heroin. I'd be very interested to learn a few more of the details of that operation.'

'Goodbye, Kurt. It's been fun.' Doyle stands abruptly, causing Rocca and the other heavy to flinch. He looks at Sonny. 'You mind if I have my piece back now?'

Rocca starts to walk toward Doyle, reaching into the back of his waistband.

'Did I say you could move?'

This from Bartok. A question dripping with threats. Rocca looks down at Bartok, who glares back at him with an intensity that could melt glaciers. Rocca slips back to his post like a scolded dog into its kennel.

Doyle says, 'It's over, Kurt. Give me my gun now, or I'm walking out of here anyway and coming back with an army.'

'Yes, because the NYPD is bending over backwards to help you right now, isn't it?'

'The gun, Bartok. Now.'

'You need help. I'm offering it to you. Take it.'

'I don't need your help. Not at that price.'

Doyle turns, and starts to walk away. He doesn't want to go without his gun, but what choice does he have?

'Then why did you come here tonight?'

The question stops him. Yes, why did I agree to come here? I know how Bartok works. If I'm honest with myself, I could have reasoned that the meeting would lead to this. So why didn't I just say thanks but no thanks?

'Twenty-four hours, Detective.'

Doyle faces Bartok again. 'What?'

'I can give you a name in twenty-four hours, max. Maybe even a lot sooner than that. You think the NYPD can match that?'

Doyle cannot help but stand there and listen. He knows he should follow his impulse to get the hell out of here, but he can't move. Bartok has hypnotized him.

Bartok continues: 'You think the NYPD is even *trying* to solve your case? While you're out of the way, nobody is getting killed. Maybe that's good enough for them. Maybe some of them *like* having you out of their hair. I mean, they're not exactly rallying around you at the moment, are they? Think about it. How often are they phoning you with updates? How often do they ask you to provide them with more leads? And even if there was a team of hotshot detectives on the case twenty-four-seven, how much hope do you have that they'll crack it? The killer's clever, from what I hear. How long do you think it'll be before they catch him? Days? Weeks? Months? Can you wait that long? Are you prepared to sit alone in your pit of a hotel, unable to see your family or anyone else for months on end? I know I couldn't do it. I don't think there are many human beings who could. We're sociable animals. The drive to interact is in our genes. Denial of such a basic need would cause many of us to self-destruct.'

Bartok pauses, allowing his message to sink in. 'I'm offering you your life back, Detective Doyle. By tomorrow night, you could be free from your personal hell, able to return to your home, your family. I think the price I'm asking is tiny in comparison to that freedom.'

'Don't dress it up in ribbons and bows, Kurt. You're trying to buy me. Another pocket cop to add to your collection. That's what it comes down to.'

'As I said, you have a tendency to be blunt about things. I prefer to think of it as the start of a long and mutually beneficial business arrangement.' He puts the tip of his finger on the desk, exactly as Doyle did earlier. 'So there you have it. It's on the table, just as you asked. What's your answer?'

Doyle stares into Bartok's questioning eyes and thinks, My answer should be go fuck yourself. Stick your offer up your ass and then wait here while I bring in a shit-load of cops to raid your club and haul your ass off to jail.

But he doesn't say any of this. For one thing, he knows he can't touch Bartok. Nobody else in this room is about to confirm that this little powwow ever took place. And for another thing, he's not sure yet that he wants to reject the offer.

Shit! Am I really thinking that? Am I really even considering the possibility of entering into a partnership with this crazy bastard? Fuck that! It's ridiculous. Absurd. I'd sell my own mother before cozying up with Bartok.

And yet . . .

'I'll think about it.'

Bartok blinks. 'You'll think about it?'

'I need time to weigh it up. You're asking a lot.'

'I'm offering a lot. It should be a no-brainer.' He sighs softly, then looks down at his finger still poised on the desk surface. 'The deal stays here until the end of the day. Midnight. After that . . .' He takes his finger away to show Doyle that, after midnight, all bets are off. 'In the meantime, I'll start to make some inquiries. By the time you call, I should have the information you need.'

'*If* I call.'

Bartok's smile is smug. He gestures to Rocca, who escorts

Doyle to the door. Doyle turns one final time to Bartok and says, 'By the way, you've got some hair out of place there.'

As he is engulfed by the throbbing music once more, Doyle smiles inwardly at the thought of Bartok scrabbling for the mirror in his desk drawer.

In the passenger seat of the Lexus, Doyle tries to get his fogged brain to think rationally about Bartok's offer. Behind the wheel, Rocca seems to read his thoughts.

'You gonna make the deal? You should. Mr Bartok's a fair man. He'll treat you square.'

Doyle looks at Rocca. 'Kurt Bartok is a conniving sack of shit. His brother should have been put down at birth. Tell me something, Sonny, why do you work for those savages? I saw the way they treated you back there.'

For a while, Rocca doesn't say anything. He keeps his eyes on the road ahead.

'Sometimes,' he says finally, 'you don't have a lot of choice, you know? When you're drowning, and there's only one guy putting his hand out to save you, you take it, right? You don't question his motives, you don't try to work out whether he's a good guy or a bad guy. You just take the hand. And from that moment on, he owns you. Even if he treats you bad sometimes, he still owns you. You get what I'm saying?'

Doyle doesn't answer. He understands exactly what his philosopher companion has just said.

Pretty much the same thought has already gone through his own head.

TWENTY-ONE

He wakes up with his clothes on. He thinks he can still hear the music from Bartok's club, but it's just his brain pounding against his skull.

He looks at the bedside clock, and is surprised to see that it's nearly ten o'clock in the morning. He remembers getting into his hotel room, lying on the bed, then trying to think through his options. At some point – he doesn't know what time – he must have dozed off.

He rolls off the bed, glances at himself in the mirror, sees that he looks like shit. He has that failed-businessman appearance – the guy who loses all his money and his job and his wife, then ends up drinking from a brown paper bag and sleeping on a park bench.

He strips off and tosses his clothes into a corner. Treats himself to a fifteen-minute shower. As he selects a permutation of the few clean clothes he brought with him, he tries to work out how long it'll be before he needs to start paying for laundry service.

Leaving the room, he drapes the 'Do not disturb' sign over the door handle. He takes the elevator down to the restaurant, has a bowl of Cheerios, some toast and coffee, then returns to his room and pulls a chair over to the window.

And then he thinks again.

He spends over two hours sitting, thinking, pacing, worrying.

And at the end of it all, he knows that there's really nothing to analyze. The choices are stark and simple. You sign your life over to the devil, with all that that entails, or you suffer in silence, waiting for the relief that may never come. You're damned if you do, and damned if you don't.

He stands up, opens the window and sticks his head out to get a look at the street below. He wants to be out there, feeling that he's doing something – anything – to accelerate this to a conclusion. But he knows how far the word has spread. Nobody will talk to him. Nobody will go near him. And even if they would, how could he bring himself to take the chance of endangering yet another life?

Shit!

He closes the window and picks up the phone receiver. He presses for an outside line and then dials a number at the Eighth Precinct.

'Lieutenant Franklin.'

'Mo, it's me. Cal.'

'Cal! How you doing?'

'So-so. Getting itchy feet – that's for sure. It's kinda hard being on the outside like this.'

'Yeah, I understand that. Bear with it, Cal. It won't be long now.'

'Yeah? You got some hot leads?'

Franklin hesitates, which says to Doyle, *No, we got nothing.*

'We're working all the angles, Cal. Don't worry, we haven't forgotten about you. The whole team is still on this.'

'Uh-huh. You track down Rodriguez?'

'Yeah. He's dead. Died of a drug overdose last month.'

'What about Lewis Stanton? He made a lot of noise about me when they carted him off to Rikers.'

'He was out, now he's back in again. Has been for a while now.'

'Maybe he reached out from his cell.'

'Nah, we don't think so. Apparently he's found God this time. He's looking to wash away all his sins.'

'Okay. So then there's Wilson Jones. He's definitely on the outside.'

'Yes, he is. But all his alibis check out, including a meeting with his parole officer at the time your CI was being butchered. When we spoke to him, he couldn't even remember your name.'

'Fuck, Mo!'

'I know, Cal, I know. When you start to go through names like that, it sounds as if—'

'So who's left, Mo? You got any suspects at all? Anyone who had the slightest motive? I mean, Jesus, even the neighbor whose window I broke when I was eleven will do. How big is the fucking list, Mo?'

Again, seconds pass. Translation: It's a list that's shorter than Lucas Bartok's temper.

'We're doing all we can, Cal. Talking to everyone even mentioned in your fives. We're even looking at relatives of those people. The perp could be someone you never met – maybe you collared his son or his father or his second cousin's girlfriend. People snap for the weirdest reasons, Cal. Maybe this is one of those, in which case it makes it all the harder to pin him down.'

'I don't think so, Mo. You read the notes he sent. He's not talking about me like I'm someone who accidentally brushed against him on the sidewalk. This guy is painting me like someone who wiped out his whole family. He hates my guts. Something major must have gone down for him to be talking that way.'

'In which case it must be something you know about. And every possibility you put our way, we're chasing up as hard as we can. You know that, don't you?'

'Yeah, sure. I know it.'

'Look, there isn't . . . ? I mean, you don't . . . ?'

'What, Mo? Spit it out.'

'There isn't something you don't want to talk about? Something that happened, maybe a long time ago, and you don't want the job to know about it?'

Doyle gets a sick feeling in his stomach. He gets the impression this isn't something that Franklin has just invented. He can imagine some of the talk at the station house. About him and Laura Marino. About him possibly keeping the truth hidden. About the odds that there may be other skeletons hidden in his closet. Without Doyle being there to deny those rumors, maybe Franklin's mind has become as poisoned as the rest of them.

'Like what?' he asks.

'I don't know. Anything. I'm clutching at straws here. But if there is anything . . .'

'There's nothing, Mo. Nothing. I told you before, I got nothing to hide.'

'Then . . . it's all good. The perp's name must be in our files somewhere. We'll get him. It's just a matter of time.'

Doyle sighs. Just a matter of time. Like the duration is of no consequence as long as the outcome is good. Never mind there's an innocent cop who's in solitary confinement all the while this remains unsolved.

'Okay, Mo. Do me a favor, will you? Keep me posted.'

'Of course, Cal.'

'I mean, you have my number at the hotel, don't you? And my cellphone?'

'Yeah, we got them.'

'So call me.'

'No problem. Speak to you soon.'

'Yeah.'

The line goes dead. Doyle looks at the receiver in his hand. You're not gonna call, he thinks. Either you've given up, or else you're too embarrassed by the fact that you're not getting any-where. You're not gonna call. I'll have to call you, and my bet is you'll still have nothing.

Bartok was right. The NYPD isn't going to solve this case. Leastways, not anytime soon.

Slowly, Doyle lowers the telephone handset onto its cradle.

He's on a stool in the hotel bar, nursing a Bushmills and wonder-ing whether the meaning of Christmas can be expressed any more profoundly than in the string of paper Santas hanging above his head. As it's only late afternoon the place is deserted, and George the Greek is his usual uncommunicative self. But then Doyle isn't here for the atmosphere.

He hears footsteps behind him. The tapping of high heels. A woman, his honed sleuthing powers tell him.

He glances across as she slides onto the stool next to his. He catches a glimpse of toned calf muscles, a plunging neckline and a smile that could make any man forget his woes.

'Mind if I join you?' she asks.

Doyle shrugs. 'If you mean do I mind if you sit there, go ahead, it's a free country.'

Yeah, look how free I am. The way I can go anywhere, talk to anyone.

All of a sudden, George is the most animated that Doyle has ever seen him. He bustles over, all smiles and arched eyebrows and hot-blooded charm. He looks ready to start serenading.

Go ahead, Doyle thinks, whip out your bouzouki and impress the girl.

She orders a Bacardi and Coke, and while George demon-strates his lemon-chopping skills, she tries once again with Doyle.

'Nothing sadder than the sight of someone drinking alone, don't you think?'

Doyle picks up his glass, gets down from his stool.

'Something I said?' the girl asks.

'Let's just say you're too young to die,' he answers. He catches the incomprehension and then the unease on her face before he walks away.

He weaves his way over to a table in an alcove at the far wall. Settles down and makes himself comfortable again.

Well, that was some line, he thinks. Bet she's never heard that one before.

He looks over at the girl. She has her back to him, sucking on a straw as she listens to George trying to work his magic.

Good luck to 'em, he thinks. She doesn't seem like a hooker. Just a lonely young woman looking for a good time. Since when did that become a crime?

He regrets the way he spoke to her. And then he's angry at the fact that he felt the need to react so strongly – that he couldn't even be civil to the girl. He has a wife, yes, and so he'd never have let things go too far, but that's not the point. There are ways of saying no that don't require a slap in the face. Is this the way it's going to be from now on? Acting like a rabid dog, snapping at people as soon as they come near?

Jesus, what a mess.

He thinks about what got him into this situation, about what caused things to get so bad. What hurts the most is that if it were anyone else on the squad in a jam like this – Schneider, even – the nature of the investigation would be wholly different. The guys would all be pulling together, all trying to steer the boat in the same direction. There wouldn't be this nagging feeling that nobody really cares if the whole thing capsizes.

But then Doyle has always been the outsider.

Ever since the events of the previous year.

TWENTY-TWO

He was driving. Heading uptown on Madison Avenue. She was riding shotgun. Hanging between them was an atmosphere you could almost bang your head against.

Doyle gripped the steering wheel so hard he felt it was about to disintegrate in his fingers. His teeth ached from all the jaw-clenching he'd been doing.

This is not good, he thought. This is precisely why the NYPD has rules about working with spouses, partners and anyone else with whom you're having any kind of intimate personal relationship. Takes your mind off the job. You lose your edge, the ability to think objectively. And ultimately, that can mean losing your life.

Not that Laura Marino was his wife or his girlfriend or even the object of his affections. Sure, she was good-looking. A real beauty, some would say. Certainly a few steps up from most of the female cops he'd ever met, despite what the TV cop shows would have people believe. But the point was he was married, she was married, and they were working partners – and she was acting like none of that was true.

'You're quiet,' she said. 'Everything okay, Callie?'

He hated the way she called him Callie. Nobody had ever called him that before. It was her own invention – something she seemed to find cute.

He should have just said, Yes, everything's fine, and got on with the job at hand, but this time he couldn't keep it in. This time she'd gone too far.

'You want the truth? No, everything is not okay. Everything is fucked up.'

'Oh,' she said. 'You wanna talk about it?'

'Yeah, I could do that. Lemme see, where do I start? How about with all the looks and the winks I got from everyone in the squad this morning? Or the way Kaplinsky kept calling me "Stud"? Or how about the way people kept asking me why I only like eating Italian now?'

Marino did the wrong thing then. She laughed. Put a hand to her mouth and made a farting noise with her mouth like this was some big joke. If she had been mortified instead – if she had exhibited the merest hint of shame – he might have been able to prevent what was coming next.

'You think this is funny? This is funny to you?'

She tried to put on a straight face, but to Doyle she wasn't trying hard enough.

'Well, the Italian thing, that *is* kinda—'

'What have you been saying?' Doyle demanded. 'What the fuck have you been saying?'

'Nothing. Take it easy, Callie. I just had a little girlie chat with Kaplinsky. Locker-room talk. You know how it is.'

'No. Tell me. Tell me how it is.'

'She's been asking for a long time now. About you and me. About how we are together. About whether we've, like, done the dirty yet.'

'Uh-huh. And of course you put her straight, right? Told her how we're just partners, like any two cops on the job. All strictly professional and platonic, right?'

'Come on, Callie. If I said that, Kaplinsky really would start wondering. Anybody can see there's a thing between us. A what-you-call-it – a chemistry.'

'No, Laura. No chemistry. Not unless it's like you're sulfuric acid and I'm getting burned real bad. Because that's how I'm feeling right now. Real burned. So what else did you say to Kaplinsky?'

'Nothing. She asked whether me and you had got it on yet, and I just smiled and walked away.'

'You smiled and walked away? That's it?' As if that wasn't bad enough.

'Yeah, that's it. Except, well, I might have made a little gesture.'

'A gesture? What kind of gesture?'

Laura hesitated for a second. When Doyle looked in her direction, she raised an eyebrow mischievously, then put her hands out in front of her, palms facing each other, about a foot apart.

'Oh, fuck,' Doyle said. 'Please tell me you didn't actually do that.'

Laura was laughing again. Doyle wasn't.

'I was paying you a compliment,' she said. 'Most guys, I'd just wave my pinky in the air. You should be grateful for me telling it like it is.'

'Like it is? What the fuck are you talking about? You've never even seen . . .' He let his words trail off.

'You oughtta try taking a walk through my head sometime,' she said. And then she was laughing again. Huskily, but to Doyle not at all seductively. In fact, this was starting to feel dark and disturbing. Inside Laura Marino's head did not seem the most inviting of places right now.

Doyle pulled a sudden left turn across honking traffic and into the only free space he could see. Which happened to be the entrance to the parking garage of the swish hotel next door.

'Hey,' Laura said. 'What are you doing?'

Doyle put the brakes on, left the engine idling. 'We need to talk, Laura.'

'And you can't talk while you drive?'

'No. Not when every brick wall I see makes me want to head straight for it.'

She pulled her neck in and squinted at him like she thought he was loopy. Like she just didn't get what all the fuss was. How could she not get that?

'So, like, okay. What do you want to talk about?'

He turned toward her on the seat, took a deep breath.

'This me-and-you thing. Don't get me wrong, Laura. I like working with you. I think we make a good team. But that's as far as it goes. The things you've been saying about me, the way you've been acting, you're going to land me in a whole heap-load of shit.'

She pulled the me-no-understand face again, and then there was another laugh. Doyle felt his fists bunching. He'd never hit a woman in his life, and now he was thinking of taking it up as a career.

'Callie! Lighten up, will ya? It's just a joke. Cops talk about other cops like that all the time – you know that. Give it a few days, it'll blow over. Anyhow, it's such a bad thing, people thinking you managed to talk me into the sack? I thought you guys liked stuff like that. Another notch on your bedpost, and all that.'

'Maybe in Neanderthal World, Laura. Maybe when we were both teenagers with more hormones than sense. But aren't you forgetting a fact or two? Like Danny and Rachel? You think they'll laugh their socks off at this big joke of yours?'

Laura rolled her eyes. 'Well, not Rachel – that's for sure.'

'Oh . . .' Doyle bit his lip, trying to hold in his fury. 'Fuck you, Laura.'

And then he was out of the car, slamming the door so hard the window almost shattered. He forced air through his nostrils and paced the ground like a mad bull on the lookout for something to charge.

A uniformed valet emerged from the dark mouth of the hotel garage.

'Excuse me, sir. Are you a resident of the hotel?'

'No. Just give me two minutes.'

Not sensing the danger he was in, the valet continued: 'I'm sorry, sir, but you can't park here. You're blocking the—'

'I said go back into your hole. Now!'

As the man skedaddled to the hotel entrance, muttering to himself, Laura got out of the car.

'Come on, Cal. We got places to be.'

She said this so matter-of-factly, as though their disagreement was over something as trivial as whose turn it was to drive. For a moment, Doyle couldn't help wondering why he was the only one feeling there was a problem here. He stepped around the car.

'Listen to me, Laura. This is serious, okay?'

'Callie, you're making this out —'

'No! Listen. To me, it's serious, even if you don't give a shit. And quit calling me Callie. The name's Cal, okay?'

She rolled her eyes again, like she was a teenager being chastised by her father for staying out late, and who has no intention of sticking to the rules he's laying down.

'Fine,' she said. 'Cal. Whatever.'

He started ticking items off with his fingers. 'First of all, it's bad enough a story like this is going around the job. I'm not talking about the grunts: they'll have their laughs and be done with it. But something like this gets back to the brass, then we got some explaining to do.'

'Cal—'

He cut her off by jabbing another finger in front of her face. 'Second of all, and more importantly, I have a family to consider. And before you start mouthing off about Rachel again, you should know that I love her and I have no intention of doing anything that would hurt her. Ever. Whatever you and Danny have between you, that's your business. You want to hurt him, go ahead. Just leave me out of it. The heat you caused between me and Rachel last time was bad enough. I don't want to go through that again. Point three—'

'Last time? What last time?'

'Last Christmas. You do remember that, don't you?'

A dreamy smile appeared on Laura's face. 'Oh, yeah. Christmas.'

They had been at a party at a fellow cop's house in Queens. Danny and Rachel were there too. Laura got drunk within the first half-hour. Kept making suggestive remarks to Doyle, pinching his ass – that type of thing. Rachel witnessed much of it in stony-faced silence. Danny seemed never to be in the same room. The last straw was the kiss: Laura with a sprig of mistletoe in one hand, the other clasped behind Doyle's neck in an embrace that lasted far too long. By the time Doyle had recovered enough from the shock to push Laura away, Rachel had disappeared and gone home. The nights that followed had been pretty lonely ones for Doyle.

'Point three,' Doyle repeated, and then got cut off again when he heard voices at his side and saw that the valet had returned with a balding man in a pinstripe suit who was making threats to call the police if the car wasn't moved.

Doyle dug into his pocket, pulled out his wallet and flashed his shield. 'Fine,' he said. 'Call the cops. And then we'll come by here and arrest you for possession of an illegal comb-over.'

As the pair retreated to consider their next move, Doyle tried again with Laura. 'Point three is maybe we should think about calling it a day.'

It took a moment for this to penetrate. 'What are you talking about?'

'I think tomorrow morning I'm going to speak to the boss about working with another partner.'

'Are you serious? Why would you want to do that?'

'Have you been listening to a word I've just said? You've gone too far, Laura. You're getting too . . . intense.'

'Intense? Really? Because this is all on me, right? I mean, you would never throw me any signals of a less-than-professional nature, would you? You would never make any comments about my figure or my hair. Nobody would ever catch you asking what color panties I'm wearing today, would they?'

There was a silence while Doyle chewed on his answer. He *had* flirted with her, that was true; but then he'd flirted with every woman he'd ever met, even the ones who looked like Shrek. He couldn't help it: it was in his blood.

'Maybe I said some things I shouldn't have. But you've taken it to another level, Laura. You've endangered my job and my marriage.'

'You go to the boss for another partner, and you endanger *my* job.'

Doyle started moving back around to the driver's side. 'Get in the car, Laura. Let's do some work.'

'Fuck you, Doyle.'

This stopped him in his tracks. It wasn't the words: she was a cop, and cops use expletives all the time. It was Laura's tone: it had a disturbing, menacing quality to it that he'd never heard from her before.

He looked across the roof of the Crown Vic at her; she glared back at him.

'You take this to the lieutenant,' she said, 'make me look bad like that, and I'll really start to let everyone know what's been going on between us. See what your precious Rachel thinks about them apples.'

'What?' Doyle said. 'Is that a threat, Laura? Are you threatening me?'

She remained silent, and Doyle started to retrace his steps back to her side of the car.

'Is that what I'm hearing, Laura? Are you trying to blackmail me?'

He kept walking until he was inches away from her, astonished that he'd never seen this side of her before. In a heartbeat she had switched from partner to perp. He could quite easily have spun her around, slapped on some cuffs, and dragged her ass to jail. A quick tune-up in some quiet alley was not out of the question either, the way he felt.

And then, in another beat, it was as if a second button was pressed in her head. She suddenly softened, and the burning died in her pupils.

'What are we doing?' she said. 'Look at us! How crazy is this? Jesus Christ, Cal, I'm sorry. I didn't mean any of that shit. Really. You just got me so . . . worked up, you know? Forget what I just said. Please. I was just lashing out. Come on, let's get out of here.'

She slid onto the passenger seat, flashing him a smile that seemed to carry no warmth. Doyle watched her every move, feeling that he no longer knew this woman, no longer understood her, that he was no longer capable of anticipating her next move. It was one of the most uncomfortable sensations he'd ever had.

'It'll be okay,' she said. 'Come on, Cal. Relax. Everything's just fine. Get back in the car. You want me to drive?'

Doyle was frozen to the spot. He had been ready for a fight, and now it had been taken away from him. He didn't know how to react to an enemy who worked like that, who was that unpredictable.

For a few seconds, Laura had let her dark side out, and now she was trying to cover up, to pretend that it was uncharacteristic. But it had been there, unmistakably so. And it had been scary in its concentrated spitefulness.

Wondering whether he needed to call in an exorcist, Doyle

returned once more to the driver's side and got behind the wheel. He looked at her long and hard, searched her face for answers. But all he got was a goofy smile.

'Chill out, Callie,' she said. 'It's hormones or something. No big thing. Let's roll.' She opened the glove compartment, pulled out a small bag. 'Here, have some M&Ms.'

Feeling like he'd just teleported to a parallel world, Doyle put the car into gear and drove off. For now, he had nothing to say, nothing that would help to make any sense of this situation. But he guessed it wasn't over.

'We'll talk about it later,' he said. 'Okay?'

She tossed candy into her mouth, nodded her head playfully. 'Sure, Callie.'

As he drove, he tried to turn his mind to the job, to give it something rooted in the real world to work on. But his subconscious had other ideas. It kept showing him reminders of Laura's face, her words, of a few minutes ago, and of how unbelievably vindictive she'd been. It kept tossing out imagined images of Rachel, crying and screaming at him, asking him why he would do such things. And it kept interrupting with questions like, So now that you know she's a crazy-ass bunny-boiler, what are you going to do about it?

Later, he would wish he'd called the whole thing off. Just aborted the mission and headed straight back to the precinct station house. Set off again when his head was straight, and preferably with a different, more stable, partner.

But hindsight can be a merciless instrument of torture sometimes.

The reason they had originally hit the streets – before all this personal shit became an unwanted diversion – was to look for a lowlife named Anton Lomax. Lomax was a junkie who'd had a relationship with a girl named Bernice Thompson. What made Lomax worth seeking was that Bernice had been found in a Harlem flophouse naked from the waist down and with a bread knife sticking out of her chest. Word was that Lomax had recently been spotted scoring dope on 125th Street, which made it a sensible place to start.

As they headed uptown, Doyle told himself he needed to focus and to stay calm. He still had a mass of pent-up anger that Laura had somehow managed to prevent him from releasing. It nestled inside and gnawed at him like a stomach ulcer. He felt as though he had not really cleared the air with Laura; if anything, their discussion had served only to bring down an impenetrable fog.

He worried that the latest rumors started by Laura were going to get back to Rachel or Danny, or both. He worried more that Laura had every intention of making the situation worse. He didn't know why she would do such a thing – he didn't understand how her mind worked – but the way she had acted earlier told him that she was capable of making his life hell if she felt so inclined.

Distracted as he was, it was Laura who was the first to spot the four young black men huddled under a streetlamp.

'It's Lomax,' she said. 'Stop the car!'

Doyle took the car across onto the next block and pulled it into the first space he found. All of his personal concerns had suddenly run for cover. He and Laura got out of their car, both pairs of eyes fixed on the knot of men, both detectives automatically checking ease of access to their handguns. With practiced, wordless efficiency, they split up and attempted to approach the gang from opposite directions.

Lomax spied them as soon as they began to cross the street, and in a flash he cut away from the group and took off.

Shit! thought Doyle, and started his own sprint. He saw that

Laura was also running, and that her trajectory was going to get her to Lomax first.

Lomax saw this too, and in the last moment before a confrontation became inevitable he cut to his left and raced up the steps of a graffiti-adorned apartment building. He disappeared inside, swallowed up by the gloom.

Seconds behind her quarry, Laura drew her gun as she too entered the building. Anxious not to get left behind and leave Laura without backup, Doyle picked up the pace and took the steps two at a time. He pulled his gun and dived into the lobby. He heard footsteps pounding up the stairs.

'Laura!' he shouted.

'Up here!' she called back. 'He's heading up.'

Panting, Doyle followed her, still jumping onto alternate steps. He listened to the heavy footfalls above him, growing louder as he closed the distance between them. Just as he thought one final push would bring him into sight of Laura, he heard the creak and slam of a door. There were more footsteps, then another creak and slam. And then silence.

'Laura! Laura! Wait!'

He practically soared over the next flight of stairs, his strides covering whole sets of steps at a time. In front of him was a brown wooden fire door containing a small reinforced window. He crashed through the door, heard its hinges squeal in complaint. From the far end of the dimly lit corridor came the sound of yet another door being slammed shut.

Ahead of him, Laura was moving swiftly toward the apartment at the end of the hallway. Above its entrance, a light flickered on and off, over and over. Each time it came on, it illuminated a faded brass plate indicating that this was apartment 4D.

'That it?' Doyle asked, finding his words difficult to force out as he simultaneously tried to suck in much-needed air.

Laura, in similar discomfort, just nodded.

'Sure?'

'Yes!'

'Okay, go!'

They would worry about the legal niceties later. About how the suspect's flight gave them probable cause to enter the apartment. About how they both remembered announcing clearly and unequivocally that they were police officers, despite what anyone else heard or didn't hear. For now, the main thing that concerned them was time. Every second they wasted now gave Lomax and whoever else was in that apartment time to arm themselves and prepare for an onslaught. Every second lost in hesitation magnified the danger several-fold.

And so Doyle hurtled himself at the door, raising his foot. He knew that Lomax had not had time to put an array of bolts and chains in place. When Doyle's foot connected, there was a loud smash and a splintering of wood, and the door almost came off its hinges as it flew open.

Sailing into the room under his own momentum, Doyle had no time to register the finer details of his surroundings. He didn't see the living room in terms of its faded and ripped green sofa or its flat-screen TV or its coffee-table collection of porn magazines. His radar was alert only to people and signs of danger. What that told him was that this room was clear. But what it also drew to his attention, as if it were lit up in neon, was the door to the bedroom.

The door was painted in cream, and a crack ran the length of one of its panels.

And Doyle could see that it was moving. It was slowly swinging shut, as though someone had just entered that room.

He was convinced of this. In that instant of time, he was surer than anything that the door was moving.

And so he called out to Laura, 'Bedroom!' and he raised his

gun in cover and watched as, in complete faith, she headed toward the room he had just indicated. She had heard the unwavering conviction in his voice, was absolutely certain now that this was where their quarry lurked, and so that's where she went, trusting to the experience and judgment and sincerity of her partner.

When Laura's back exploded, the universe disappeared for Doyle.

If he was unaware of his surroundings before, they had now winked out of existence.

What remained was . . .

. . .Laura, a huge hole punched into her back, falling and twisting, her face contorting in pain . . .

. . .the sound. A blast that filled the room, its shockwaves bouncing and rebounding off the walls . . .

. . .and Lomax. Standing in the doorway of the room to Doyle's left.

That room being the bathroom.

Not the bedroom. Not the room into which Doyle had just sent Laura. Not the room with the cream door and its cracked panel. The door that was moving. Because, so help me God, it was most definitely moving.

Lomax was not alone. He had a gun for company. A sawed-off double-barrel shotgun, one of its dark deadly eyes still smoking after its look at Laura.

And now the other eye, the one still capable of seeing, was turning in search of another victim. The gun was swinging in an arc that, in the next fraction of a second, would bestow upon that eye full sight of Doyle.

In the moments which followed, Doyle discovered something profound. He found an understanding that had eluded him before – something that is likely to elude anyone who has never looked death in the eye before.

What was revealed to him was that, in a situation like this, you lose control of your body. You lose the ability to think, to rationalize, to make conscious decisions. You become an entity that functions solely by reflex, a biological unit within which every muscle, every sinew, every neuron is acting in unison to the tune of one overriding message. And that message is to survive. At any cost.

And if that objective entails the complete obliteration of another human being, then so be it. There is no morality here. No appeals to God or to humanity. There is only the law as laid down in our veins through millions of years of evolution.

What Doyle found himself doing was pulling the trigger of his Glock not just once, or twice, or any accountable number of times. He found himself pulling that trigger again and again and again, absorbing the kick of the Glock as it spat its fire and took chunks out of the man in front of him. He found himself moving toward Lomax, every fiber of his being saturated with the necessity of wiping that motherfucker from the face of the planet. To Doyle, Lomax was not a man with thoughts and feelings; he was just a threat to his own existence.

Even when Lomax was on the floor, blood pumping from the holes already in his body, Doyle kept on firing, his eyes observing dispassionately as Lomax's dying form jumped with each bullet. He tried to shoot long after the gun was empty, long after the sounds of its explosions had faded. His trigger finger just kept on twitching. And even when his subverted consciousness began to exert some kind of control, he still experienced an almost irresistible impulse to continue the devastation.

He understood then. He had never killed before, never come so near to being killed. And now he understood.

There have been numerous times that cops have been vilified by the media for being apparently trigger-happy. Even Doyle himself, despite being a police officer, had occasionally wondered whether such extensive lethal force had been necessary.

But here he was, holding his Glock 19, now empty of the fifteen rounds it held in the magazine and the additional one in the chamber, and still he felt the urge to ram its butt into the skull of the corpse beneath him.

Shoot the gun out of the man's hands? In your dreams. A clinical and effective double-tap? Yeah, right. Fire three times and assess? Sure. Try standing here in my shoes and saying that afterwards.

Yes, he understood completely. And he would never be the same again.

It took some time before the world materialized around him once more, before he could tear his eyes away from the lifeless form of Lomax. He was that wired, it came almost as a surprise to him to see the second body in the room. He found it difficult to work out what he should do next. All of his police training seemed to have deserted him.

When he finally fished out his cellphone, he issued a garbled call for an ambulance, and then he went to his partner. She was showing faint signs of life, but she was a mess. The whole of her back was stained with her dark wet blood, and a puddle of it was growing next to her.

He didn't know why, but he felt a need to gather her up in his arms. He sat in the warm wetness of her blood and held her close, rocking her gently.

And when the time finally came for her to leave, he told her how sorry he was.

It was only the beginning.

In the days, the interminable weeks that followed, truth became lies and lies became truth. Without Laura to retract them, her rumors became fact. To Doyle's colleagues, to Internal Affairs, and even to Rachel.

He'd been having an affair, they concluded. It was becoming public knowledge and he wanted a way out, they surmised. He was responsible for Laura Marino's death, they decided.

He knew they were all wrong. But when you believe one thing and everybody else believes another, you start to lose confidence. You start to have doubts. You start to wonder whether your own mind is deluding you.

And when that happens, you start to ask yourself whether, in fact, a tiny hidden part of you really did seize upon an opportunity to rid yourself of what was becoming a major problem.

And occasionally – in the dead of night when nobody else is listening – you ask yourself whether, in fact, that cream door with the cracked panel really was moving.

TWENTY-THREE

Doyle throws down the dregs of his drink and leaves the table. On the way past the bar, he feels he should say something apologetic to the girl with the legs-cleavage-smile combo, but she has already moved on from George and engaged another guy in conversation. The whiskey-drinking loser with the socialization problems is probably already a distant memory.

He goes back upstairs to a room that's starting to feel the equivalent of a prison cell, except without even the company of a psychotic, tattoo-adorned Nazi to break the monotony. He picks up the phone again and makes another call.

'Cal!' Rachel says. 'Just a minute. Amy wants to talk to you.'

There is a moment of confused fumblings and whispers of 'Talk to Daddy,' before Amy's breathy voice comes on the line.

'Daddy!' she squeals. Her tone sounds several octaves higher than normal, its intense childish innocence punishing him more than he would like.

'Hi, sweetie,' he says. 'How you doing? Are you being good for Mommy, like I asked you?'

'Yes, Daddy, but, but, but . . . I am a *little* bit sad.'

'Sad? Why's that, honey?'

'Because, because I have to go to bed soon, and I asked

Mommy if you were coming home tonight, and she said she didn't think so, and I said I wanted you to be here because of the burglars. And then Mommy said—'

'Hold on, hon. What burglars?'

'The burglars who come into people's houses and take all your toys and stuff. My friend Ellie, who isn't my friend anymore because she's always nasty to me, she said that burglars break your windows and come into your house at night when everybody's asleep, and they take all your things, even your best toys and Christmas presents, and I said they won't come in our apartment because my Daddy's a policeman and he'll put them in jail, and she said yes they will because your Daddy's not there anymore, and I said—'

'Amy, listen to me. The burglars won't come. You know why?'

'Why?'

'Because I've told all the other policemen to watch our apartment from outside. At night, when you're asleep, they sit outside and watch, and they make sure no burglars will come. And they'll be there every night until I come home.'

'Well, I want *you* here. You're the best policeman and the best Daddy, and that's why I couldn't sleep last night and I had to get into bed with Mommy.'

'You couldn't sleep?'

'No. I got scared, and I . . . I . . . I . . . wet the bed a bit.'

There is a silence between them then. A few seconds that are devoid of sound but which, for Doyle, are bursting with barely contained anguish. As his vision blurs, he thinks about what he is doing to his family.

'It was only a little bit,' Amy adds hastily. 'That's okay, isn't it?'

'Yes, sweetie, that's okay. But there's nothing to worry about. I'm coming home real soon. I promise.'

'When?'

'Soon. Maybe even tomorrow.'

Amy's voice drops in volume then, but only because she has turned away from the receiver and is talking to her mother. 'Yay!' Doyle can hear her saying. 'Daddy's coming home! Daddy's coming home!'

And then there is more fumbling with the phone, and when Rachel's voice comes on the line there is an unexpected sternness to it.

'Is that true, Cal? That you're coming home? Because if it's not, then you're being so unfair to Amy.'

'Rach. It's true. There's been a break in the case. All goes well, it'll be over by the morning.'

There is another period of silence, and then comes an audible sigh of relief from Rachel.

'Thank God!' she says.

Well, thanks to someone, Doyle thinks. But God is probably the last one on the list on this occasion.

For the next few hours, he resumes his pastime of sitting and waiting and thinking. His mind hunts in desperation for alternatives to the decision he has made, but the only one it can find involves waiting some more, and he doesn't think he can do that any longer. Not with the lack of progress the NYPD is making. Not with the pleading voice of Amy still ringing in his ears.

At two minutes before midnight, he picks up the phone and dials the number on the card that Sonny Rocca gave him.

'You're cutting it fine, Mr Doyle,' Rocca says.

'I'm a last-minute kinda guy. I like to keep people guessing. It adds to my mystique.'

'You sure you want to do this?'

'What, you trying to talk me out of it now?'

Rocca chuckles. 'I'll be right over.'

'Some days are special,' Rocca says as he drives. 'Red-letter days. Days that change your life forever. You know what I mean, Mr Doyle?'

In the rear of the Lexus, Doyle stares at the back of Rocca's head.

'You think this is one of those days?'

'I *know* it is. Soon as I heard your voice on the phone, I thought, this is it. This is where it all starts to change.'

'Remind me to make a note in my diary,' Doyle says. 'I'll send a thank-you card to the Bartoks every year.'

Rocca laughs. 'You're a funny guy, Mr Doyle. A real comedian.'

Doyle wonders, What's Rocca got to be so happy about? He hoping we'll be some kind of blood brothers now? Another addition to the family of oddballs?

And I could do without all the fuss he's making. Like it's some kind of historic victory or major coup for the Bartok clan.

But then who am I kidding thinking this is just a five-minute pact? What am I expecting – that I'll just pass some info to Bartok and he'll give me a name, and then I'll never see him again? Do I really believe that it'll stop there?

Doyle knows it won't. He knows that once he's in Bartok's pocket he's there to stay, like a handkerchief, waiting for Bartok to pull him out and blow his nose on him whenever he feels like it.

Rocca pulls the Lexus into the narrow alley next to Bartok's club, parks it tight against the wall like he did the previous night. He gets out first, and like a chauffeur, opens the rear door to let

Doyle out. Doyle steps out onto the cobblestones, already feeling slippery beneath his feet. He guesses that, by the morning, the city will be covered in a film of frost.

He waits for Rocca to lead the way toward the club, but Rocca just stands there, a dumb smile on his face as he stares at Doyle.

'What? Having second thoughts? And after all the drinks I bought you? You men are all the same.'

Rocca's laugh forms a cloud in front of his face. 'Two things, Mr Doyle. First, your piece.' He holds out his left hand, sheathed in a tan leather glove.

Doyle looks around as he hesitates. Giving up his gun is anathema to him. It's one of the few things that's become ingrained in him since his days in the Academy: never give up your sidearm. Last night was different: Rocca took the gun while he was asleep. But now he's being asked to surrender it voluntarily. He would rather hand over very item of clothing he's wearing if it meant he could keep his Glock.

'Bartok still doesn't trust me?'

Rocca shrugs. 'Maybe after tonight he will.'

Because he'll have something on me, Doyle thinks. He sighs another cloud of vapor and, with reluctance, plucks his Glock from its leather holster and slaps it onto Rocca's gloved palm. It seems to Doyle an immensely symbolic act; he almost feels like he should offer his gold shield too.

Rocca drops the gun into a pocket of his overcoat. It's a stylish gray coat; Italian, no doubt.

'The other thing: I have to search you.'

'I ain't wired, if that's what's worrying your boss.'

Rocca just shrugs again, as if to say that he has his orders and so there's no point debating it.

Doyle puts his arms out, in invitation for Rocca to go ahead.

While he's being patted down, he says, 'Tell me something. Your boss not worried about the risk he's taking by talking to me? Could be he's putting himself right at the top of some sicko's hit list.'

Rocca laughs like this is the best joke ever. 'You've seen how Mr Bartok operates, how careful he is. You think me frisking you like this is just for kicks? Wherever he goes, he practically has a whole army with him, me included. You don't get near to Mr Bartok unless he wants you to.'

'Just asking. So far, this whacko's been pretty resourceful.'

'Yeah, well, don't you worry about it. Besides, aren't you forgetting something?'

'What?'

Rocca completes his search, and pulls Doyle's lapels neatly back into place. 'Mr Bartok *knows* who this guy is. It gives him a certain . . . *leverage*. Anytime he wants, all he has to do is click his fingers and the guy is history.'

As they start walking round to the club entrance, Doyle says, 'Do *you* know who the guy is?'

Rocca halts and turns, that disarming grin on his face. 'You know, I do like that coat of yours, Mr Doyle. I think I might get me one just like it.'

For a Sunday night, it seems to Doyle as though there's a heck of a lot of people who don't seem worried about having to get up for work the next morning, the dance floor being as overcrowded and as noisy as it was the previous night. And then he realizes what an old fart he sounds like.

Bartok's goons don't appear any more relaxed either. They stand glued to their stations throughout the club, monitoring the patrons and waiting for their opportunity to knock a few heads together. The closer Doyle gets to Bartok's office up all those stairs, the more menacing the heavies seem to get, as though

Bartok has positioned himself at the apex of some kind of hierarchy of malevolence. It crosses Doyle's mind to tell them to chill, that he's one of them now, but it's a thought that seems bitter rather than funny.

Rocca knocks and enters, Doyle trailing behind. Facing them on the other side of his expansive and expensive desk, Kurt Bartok sits observing their entrance as he sips from a cocktail glass. The thick drink looks like partly congealed blood.

'Detective Doyle! How nice of you to drop in again. Bruno, make yourself useful and fetch the man a seat.'

Looking as though he hasn't shifted an inch from his spot behind Bartok since the previous night, the big bodyguard hefts his muscles over to a solid oak chair against the wall, picks it up as though it's a matchstick, and puts it into place at Bartok's desk. All the while, his eyes are fixed on Doyle as though he's debating whether there's enough meat there for his next meal. Bruno's a good name for him, Doyle thinks. A bear's name. A name for someone who could crush you with a hug, or cave in your skull with one swipe of his paw.

Doyle sits himself down. As if he's just provided a cue, Rocca and Bruno take up their customary flanking positions behind Bartok.

'Don't you people ever sleep?' Doyle asks.

'Sleep is for losers. There's far too much to be done.'

'Why? You one of Santa's helpers?'

Bartok smiles and smacks his lips. He tips a manicured hand toward his drink. 'Can I get you something? A little refreshment? I hear you're a Bushmills man.'

'Not for me, thanks. It's past my bedtime.'

Bartok leans back, touches a hand to his beloved hair. 'Speaking of Santa, I assume you've come here to exchange presents.'

'Or you could just give me mine. The joy is in the giving, you know.'

'Is that so? I've always found receiving much more pleasurable. Especially when it comes to receiving knowledge. A snippet of information I never knew before. You'd be amazed at how little of that it takes to make me happy.'

'I'll send you an encyclopedia for Christmas. Keep you going for years. Me, all I want's a name. How about it, Santa? You want me to sit on your knee while you whisper it in my ear?'

Doyle detects a slight tensing in Rocca and the other guard-dog standing behind Bartok. They're not used to hearing people being so impudent with their master. Any minute now they'll start barking.

Bartok picks out a cocktail stick from his drink. He slides the pierced olive into his mouth and spends a minute rolling it around before chewing and swallowing.

'My brother hates olives,' he says. 'He calls them phlegm-balls. I don't think he'll ever make it in marketing. So often the money is in choosing the right name, don't you agree? Take the name you're interested in, for example. What would you say that's worth?'

What's it worth? How do I measure something like that? What's it worth to get your life back, to be able to see your family again?

'Depends. If it's the name of someone who's already dead or out of reach, then not very much.'

'And if it's someone who's very much alive? Someone not so far away? Someone who is still determined to keep you in this state of extreme isolation? What's it worth to hear that name, to know that you can leave here and go straight to that man and arrest him or kill him or torture him or do whatever else you need to get your revenge?'

It's the first time Doyle has been presented with any realistic prospect of confronting his persecutor. Would I, he wonders, just collar him? Would that be enough to give me closure?

He doesn't think so. He thinks too much hatred has built up

inside for him simply to follow the rules like this was any run-of-the-mill criminal.

But he'll worry about that when he gets the name.

'How do I know you've got the right guy? The NYPD have been on this twenty-four-seven. I got snitches out there who could tell me who shot JFK quicker than they can get me a name for this perp. So what's so special about you?'

Bartok takes another dainty sip of his drink, then puts the glass down and twirls the stem between his fingers.

'As I told you last night, Detective, my commodity is information. I have a lot of data on a lot of things and a lot of people. Sometimes it comes in useful, sometimes it doesn't. But just in case, I never throw any of it away. It all gets filed, most of it up here.' He taps his temple, then smoothes down his hair on the off chance he's just disturbed it. 'On this occasion we have . . . *serendipity*. You want something; I heard that you want it; I now have it. It's nice when things fall into place like that, don't you think? Makes you want to believe in fate.'

'If you're giving me the runaround . . .'

Bartok flops back in his chair. He looks irritated now. 'Detective Doyle, this is starting to become tiresome. I made you an offer in good faith. My assumption was that you came here tonight because you decided to accept that offer. If you've changed your mind, then feel free to leave and go back to your scant existence in your miserable flea-pit of a hotel. It's time, as the saying goes, to piss or get off the pot.'

So there it is, thinks Doyle. What's it gonna be? Haven't you already made up your mind? Are you really gonna get up and walk out of here without that name?

'You want to know about Ramon Vitez.'

Bartok says nothing. He purses his lips slightly and waits.

Doyle says, 'I'm not involved in that operation.'

He sees the fury igniting in Bartok's eyes, a twitch appearing on the corner of his mouth.

'But,' Doyle adds, 'I know one or two things.'

Bartok continues to wait. The room is silent, save for a steady pounding. Doyle isn't sure whether it's from the dance floor or his own heart. He opens his mouth, finds himself choking on his own words. This goes against everything in which he believes, everything he is.

'New Year's Day. Seven a.m. When all the revelers are still sleeping it off. East River Park. The handover will take place at a bench under the Williamsburg Bridge. That's all I know.'

More silence. Bartok finishes his drink and passes a reptilian tongue over his thin lips, then smoothes his hair again.

'Good enough?' Doyle asks.

'It's a start,' Bartok answers, and Doyle can see the devilish glee on the man's face.

Stay calm. He's fucking with your head. Stay calm.

'The name, Kurt. Give me the name.'

'In a moment. I need a little more . . . persuading.'

Doyle leans forward suddenly, almost coming off his chair. Again he notices how Rocca and Bruno brace themselves.

'Persuading is the last thing you want me to do, Kurt. You haven't seen how I can persuade people. I've given you what you asked for, so you—'

'You've given me nothing,' Bartok says. He reaches for a drawer, slides it open. He pulls out a notepad and pushes it across the desk. On the top sheet of paper it says, 'Ramon Vitez. East River Park. Jan 1.'

Doyle stares at the sheet for some time, then raises his gaze to Bartok. 'What the fuck is this?'

'Call it a test. A validation of your sincerity. You'll be glad to

hear that you've passed with flying colors. Now, tell me something
I don't know.'

Doyle leaps to his feet so fast, the heavies are almost caught
off guard. He sees them reach beneath their jackets and start
toward him.

'Fuck you, Bartok!' Doyle says. 'You want to play games, do
it with someone who's prepared to lie down and roll over. I'm
outta here, and when I come back, all the data in the world ain't
gonna save you from what I got in mind.'

He starts toward the door, wondering how far he's going to
get. Wondering whether they're prepared to let him leave. Once
again, he's regretting giving up his gun. He gets to the door,
reaches for the handle . . .

'He's close, Detective Doyle.'

Doyle halts. Despite himself, he wants to hear what Bartok has
to say.

'He's close,' Bartok repeats. 'You know him, in fact. And he
knows oh so much about you. Don't you want to know who it is?'

Doyle lowers his hand. I have to know, he thinks. I've come
this far.

He turns to face Bartok. Rocca and Bruno are toward the
front of the desk now, their hands still inside their jackets. A
sneer on his ugly face, Bruno is straining against his leash, anxious to release some pent-up violence. Rocca's face is impassive.
He has no axe to grind, but there is no doubting his loyalty or
conviction.

'Come on, Detective. You're already committed. Whether I
knew about Vitez or not, the fact that you told me about him is
enough to lose you your job and get you put in jail. You've
proved yourself. All I'm asking for now is for you to demon-
strate your usefulness. Please, sit down. Finish what you came
here for.'

215

It's true, Doyle thinks. He has me. I'm in. You can't get back in the plane once you've jumped.

Slowly, he walks back to the chair. Bartok flicks his wrist and his guards back away, Bruno looking like he's just had a prime steak snatched away from him.

Doyle sits down. Tries counting to ten before saying, 'What do you want to know?'

Bartok waves his hand. 'I'll leave it to you. Surprise me.' He says this as though he's a food critic inviting a restaurant owner to impress him before he writes his review.

Doyle consults his mental menu and tries to avoid the expensive items.

'Tito Sloane, one of Blue Tucker's soldiers. Took a hit last month in a Chinatown parking lot. Tucker blames your crew for the hit, saying you claim he ripped off one of your mules.'

'Ah, yes, Mr Tucker. Such a fantasist, and yet he's determined to cause me a lot of problems at the moment.'

'It's gonna get worse. Tucker plans to even the score by acing one of your own operatives.'

He sees the sudden concern on Bartok's face.

'Who? When?'

'I don't know. Soon. Story is he's psyched up for a war.'

Bartok blinks several times in a way that suggests he's trying to bat away his anger. 'The future killing of an unnamed associate at an unknown time and place, coming from a man who is widely known to despise me, is hardly one of the most valuable or even interesting pieces of information, Detective. You'll have to do better than that.'

'I'm not done. Suppose I told you I know a way to take the heat off?'

'Go on.'

'Have a word with Lionel Dafoe. He was the one who offed

Sloane. Something about a beef over his girlfriend. It was also him spread the rumor it was down to you. You want proof, the nine he used for the hit is still in his apartment. The girlfriend will also confirm the story.'

Bartok thinks about this for a minute. Doyle wonders whether it's enough. Because what he hasn't told Bartok is that Dafoe has already fled to Mexico. Giving Bartok some proof that will take Tucker's heat off him is one thing, but he's not going to be responsible for setting up Dafoe to be killed.

Bartok says, 'And you know this how?'

'From a CI of mine, whose information was always reliable.'

'*Was?* That wouldn't be poor old Spinner, would it? Such a shame about him. I hear that his wasn't the quickest or most painless of endings.'

Doyle doesn't want to talk about Spinner. Not with this monster.

'Your move, Kurt. You've been paid. I want my goods.'

Bartok smiles. He makes Doyle wait that little bit longer.

'Yes, I think you've earned your stripes. Perhaps now you'll join me in a little drink to celebrate our new relationship?'

'The name,' Doyle says, and will keep on saying until he gets it.

'All right,' Bartok agrees. 'The name. As I said, it's a man you know already. You can stop digging into your past because—'

He doesn't get any further.

Primarily because his throat has just exploded.

A hole has opened up in his neck, sending a fountain of blood spurting across his desk and onto Doyle's leather jacket.

Bartok looks surprised that he can't speak any longer. He sits there, his mouth moving soundlessly, seemingly unaware that the source of all that gushing blood is himself.

Doyle's reaction isn't exactly immediate either. He doesn't know what has just happened here. The shock of what he has just witnessed has confused and paralyzed him. And then he zooms out, takes in the wider picture, sees the movement behind the man choking to death on his own blood.

Bruno is also clearly puzzled. His arms come up and his fingers grapple comically with thin air as though he's operating some complex invisible machinery. By the time he works out that he should be reaching for his gun, it's too late. Sonny Rocca is already on him, his gun arm outstretched, his silenced weapon making phut-phut sounds as it spits. Bruno stares uncomprehendingly while his chest is drilled. When anger finally appears on his face, it is there for the fleetest of moments before being obliterated by a salvo of bullets that take out his teeth, then his nose, and then his right eye. Bruno stiffens, leans back like a toppling domino, and crashes to the floor with the force of a felled elephant.

Doyle is already on his feet. His hand dives automatically under his coat, finds itself clawing at the empty leather of his holster. He starts moving toward Rocca, no thought yet as to what he might do when he gets there. Rocca whirls on him, aims his gun at Doyle's face.

'Back!'

Doyle brings his hands up, takes a step in reverse. He watches as Rocca moves calmly back to Bartok, now clutching at his neck, trying in vain to plug the hole there as he coughs and splutters.

No, thinks Doyle. Don't.

Rocca observes his boss for a second or two, not a hint of compassion on his face. It's like he's studying the behavior of an amoeba under a microscope.

Please don't.

With casual ease, Rocca raises the dark semi-automatic again, and Doyle can only look on helplessly as bullet after bullet smashes into Bartok's head and face. Even when Bartok's body slides lifeless from his chair and lies crumpled on the wooden floor, Rocca stands over him and continues with the steady eradication of his ex-employer's features.

I have one chance, Doyle thinks. And it will come only if Sonny Rocca hates his former boss badly enough.

So he watches and waits, listening to the muffled explosions, the clatter of empty cartridges hitting the floor, thinking that the destruction seems to be going on forever.

And then it happens. The slide on Rocca's gun jerks back and stays there, announcing that its work is done: there are no more bullets to be fired.

Doyle makes his move. He believes it's the fastest he's ever shifted. His high-school sprinting instructor would have been proud of him.

He manages to cover all of one yard.

Rocca is ready for him. His other hand, which Doyle hadn't even noticed dipping into his pocket, now comes up and points at Doyle. And it's not empty.

The soles of Doyle's shoes squeal as he applies his brakes. For the umpteenth time, he mentally slaps himself for agreeing to surrender his Glock. He thinks, finally, that he's learned his lesson. Certainly he'll never do it again.

Because now, for the first time in his life, he's staring into the business end of his own gun.

'Back!' Rocca says again. He twitches the gun muzzle to one side. 'Back in the chair.'

Doyle takes a few steps backwards, his eyes never leaving Rocca's.

'Why, Sonny?' he asks. 'What the fuck's this about?'

Rocca doesn't answer. He swaps his guns over, putting the

loaded Glock into his right hand. Then he steps over Bartok's corpse, edges around the desk, the Glock aimed squarely at Doyle's forehead. He comes to a halt. Continues to point the gun. He stands like that for several seconds, as if allowing Doyle the opportunity to say a final prayer.

'I was beginning to like you, Mr Doyle,' Rocca says. 'So long.'

Doyle senses the change in Rocca. He realizes that Rocca has just made his decision. He sees the whiteness of Rocca's knuckle as he tightens his trigger finger.

Doyle closes his eyes and thinks of Rachel and Amy.

TWENTY-FOUR

When Doyle opens his eyes again, Rocca has disappeared from in front of him.

He twists in his chair and sees that Rocca is now standing at the door.

'Sonny . . .' Doyle says.

'I got no instructions to kill you, Mr Doyle,' Rocca says. 'Quite the opposite, in fact.'

There is a trash basket next to the door. Rocca holds the empty, silenced gun over the basket and allows it to drop in. His left hand now free, he reaches into his inside breast pocket and pulls out an envelope. A white one. There is typing on the front, and even though Doyle can't read it from here he knows that it will be addressed to him.

'A message for you,' Rocca says, and lets the envelope float down to join the gun.

'You're not thinking this through, Sonny. They'll hunt you down. You know that, don't you?'

'We'll see. Goodbye, Mr Doyle.' He reaches for the door handle behind him.

'Sonny! The name. You know who it is, don't you? Please, this was my last chance. Give me the name.'

Doyle hears the desperation in his own voice, but he doesn't care. Right now he thinks he'd get down on his knees and beg if it'd get him the name.

Rocca hesitates. 'I'd like to help you, Mr Doyle. Really I would.'

But he's not going to, Doyle realizes.

In one smooth motion, Rocca drops the Glock into the trash basket, swings open the door, and leaves. Doyle jumps from his chair, but even before he's anywhere near the door he hears a key turning in the lock.

He grabs the handle and tries turning it. Realizes that he's well and truly imprisoned.

'Shit!'

He reaches into the basket, removes his Glock and the envelope. He stuffs the unopened envelope into his pocket, points his gun at the door-locking mechanism . . .

What the fuck? he thinks. What am I going to do? Blast the door open, and then what? With all those human tanks out there, I won't even get down the first flight of steps before someone blasts me out of my shoes.

Shit!

He lowers his gun and begins to pace the office. He glances at the mutilated figures of Bruno and Kurt, leaking their bodily fluids all over the polished floor. He can still smell the acrid odor of gunpowder in the air.

Why the fuck couldn't you speak a little faster, Kurt?

It makes sense now. Sonny in his big heavy overcoat to hide his armory. His gloves to avoid putting fingerprints on the gun he used for the hit. And let's not forget his demeanor. His cheerfulness tonight. His little speech about red-letter days, the start of a new life. He wasn't talking about me, Doyle realizes now; he was talking about himself.

Doyle moves back to the door. How the hell am I going to do this?

He knows he can't stay here for much longer. Any second now, someone could come through that door. Maybe even Lucas Bartok, and my, won't he be in a good mood when he sees what happened here? How am I going to explain that one? Me locked in a room with his dead brother and his dead bodyguard, and oh yes, that murder weapon in the trashcan – that's nothing to do with me. How long is Lucas or one of his heavies going to stand there and listen while I try to wriggle my way out of that one?

Fuck!

He paces again. Takes another look at Bartok. He had the name, goddamnit! He was on the verge of giving it to me. The only man walking this earth who . . .

Well, that's not quite true. Sonny Rocca knows the name, doesn't he? Sonny Rocca, who is probably right now heading for a flight to Rio if he has any brains, knows who the sonofabitch is.

Doyle leaps over Bartok and stands at the window behind his desk. Straight ahead is the uniform blackness of a featureless wall. Below, he can just make out the dimly lit alley in which they parked.

Doyle holsters his gun and flips off the catch on the window, which looks old and covered in a million layers of paint. Please let this open, he thinks.

He manages to force the window up an inch, then slips his hands through the gap. The ice-cold air from outside almost freezes his hands to the frame as he strains to pull the window upwards. Eventually, he raises it by about a foot or so – just enough, he hopes, to squeeze through.

He pushes his head outside, feels the sting of an icy blast of wind. It looks one hell of a long way down. He has never thought of himself as a sufferer of vertigo, but his head swims at the thought of putting his center of gravity any closer to that sheer drop. He turns his head and sees that the nearest fire escape runs under the adjoining office. The only thing that will take him anywhere near it is a drainpipe that runs from above his window and gently angles down toward the front corner of the building. It's hard to tell in the darkness, but there's a slight gleam on the pipe that makes it look as though it's been recently painted. What lurks beneath the paint is another matter. As escape routes go, dangling from a length of decades-old rusty pipe two floors above the ground would not be high on his list of preferred options.

Not that you got all that many options here, Doyle.

He swings his right leg up and slides it onto the narrow outer ledge. Slowly, cautiously, he edges his torso sideways through the window. Keeping his left arm hooked under the window, he starts to pull his outer leg under his body. Inch by jittery inch, he transfers his weight onto that single leg, as he brings his other leg out and twists himself to face the building. He eventually gets into a standing position, his face pressed hard against the freezing glass as he tries to stop his knees wobbling. Remind me not to become a window cleaner when they throw me off the job, he thinks.

He slides his hands upwards along the window and brings them above his head. He feels them hit the brickwork, and continues to push them over the rough surface. He flexes his fingers, searching for the drainpipe.

Nothing.

Reluctantly, he unpeels his face from the glass and leans his head back as much as he dares, then rolls his eyes upwards. He sees that the pipe is inches above his fingertips. He straightens up again. Begins to raise his heels from the ledge. When he is on his tiptoes he stretches his arms until it seems they're about to leave their sockets.

He feels like an Olympic diver about to do a backward jump into the pool. He has never been in such a precarious position. One gust of wind is all it'll take to knock him from his perch. Despite the cold, he starts to perspire.

He extends himself another couple of millimeters. Feels his fingernails just scrape the lower surface of the pipe. But it's not enough. He comes down onto his heels again, relaxes his muscles, allows his joints to click back into place. There's nothing for it, he thinks. I'm gonna have to jump.

He looks up again, fixes his gaze on the drainpipe, flexes all his fingers. Another couple inches – that's all I need. If I don't make it, or I do make it and the pipe doesn't hold . . .

He casts such thoughts out of his mind. There is no time to debate this. It has to be done now, and it has to be done with utter conviction.

He brings his arms up again, then starts to bend at the knees. There's no room to take his knees forward, and so he has to bow them out to the sides, like he's a ballet dancer.

He gives himself a three-count: *Three* . . .

It's a lot lower than the basketball hoop in high school, he tells himself, and you could reach that.

Two . . .

Except I was a lot younger then. And fitter. And I weighed less.

One . . .

And it was always a running jump, never from a fucking bandy-legged nutcracker position like this.

Go!

He hears a starting pistol go off in his head, and suddenly he's shooting up like a rocket, willing himself up and up. He imagines himself back at school, stretching for that basket, seconds left to win the trophy for his team. At the apex of his jump he gives a loud grunt of exertion . . .

His hands snap into position around the pipe. He hears the metal groan at the sudden burden, but it doesn't give way.

The pipe is so cold it burns Doyle's hands. He knows he can't stay in this position for very long. Not that that was ever his desire.

He slides his left hand along the metal, feeling as though he's leaving a layer of frozen flesh behind, then follows it with his right hand. His legs dangle and swing freely below him, cold air fluttering up the inside of his pants. He continues his motion sideways and slowly downwards, trying to ignore the pain in his hands, his arms, his shoulders. You're okay, he tells himself. Focus and keep going. We're gonna do this.

He moves again, and hears more squeals of complaint from the drainpipe. 'Don't you dare,' he hisses at it. 'Don't you fucking dare!'

He keeps going. Another couple of feet, then another. How come that damned fire escape doesn't seem to be getting any closer?

There is a sudden outpouring of noise from below. He stops moving and looks past his armpit to the alley that still appears a thousand miles down. Light spills out from an open doorway, and the night is filled with voices and throbbing music. Some kind of side entrance to the club, Doyle realizes.

A lone figure exits the club and closes the door behind him. He is tall, with dark hair and a *Saturday Night Fever* swagger. He wears a heavy gray overcoat and gloves.

Sonny Rocca.

Rocca heads toward his Lexus, almost directly below Doyle. Don't look up, Doyle thinks. He hangs there in space, praying that his arms don't pop out of their sockets. His hands burn like they're on fire, like they're becoming fused with the drainpipe.

Rocca opens his car door, climbs behind the wheel, closes the door.

Shit, he's gonna get away! The only man who can help me now is about to take off, probably never to be seen again.

He starts moving again with renewed vigor. I have to get down there, he thinks. I have to stop him.

The drainpipe creaks more loudly now. Doyle is certain he feels it give slightly, but he can't slow down now.

Below, Rocca starts up his engine.

Doyle puts everything into one last desperate push. The fire escape is just feet away.

Rocca backs the Lexus up, just enough to give him clearance to pull out.

Come on, Doyle tells himself. Get the fuck down there!

And then, as if granting his wish, the drainpipe gives out a loud crack and breaks away from the wall.

There is no time for thought, no time for any reasoning along the lines of Okay, I'm plummeting to my death, here's what I should do . . . All that Doyle can do is live the experience of his body twisting in free space, register the unusual sight of a car's roof hurtling toward him at God knows how many miles per hour.

He lands on his side, smashing into the roof of the Lexus. He feels it crumple below him, absorbing his impact. There is an explosive sound as the metal collapses and the windows blow out, showering fragments of glass in all directions.

Doyle lies there for a second, appreciating the fact that he's still alive. He feels pain in his ribs and in his leg, and wonders if any bones are broken. He looks around him, realizes that he's landed on the driver's side, and that the roof on that side is now almost level with the car's hood.

Rocca! Jesus Christ, have I just killed him?

He drags himself forward and peers upside down through the shattered windshield. At first he's not sure what he's looking at, but then he sees motion. The face of Rocca looks straight at him, rivulets of blood streaming down past his eyes and mouth. There is more movement. Rocca's arm comes up, his gloved hand comes into view, and . . .

Shit!

Doyle rolls sideways off the car just milliseconds before Rocca starts shooting upwards through the roof. He lands heavily on the cobblestones, agonizing jolts of pain firing through his bones.

He keeps rolling, putting distance between himself and the car. When the shots cease, he stops too. He gets up on one knee and fumbles for his Glock. Ahead of him, Rocca has begun squeezing himself through the passenger-side window, forcing himself up the narrow gap between the crushed Lexus and the wall of the nightclub. He looks on the edge of consciousness, barely aware of his surroundings.

Doyle takes up a two-handed stance and steadies his aim.

'Sonny! Drop the gun, man!'

Rocca pauses in his struggle. Shakes his head as if to clear his blood-filled eyes and his addled brain. His gun waves lazily in Doyle's direction.

'Don't do it, man!'

As if working by echo location, Rocca homes his gun in on Doyle's voice, leaving Doyle with no option.

It's not like it was with Lomax. It could be just a matter of physical distance, Rocca not being right on top of him like Lomax was, or the fact that Rocca doesn't appear able to shoot straight. Maybe it's because he quite likes Sonny Rocca, whereas Lomax was just a worthless piece of shit. Maybe it's because he doesn't want Rocca dead, because he is so much more valuable alive. Or perhaps it's because Doyle has already killed once, and now finds it easier to tell when to pull on the reins.

Whatever the reason, he stops firing after four rapid shots. He sees Rocca loll back against the brick wall, the gun dropping from his hand. Doyle gets to his feet. Fights the pain racking his body as he limps across to the car. He climbs onto the hood, feeling fragments of glass crunching beneath his feet, then gets onto the roof. He cups a hand under Rocca's blood-soaked chin and turns his face toward him. The man's alive, but only by a thread.

'Sonny. Who got to you? Who put you up to this?'

Sonny opens his mouth and releases a dribble of scarlet. 'I was gonna go someplace nice,' he croaks. 'I was thinking of Europe. Maybe even Ireland. I hear it's nice there, right, Mr Doyle?'

'The name, Sonny. What was Bartok about to tell me?'

'Bartok? Bartok was scum. Shoulda . . . shoulda whacked him a long time ago. He gave me money, you know that? A lot of money.'

'Who? Who gave you money?'

'I made him an offer. He . . . he made me a better one. And you know what? Now I know how it feels, I'da done it for free.'

Doyle grabs him by the lapels and shakes him. 'He give you enough to die for? You ready to go out of this world for that garbage? Give him up, Sonny. Make it right.'

A twisted smile crosses Rocca's lips. 'I like you, Mr Doyle. You're a funny guy.'

Doyle feels the life leave Rocca's body. It floats from his form, leaving him sagging and heavy in Doyle's grasp. Doyle takes his hands away. Looks at Rocca's blood staining them. He stays there longer than he should, just staring at his hands.

Red-letter day.

When he finally comes to his senses he climbs down from the car and, like a deformed criminal from an old B-movie, limps away into the night.

He doesn't know how long he's got, but he can't stay here.

He races around his room, yanking open drawers and closets and tossing the contents into the case yawning open on his bed. Rocca and Bartok knew where he was staying. That means there may be others in the Bartok organization who know where he's staying. And if that set of people now includes Lucas Bartok, it won't be long before hell descends on this place.

He thinks it was bad enough when he was being isolated, but now that he's got people actively trying to kill him too . . .

Shit.

He locks up his bag, performs one last check of the room, then gets the hell out of there.

The door still has yellow crime-scene tape stuck across it. Doyle tears some of it away; then, after a quick look up and down the hallway, he kicks the door open. Somewhere in the building a dog barks, but at least the big black woman in the neighboring apartment seems to be a sound sleeper.

Doyle steps inside and feels for a light switch. He flicks it on, and a bare bulb shows him his new home. Not exactly the Ritz, he thinks, but then Spinner led a pretty spartan existence.

He closes the door again and puts a couple of Spinner's locks into place. He looks around. There is an unpleasant odor in the air which Doyle decides it might be better not to identify, and the bleak apartment looks as though it has been devoid of occupants for months rather than days. Much of the clutter that used to be here has gone. All of the boxes of electronic equipment have disappeared. Impounded as evidence, presumably, although Doyle can't help thinking that there may be one or two cops or technicians who are giving nice DVD players for Christmas this year.

Also gone are the chair, table and tape recorder that formed the centerpiece of the living room the last time Doyle was here. For that he is grateful, although there are other reminders. The vast dark bloodstain on the carpet, for example.

He is not a believer in the supernatural, but knowing what happened here colors his normally skeptical view. There is a feeling of unearthly presence here. A sharp coldness like a razor blade scraping the hairs from the nape of his neck. A sensation of things left unfinished.

He doesn't want to be here. He can still picture Spinner, still hear his screams. The emptiness of the room and the lateness of the hour serve only to amplify these mental sounds and images.

'It's me, man,' he whispers to the ceiling. 'Doyle. I got nowhere else to go, man. Look after me, okay?'

He knows he must appear crazy saying these things. When dawn arrives and its light chases away the shadows and shows him the truth, he knows he will rebuke himself for acting like an idiot. But right now talking to walls doesn't seem so absurd.

He walks over to the bathroom, switches on another naked bulb. In the corner, something small and black scuttles behind the bath. Doyle tries to overlook the obvious fact that this room is a stranger to cleansing products.

He steps over to the shower control and turns it on full blast. Another memory jumps to mind, of him almost drowning Spinner beneath this jet of water.

As the steam rises and begins to fill the room, Doyle strips off and does his best to take a look at himself in the grime-caked mirror over the sink. Almost the whole of his left side is swollen and tender. Tomorrow it'll be one enormous bruise. He touches his ribs and feels a stab of pain. It hurts to breathe, to walk, to lift his arm. Shit, it hurts to live.

He steps into the bathtub, then moves under the water. It's hot, and it stings at first, but gradually he becomes accustomed to it. He lets it wash over his body, soothing his tired aching muscles.

When he's done, he climbs out and picks up one of Spinner's old towels. It feels cold and damp, and has the stiffness of fabric that hasn't been washed for weeks. As he rasps it over his body, he closes his eyes and tries to imagine that it's one of the white fluffy ones from his hotel. If he'd been thinking ahead, he would have stolen one before he left.

He walks back into the living room and opens his case. Pulls out some clothes. He's worn them before, but they'll do for tonight. He has the feeling he needs to be dressed. Just in case.

When he's got his clothes on, he reloads his Glock, ensuring there's a round in the chamber. Just in case.

He picks up one of Spinner's chairs, turns it to face the door, then sits down. It doesn't escape him that he's in almost exactly the same position that Spinner was when he found him.

A thought occurs to him. He goes back to the bathroom, where his jacket is hooked on a door peg. He reaches into the pocket and pulls out the white envelope that Rocca delivered. He brings it back to his chair, studying the familiar lettering of his name typed across the front.

He sits down, rips open the envelope and begins to read.

Dear Detective Doyle,

Are you finally getting the hang of this now?
Has it finally sunk into your dim policeman's

```
brain? Do you need any more deaths to convince
you?
    Wherever you go, I know about it. Whoever
you speak to, I know about it. I don't care if
they're good or evil. Make them your friends,
and they're dead. That's the sickness you carry
with you. There's no cure. You need to be
quarantined for your own good.
    I think you're starting to feel it now,
aren't you? You're starting to understand
what it's like to be me.
    We've almost become one.
    Merry Christmas, Detective.
```

Doyle crumples up the letter and throws it across the room. It seems a pitiful gesture of defiance, but it's all he has. Every battle has been fought and lost. The war is over. Here he is, stuck in a bare decrepit room amid the stench and the aura of death. Hidden away like the mad relative in the attic. Separated from the rest of humanity so that he can't hurt them and they can't hurt him.

He stares at the door and waits, praying that sleep will overtake him and provide some brief respite from this hell that is a man truly alone.

TWENTY-FIVE

He comes awake to the sound of a bang. He doesn't know whether it's real or imagined. Perhaps his mind is replaying one of the many gunshots it's witnessed recently. At first he doesn't know where he is, his eyes scanning the apartment, wondering what happened to his hotel room. Then, with a groan, he remembers and wishes he'd never woken up.

He looks down at his watch, feeling a painful tug in his neck after being stuck in such a peculiar position all night. It's seven-thirty in the morning. A cold gray light filters through the dirt on the windows. He rises from his chair, wincing with the effort of moving joints and bones and flesh that have been pounded against metal at great speed. He hobbles over to the bathroom. Treats himself to another hot shower and another session with Spinner's delightful towels.

As he re-dresses, he hears the drone of the neighbor's television through the walls. It stops suddenly, to be followed by the click and slam of a door. Doyle steps over to his own front door and puts his eye to the spy-hole. As the figure of the huge woman comes into view, it fills the whole of his field of vision, the distortion of the eyepiece making her appear even more spherical than she is. She pauses for a second and turns her head toward Doyle, staring directly at him it seems, before resuming her waddle along the hallway.

Doyle gives her ten minutes to get out of the building, then leaves. Outside, he turns up the collar of his leather coat, partly against the cold but also to hide his face. Feeling like an over-dramatic spy, he takes a good look around him before setting off down the street. On the next block he finds a small burger joint. He buys a bacon and egg muffin and some coffee, and takes them back to Spinner's apartment.

Before he settles down to his breakfast, he switches on Spinner's television. It's an old portable, not worth enough to sell for drugs. As he eats, he flicks through the channels, on the lookout for any local news. He sees nothing about Rocca or Bartok. Nothing about any killings or shootings in the Meatpacking District. All of which tells him that Bartok's men must have been the first to discover Sonny Rocca's dead body. It's not something about which they would have wanted to make public announcements.

Doyle is ashamed to admit that it comes as something of a relief. He thinks, I'm a cop, involved in a string of fatal shootings, and all I can think about is keeping it under wraps. That stinks, Doyle. That's really low, man.

But then how much lower can I get? Look at me. I hand con-fidential police intelligence over to known criminals. I get smashed up on a car. I kill a guy and then run away. I camp out in a shit-hole owned by a dead junkie fence. I got mobsters out looking to waste me. And I got this unknown perp willing to waste everyone I so much as look at. A guy who has this uncanny ability to follow my every move.

Speaking of which, how the fuck does he do that? How does this guy always seem to know what I'm doing? How is it possible for him to have eyes everywhere like that?

Doyle walks across the room, his eyes scanning the floor. He kicks aside a cardboard box, then bends to pick up the ball of paper he threw last night. As he goes to straighten up, something on the box catches his eye. A picture of a bird stamped onto it in red. He'd noticed the same picture on many of the boxes when he came here to ask for Spinner's help. What is it about that bird?

He shakes his head, then turns his attention to the piece of paper as he unfurls and rereads it.

Wherever you go, I know about it. Whoever you speak to, I know about it.

Okay, so how?

Doyle is certain nobody knew about his meetings with Bartok. Not his wife, not his squad. Nobody. So how could the killer know? How could he be watching Doyle that closely, that carefully, that Doyle never sees him, never knows he's there? How is that possible?

And then there's Spinner. Okay, there were a few people who knew about their first meeting at the boxing gym, but Doyle told no one when he came to see Spinner here at his apartment. He was extra careful to make sure nobody followed him here, and Spinner made it clear that he wasn't too happy about a walking bullet-magnet being in his vicinity, so he wouldn't have blabbed about it either. So how did that news leak out?

It's like the perp has superhuman powers, Doyle thinks. Like maybe he's there in the room with me, but he's invisible. Or maybe he can see through walls or listen from a great distance.

And he's not the only one. Take Kurt Bartok. How did he get the killer's name so quickly? When the various divisions of the NYPD working flat out on this case were getting nowhere, how could Bartok be so confident he could get the name in just a few hours? And who the fuck was he getting the name from?

Sonny Rocca knew the name too. The killer bought him off – paid him to whack Bartok. It was a very clever move. He couldn't get close enough to Bartok to do it himself, so he paid someone else to do it. Nice.

Except, how did he know to do that?

Suppose I'm the perp, Doyle thinks. Psycho that I am, I follow the detective around, acing each and every one of his friends as I go. News reaches my super-sensitive ears that Doyle is now talking to one Kurt Bartok, so naturally Bartok is next on my list.

I don't care if they're good or evil. Make them your friends, and they're dead.

Problem is, Bartok isn't like the others. This is a man who expects attempts on his life as a hazard of his profession. This is a man who surrounds himself with an army to prevent any such efforts reaching fruition.

So what do I do? I know, I'll approach one of Bartok's closest bodyguards, offer him a shit-load of money, and he'll do the job for me.

Yeah, like fuck.

How did the perp even know who Sonny Rocca was, let alone that he was disgruntled with his boss? What made him think he could trust Rocca? What made him so sure that Rocca wouldn't cap him as soon as he even broached the idea, or that he wouldn't immediately spill the beans to Bartok? How did he know there was the remotest chance his offer would be accepted?

His offer.

What was it Sonny said just before he died?

I made him an offer. He made me a better one.

Sonny Rocca made the killer an offer. What kind of offer?

Whatever it was, it means that the killer didn't need to work out whom to approach to do his dirty work.

Sonny Rocca had already come to him!

Why? Was he acting on Bartok's behalf? If so, what would Bartok possibly want from this lunatic?

Doyle crumples the letter up again and tosses it to the floor. He doesn't see the logic in any of this. None of it makes any sense.

He starts to pace. His foot kicks the empty cardboard box. He looks down at it, and sees that bird looking right back at him. He bends down and picks up the box. It used to contain a CD player, manufactured by a Japanese company. The image of a bird is not part of the original packaging; it was stamped onto it at a later date. Doyle spins the box around, examining each of its sides. On one end is another stamp, giving details of the consignment. Amongst other things it gives the name of the company that has received this item and will be selling it in its stores.

Trogon Electronics.

And then it all comes back to him.

A conversation. Part of an investigation. Doyle talking to one of the managers at Trogon. Asking him, 'What the fuck is a trogon, anyhow?' And the manager replying that it's a bird found in Central and South America. Hence the company logo.

You learn something every day.

And the reason Doyle was talking to this guy in the first place was . . .

Doyle races across to his jacket, whips out his cellphone. He speed-dials a number.

'Eighth Precinct. Detective LeBlanc.'

'Tommy, it's me. Cal Doyle.'

'Cal! How you doin', man? Making the most of the hotel hospitality?'

Doyle looks around at the peeling paint, the threadbare curtains. 'Uh, yeah. It's nice to be waited on like this, you know? Listen, Tommy, can you do something for me?'

'Sure, buddy. What is it?'

'You remember that hit on the Trogon Electronics warehouse a couple months back?'

There's a moment's pause, like LeBlanc doesn't know where Doyle is coming from with this.

'Yeah?' he drawls.

'Somewhere in the fives there's a list of item numbers of the stolen goods. You think you can look those out for me and call me back?'

'Uh, well . . . Look, Cal, I want to help you and all, but aren't you kinda off the job right now? I mean, why do you need this shit?'

How much to tell him? Can I trust him? Can I trust anyone?

'Tell you the truth, Tommy, I'm bored stiff in this place. I'm going out of my mind waiting for you guys to rescue me. So I'm working through some old cases, just to keep me occupied. You don't mind, do you?'

Another pause. 'I guess not. Give me five minutes.'

Doyle ends the call, but keeps the phone in his hand. He returns to his chair and waits. It's more like fifteen minutes before LeBlanc calls him.

'Yeah.'

'Cal? Where are you?'

'What do you mean? I'm in the hotel, like I told you.'

'Yeah? Well, I been calling you on your room phone for the last five minutes.'

Shit.

'I, uh, I'm sorry, Tommy. I shoulda said. I'm not in my room. I'm down in the bar. I was calling you on my cell. You get the numbers?'

'Uh, yeah, yeah. I got 'em. What do you want to know?'

'CD players. You got a bunch beginning with the letters CDX?'

'Yeah. About a dozen of 'em.'

'Okay. Read them out to me.'

While LeBlanc reels them off, Doyle stares at the number on

his carton. When nine or ten numbers have been called, he begins to think he's got it wrong.

'Wait. That last number. Read it to me again, slowly.'

LeBlanc sounds out the digits, Doyle moving his finger steadily along the box.

Bingo.

'That's great, Tommy. Thanks.'

'That it? That's all you wanted?'

'Like I said, I'm just trying to tie up a few loose ends on old cases. No big deal.'

'Oh. Okay . . . Listen, man, I hope you can get back on the job soon. I mean it. We're doing all we can to find this guy. It's just, well . . .'

'Yeah, I know. Thanks. I'll see you soon.'

He ends the call. He doesn't want to hear any more about how the squad is putting all its efforts into his case. It's starting to make him want to vomit.

He looks again at the box, as if doing so will help him to fit this new piece of information into the puzzle. The CD player was stolen in a raid on a warehouse owned by Trogon Electronics. Three months ago, Doyle collared a crew he believed responsible for that robbery, but their shyster lawyer got them off the hook faster than you can say *habeas corpus*.

The crew comprised the Bartok brothers and Sonny Rocca.

And now one of those purloined items turns up in the home of Mickey 'Spinner' Spinoza – a man who, like the Bartoks and Rocca, also became tangled in the web of Doyle's persecutor and died because of it.

Coincidence? My ass!

Spinner was fencing goods for the Bartoks. That means he knew them, and they knew him – well enough to entrust him with selling on their ill-gotten gains.

Something Spinner said on the phone . . .

I got a meeting fixed up. Some people I know. They want to talk about who whacked your two partners.

Could those people have been Bartok and Co.?

Until now Doyle has always assumed that the meeting was a sham, that the killer somehow pretended to be someone that Spinner knew and trusted, in order to bring him into his clutches.

But Spinner was no idiot. Good snitches like him don't stay on this earth for very long unless they possess a substantial amount of street smarts. It would not have been easy to get him to walk blindly into a trap like that.

And there's something else that bothers Doyle. Why bring Spinner back here? Why would the killer trick Spinner into coming to him, only to drag Spinner back to his apartment to torture and kill him?

So what if he really *was* on his way to a meeting? He talked about *they* – plural. Could *they* be Bartok and Rocca?

Think it through, Doyle.

Okay, so Spinner is asking around on his behalf, trying to find out who's giving him all this grief. The mistake Spinner makes is talking to Bartok or one of Bartok's men – those good old buddies of his. They say, *Sure, come on in; we'll give you the name.*

Two things. First of all, why? Why would they offer to give Spinner the name? What was in it for them? Were Spinner's services as a fence of such great value *to them?*

Thought number two: if Bartok wasn't bluffing about the name, then that means he knew it well before he called Doyle in and told him he could get hold of it. So why didn't he just say, *I know the name you want, and here's my price for it?*

Answer: Because he didn't want Doyle connecting him with things that had gone on before.

He didn't want me linking him to Spinner's death!

The perp didn't need X-ray vision or a cloak of invisibility to know about Doyle's meeting with Spinner. He was told by Bartok about Spinner's interest. Spinner wasn't killed because he got too close to Doyle, but because he knew, or was about to discover, the killer's name. Same probably goes for Doyle's meetings with Bartok. The perp didn't have to be watching him around the clock. Bartok or one of Bartok's men told the killer that Doyle was talking to them.

But why would Bartok go to all the trouble of bringing Spinner in to give him the name, then hand him over to be tortured and put to death? It doesn't make sense.

Unless . . .

Unless it was a way of putting pressure on the killer. Because the thing that Bartok was offering was his silence in return for the killer's cooperation.

Bartok was saying, *I know your name, and unless you do what I want, I'm giving it out.*

Only the approach backfired. Twice. The second time fatally for Bartok.

Which brings us back to the earlier question: What form of cooperation did Bartok want? Why was this guy of such interest?

Doyle reaches for his phone again. Dials another number.

'Hello?'

'Hi, hon. It's me.'

'Cal! Where are you? Are you coming home?'

He doesn't want to tell her where he is. He doesn't want her to know he's hiding away in this shit-heap, doing his best to stay alive.

'Soon, Rach. I'll be home as soon as I can. Something came up. A snag.'

Ha, he thinks. A snag! If that's a term you can use to cover three more people dead and me trying to get into a Lexus through its roof.

'At breakfast, Amy wanted to know why you weren't there yet. She drew a lot of new pictures for you last night. She's desperate for you to see them. I didn't know what to say to her.'

He doesn't want to hear this. It's too painful.

'Honey, I need you to do something for me.'

'What?'

'You know that little address book of mine in the bureau? Could you go fetch it for me?'

'An address book. Cal, have you been listening to a word of what I've just said to you?'

What to tell her? That maybe his life is hanging on this? That if this doesn't pan out as he hopes, she may never see him again?

'Rachel, please. It's important.'

He hears her put the phone down and walk away. Seconds later she's back.

'All right, I've got it.'

'Go to the P section.'

He hears her tuck the phone under her chin, then her trying to steady her breathing as she flicks through the pages.

'Okay. Now what?'

'I need a cellphone number.'

'Cut to the chase, Cal. Whose number do you want? And it better not be an old girlfriend.'

He tells her, then waits out the expected shocked silence.

'Cal, what is this?'

'I just need to call him, that's all.'

'You want to talk to that bastard?'

'Yes.'

'The man who nearly destroyed you? The man who nearly broke up our marriage?'

'Yes.'

There comes an exhalation of redirected anger. 'I hope you know what you're doing, Cal. And when you see Paulson, you can tell him from me he can go fuck himself.'

TWENTY-SIX

Says Paulson, 'Coffee and donuts.'

Says Doyle, 'Look, Paulson, all I want to do is ask you a lousy question or two. We can do this on the phone.'

Paulson sighs. 'Last time we spoke, you said you wouldn't go for coffee and donuts with me. I was insulted. Hurt, in fact. Now you need something from me, I think it's only fair you make amends. Coffee and donuts.'

Doyle thinks on it. A date with Paulson has never ranked high on his list of ambitions.

'You know my circumstances. Being around me is even worse for your health than those high-tar cigarettes you keep puffing on. I should carry a warning from the Surgeon General.'

'You know my circumstances too. My line of work, other cops tend to be a little shy in making the first advance. It's nice when guys like you realize what a valuable service we perform. Come on, Doyle, pop the question. I promise I won't be a prick-teaser.'

Fuck him, Doyle thinks. He wants to be the next rat in the trap, so be it. This time the perp may actually be doing me a service.

'Where and when?'

The *when* is four-thirty in the afternoon. It's the earliest Paulson can make, which means that Doyle has no choice but to bide his time in Spinner's palace, switching his gaze between daytime TV and the cockroaches and trying to decide which has more entertainment value.

The *where* is Kath's Koffees on Eighth Street, a place which Doyle feels is uncomfortably close to the precinct station house and people who might recognize him. But then, anywhere in the state of New York seems too close to the station house right now.

When he arrives, Paulson is already seated in a booth. It's a window booth, so Doyle couldn't be any more visible to passersby. Sighing, Doyle takes a seat opposite Paulson.

The IAB man is pouring a packet of white sugar into tar-black coffee. The remnants of several other packets are scattered around the table, meaning that either Paulson has had several cups already, or else he likes his coffee tooth-achingly sweet.

'Nice place,' says Doyle. 'You come here often?'

Paulson dips a spoon into the murk and begins to stir. It looks like he's struggling to push it through the molten sugar.

'It has a certain ambience.'

'I think the word is ambulance, for after you've eaten here.'

A waitress scrapes her shoes across to the table and asks for his order. Doyle requests a coffee.

'And donuts,' Paulson says. 'We agreed donuts.'

Doyle nods his assent to the waitress and she shuffles off again.

'We could have done this on the phone,' Doyle says.

'No, we couldn't,' Paulson responds. 'Sure, we could have traded questions, information, facts, whatever. But true social interaction – you can't get that in a phone call. That's the tragedy of today's cellphone culture. Too many people think they're socializing when in fact they're avoiding it. It's a sad situation. I mean, look at us here. The two of us, drinking coffee, eating donuts, passing the time. There's no substitute for that, is there?'

'What do you want me to say, Paulson? That this is the highlight of my week? It ain't gonna happen. There's too much shit gone under the bridge for that. I came to you because I got a question that maybe you can answer. I thought maybe, just this once, you might be willing to try and help a cop out instead of doing what you can to get him jammed up.'

Paulson takes a sip of his coffee, licks his lips, then nods as if in satisfaction with the drink's consistency and flavor.

'What is it with cops like you, Doyle? How is it you manage to see everything in black and white? Where does this notion of simplicity come from? The boys in blue, the precinct DTs – they're all good guys, right? Doing everything they can to put the world to rights. Doing it on piss-poor pay, too, and under conditions of service that get lousier every time the commissioner puts pen to paper. And then you got people like me. The ones who crossed to the dark side. The ones who will use any means at their disposal to hurt honest, hard-working officers. That about sum it up for you, Doyle?'

Doyle nods, more to humor Paulson than anything else. He's not in the mood for joining a debating society right now.

'Something like that,' he mutters.

Paulson takes another sip. 'You know what I was doing two weeks ago today?'

Doyle wants to groan in despair. He just wants to lay down his questions and get out of here.

'I dunno. Helping old ladies cross the street and then asking them what their cop grandsons do when they're off duty?'

'No. I was arresting a cop. I made the collar personally. Even put the cuffs on myself.'

'Well, that sounds like a good day's work. Shame on me for thinking badly of you.'

'You want to know what the guy did?'

Not really, Doyle thinks. 'He take home an official NYPD pencil? That would be pretty serious, I think. Hard prison time for that one. Maybe even the death penalty if you play your cards right.'

'I'll tell you what he did . . .'

Paulson pauses while the waitress brings over Doyle's coffee and the two donuts. Paulson takes a bite of his donut and gives another nod of satisfaction. Doyle wonders how long it'll be before Paulson goes hyper when the sugar and caffeine rush kicks in.

'I'll tell you what he did,' Paulson repeats. 'Porn. On his computer. Masses of it.'

'Well, thank God you uncovered that one, Paulson. You never know, could be the guy was even planning to jerk off sometime. Where would we be then?'

Paulson stuffs another chunk of food into his mouth, but doesn't let it stop him from speaking. 'I'm talking thousands of images here. Movies, even. Some of them pretty hardcore stuff. Stuff that would make your hair curl.'

Doyle flicks particles of jettisoned food from his jacket sleeve. 'Yeah, well, don't let it worry you too much. One of these days you'll get a real live girlfriend of your own and you'll realize it's not so disgusting. Some of it is actually pretty good fun.'

'I'm talking kiddie porn,' Paulson says.

Doyle stares at him, but Paulson isn't even looking back. He's raising his coffee cup, blowing across the surface of the steaming liquid. Doyle realizes he's just been led into a well-prepared trap.

Paulson continues: 'Kids of all ages, both sexes. Far as we can tell, the youngest is about six months old. You shoulda seen the look in her eyes. I'll never forget that look.'

Doyle fills his own mouth with coffee, providing himself with an excuse for not speaking. He gulps audibly and feels the burning run down to his stomach.

'And you know what the worst of it was?' Paulson says. 'The thing that made me want to be there for the collar? The thing that gave me so much pleasure to slap on the cuffs and tighten them so they practically cut off his circulation? It was him, Doyle. In the pictures, in the movie files. It was the cop. The worthless piece of shit who defiled the bodies and destroyed the souls of little children – he once wore a uniform and a badge. Now you tell me which one of us was wrong, Doyle. Tell me which one of us wears the black hat and which one wears the white. Maybe all hats are just shades of gray.'

Almost a full minute passes before Doyle answers. 'Okay, Paulson, you got me with your little story there. You convinced me that you're a force for good, that you provide a useful and valuable scrvice. That what you wanted to hear? Feeling good about yourself now? Can we move on? Can I ask my question and get the fuck outta here?'

And then Paulson does something unexpected. He brings his fist crashing down on the table so hard that the coffee cups and plates do a little jig, and the head of every other customer turns to glance at them.

'Fuck you, Doyle!' he spits. 'You want something from me, then you stop acting like a fucking asshole. You stop pretending that everyone can be put into neat little boxes, and you start accepting that some of us do what we do because it's right, not because it's easy.'

In that moment, Doyle sees something in Paulson he has never seen before. A spark of humanity. In that flash of emotion, Doyle sees vulnerability, outrage, morality and devotion to a cause, all combining to make Paulson something more than the obsessed automaton he has always appeared. Despite his antipathy, Doyle finds himself no longer able to be so dismissive of Paulson, no longer able to prevent himself from engaging with his old adversary.

'Because it's right? You gave me one chapter, Paulson. A few pages where things worked out for once, where you really did end up catching the bad guy. Well done to you. Good catch. But what about the rest of the story? What about all the other times you and your IAB pals made life miserable for cops who never did so much as accept a cookie without paying for it? What about all the cops who ate their guns because of pressure from IAB? What about me? You forget about that? You forget about how you told me I was no better than a cop killer? Saying to me that maybe I didn't pull the trigger, but I damn well may as well have done? Telling me about how you were going to talk to my wife about all those nasty rumors going around? How you were going to interrogate her about my sex life? Any of this coming back to you, Paulson, or do you have some kind of selective memory in that head of yours, only able to remember the cases that fall right for you?'

Doyle pauses for breath, and notices that the waitress is at his elbow.

'Guys,' she says. 'You mind calming it down a little, please? You're making the other customers a little uncomfortable.'

The way he feels, Doyle is on the verge of yelling at the rest of the dump's clientele to mind their own fucking business, but the waitress's practiced smile defuses his anger. He nods at her, then distracts himself with his coffee, the cup in his hand trembling with the memories that have resurfaced.

When he speaks again, Paulson's voice is quieter, more reasoned. 'This is where I say something like I was only doing my job, and you say something about Nazis, right? So let me say this instead. Suppose you *had* been cheating on your wife. Suppose you *had* been responsible for the death of that girl.'

'What?'

'I'll make it easier for you. Take yourself out of the equation. Suppose you'd heard that another cop had been making whoopee with your partner Laura Marino. Suppose that same cop had gone into a building with Laura, and he'd come out alive and she'd come out in a body bag. What would you have me do? Should I say to the cop, "Hey man, you're wearing a badge, so you must be okay, have a good day, officer?" Or, given that your partner's now six feet under, would you prefer I push him a little bit more than that? What about our Kindergarten Cop? Should I maybe have given him the heads-up? Give him a chance to wipe the porn from his computer because, hey, after all, he's one of the good guys, right?'

'Sometimes,' Doyle says, 'it's not what you do, it's the way that you do it. There are ways and means, Paulson.'

'Really? I know it hurts, but think back over those talks we had a year ago. Look at them really closely, replay the words in your mind, and then tell me I was any more brutal than you've been with perps in the interrogation room.'

'Difference is, I'm not a skell. I'm a cop. I'm NYPD. And so are you.'

'And so was a child rapist. All the more reason to have people like me on the job, wouldn't you say? People who aren't afraid to squeeze balls just because they belong to another cop. Like I said, I don't do this to make me Mr Popular. I do it because it's necessary.'

Doyle drains his cup. 'Okay, Paulson.'

'Okay what?'

'Just . . . okay.'

Paulson stares into Doyle's eyes. It takes a while, but finally he gives one more of his nods. What do you know, Doyle thinks; he finds me as acceptable as his donut.

Paulson says, 'Your turn.'

'My turn for what?'

'To tell *me* the point of this meeting. I gave you my reasons. What are yours?'

'I been telling you all along: to ask you some questions.'

'Must be pretty big questions, you agreeing to meet me here, listen to me preaching like this.'

'Actually, yes. Finding the guy who's whacking everyone around me, that's a pretty big issue.'

'You're not even on the case, Doyle. What sort of questions come up when you're watching adult cable and drinking the contents of your mini-bar?'

'I got a lot of time to think, and I got more at stake than most.'

Paulson taps his fingernail against the handle of his cup for a few seconds.

'I think we're done here.'

'What?'

'I said we're done. Don't forget to pay before you leave. You're the host, remember.'

'What are you talking about? We're not done. Not until you start answering—'

Paulson brings his fist down again, but with a lot more restraint this time.

'Damn it, Doyle. I was straight with you, now you start being straight with me. Otherwise this ends now. I called your hotel after you phoned me. They said you checked out in the early hours of the morning. I made them give me the home phone number of the night clerk, and guess what? She said that not long before you checked out, you arrived at the hotel looking hurt and with blood on you. Then tonight you limp in here looking like you've been hit by a truck. So cut the crap, Doyle. You're investigating, aren't you? You're working the case.'

Doyle hesitates, but he knows he can't quit now. 'Yeah, I'm working the case. I'm about the only fucking one, far as I can tell. And it wasn't a truck, it was a Lexus.'

Paulson smiles slightly. 'Pardon me for denigrating the

252

offending vehicle. You mind telling me how you came to be knocked down by a Lexus?'

'It didn't hit me; I hit it. Don't ask – it's complicated.'

'You up to something you shouldn't have been?'

Doyle thinks about his meeting with Bartok, his handing over of confidential intelligence. He looks into Paulson's eyes and somehow knows that he will detect a lie.

'Probably.'

Paulson stares back, and for once Doyle sees something there that is more cop than cop hunter.

'Ask me,' says Paulson.

Doyle gathers himself. 'The other day, outside the boxing gym, you said the reason you turned up was because you already had a vested interest in the precinct. I think those were your exact words.'

'Vested interest. Yeah, that sounds like something I might say. That your question?'

'An interest in the precinct. Not in me. In the precinct. When you said you thought there was nothing to find on me, I thought you were just yanking my chain, but you were serious, weren't you? I also thought that Schneider called you in because of me, but he didn't, did he? You were already looking at the Eighth Precinct for other reasons.'

Paulson raises his thick eyebrows. 'Maybe.'

'Come on, Paulson. Are you gonna talk to me, or what?'

'You know better than that. You know I can't talk about an ongoing investigation.'

Doyle pushes himself back in his seat. 'What the fuck? This is you being straight with me? I'm wasting my fucking time here.'

He starts to slide out of the booth.

' 'Course,' Paulson says, 'what I would do is deny anything I know to be totally inaccurate.'

Doyle halts, sits down again. So that's how he wants to play it. Cloak-and-dagger stuff. Plausible deniability. The old Deep Throat routine.

'All right,' Doyle says. 'So you're looking at a cop. There's a dirty cop in the Eighth.'

Paulson shrugs. 'You wanna pay the bill now? I'm dying for a smoke.'

No denial. So it's true.

Doyle digs out his wallet, finds some bills to throw on the table.

'And I'm not in your sights this time?'

'Not this time. Not unless you wanna confess something.'

'So who? Who's the cop?'

'Come on, Doyle.'

'Someone on patrol? Anti-Crime? The detective squad?'

'I dunno.' He sees the look on Doyle's face. 'Seriously. I don't know. And I couldn't tell you even if I did. Come on, let's get out of here. You want that donut?'

Shit, thinks Doyle. It's something, but he could do with more. A lot more.

They stand and head out of the coffee shop. Outside, the cold air hits Doyle hard, and he rubs his hands together. His mind is racing ahead.

'You get what you wanted?' Paulson asks, starting on Doyle's donut.

'Some of it.'

'Maybe you haven't asked all the right questions.'

Doyle looks at Paulson. There's a twinkle in the man's dark eyes. A hint of something hidden there that he is daring Doyle to pursue.

'They're all the questions I got.'

'Maybe next time,' Paulson says. He puts out his hand.

Doyle stares at the hand and wonders whether he has forgiven the man for what he did to him.

'Maybe next time,' he says.

He turns, starts to walk back to his car.

When he hears his name being thrown after him, it's not just a casual call.

It's a yell.

A scream, in fact.

When Doyle whirls, he sees Paulson running straight at him, his arms coming up, the donut dropping from his hand, his teeth bared as though he's about to bite Doyle's face off.

TWENTY-SEVEN

It happens too fast for Doyle to reach for his gun. Too unexpected for him even to step out of the way. As Paulson slams into him at gut level, bringing him up and off the sidewalk like he's stopping a winning touchdown, Doyle hears a long burst of noise and thinks his eardrums are exploding with the air being punched out of him. He turns his head as he crashes to the ground with Paulson on top of him. Sees the black sedan cruising by, flame leaping from the stubby muzzle of a sub-machine gun poking through the vehicle's rear window. He hears glass shattering above him, then feels needles of it raining on his face and puncturing it.

He rolls Paulson off him and scrambles to his feet. He snatches out his Glock, but the car is already screeching around a corner. He can't see who's inside, but he knows who's pulling their strings.

He turns back to Paulson, who is still on the ground, a twisted smile on his face.

'You okay, Paulson?'

In reply, Paulson displays his open palm. It's red and slick.

Doyle crouches down next to him and pulls the man's coat aside. The shirt over Paulson's abdomen is soaked in his blood.

'Shit, Paulson. What the fuck do you think you were doing?' He looks both ways along the block, sees that someone has dared to show his face through one of the doorways. 'Call 911 now! Ask for an ambulance and police. Tell them there's been shots fired and there's a cop down. A cop down, understand? Do it!'

He examines the wound again. 'Bullet's gone right through. There's an ambulance bus on its way. You're gonna be okay, Paulson. You hear me? You're gonna be okay.'

Paulson's face is so white it reflects the neon signs from the storefronts. He says, 'Life's never dull when you're around, is it, Doyle? Maybe I should have answered your questions on the phone like you wanted.'

'Would have been a whole lot safer.'

'Yeah, but then I would have missed out on our cozy little chat. Worth it, don't you think?'

'Sure, Paulson. Hang in there, okay? Hang in there.'

'You get a look at your man in the car?'

'Uh-uh.'

'Pity.'

'Put your hand here. Try to stop the bleeding.'

Doyle hears sirens in the distance. They're growing closer, their urgency fueled by the 10-13 call. Doyle knows he's going to have a lot of explaining to do. It's time he doesn't feel he can spare right now.

Paulson sees the expression on his face. He says, 'Why do I get the feeling you don't want to be here when the cops arrive?'

'I got this aversion to authority figures. Now shut the fuck up and save your energy.'

'You worked out the question yet, Doyle?'

'What?'

'The question you should have asked me.'

'No, I . . . no.'

'For fuck's sake, do I have to do all your thinking for you? Ask me how I know there's a dirty cop in your precinct.'

'Okay, how do you know about the dirty cop?'

Paulson's body jerks, and he groans with the pain in his abdomen.

'I can't tell you that.'

'Jesus Christ, Paulson. This is no fucking time for games.'

'It's an ongoing investigation, Doyle. Give me something I can deny or not. A yes-no question.'

The sirens are louder now, just blocks away, probably trying to fight through the traffic.

'Okay, uhm . . . let me think . . . uhm, an operation. It went south. An intelligence leak.'

'I couldn't comment.'

No denial.

'And the outfit involved, the crew that got away because of the leak. You know who they were.'

'You do too, don't you, Doyle?'

Doyle almost can't bring himself to utter the name.

'Kurt Bartok.'

Paulson coughs. 'No comment. Now get the fuck out of here.'

Doyle looks down the street. He can see flashing lights bouncing off the buildings.

'I'm staying with you.'

'I can tell you got other things to do, and I don't need you, so go!'

'You saved my life.'

'And now I'm saving your ass. Don't worry, I'm not jamming you up. Last time I checked, I was a sergeant and you were a DT Second Grade, so take this as an order to leave. Go, will ya!'

Doyle stands and looks around, sees the approaching RMPs and an ambulance. Before he leaves, he performs one last act.

Reaching down to Paulson, he takes his free hand and shakes it firmly.

He's out of time.

He's pacing up and down in Spinner's apartment, trying to think, and all he can hear is a tiny voice telling him he has no more time.

Bartok has found him once, he'll find him again. And next time he won't miss. In a period of less than one day, Doyle has twice washed the blood of others from his hands. It's only a matter of time before they're covered in his own.

The cops will be searching for him too. They'll want to know why he was talking to IAB, and why he booked the scene when Paulson was shot. If they haven't done so already, they'll check the hotel and discover that he's abandoned it and gone into hiding. At some point, either the cops or Bartok will have the presence of mind to look here, and then it'll be too late for him to do anything.

So concentrate, goddamnit!

Okay, what do we have? Somehow Kurt Bartok found out the identity of the guy who's been terrorizing me. He gets Sonny Rocca to approach the killer with an offer. Bartok will keep his identity under wraps in return for . . .

For what?

What use is this guy to Bartok?

Doyle knows the answer. It's something he should have realized a long time ago, but even now he finds it hard to accept.

Bartok was just doing what he always did. It was second nature to him. The value of the killer to Bartok was his information.

Because the killer is a cop.

Much as Doyle doesn't want to believe it, it's the only glue that can hold all the pieces together. Bartok's commodity was information, most of which came from cops. He already had at least one Eighth Precinct cop in his pocket – Paulson confirmed that much.

Suppose the crooked cop finds something out about another member of service. Not necessarily that he's a killer – this is probably way before Parlatti is murdered. Just a juicy tidbit of information that maybe could be used as leverage. Dutifully, the dirty cop passes it on to his unofficial employer, Kurt Bartok, and Bartok files it away in his vast mental storehouse. Only later, when the killings begin, is Bartok able to slot the data into the right place and see it for what it really is: a pointer to a man who is slaughtering and persecuting his own brothers.

What Bartok has now is the perfect opportunity for turning another cop. It's not something he's going to ignore. So he sends Rocca out to talk to the cop, to make him that offer.

Only the cop doesn't fall for it. He bounces Rocca back with instructions to Bartok to go fuck himself.

Now Bartok doesn't know what to do. Nobody's ever called his bluff like this before, but he doesn't want to give up this chance of gaining another source of his precious data.

Which is where Spinner comes in.

To Bartok, Spinner is just a pawn. Expendable. His only use is to put pressure on the cop. Bartok calls Spinner in to give him the name, but he lets the cop know about it, hoping that this time he'll cave in.

Only he doesn't. What he does instead is to track down Spinner and eliminate him. Whether Spinner actually learned the name or not is irrelevant. The point is that the killer *believed* he knew it.

And still Bartok doesn't give up. He sends Rocca back yet again, this time with the message that he's going to hand the killer's name directly to the victimized cop, Doyle. It seems a win-win situation to Bartok, because he gets either the killer or Doyle as a new addition to his stable.

But the killer is always just that one step ahead. Being a cop, he may already know about the bad relations between Rocca and Bartok. He's also had several opportunities to sound Rocca out about his employment prospects. So he makes Rocca a counter-offer, and it's bye-bye Bartok.

Doyle stops pacing. He puts his hands over his eyes, the enormity of the truth shocking him to his core.

A fellow cop! Jesus Christ.

He wants to look for reasons to reject it as fact, to find alternatives, but he knows that nothing else will fit.

It explains so much: how the killer knew Doyle was at the boxing gym, and which was his car; how he knows Doyle's wife and child, his address, the car that Rachel drives; how he knew Joe's pool-night routine so well.

And there's something else, too. When this guy phoned Rachel, pretending he was a doctor at Bellevue, he put on a fake Indian accent. The only reason for doing that is because there was a danger of Rachel recognizing his voice.

This isn't just any cop.

This is a cop close to home.

So who?

And why is he doing this to me?

Which cops have I hurt so badly that he would go to such lengths to get back at me?

Marino? Sure, he hates my guts, but would even he stoop to this? Killing other cops just to isolate me? What kind of perverted justice is that?

Doyle collapses onto a chair, his head still in his hands. Around him are the noises of a building come to life: televisions, slamming doors, footsteps in the hallway, barking dogs, crying children. But he is oblivious to them all. He doesn't move for a long time. He just sits and thinks, replaying recent conversations a thousand times each in his head. Looking for signs. Looking for hate. Looking for reasons.

And when his brain can take no more, he experiences utter despair. Sadness overwhelms him.

Not because the answers evade him.

But because they come to him. In a form more shocking than he would have believed possible.

He has work to do. He has people he must speak to.

If he is wrong, he may be putting their lives at risk.

That's if he can stay alive long enough to get to them.

TWENTY-EIGHT

The house is situated near the New Croton Reservoir in Westchester County, about twenty-two miles north of the city. The body of water used to be known as Croton Lake, which, back in the mid-nineteenth century, fed a distributing reservoir located in mid-town Manhattan. Today's users of the New York Public Library on Fifth Avenue might be surprised to learn that, a century and a half earlier, their ancestors were promenading above them and delighting in the view of the moonlight bouncing off glassy waters.

The property is a huge two-story affair in white clapboard, with not a neighboring building in sight. A perfect vertical line of chimney smoke betrays the stillness of the crisp air. Christmas lights are strung like icicles along the eaves, and a ghostly plastic snowman looks out from a window, a friendly smile on its big moon-like face. Somewhere in the many acres of woodland beyond the rear of the property, an animal or bird screeches. It's a quiet, peaceful place, so different from the frenetic bustle of the city.

Doyle steps onto the wooden porch, sucks in an icy breath that stings his windpipe, then thumbs the doorbell.

A light comes on inside, and a shadow looms through the glass pane of the door. The door opens, and a woman peers at him through the porch screen. She seems surprised – shocked even.

'Cal!' she says.

Doyle wishes he could find a smile for her, but he can't.

'Hello, Nadine,' he says.

She leads him through a paneled hallway. Ornamental plates on the walls. A pendulum clock beating out the house's pulse. A tastefully decorated Christmas tree in one corner.

When he shambles into the light, she sees what a wreck he is.

'My God, Cal. What happened? Did you take up boxing again?'

'Yeah. Only now I fight three at once, just to make it a challenge. Is Mo in?'

'Not yet. It's just another lonely night.'

Another lonely night. She could have been saying, Oh, for some male company to keep me warm on this bitter winter night. But this is Nadine the Siren. She makes men read such things into her words.

She adds, 'He's driving up later, but he won't get in till after ten. Believe it or not, he's actually taking a day's leave tomorrow. I think he really needs it. He's looking pretty tired lately.'

She escorts him into a spacious living room. Its centerpiece is a colossal stone fireplace. A log fire crackles and pops and throws out its cozy glow. She gestures for him to take a seat in one of two massive armchairs angled toward the fire, a lace-covered oak coffee table between them. As Doyle sits, she gets onto the other chair and curls her bare legs beneath her. Dwarfed by the chair, and with the sleeves of an oversized woolen sweater hiding her hands, she looks like a child waiting to be read a bedtime story.

'So,' she says, 'how did you know I was up here?'

'I didn't. I went to your Manhattan apartment first. Your neighbor said you'd traveled up here.'

'You should have phoned me. I could have told you where we were. Saved you all the trouble.'

He doesn't answer. He looks around at the antique furniture, the sepia photographs on the walls. 'Last time I was up here, it was summer. The barbecue, remember?'

She laughs girlishly. 'I do. You pushed Schneider into the swimming pool and then claimed it was an accident.'

Doyle shrugs. 'I'd had too much to drink. Joe Parlatti and Tony Alvarez were up here too. Remember that?'

Her smile fades in an instant. 'Listen, Cal. It's always a pleasure to see you – don't get me wrong, I think we've become real good friends, but . . . should you be here? I mean . . .'

'It's okay, Nadine. I wasn't followed. Nobody knows I'm here. You're safe.'

He remembers giving a similar guarantee to Spinner, and look how that turned out.

'I'm sorry, Cal. I didn't mean to sound rude. It's just that . . .'

'Yeah, I know. A lot's been happening. You've every right to be concerned. I just . . . needed to see you.'

She glances at the mahogany-cased clock on the mantle. 'Well, like I say, I think it could be some time before Mo gets here . . .'

'Actually, Nadine, I think maybe I need to talk with you first.'

She stares at him with those ice-blue eyes of hers. Christmas is all wrapped up in those eyes.

'You must be freezing,' she says finally. 'Let me get you something. I make a mean hot chocolate. Marshmallows and everything.'

She starts to get up, but Doyle stops her with a raised hand.

'No, please. Not for me. Can we just talk for a while?'

She sinks slowly back into the cushions. 'Now you've got me worried. What's going on, Cal?'

Doyle tries to find the words. He's been trying to assemble them all the way up the Parkway.

'I've been through a lot these past few days. I'm tired. Maybe I got this all wrong, but some things are bugging me.'

'What kind of things?'

'This guy. The one who's been following me around, picking off my partners and my friends, threatening to hurt my family, doing everything he can to cut me off from people because of some crazy idea he has that I wronged him in the past . . .'

'What about him? Have they caught him? Do they know who he is?'

'No. See, that's the problem. They haven't caught him. They haven't got a name for him. They can't find a shred of evidence that pins anything on any of the people I've collared or had beefs with in the past. For a while now, I've been thinking that the job doesn't really care about me. The shit I'm carrying around, there are some cops who don't care if I live or die. The longer I'm off the squad the better, far as they're concerned.'

'Cal, that's nonsense. Sure, there are a couple of cops who won't be sending you Christmas cards this year, but they're not all like that. I know. I've talked to them. Mo's talked to them too.'

Doyle nods. 'Yeah, I'm beginning to believe that. I'm beginning to believe that they really are doing their damnedest to catch this guy, or at least work out who might hold such a grudge against me. Me too. I've been going through lists of perps in my mind over and over again. The most likely suspects are either dead or locked up or have ironclad alibis. The rest . . . well, to be honest, I just don't see it. I don't want to sound like I got no modesty or anything, but I just can't see any of these people hating me enough to do this.'

'Yeah, but Cal, you're forgetting how people can change. The guy you locked up ten years ago is probably not the same guy today. He's had time to brood. Maybe things happened to him in prison that he blames on you. And then there're the lunatics. The people who see you through their crazy eyes as someone who was responsible for a lot more than you did. They could blame you for 9/11 – who knows with these people? Or maybe it's a relative of a perp you put away – someone who sees himself as a victim of yours even though you've never met him. There are a lot of possibilities, Cal. Maybe you just need to give it more time.'

'Yeah. Mo said similar things to me.'

'And he's right.'

'Yeah, maybe,' Doyle says, but the doubt is evident in his voice.

'You don't buy it, do you? So what's the alternative?'

Doyle looks at her. Her logic seems so impeccable, it almost seems ridiculous to suggest anything else.

'The alternative is, the reason nobody can identify this guy, me included, is that . . . is that he doesn't exist.'

He watches her face for the reaction. She looks as though she hasn't heard him. As if she's still waiting for him to say something. Or at least something intelligible. Finally, she blinks several times as if coming out of a hypnotic trance.

'Cal, what are you talking about?'

He has to look away from her, so as not to let her expression of incredulity prevent him from voicing his train of thought.

'I met a guy last night. He knew the name of the person doing this to me, but he was killed before he could tell me. The very last thing he told me was that I could stop digging into my past. At the time, I thought he meant there was no need to keep looking through the files because I was about to discover the name. But now I think what he was telling me was that I was looking in the wrong place. That it had nothing to do with my past. That maybe it didn't even have anything to do with *me*.'

There's a silence, and he has to slide his eyes to her again to try to discern her thoughts. He decides that she still assumes he's gone ga-ga.

'Cal, I seriously think you need to get some rest. How can one ambiguous statement from a guy who's now dead make you start to think that none of this is real? Look at what's happened. To *your* partners, to *your* wife, to *your* friend Spinner, to this guy *you* were speaking to last night. That's not imaginary, Cal. Horrible though it all is, you have to start accepting that you're the common factor in this or you'll lose your mind.'

'Yeah, I admit that's how it looks . . .'

'That's how it *looks*?'

' . . . but when you break it down I'm not so sure. The guy last night was killed to shut him up. Spinner was also killed because he knew too much, not because he was close to me. Rachel wasn't even hurt; I was just tricked into thinking she was. Take all of them out of the equation, and that just leaves Joe and Tony.'

'Aren't they enough? And anyway, it's not true. What about the two hookers who died, and that pimp?'

'Cavell. Yeah, I been thinking about them too. You know what the funny thing is? All along, people kept asking me, "You got the cop killer yet? You got the guy who whacked your partners?" It would get me so pissed off, I would say to them, "Don't forget the hookers and the pimp; they died too, you know. They were human. They mattered." And you know what? I was wrong and they were right. To most people, the killer included, they didn't matter. They didn't count. Their only use was as bait to set traps. The problem was, I couldn't see that I was wrong. I kidded myself that I was on some kind of moral high ground. Hell, I never even bothered to find out that second hooker's name, that's how much I cared about her.'

'But that still leaves Joe and Tony. *Your* partners. Or do you have a way to cross them off your list too?'

'Sure, Joe was my partner. But Tony never was. Not really. I worked with him for a few hours, that's it.'

'So what are you saying? That it's just pure coincidence that you happen to be linked to all these people? Come on, that's kind of a stretch.'

'No, what I'm saying is that somebody killed Joe and Tony, and then made it look like just a part of a greater plan to hurt me. That's why the killer sent me revenge messages: to make me and everyone else think I was the focal point.'

'Why? Why would they do that?'

'To shift the attention away from Joe and Tony as the real victims. And it worked. Nobody is looking for links between Joe and Tony because they're all too busy looking at me.'

Nadine stares for a while, then shakes her head. 'I don't know, Cal. To do all this, just as a diversionary tactic . . .'

'What, you don't think escaping the death penalty is sufficient motive? The killer's got the whole NYPD looking in the wrong direction, and that means they're never going to find him. I'd say that makes his efforts pretty damn worthwhile, wouldn't you?'

Seeing that Nadine still looks doubtful, he says, 'Look, if this guy really wanted to hurt me, why didn't he just kill Rachel and Amy rather than go through that whole charade of making me think they were in trouble? Why didn't he kill Spinner after my first meeting with him, rather than wait until Spinner became a danger to him? Where's the consistency?'

Another pause from Nadine. 'If you're right, and I still think it's a huge if, then that still means somebody wanted Joe and Tony dead. Why would they do that? You knew Joe better than most. Why would someone want to kill a nice guy like that?'

Images of Joe Parlatti laughing and smiling jump to Doyle's mind. He feels slightly guilty that the events of the past few days have not allowed him more time to think about his partner. Yes, Joe was a nice guy. One of the nicest. His wife, Maria, said the same. She said a few other things too.

'I don't know why,' Doyle says, although he could venture a guess. 'But I got some ideas as to who.'

Nadine's eyes narrow. He can almost feel the touch of her gaze flicking over his face, searching it for clues.

'Are you going to let me in on it?'

'A cop.'

'A cop. Any particular reason?'

'Several, actually. The details don't matter.'

'Ooo-kay. Any particular cop?'

And this is where it gets difficult, thinks Doyle. This is where friendships are tested. This is where bonds are stressed to their breaking point. This is where hearts are broken.

'You remember the night after Joe was killed?' he begins. 'When I came home, and you were there with Rachel?'

Nadine doesn't move. Her eye-line doesn't shift even a degree away from Doyle's face.

'Go on,' she says.

'I told you that Mo was on his way home, because that's what he told me. And you seemed surprised at that, like you weren't expecting him home until much later.'

This time she says nothing. Just waits.

'So was he there when you got back? Or did he get in much later?'

'Does it matter?'

'Was he in the apartment when Tony Alvarez was being killed?'

So there it is. He's crossed the line, and he can see as much on Nadine's face.

'Cal, are you suggesting what I think you're suggesting?'

Doyle has no choice but to press on. 'What about the previous night, when Joe was killed? Was Mo home then?'

'He works hard. You know that. He's a hard-working, hands-on cop. He's out all kinds of strange hours, just like you are, Cal. Now before you say another word, I think you need to—'

'What about Saturday, Nadine?'

'Saturday? What about it?'

'That's the day Spinner was killed. According to Mo, he was in a meeting at police headquarters that afternoon.'

'And?'

'You're right. Nothing unusual in that. No reason to doubt him. Except that he said something else too. He said that directly after leaving 1PP he met up with you to do some Christmas shopping.'

Nadine's silence says everything.

Doyle continues: 'All perfectly normal too, right? Nothing suspicious there. In fact, it was only today that it clicked with me. He couldn't have gone shopping with you.'

Nadine is angry now. Angry and fearful. 'Why, Cal?' she snaps. 'Why couldn't he? Suppose I say he *was* shopping with me? What then?'

'You'd be lying. Saturday evening was when Amy was in the dance competition. And you were there. I remember Rachel telling me you were going to be there. You weren't available to go shopping because you were at the dance competition. Am I wrong about that, Nadine? Am I?'

Nadine's eyes well up and glisten with the reflected light of the fire. Through tight, trembling lips she says, 'Do you know what you're accusing him of, Cal? I heard about what happened to Spinner. He was tortured. For a long time. And then his throat was cut. Do you really believe that Mo is capable of such a thing? He's my husband, Cal. Your boss. He's always said great things about you. You brought a lot of baggage with you to the Eighth, and he's always defended you. Do you think he could turn on you like this? Do you think he deserves this kick in the teeth from you?'

'I don't want to believe it, Nadine. Really I don't. But it all fits. The person who's doing this is a cop, and it has to be a cop who knows a lot about me. He had to know a lot about Joe too, and the fact that Tony had interviewed Cavell. And there's something else . . .'

Nadine sniffs. 'What?' she asks, in a tone that suggests she doesn't really want to hear the answer.

'Something else that Mo said on Saturday, when he came to Spinner's apartment. He was giving me a hard time, letting rip at me for all the mistakes I was making. One of the things he didn't like was the fact I had an unlogged meeting with an informant.'

'So?'

'I hadn't told him about that meeting. I hadn't told anyone about it. The only way Mo could have found out about it is if he was the one who killed Spinner.'

Nadine shakes her head, gets to her feet.

'You're wrong. There has to be another explanation. Mo couldn't do all this. You're wrong.'

She moves closer to the fire. She slides a poker from its beaten-copper holder. Idly, she pokes it into the logs. They hiss at her like disturbed rattlesnakes.

Doyle stands up. 'The guy I met with last night? Someone paid a lot of money to have him killed. Most cops I know don't have that kind of money. Mo does, though. This house, the inheritance from his mother. He must be worth a fortune now. I hear he plans to retire next year.' She stabs at the logs more vigorously. Doyle takes a step closer. 'I'm sorry, Nadine, but it all fits. It's the only possible answer.'

She whirls on him, brandishing the poker. The glowing red tip is a foot from his face.

'Then answer me this,' she yells at him. The tears are streaming down her face now, and he hates that he's doing this to her. 'Why, Cal? Why would Mo do it? Why would he want to kill Joe and Tony?'

Doyle looks at her pain. Sees beyond it to the understanding and the damage it has done.

'I was hoping you could tell me.'

They stand there for a full minute, either side of a broken friendship, until Nadine's arm begins to shake with the weight of the outstretched poker. Finally she lowers it and pushes it back into the fire, coaxing new life from it.

Doyle waits patiently for her response. He waits for words that will either form the last piece of the puzzle, or else will leave him wondering whether he has somehow got this terribly, horribly wrong.

'I'd like you to leave now, Cal,' she says, giving him neither.

TWENTY-NINE

She waits alone in front of the fire. Even though the logs are now just glowing embers, she has removed the woolen sweater that was covering her white silk shirt. She has also slipped on some shoes and combed her hair. Because for some reason she doesn't want to feel cozy and snug and Christmassy. She wants – *needs* – to be businesslike and objective and distanced from that precipice which seems so perilously close to her feet.

She curses Doyle for coming here tonight. He was supposed to be a pariah. He should have acted like one. He should have stayed away.

But he didn't. And the demons followed him, bringing not death this time but destruction and misery of a different form.

She hears the car approaching, sees the flash of headlights across the drapes. The slam of a car door. The jangle of keys. The unlatching of the front door. The steps across the hallway.

She manufactures a smile as he enters the living room.

'Hey,' he says.

'Hey,' she echoes.

'Long day.'

'When isn't it? You eaten?'

He looks at her, puzzlement and suspicion in his gaze.

'Yeah. I grabbed something earlier. Are you . . . is every-thing okay?'

'Mo, can I talk to you, please?'

For a long time he doesn't answer. He puts his hands on his hips and looks her up and down, appraising her. As if thinking, What is this? What is this woman doing, getting above her station like this? Where's the welcome-home Scotch and the sexy negligee and all the other things in our contract? Where did it say she could ask for a damn conversation, for Christ's sake?

'Sure. What's wrong?'

She sits down on one of the armchairs, then gestures for Mo to do likewise. Mo stares at the chair like it's haunted, before finally stepping across the room and lowering himself onto it.

She studies his face. She sees the tiredness there. But more than that she thinks she sees turmoil. An immense tension inside, pulling him in on himself, making him appear small and withdrawn and incredibly old.

'I had a phone call tonight,' she lies.

'Who from?'

'Cal Doyle.'

'Cal? Is he okay? Has he been trying to get hold of me?'

He reaches into his pocket and produces his cellphone, then starts checking it for messages.

'No. He wanted to talk to me. He has a lot of worries. About what's happening to him. About the lack of progress on his case.'

A sigh. 'I already talked to him about this. It's a tough case. He's just gotta hang in there.'

'Yes. That's what I told him too. Only he's got some new theories about it. Some idea about the only true targets being Joe Parlatti and Tony Alvarez, with everything else being just stage fog.'

He barks a mirthless laugh. 'What? Is he crazy? What's he talking about? And why you, Nad? Why's he telling you all this? If he's got something to discuss about the case, why doesn't he come to me?'

She listens to his dismissal. There's a hollow ring to it that sickens her.

'Could he be right, Mo? About all this boiling down to the murder of two cops? Is there any reason why someone would have wanted Joe and Tony dead, other than to hurt Cal Doyle?'

'What? No. We would have picked it up already, the manpower we have on this.'

'Even with everyone looking the other way because of Cal? Has it ever crossed *your* mind, Mo? Have *you* looked into that possibility, or asked any of your squad to do it?'

'Well . . . no. But only because it's so ridiculous.'

'Or because you didn't *want* anyone to look into it.'

The silence then is ominous. Her thoughts came out faster than she wanted them to, her accusation more direct than she intended. Her words hang in the air like a death knell.

'What are you saying, Nadine?' His voice is gruff now. Stern.

'Mo, I have to ask you this. Did you have anything to do with the deaths of Joe and Tony?'

She wants a sudden explosion of denial. An outcry of indignation. A burst of emotion that is real and from the heart and believable. What she gets is a silent stony glare that splinters her heart.

'How could you ask me that?' he says. He gets to his feet and averts his face, unable to meet her eyes any longer. To Nadine it's just another telltale sign.

She stands up too, but doesn't go to him. 'Mo, I'm sorry, but I need to know. I need you to tell me you had no involvement in this. I need you to convince me.'

He shoves his hands into his trouser pockets, but still faces the wall. 'I shouldn't have to say anything, Nadine. You should trust me enough not to be asking these questions. My guess is you've already made up your mind. My guess is there's nothing I can say that will save me in your eyes.' His head snaps toward her and his gaze locks on her again. 'Am I wrong? Haven't you already tried and convicted me? Are you even willing to listen to anything I say in my defense?'

He looks away again. She can see his jaw muscles flexing as his anger builds.

'I'll listen, Mo. So tell me. Tell me where you were when Joe was being killed. Tell me why you had to work so late on the night Tony was murdered. Tell me what you were doing when that man Spinner was being tortured to death. Explain to me why you told Cal you met up with me to go shopping on Saturday.'

Mo shakes his head. 'Boy, Doyle did a real number on you, didn't he?'

'Tell me, Mo.'

'Jesus, Nadine, listen to yourself. Listen to how insane this all sounds.'

She takes a step closer to him. 'Tell me. Tell me you didn't kill those two detectives. Tell me you didn't kill those other people. Tell me you didn't hurt Cal and his family. *Tell me!*'

When he turns on her, he is like a ravenous Rottweiler taken off its leash. His hands fly from his pockets and his face contorts into a mask of fury. His wiry frame seems suddenly energized and ready to spring. Nadine cannot help herself from jumping back in fright.

'And you give me a *reason!*' he yells at her. 'Give me one good fucking reason why I would want to kill two of my own men. Two young, ambitious detectives who I saw as my friends. What reason would I have, Nadine? What possible fucking reason could that be, huh?'

And in that rant he gives her what she dreaded. In what appears to be a series of questions he is really giving her an answer.

She takes another step back, the tears flooding down her cheeks. When she finds her voice again, it is but a whisper.

'You killed them.'

He sighs again. 'What do you want from me, Nadine?'

'I want to hear you say it. I want you to tell me that you killed Joe and Tony. I want you to admit to me what you did to Cal.'

He lowers his head, as if in defeat. He seems drained again. He looks almost relieved at this chance to unburden himself.

And so she is unprepared when he suddenly closes the gap between them and grabs hold of her shirt.

She gives a short yelp and tries to pull away, but he grits his teeth and rips open her shirt, sending buttons pinging and exposing her breasts.

She stares in wide-eyed fear as he looks down at her chest and then slowly brings his gaze up to her face.

'You bitch!' he says. 'You fucking bitch!'

He lets go of her shirt with one hand, uses it to punch her hard in the face. Her head bounces backwards and forwards like she's a toy, and her brain struggles against the internal fireworks as she tries to come up with a plan to save herself.

But her husband has already decided how things will be.

'Get in here, Cal!' he yells into the microphone taped below her left breast. 'Get in here now, or she dies. And bring the recording equipment with you.'

THIRTY

Doyle leaves his car in its hiding place in the woods, and approaches the house on foot. When he reaches the porch he sees that the front door is already open. He stops and peers through the mesh of the porch screen. Franklin is in the hall, one arm around Nadine's neck, the other holding a gun to her temple. Nadine is clearly struggling for breath. One of her hands paws at the arm which is choking her, while the other tries to keep her shirt closed over her torso.

'Inside, Cal!' Franklin commands. 'Keep your hands where I can see them.'

Since Doyle is carrying the recording equipment, it's easy to comply with the order. He moves into the hall, follows Franklin as he shuffles backward, dragging Nadine with him. Her face is almost purple, her eyes bulging.

In the living room, Franklin flicks his gun muzzle toward a small table near the window.

'Put the gear on there. Then your gun. Slow and easy.'

Doyle groans mentally at the thought of surrendering his weapon yet again, but does as he is told.

'Move away,' Franklin says.

Doyle takes a few steps to his right, his hands raised slightly, his eyes fixed on the man who has been both his boss and his persecutor.

Franklin lifts a foot from the floor, and kicks one of the arm-chairs so it now faces away from the fire. He spins Nadine around and shoves her down into the chair. Her shirt flaps open and she clutches it around her again.

'Sit!' he tells her. 'Don't move!'

Doyle says, 'What now, Mo?'

Franklin doesn't answer. He walks over to the table, picks up Doyle's Glock and slides it under his waistband. He presses a button on the black box that Doyle set down. A small door flips open, and Franklin takes out the cassette. He moves back to the fire-place and tosses the tape onto the glowing logs. Within seconds, flames lick around it and it softens and melts. Black, poisonous-looking smoke rises up the chimney.

'I asked you a question, Mo. Where do we go from here?'

Franklin licks his lips, seemingly at a loss for an answer. 'I don't know. I never planned for this. It wasn't supposed to go this way. You . . . you fucked it all up for me, Cal.'

'So there was always a grand plan, then?'

'Actually no. Not at first. The only thing I wanted was to see Joe and Tony dead. That was it. End of story. You didn't enter into it. The only thought I put into Joe's death was how to make it look like it was done by someone he didn't know too well. Someone who couldn't get close enough to pop him in his house or his car or whatever.'

'So what changed things?'

'You did. You and your history with Laura Marino. As soon as the news spread about Joe, it was clear that some people were just itching to bring you into it – even to put you at the center of it. But even then I had no idea what I was going to do with all that. I guess it sort of entered into my subconscious, changed the way I did things. When you asked for the Parlatti case, it was already a done deal in my head. Normally, I wouldn't let a detective anywhere near a case involving his own partner. But somehow, without me even being aware of it, my brain was already evolving a scheme that could put the blame on you. That's why I partnered you up with Alvarez.'

This comment puzzles Doyle. He had always thought that Alvarez had chased after him under his own steam.

'What do you mean, you partnered us up?'

Franklin gives a rueful smile. 'You didn't know that, did you? Yeah, that night, the night of Joe's death, I sent Tony running after you. It was just a spur-of-the-moment thing. My brain telling me to make the link between you and him.'

Doyle thinks about this. If it hadn't been for that single impulse, that snap decision to forge a bond between him and Tony on that night, perhaps none of this nightmare could have been possible.

'So that was the seed.'

Franklin nods. 'And then it grew. You were now the obvious common factor. Everyone could see that. Even you. You said as much yourself in the squadroom.'

'So you started sending the notes, just to confirm the suspicions. And then, when that wasn't enough, the killings had to continue.'

Something flashes in Franklin's eyes. 'The only others I killed were pond scum. Whores, junkies, pimps, criminals. I didn't hurt any other cops or their families, or any innocent civilians. I wouldn't do that. There was a line I wouldn't cross. Your family was never in danger, Cal.'

Sure, Cal thinks. You wouldn't hurt another cop. Kind of a loose definition of the word 'hurt', wouldn't you say?

'Joe Parlatti was a cop. Tony Alvarez was a cop. Good cops. What was their crime, Mo?'

Franklin looks down at Nadine. She's shivering. There's a

painful-looking swelling beneath her eye. With her torn clothes she looks like a homeless undernourished waif.

'*She* knows,' Franklin declares. 'Why don't you ask her?'

Nadine stares at her husband, and then turns her injured face toward Doyle. He sees the grief, the guilt, the acceptance of her part in all this. She was the spark; Franklin was the flame she ignited.

Doyle says to Franklin, 'How did you find out?'

Franklin's expression is one of disgust at the memories he unearths. 'There were signs. Around the apartment. Here at the house. Changes in Nadine's behavior. She thought I didn't notice, but I did. I couldn't be sure – I guess I didn't *want* to believe – so I checked it out. I bought one of those nanny cams – you know those tiny hidden cameras? – and put it in a shoe box on top of the closet.'

'Oh, my God,' Nadine says. 'You filmed me?'

When he turns on her then, there is loathing and agony in his eyes and his voice. Spittle flies from his mouth as he confronts her with his truth.

'Yes, I filmed you. I filmed you with Parlatti and I filmed you with Alvarez, and I still sometimes wonder if there were others I didn't catch you with. I saw what they did to you, Nadine. To *my* wife, and on *our* bed. I saw what little respect they had for me. I saw them stripping your clothes off. I saw them running their grubby little hands over your body. I saw . . . I saw everything. And I knew I couldn't let them live after that.'

Doyle says, 'Did you really think you'd get away with it?'

Franklin's turn back to Doyle is slow. The hatred seems to fade from him and his expression becomes one of calm reason again. Doyle realizes then just how unstable this man has become.

Franklin shrugs. 'Back then I didn't really care either way. I just wanted them dead. But when you became involved, then yes,

I started to think it might just work. At least, I did until Sonny Rocca showed up.' He tilts his chin at Doyle. 'There's a dirty cop in the precinct, did you know that?'

But not as wrong as you, thinks Doyle. 'Yeah, I heard that.'

'Whoever he is, I don't think he knew what I was doing. I think he just heard something in the locker room about Joe or Tony with my wife. You know how these things start.'

Doyle nods. Oh, yeah, I know all about the way rumors can start and then wreak havoc.

'Whatever, he passed it on to Bartok. To be honest, I don't think even Bartok was sure about me at that stage. When he sent Rocca to me, I got the feeling he was just testing the waters, so I told him to get the fuck out of my face or I'd collar him for extortion.'

'But when Bartok called Spinner in, you knew he wasn't going to leave you alone. Was it really necessary to torture Spinner like that?'

'I . . . I had to find out what he knew, and also who else he'd spoken to. He was just a junkie, Cal. A junkie and a fence and God knows what else.'

So that makes it okay, Doyle thinks. This whole project was executed according to some warped moral code that makes it all okay. Provided you draw a line in the sand and you don't cross it, everything is hunky-dory.

'So where does it end, Mo? What's the final act in this big scheme of yours? Were you planning to keep me in isolation forever?'

'No. I never really had an ending. I guess I thought I'd just let it fizzle out. The NYPD would keep looking until it ran out of steam and the brass called it a day. You'd slowly come out of hiding, start making contacts again. Gradually you'd reintegrate and everything would return to normal.'

'Happy ever after, huh? What about me looking over my shoulder every minute in case this guy's still around? What about me worrying about my family? What about people still refusing to come near me in case they get whacked? You really think that it would all just go away? You think it's okay to let me live like that, never knowing whether each day is my last?'

'I had no choice. I was never going to hurt you or your family, but I had to make you and everyone else believe I would. I'm sorry, Cal. Really. I know what you went through, but it would've been okay for you in the end. It just would've taken time.'

'And now?'

Franklin looks puzzled. 'What do you mean?'

'You keep saying "would have". If your plan *would have* worked. But it didn't, Mo. It fell to pieces. So I'm asking you what I asked earlier. What happens now?'

Franklin lowers his gun slightly, but doesn't take his eyes off Doyle.

'I can't undo it,' he says regretfully. 'I can't stop it now. It has to play out.'

The unease creeps into Doyle's bones. 'Play out how?'

'The same way it's gone all along. Death following you around like it always does. You chose to come here tonight, Cal. You know what that means.'

It's only as Franklin says these words that Doyle understands. And then it is too late. Too late to do anything except watch as Franklin pulls Doyle's Glock from his waistband, turns it on Nadine and puts a bullet between her eyes.

Blood, skull fragments and brain matter explode onto the headrest behind her, and her arms fly apart, baring her upper body as she twitches in a macabre dance to her death.

'NO!' Doyle cries. He starts forward, but is stopped in his tracks by the sight of two gun barrels aimed straight at him. It's the second time his own gun has been trained on him, and the second time he believes it to be his last.

'Fuck!' Doyle says. 'She was your wife, for Chrissake! You didn't have to do that.'

'You're wrong. I should have done it in the beginning. Instead of all that complicated shit, I should have just killed Nadine. I thought I could fix things, but I couldn't. I should have kept it simple. I think she knew the truth anyhow. The way she acted after Joe and Tony died, I could tell she knew it was me. Of course, she couldn't say anything without giving up what she'd done. When I started making it look like it was about you, she latched onto that. She really wanted to believe it had nothing to do with her own infidelity. We were both living a lie, Cal. It couldn't have lasted.'

Doyle glances again at Nadine's body. It's motionless now. Blood trickles down from the hole in her head and into her part-open mouth. Her eyes are wide; they stare at Doyle as if to say, *Look at what you've done*. Doyle breathes like he's just run a marathon; his heart seems to pound the blood through at the rate of a machine gun. He wants to move, to take some kind of action.

'How the fuck are you going to explain this, Mo?'

Another shrug. 'She was killed by your gun, Cal, not mine. There'll be forensic traces that you were here – I'll make sure of that. You came here, you killed her, you disappeared. Weird, I know, but then your behavior has been pretty erratic lately. I mean, the way you just *happened* to turn up at Spinner's place and find the body. That was pretty coincidental, don't you think? Then there was the meeting you had with known criminals – again, I'll make sure we find confirmation of that. Maybe the hotel staff saw you leave with one of 'em? I don't know – I'm sure we'll find something. Oh, yeah, and then you go and check out of your hotel without even informing anyone. You just up sticks and leave.

Pretty strange, all right. Why kill Nadine? Who knows. Maybe you were having a little thing with her. Wouldn't be the first time you've been suspected of cheating like that. Or maybe she found something out about you, along the lines of you engineering this whole anti-Doyle scheme yourself. We'll see what the NYPD manages to come up with.'

'With you directing the investigation, naturally.'

'Naturally.'

'For a last-minute change of plan, that's pretty good.'

'Thank you. I think better under pressure.'

'Only, I didn't like the bit about me disappearing after I've been here. Can we change that?'

'Sorry, Cal. That stays.'

Doyle nods. 'I thought it might.'

Franklin nods too, then stands there for a while. He tucks Doyle's Glock back into his waistband, then gestures with the other gun.

'Let's get this over with.'

THIRTY-ONE

Franklin leads Doyle through a large kitchen to the rear door of the house. He unlocks it and motions Doyle out into the backyard. He picks up a spade resting against the wall of the house and tosses it to Doyle. Then he grabs a flashlight resting on the windowsill and aims it away from the house without turning it on.

'Walk,' he says. 'That way.'

Doyle looks down to the bottom of the yard. The moon overhead is almost full; it bathes the scene in an eerie gray light. He begins to walk, his feet crunching on the coarse white gravel path. Halfway down, he hefts the spade in his hands, debating whether he can swing around fast enough to smash it into the face of the man behind him.

'Don't even think about it,' Franklin says, and Doyle stops doing so.

They reach a fence separating the yard from the woods beyond. Franklin tells him to unlatch the gate, then switches on the flashlight and shines it into the trees.

'Through there.'

The way he's indicating is straight into the thick of the woods, away from any well-defined path.

Doyle pushes on. Without a flashlight of his own it's slow going. He frequently trips on gnarled roots or gets poked in the eye by a branch. At every step, small forest-dwellers in the blackness ahead of him scurry for cover.

After ten minutes of fighting nature, he halts and turns toward Franklin, who responds by shining blinding white light into his eyes.

'You don't think we should be leaving a trail of breadcrumbs or something?'

'Not much farther, Cal. Straight ahead.'

Doyle continues his struggle for another few minutes as the ground begins to slope downward toward the banks of the reservoir. Then, after unsnagging his pants from a particularly stubborn tree, he stumbles into a small clearing. Following behind, Franklin switches off the flashlight and allows the moonlight to take over the illumination of this stage upon which Doyle figures he is to play out his final moments.

Franklin circles the arena, then hops onto a large rock and sits himself down. It's clear from his sure-footedness that he's been here before.

'I come here alone sometimes,' Franklin says. 'Just to think, to get away from the world. I'm sure there's hardly another soul even knows it's here.'

Doyle sniffs against the cold. His nose feels like it's on fire. 'I'm honored you feel you can let me in on it. Why don't you do some more of that being-alone business while I head back to somewhere a little warmer?'

'A little exercise will soon warm you up. Start digging, Cal.'

Doyle looks down at the ground. With the tip of the spade he scrapes a hole in the carpet of dead leaves, then taps the hard soil beneath.

'This ground's frozen, Mo, and I'm not in the best of shape right now.'

'I'll do it myself if I have to, Cal. But only after I've put a bullet in you.'

'Never mind. I've just remembered how much I like digging.'

He puts his foot on the edge of the spade's head and transfers his weight onto it. He's surprised at how easily the blade sinks into the soil once it breaks through the top crust.

Which means that this isn't going to drag on as long as I hoped, he thinks. Great.

He throws out a few mounds of earth, wincing against the pain in his side with each swing.

Franklin says, 'Hurry it up, Cal. I'll be arriving home soon, crying out at the sight of my poor murdered wife.' He pauses for a second. 'Or maybe I had too much work to do and decided to stay in my Manhattan apartment. Hmm, I'll have to think that one over.'

Doyle continues to dig. Sweat trickles from his brow, and now his whole ribcage seems to be throbbing with the pain.

He pauses for breath, one hand resting on the end of the spade, the other pressed to his side.

'What's the matter, Cal? Young guy like you shouldn't have any trouble doing this.'

Doyle doesn't answer. He sniffs again, smells the resin from the trees surrounding him. He looks hard at those trees. Looks for a way out of this. Looks for some hope. Finally, he puts his hands down and faces Franklin. The upright spade topples and falls to the ground.

'What are you doing, Cal? That's not nearly deep enough.'

'It's over, Mo.'

Franklin raises his gun and points it at Doyle. 'It's over when I say it is. Now keep digging or I'll shoot you. Makes no difference to me whether I kill you now or when you're done. Just thought you'd appreciate a few more minutes to make your peace with the Lord. You're a Catholic, aren't you?'

'Lapsed. I got the feeling He wasn't listening to me. Somebody else has been, though.'

Franklin says nothing for a few seconds. Doyle senses the alarm creeping into the man's bony frame.

'What? What the fuck are you talking about?'

'Back at the house. I wasn't the only one listening in to that microphone strapped to Nadine. You may have got my recorder and my tape, but the wire was still running, Mo. Still pumping it out to another machine. All that stuff you said after you brought me into the house. It's all been recorded. You're finished, Mo.'

Franklin stands up on the rock. His gun is still aimed at Doyle, but his eyes scan the woods nervously.

'Don't try to mind-fuck me, Cal. As an attempt to save your ass, it's pretty pathetic. You're the loneliest man on the planet. You dropped off the face of the earth, and even if you hadn't, there isn't another cop who'll knowingly come within a mile of you.'

'Who said anything about cops?' Doyle asks.

The crack of the gunshot sounds like a huge branch snapping off one of the trees. Doyle's whole body jumps.

But he's not the one who's been shot.

Franklin's gun hand jerks to his left, the Glock flying from it and clattering onto the rocks. The woods are suddenly alive with the sounds of animals and birds scampering and flapping in panic. Franklin clutches his arm, looks down at it in disbelief and agony.

Then, from behind Franklin, another figure appears and steps up onto the rock. He walks casually, a sniper rifle with telescopic night sights in his hands. Franklin whirls on the intruder.

'Who the fuck are you?' he asks.

The man's response is to slam the butt of his rifle into Franklin's face. Franklin spins away and drops heavily from the rock. Without hurry, and seemingly without emotion, the man follows Franklin down and aims his rifle at him.

Another man comes into view from around the rock. He's not

holding a gun, but Doyle knows that he is definitely the most dangerous man here.

He steps over to where Franklin is lying on the ground.

'Stand up.'

Franklin staggers to his feet.

The man says, 'You know who I am?'

Franklin rubs his injured face. 'You're Lucas Bartok.'

Bartok nods. 'And you're the man who had my brother killed.'

Franklin hesitates. He knows it's the end, Doyle thinks. He hopes his boss will choose to go out like a man.

'Your brother was a stinking piece of shit,' Franklin says. 'And you're a stinking piece of shit who can't even see straight 'cause he jerks off too much. Get it over with, Squinty.'

Like a man, then, Doyle thinks.

Bartok doesn't argue and doesn't wait for a second invitation. His arm shoots out into Franklin's face, and for a brief moment Doyle wonders why he leaves it there.

And then he remembers something about Bartok.

He remembers that he likes to use a meat hook.

And right now that hook is embedded in Franklin's left cheek like he's a fish.

With a roar of anger, Bartok yanks Franklin toward him, spins him right around, and then flings him toward the rock. As Franklin goes one way, Bartok wrenches the hook in the other direction. Franklin's cheek explodes as he hurtles back against the rock.

Doyle takes a step forward, but Bartok's henchman raises his rifle, smiles, and shakes his head.

Bartok advances on Franklin, and again his arm whips out. This time the tip of the hook sinks into Franklin's eye.

Franklin's high-pitched scream scythes through the night air. He claws frantically at the metal thing protruding from his skull as

Bartok drags him away. They disappear behind the rock, and even though they are now out of his sight, Doyle finds that he has to fix his eyes on the ground. He has to stare into the hole he has been digging and concentrate on that blackness to shut out the images. He tells himself that the noises he hears are wild animals fighting and calling to one another. It's nature, that's all. Just the animals. They sound like that sometimes. Almost human.

When it ends, Doyle feels faint with relief. The clearing is so chillingly silent he wonders if his fervent desire to cut out the screams has made him go deaf.

Bartok reappears looking like something from a zombie movie. In the moonlight, the blood that covers him from head to toe looks black. He walks toward Doyle, panting with the effort of his labors.

'Talk about cutting it fine,' Doyle says.

Bartok's arm lashes out again. Doyle starts to dodge, but isn't quick enough to avoid the cold steel connecting with his face. He drops to the ground, rolls to get away from Bartok's onslaught. But when he looks up at Bartok, he sees that the man is no longer carrying his meat hook. What he struck with was Doyle's own Glock.

Doyle touches his cheek. He feels warm blood there, but nothing as bad as he expected.

'That's for when you arrested me and my brother,' Bartok says.

Doyle can sense he's not done, though. When Bartok's foot comes up, Doyle is ready to block it, grab it and push upward and back, knocking Bartok off balance.

But he doesn't.

He doesn't because that would mean his death. It would mean a salvo of bullets piercing his body within a split-second of any reaction against Bartok.

And so he takes the lesson, lets Bartok get it out of his system. Allows Bartok's shoe to collide with his face, splitting open his lip.

'And that's for being a wise-ass.'

Doyle gets to his knees, tastes the blood gushing into his mouth. He spits it out onto the ground.

'You done?' he asks. 'We finally quits now?'

'Put your hands behind your back.'

'What?'

'You heard me, you dumb Irish fuck. Put your hands behind your back.'

Doyle looks at Bartok. Wonders why it is that the end of one predicament always seems to lead straight into another.

When Doyle has clasped his hands behind him, Bartok signals his goon to approach. The man slings his rifle over his shoulder, then pulls a length of cord from his pocket and begins to tie Doyle's wrists together.

'What the fuck's going on?' Doyle asks.

'Shut up,' says Bartok. He snaps his fingers at the other man, who tosses him something soft and dark. Bartok moves behind Doyle, slips the cloth bag over his head.

Oh, Jesus, Doyle thinks. Not like this. Not after all I've been through.

He feels something hard press into the back of his skull.

'You know what this is?' Bartok says, his voice muffled through the cloth.

'A gun.'

'Yeah, a gun. *Your* fucking gun.'

My gun. Aimed at me again. This is starting to get repetitive.

'We made a deal, Bartok.'

Ah, yes. The deal. Me getting my life back in return for handing Bartok the killer of his brother. Lucas sure got a shock tonight when I turned up at his door offering that one. Now where did I get the idea he could ever be a man of his word?

'You think I'm stupid, don't you, Doyle? Think I don't know

shit. To you, Kurt was the brains and I was just the dumb side-kick. Ain't that right, Doyle?'

'No, actually your dastardly ruse never fooled me for a minute. I always suspected you were the criminal mastermind and Kurt was just your puppet.'

For his impudence, Doyle receives another smack in the mouth, rattling his teeth.

'Oh, you are so pushing it, Doyle. You are so asking to die here.'

'What's the difference?' Doyle asks, finding it harder to speak now. 'You're gonna kill me anyhow.'

The laugh from Bartok seems to fill the clearing. Doyle can picture the forest denizens deciding they want nothing to do with whatever insane creature is issuing that fearful noise.

When Bartok speaks next, his voice is just an inch from Doyle's ear. Doyle can feel the man's warm breath pushing through the cloth.

'Kill you? I ain't gonna kill you, you stupid fucking mick. I want you alive. And you know why? To show you that I'm smarter than you think. I'm gonna help you, Doyle.'

'I don't need your help.'

'Oh, yes, you do. Think about your situation. Think about your ex-boss lying in pieces behind that rock over there. Think about his missus with your bullet in her brain. She's got great tits, by the way – I copped a feel on the way out.'

Doyle tries to suppress his anger. His mind struggles to work out where Bartok's going with this.

Something – probably his gun – taps against his skull.

'This,' says Bartok, 'gives you a story. You say that the lieutenant tied you up and put the hood on your head. That he was going to shoot you and dump you in that hole over there. And then somebody else came along. You have no idea who. You heard noises and that's it. You got that, Doyle?'

Doyle doesn't answer. He feels his coat being opened, a hand reaching into his inside pocket.

'And this,' Bartok continues, 'gives you the rest of what you need to get out of the fix you're in.'

'I don't want it. Whatever it is, I don't want it.'

Bartok laughs again, but it's more of a chuckle this time.

'We *were* quits,' Bartok says, 'but now you owe me. You owe me big time.'

Doyle swallows down some blood. 'I don't owe you shit. Take your crap out of my pocket. I'll take my chances.'

'It stays, Doyle. And I think you'll use it. But even if you don't, you still owe me.'

'Yeah? How d'you figure that?'

Another cruel laugh. 'Because I got something else up my sleeve. Something you don't want anybody to know about. Any ideas yet?'

Doyle's mind races, but doesn't seem to get off the starting line.

Bartok's voice drops to a whisper. Although carried on lungfuls of air that feel almost burning against Doyle's ear, the words themselves chill him to the bone.

The breathing moves away. When Bartok speaks again it sounds as though he's standing up again.

'Think about that, Doyle. Not so much the dumb brother now, huh? We'll talk again soon. Oh, and one other thing before I go . . .'

Doyle waits for more words he doesn't want to hear. What he gets is something hard smashing into the side of his skull, and then a feeling of sinking into the soil as though it's quicksand, swallowing him up and closing over him.

He thinks he's dead.

When he opens his eyes he sees nothing, feels nothing. His brain sends out commands to the rest of his body, but nothing responds. It's like he's become some kind of disembodied soul, floating in a featureless limbo.

Gradually, he realizes that his limbs are moving, but the cold has numbed them – turned them into unfeeling slabs of frozen meat. He manages to roll into a sitting position, then starts pumping his legs along the ground to get the blood circulating again.

Next, he flexes his biceps, rubs his arms up and down his back, wrings his hands together until they start to thaw a little. When he has finally re-established the perimeter of his own body, he goes to work on the cord binding his wrists. He frees his arms more quickly than expected, and when he pulls off the hood he sees why: the lack of sensation in his hands meant that he didn't notice he was sloughing off layers of skin as he pulled and twisted them against the rope.

He stands up. Shakily at first, he stamps his feet and slaps his arms across his body, trying to dispel the iciness that seems to have sunk right down into his bones. Each movement sends jolts of pain coursing through his battered body.

He burrows his hands deep into his pockets, then scans the clearing. It's so quiet, so peaceful here. It's almost impossible to believe that this place was recently witness to such extreme, sickening violence.

He knows he has to look, has to confirm what he already knows to be true. He's a cop. He has seen numerous corpses, in various states of decay and putrefaction. But as he circles the rock and glances at what lies behind, even he feels the bile rise in his throat.

He performs a quick search of the area. There's no sign of either his gun or the lieutenant's, but what he does find is Franklin's flashlight. He switches it on, but just before he aims for the woods he takes another look at the hole he started digging. The site that almost became his grave.

With no idea of the route, and nothing that looks familiar, it takes him a long time to get back to the house. When he finally arrives, he stamps across the back porch, enters through the kitchen, then goes straight to the living room. He wonders why he finds it surprising that Nadine is still there in the armchair. Still half-naked, still staring sightlessly, still dead.

There's one slight difference: Nadine's skirt is pushed up around her waist, and Doyle's Glock has been tucked under the waistband of her panties. A parting message from Bartok.

'Sonofabitch!' Doyle mutters.

Gingerly, he retrieves his gun, then smoothes Nadine's skirt back into a more respectable position. As if it makes any difference to her.

He looks long and hard at the face of Nadine, tries to see past the mask of blood she now wears. He pictures her laughing, smiling, teasing, flirting. He tries to comprehend how such a vision of beauty can be the trigger for such a tidal wave of destruction. How she could possibly have acted as the inspiration for all that hate, all that evil. He wonders, too, whether she managed to convince herself that it was none of her doing, or whether she suspected the real reasons for what was happening to Doyle and chose to say nothing.

He reaches into his inside pocket, takes out Bartok's present.

A cassette tape. Presumably containing a record of everything said in this room since Franklin arrived home.

Doyle goes over to the tape recorder he left on the table. He slips the tape in, rewinds it a little, then hits the play button. He hears Franklin's voice telling how he used a nanny cam to confirm his wife's infidelity, how he was convinced that Parlatti and Alvarez couldn't be allowed to live after that. And then . . .

Nothing.

Just hiss. Nothing about Rocca or Bartok. Nothing about the dirty cop in the precinct.

When a voice cuts in again, it's Doyle asking what happens next.

So, okay, Lucas, you're not so stupid after all.

He ejects the tape, holds it in the air and looks at it questioningly. And what, he thinks, do I do with this? Destroy it? Consign it to the fire like the other one?

What the hell. Bartok was right. This tape is the only proof of what really happened. Much as Doyle hates to admit it, this tape saves him. Unless Bartok's whispered message was a bluff, destroying the tape gains him nothing and could lose him everything.

Sighing, he pockets the tape and reaches for his cellphone.

THIRTY-TWO

It's one of the longest days of his life.

The Westchester County police get him first. They bring in a doctor to look him over. After listening to the parts of the medical assessment that suit their purpose, they pummel him with questions until he feels he's just gone ten rounds in the boxing ring.

The cops from the city get him next. To the obvious relief of the Westchester guys, who seem overjoyed not to have to deal with such a complicated case, his ass gets dragged down to One Police Plaza, where he undergoes another grueling sequence of interviews. Despite the fact that he's had no sleep, and that he keeps telling this to everyone he meets, the questioning continues throughout the day. The Puzzle Palace, as the police headquarters is affectionately known, is like a hornet's nest which has been hit by a big stick. All kinds of people, some wearing polished brass, some just in neat blue suits, keep dropping in on him and asking him the same damn questions, again and again. It's clear from the consternation that they are worried about damage control. It was bad enough when cops were just victims; but when one of them – a lieutenant at that – turns out to be a serial murderer . . .

What's also clear is that the tape of Franklin's confession is making all the difference. Without it, Doyle suspects that there would be strenuous efforts to pin the blame on him – or at least to cast doubts on his version of events. Even so, there is a lot of emphasis on certain unanswered questions. They want to know, for example, what Franklin is referring to when he says on the tape that Doyle consorted with known criminals. Doyle's answer is that he talked to a lot of known criminals in his efforts to unmask his persecutor; other than that, he has no idea what the hell Franklin is babbling about.

So what, they ask him, about Franklin's death? Who was responsible for his brutal murder, and why? On that one, Doyle pleads ignorance. Obviously, Franklin must have made himself some vicious enemies in the course of his nefarious dealings. A stroke of luck that they caught up with him when they did, hmm?

Lucky also, they remark, that Franklin didn't notice that the tape recorder was still running when you brought it into the house, him usually being so meticulous and all.

Yeah, says Doyle, I really got the luck of the Irish there, didn't I? Except for that small malfunction in the middle, the wire seems to have picked up damn near everything.

When it becomes apparent that there are no more answers to be had – at least for today – they tell Doyle he can go. They also inform him that he remains suspended for the time being, and that he needs to remain available for questioning in the next few days.

Doyle nods his consent to one and all. Anything to get out of there.

There's only one place he wants to be right now.

He puts the key in as slowly and quietly as he can. Pushes the door gently open.

There's nobody in the living room, but he can hear them in Amy's bedroom – Rachel helping their daughter out with a tricky part on her Nintendo game.

He softly closes the door behind him. And waits.

When Rachel walks out and sees him, she jumps with the shock, her hands leaping to her mouth. That's when he thinks maybe the surprise idea wasn't such a good one, him looking like a man who's just walked out of a train wreck.

But he forgives himself when he hears her call his name and sees her fly across the room at him and feels her crushing his bruised, battered body until it feels like his organs are about to pop out.

And when Amy pokes her head out to discover what all the commotion is, and sees her Daddy – the man who chases the burglars away for her – she too clings to him with arms too tiny to go all the way around and yet powerful enough to squeeze every last teardrop out of him. Later he will tell her that he has something for her – a huge cuddly toy rabbit called Marshmallow – but right now he doesn't want her to let go.

He would skip and dance with his wife and daughter like he did all that time ago at the hospital, but he hasn't an ounce of energy left, so instead he dances with them in his mind, and he pictures himself dancing with them every day from now until at least Christmas, when he will give thanks for the presents that have come slightly earlier this year.

The man in the hospital bed flicks through the pages of his magazine before tossing it with disdain to the foot of the bed. He adopts a more quizzical expression as Doyle comes over and plonks a brown paper bag onto his bed table.

'You look worse than me,' says Paulson. 'I think maybe we should trade places.'

'This is nothing,' Doyle says. 'You shoulda seen me in my boxing days. I was just one big bruise.'

Paulson aims a finger at the table. 'What's in the bag?'

'Coffee and donuts. On me.'

'I don't know if I can drink coffee. I think it might come pouring outta the hole in my side.'

'Saves going to the bathroom, I guess. Maybe you could plug it up with the donut.'

'Yeah. I might try that. Thanks.' He gestures at his magazine and frowns. 'I don't suppose you thought to bring me any porn?'

'Hey, have you seen the nurses in this place? Who needs paper when you've got it all in 3D?'

'True. Remind me to pass on your thoughts to the staff before you leave. Especially the hairy one with three eyes and a humor bypass.'

'How's the . . . the uhm . . .'

'The massive injuries I sustained while heroically throwing myself in front of an assassin's bullet meant for you? Bearable, I suppose, although I still get twinges when I do too many backflips.'

'You seem pretty upbeat.'

'Yeah, well, 'tis the season to be jolly, and so forth.'

'They letting you out for Christmas?'

'I hope so. I'm supposed to be moonlighting as Santa at Macy's. Good thing it's a sit-down gig.'

'No, seriously. You coming out?'

Paulson nods, but Doyle detects a sadness there. Like maybe he hasn't got much to look forward to when he gets out of here.

Paulson pulls on a happier mask and clears his throat. 'Yeah. A day or two. I should be back trying to put your ass in jail before you can say Internal Affairs.'

Now it's Doyle's turn not to see the funny side. 'Maybe you won't have to worry about me.'

'You planning to deprive me of the one thing keeping me going? What are you talking about?'

Doyle shrugs. 'I'm not sure the job's gonna take me back. In case you didn't hear, I raised a pretty big stink. There are some who think it'll always follow me around.'

Paulson stares at him for a while. And then he starts laughing.

'Ow! Don't do that to me, Doyle. The doc tells me I can turn myself inside out if I laugh too hard.'

'What's so funny?'

'You. You're so fucking pessimistic. Try flipping it over, will ya? You're a hero, goddamnit. You were victimized, driven to the depths of loneliness and despair, but you rose above it and uncovered the identity of a cop killer. What's not to admire?'

'There's a lot of cops won't hang those clothes on it.'

'Well, fuck 'em. They don't know shit, and they don't deserve to be cops if that's how they decide to treat a brother.'

Doyle notices something in Paulson's tone. Bitterness, maybe. Something that suggests he may not be talking just about the man sitting at his bedside.

'Besides,' Paulson adds, 'I *know* they're gonna take you back.'

'Yeah? You read my horoscope in your magazine there?'

'I been asking around. Just because I'm confined to bed, it don't make me totally incommunicado. When Mohammed can't go to the mountain, et cetera.'

'Paulson, what are you talking about?'

'You're not my only visitor, you know. It can get pretty crowded around this bed at times. Admittedly, a lot of them just want to ask about you.'

'Me?'

'Don't act so modest. They want to know why you came to see me. They also want to know why you booked the scene after I got shot.'

'What'd you say?'

'On the first count, I told them you were working on the notion

303

that the guy doing the number on you might be a cop, and so you asked me if I had intel that might point to that. On the second count, I told them that, despite my orders to chase down the perps who shot me, you insisted on staying with me right up until the medics arrived. Only when I was in safe hands did you then go after them. It'll all be in my report.'

Doyle finds it hard to believe that the man in the bed is the same guy who, only a year ago, chewed him up and spat him out. It's like he's experienced some kind of epiphany.

'Thanks. You didn't have to do that.'

'Can the gratitude. You're making me start to doubt my vocation. Anyway, while they were asking me questions, I fired a few back at them. Story is they're about ready to bring you in from the cold. My guess is they'll put you on modified duty at first, but if you can put up with being a house mouse for a while, it'll soon blow over.'

Will it, Doyle wonders, be as straightforward as that? But then maybe Paulson's right. Maybe that's my pessimistic streak showing itself again.

He glances at his watch.

'Listen, I gotta go. More Christmas shopping. We already got a freezer busting at the seams, but who am I to argue, right?'

'Sure,' Paulson says, and when Doyle stands up he adds, 'You mind if I ask you something?'

'Go ahead,' says Doyle.

'Why'd you come here today?'

'You have to ask? You saved my life.'

Paulson nods, apparently satisfied with the response.

Doyle starts to turn away, then pauses. 'You mind if I ask *you* something?'

'What?'

'Why are you being so nice to me? Why all the help?'

Paulson looks back at him for a long time, as if debating whether to give him the full or the condensed version.

'You bought me coffee and donuts.'

Doyle narrows his eyes. 'Is that all?'

'Sometimes that's all it takes.'

Doyle thinks this over, then completes his turn and heads for the door. Paulson's parting shot floats after him.

'Merry Christmas, Detective Doyle.'

'Yeah,' says Doyle. 'You too, Sarge. You too.'

He goes back to work on the first day of the year. A fresh start and all that. His New Year's resolution: to take whatever's coming and make the best of it.

He barely has a foot through the door of the station house before he starts to think that resolutions are the most ridiculous invention known to man.

The atmosphere reminds him of the night this all began – when they clustered around the body of Joe Parlatti. The stares, the nudges, the winks, the muttered asides. It starts with the desk sergeant, who looks goggle-eyed at him like he's an alien invader, then spreads from there in a wave. Even a pair of handcuffed skells seem to sense deep in their coke-addled brains that something is amiss with the new arrival.

He takes the steps to the second floor, passing a couple of undercovers who stop in their tracks and follow him with their eyes. Along the hallway, clerical workers glance out through the glass windows of their offices and call to their colleagues to bring their attention to the phenomenon drifting by.

At the entrance to the squadroom he has to pause and draw a deep breath before continuing. Ignore them, he tells himself. Whatever they want to say, whatever bullshit comments they want to make, don't react. Just let them get it off their chests.

The room is busier than usual. A *lot* busier. In addition to the regular day-tour detectives, there are the Robbery Apprehension guys, there are cops from Anti-Crime, there is a gaggle of uniforms who all chose this very moment to drop off some paperwork. All come to see the freak show.

The gang's all here, thinks Doyle. Let's get this party started.

He aims for his desk and starts walking like he's heading for the hangman's noose. Silence descends on the room. No clacking of keyboards, no wisecracks, no coughing, no cursing. Eerily, even the phones stop ringing, as though the whole city has been notified to observe a minute's silence for this event.

Doyle takes a seat on his familiar chair – the one with the splatter of paint on its arm. He casts his gaze over his familiar scarred desk – the one with the left-hand drawer that doesn't open. He looks at his stack of Guinness beer mats, the bobble-headed leprechaun.

And then it starts.

One guy at first. Then a few more. Then practically everyone.

They are applauding.

They are clapping loudly and without sarcasm. They are showing their support for one of their own. They are welcoming him home.

Doyle keeps his gaze fixed on his desktop. He is certain there will be one or two cops – Schneider amongst them – who will not be applauding. But right now he doesn't want to know who's for him and who's against him. He just wants to absorb the overriding sense of acceptance.

They approach him then. Shaking his hand, slapping his back and shoulder, issuing pat phrases that could come straight off greeting cards. To Doyle it's a blur of faces and a bombardment of words that all sound different but which all convey essentially the same positive message.

And then they drift away. Back to their desks, their offices, their work. A file cabinet squeaks open. Someone starts bashing at a keyboard. A phone starts ringing. Normality reigns once more.

Except it isn't normal. How could it be normal?

All those people dead. The empty desks in the squadroom. The things that Doyle himself did and of which he cannot speak. And, of course, the message from Lucas Bartok. Those whispered words of his, seared into Doyle's brain:

'I got a corpse. The body of a guinea named Sonny Rocca. Still with your bullets in him.'

Which tells Doyle that Bartok hasn't stepped out forever. He's coming back. Maybe not tomorrow, or next week, or even next month. But he'll be back.

Doyle knows his life will never be the same again.

THE HELPER
By David Jackson

The furiously fast-paced, totally unpredictable and unforgettable next novel from the acclaimed author of *Pariah*.

*'I can help you, Cal. I can help you solve
the murder of Cindy Mellish.'*

A grisly murder in a shabby New York bookstore seems to hold a special significance for Detective Callum Doyle: the victim's been marked with a message that could have been left especially for him. But why?

Then the sinister phone calls start. Doyle is told more deaths are planned but the caller will give him clues – on condition he keeps them to himself. So begins his dilemma. If he turns the offer down he will have nothing to go on. But if he accepts and gets it wrong, he will have concealed knowledge that could have stopped a killer.

As more deaths follow, increasingly vicious and apparently random, the pressure on Doyle to find a link becomes unbearable. Does he continue to gamble with people's lives? Or must he sacrifice everything to defeat a ruthless and manipulative enemy?

An extract follows here.

ONE

She doesn't know it yet, but she needs his help.

The special kind of assistance only he can provide.

He's in a used bookstore, pretending to browse. She's behind the counter, pretending she hasn't noticed that her favorite customer has graced her with his presence. Which would be difficult, seeing as he's the only customer here. He was the sole customer here last time, too. And the time before that.

He wonders how the hell this place manages to stay in business.

It's called Brownlow's Book Emporium, which makes it sound like something straight out of a Dickens novel. Not that Mr Fuzzypubes or Ebenezer Scrotum or whoever would seem out of place in an antiquated dump like this. Listen carefully and you'll swear you can hear the scratching of ink-dipped quills on parchment.

The tiny store is squeezed incongruously between a Laundromat and a massage parlor, here on East Tenth Street. Farther along the street there's a place offering tarot reading. The owner of Brownlow's might be well advised to drop in there for a quick peek into his future. Alternatively, he could compare the present with the past by turning the corner onto Fourth Avenue. The stretch running from Astor Place up to Union Square was once known as Book Row. In its heyday it offered a home to something like four dozen bookstores. Now they're all gone, which says something about the book trade. And when even the big players like Borders are struggling with the recession, how the hell does the owner of Brownlow's Book Emporium even manage to pay the staff?

The man wonders if there is something about the book-buying business of which he remains blissfully ignorant. Some special time of day when a plague of frantic bookworms descends and purchases every dusty volume on the shelves. Maybe he should ask the girl.

She's looking at him.

Even when she's not looking at him, she's looking at him. She's one of those people who can keep their head in a fixed position while their eyeballs roam around and take in the surroundings. Like a gecko or chameleon or some other creepy reptile.

Not that she's repulsive. She wouldn't shatter a camera lens. But on the other hand she'll always be a stranger to the catwalk. For one thing, she has no bone structure. Her contours are buried beneath a thick layer of pallid flesh. And a million freckles congregate around the bridge of her nose like they've come to hear the sermon on the mount.

These things he could overlook. He could easily while away a few hours talking to a girl whose primary drawback is a spherical dotted head.

But the sniffing, no. Not the sniffing.

She does it every few seconds. She does it so often it's a wonder she isn't dizzy with oxygen overload. It's probably the reason her face looks so inflated.

Stop the sniffing, girl. Let some of that air out so we can see your cheekbones.

He guesses she's not aware of the habit. That it has never occurred to her that her frequent snorting just might be a source of intense irritation to others. That maybe it's one of the reasons she's stuck behind the counter of this dingy little bookstore in the East Village.

Nonchalantly, he reaches at random for a book. *Moby Dick*, it's called, and it's not even pornographic. Although it could be called obscene. Heading out to sea to kill a big whale just because it's, well, big. And things aren't much different now either, the way those so-called 'research' programs involve hunting down those innocent blubbery creatures.

Speaking of which . . .

No, that's too cruel. She's not fat. Not even especially over-weight, in fact, although she could do with a little more muscle tone. She should try hefting a few of these books around instead of sitting there scribbling in her little notebook all day.

He opens the first page of his book and reads. *Call me Ishmael.* Well sure, if that's your name. Pleased to meet you, Ishmael. My name's . . .

What is my name today?

It needs to be something with a hint of mystery, an undercur-rent of danger. A name a spy might have. Or the hero in a cowboy movie. Something like John Rambo or James Bond.

Hi. The name's Gordon. Flash Gordon. Wanna see why I'm called Flash?

He feels her eyes on him.

They're her redeeming feature, those eyes. Huge and wide and wet, they make Bambi look shifty in comparison. She doesn't real-ize what an asset those peepers are. She should use them to her advantage a little more often.

Her tits too. That's quite a rack she's got there. If she unfas-tened a couple of buttons she'd have guys eating out of her hand and drooling into her cleavage.

He looks across at her and she bows her head even further. She brings pen to paper, pokes out her tongue in mock concentration. But he knows that in another few seconds her head will tilt slightly upwards and her eyes will roll around in their sockets until they can lock onto him again.

She's smitten, is what she is.

He's not surprised by this, and he acknowledges it without arrogance. Girls go for him. They find him attractive. Years ago he went to live in Paris, France. The only thing he was good at was languages – science and technology just never interested him – so moving somewhere where his forte might actually come in useful seemed a potentially fruitful idea at the time. He ended up teaching English at a girls' school.

Now *that* was an experience.

It began with the suggestive remarks. Passages of text would be deliberately mistranslated to give them lewd overtones. Some of the girls would exploit any opportunity to sit next to him, sidling up close and sucking on their pencils, one too many buttons unfastened on their virginal white blouses. Others would jockey for position at the front of the classroom, affording them an optimal view of the shadowy region beneath his desk. They would sit there, whispering and giggling and constructing their fantasies.

He let it all pass him by. He knew what they were doing, but was never tempted to succumb. He saw them initially as childish, later as faintly ridiculous, later still as irritating and even despicable. They held no attraction for him.

Not those girls, anyway.

There were others, however. The less than beautiful ones. The quiet ones. The girls who would sit at the back of the class, hiding their faces and their fears and their very presence. The vulnerable ones. They were the ones who fascinated him. He would go out of his way to talk to those girls, much to the chagrin of their more assertive and voluptuous classmates. When he could do so without inviting criticism of his motives, he would chat to them in private. And what he quickly discovered was that he had a talent for getting them to open up to him. It was as if he possessed a magic key which, when he turned it, released a flood of emotions and tales of personal woe. His secret was to listen intently, with an interest that was never feigned, and he knew that they relished the attention from this dashingly handsome teacher. This was when he first became aware of his ability to help life's unfortunates.

Like the bookstore girl.

He decides it's time.

He tucks the book under his arm, picks up his sports bag and starts toward her. She continues her pretense of being unaware, but he knows that his every footfall is the first beat of a whole bar in her fluttering heart.

When he reaches the counter, and any further denial of his presence would be so obvious as to be rude, she looks up at him and blinks myopically.

Those big eyes.

She gets off her chair, smoothes down her skirt, affixes a warm smile. He notices how round-shouldered she is. Throw 'em back, he thinks. Stick that chest out. You wanna shift some of this paper, then give the public a reason to come through the door.

'Hi,' she says. 'Found something you like?'

He wonders if this is meant as a *double entendre*, whether she has spent the last few minutes slaving over that opening line. If so, it's a stinker.

He drops his bag, holds the book up so that she can see the cover. 'I'm trying to work my way through all the books I should have read when I was younger.'

'That's a worthy ambition. You shouldn't speed-read them, though.'

'Excuse me?'

'*The Grapes of Wrath*. You finish it already?'

The book he bought the last time he was in here. Two days ago. Obviously he made an impression.

'You remember.'

She reddens as she wrestles with her answer. 'I, uh, I have an excellent memory when it comes to books.'

Good recovery, he thinks. Now my turn for a plausible response.

'My mother took the Steinbeck. Saw it in my hands and thought it was a gift. Yanked it from me so fast I got paper cuts.'

He laughs and she joins in. Which makes it even funnier to him because she doesn't appreciate the real joke. Not yet, anyhow.

'Maybe you should put on gloves next time you visit your mom,' she says, trying to continue the humor.

He stops laughing. That's not funny. It's just stupid. It's such a lame riposte that he finds himself feeling embarrassed for her.

She looks confused now, out of her depth, so he gestures toward her spiral-bound notebook.

'You mind me asking what you're writing there? You seemed really lost in it.'

'This? Oh, it's nothing. Just a little poetry. Helps pass the time.'

'Poetry? Really? I love poems. Could I hear some?'

He doesn't want to hear any. He suspects they're shit. But when people need your help you sometimes have to make sacrifices.

She grabs up the notebook, clutches it to her ample chest, flutters her eyelids at him, sniffs a couple of times. 'Oh no, I couldn't possibly. It's way too personal.'

He finds it hard to maintain a smile. He knows what she wants him to do. She wants him to plead to see her outpourings. She wants him to keep on asking so that she can keep on saying no, no, no, until he just wants to rip the fucking pages from her hand.

But he manages to hold on to his civility. 'What, you mean it's hot stuff?'

She looks shocked. 'No. What do you . . . No.'

'I'll bet it is. I bet I'd never be able to look you in the eye again once I'd found out what goes on in that head of yours.'

'Well, you're just going to have to keep on wondering, aren't you?'

He studies her. Watches the way she tilts her head to one side while she beams her wouldn't-you-like-to-know smile.

'Tell you what. If I guess your birthday, you have to let me read your poetry.'

She considers this. 'My birthday? The exact day of the year?'

'Give me a sporting chance. Allow me two days either way.'

'All right. You're on.'

He folds his arms, looks her up and down. She seems to enjoy the scrutiny. Probably the most rigorous inspection she's had in a long time.

'First of all, I'd say you're a Pisces. Am I right?'

'That's pretty good. How'd you figure that one out?'

'Pisces people are creative and imaginative. You'd need that for the poetry.'

They're also weak-willed and gullible, he thinks.

'Okay,' she says, intrigued now. 'Go on.'

'I'd say . . .' He pauses for effect. David Blaine, eat your heart out. 'I'd say March rather than February.'

She's shifting from foot to foot now, like she's about to pee herself.

'The tail end of the star sign,' he intones. 'Yeah, right toward the end.'

She lets out a tiny squeal of excitement. He thinks she's easily entertained. He thinks that if he gets this right, she's going to have an orgasm.

'March the . . . the seventeenth.'

Anti-climax. She lets out a puff of air in disappointment. Her face says, *Don't worry about it, it happens to all guys at one time or another.*

'Close,' she says, holding her finger and thumb apart like she's commenting on his manhood. 'It's the twentieth. That was pretty impressive, though.'

He smiles. Not at the compliment, but at how far a deliberately wrong guess can get you.

'So I suppose I don't get to see your poems then?'

'No. Not this time.'

Oh? A hint of opportunities yet to come? How daring of you, young lady.

'In that case,' he says, 'you don't get to see mine.'

'Your what?'

'My writing.'

Her eyes bulge. 'You write? Poetry?'

'Fiction, actually. Short stories mostly, although I'm trying my hand at a novel. It doesn't come easy to me, though. You know what somebody once said about writing? All you have to do is sit at a typewriter and open up a vein. That's kind of how I'm finding it.'

'I know what you mean,' she says dreamily, like he's her new-found soul mate. She doesn't know he hasn't written a single line of fiction since he graduated from school.

She sucks up another deep lungful of the musty air. 'Maybe we could do a trade. One of your stories for one of my poems. Next time you drop in.'

Here we go . . .

'Or sooner.'

She blinks. 'What?'

'I'm not in this area too often. I live upstate. But maybe . . . well, I was just thinking . . . if I could call you or something . . .'

Her mouth opens and closes like she's a landed trout. 'I . . . I'm not sure . . .'

'That's okay. I understand. Why would you give your number out to a perfect stranger? Tell you what: I'll give you my number. If you want to call me, that's fantastic. If not, then, well, I understand.'

He fishes a pen from his inside pocket, makes a show of looking for a piece of blank paper. Before she can find one he points to her arm. She's wearing a woolen sweater with sleeves that reach only to the elbow. Perfect.

'Give me your arm. Come on, that way I know you won't lose it.'

She hesitates, but only for a second. Smiling, she lays her arm on the counter. What harm can it do, right?

He clicks his biro, scribbles a number in blue ink across the inside of her wrist.

'No washing until you call me, okay?'

She laughs as she glances at the number, then follows this up with a frown.

'What?' he asks.

'I, uh, I don't even know your name.'

He motions for her to surrender her arm again. 'Close your eyes,' he says. 'No peeking. You can look at it when I'm gone.'

'Why? Is it that bad?'

'It's . . . unusual.'

She sighs, then sniffs, then does as she has been asked.

He looks down at the column of white flesh with its network of blue-green veins. Like marble.

It's the moment. His plan has worked. He's surprised at how

easy it's been. Perhaps it's because, even though she's not conscious of it, her soul is crying out for help.

It's okay, he wants to tell her. I'm here now.

'What's taking you so long?' she asks with a giggle.

He does it then. One swift motion.

Her eyes pop open. He sees the total lack of comprehension in them as her brain struggles to switch context, to make sense of this unexpected phenomenon.

Because what she sees is a geyser of blood spurting from her wrist.

And when the pain strikes home and her brain realizes that something is seriously wrong here and she opens her mouth to scream, he tightens his grip on her wrist and strikes again with his scalpel. And again, and again, moving higher and higher up her bare arm.

And when her hand becomes so slick with her hot blood that she is able to wrench it out of his grasp, he steps around the counter and continues his methodical onslaught. The screams continue as he slashes at her face and neck, at her full, ripe breasts, and when she finally spins away he stands and watches as she whirls and crashes into walls and bookshelves, the blood spraying from her body onto all those books, all those words.

When her heart has almost nothing left to pump and her brain has decided the fight is over, she collapses in a corner of the room. The blood leaks more slowly now from the gaping mouths in her flesh.

He walks over to her, looks down at her twitching figure.

Paper cuts, he thinks. It was a hint.

Sit at a typewriter and open up a vein. Another hint.

Hell, I practically told you why I came here.

He knows the precise moment when life leaves her. He's witnessed it before. It's as if every cell of the body sighs with the lifting of its burden of coping with the world.

For a couple of minutes he absorbs the peace of it all, allows the calm to percolate through his system.

He surveys the scene. Messy, very messy. But it had to be this way.

He's drenched in her blood. It's on his face, his hands, all down his nice white shirt. A drop of it trickles down his cheek and onto his lips. He licks it away.

He walks over to the front of the store, his shoes squelching on the carpet. He turns the lock on the door, flips the sign to 'Closed', then moves back to the counter and retrieves his bag. Carrying it into the small office at the rear, he strips, washes himself down at the sink, then changes into the clean clothes he brought with him. He puts the blood-soaked garments into the bag and re-traces his path to the front door.

When the street seems momentarily clear, he unlocks the door, steps outside and walks without hurry to his car.

As he fires up the engine he takes a last look at the bookstore. It looks so small, so dull, so lacking in energy and adventure. So absent of life.

God knows how they stay in business, he thinks.

extracts   reading groups
competitions   books   new
discounts   extracts
competitions
books   new
events   books
extracts
new   reading groups
interviews
events   extracts
discounts
new books   events
events
www.panmacmillan.com
extracts   events   reading groups
competitions   books   extracts   new